MW01167149

DEMON UNTAMED

Published by Kiersten Fay
Edited by Rainy Kaye

Copyright 2013 by Kiersten Fay.
www.kierstenfay.com
All rights reserved.

This book is a work of fiction. All of the characters, names,
and events portrayed in this novel are products of the
author's imagination.

ISBN- 0-9835733-7-9
ISBN-13: 978-0-9835733-7-1

The scanning, uploading, and distribution of this book
without the permission of the publisher is illegal and
punishable by law. Your support of the author's rights is
appreciated.

This book is dedicated to the fans. Thank you for your amazing support of authors such as myself. We work hard to create entertaining stories for you, and will continue to do so as long as you are there to read them.

Mel —
you are sort of
the most amazing person to
I've had the pleasure
get to know ♡
Kiersten Fay
P.S. love you lots!

DEMON
UNTAMED
Shadow Quest - Book 4
by
Kiersten Fay

Chapter 1

Sonya's latest concoction oozed out of the carafe as she poured it into a serving mug. The soft floral color gave it a pleasing façade. The plopping sound it produced upon landing? Not so much.

"What *is* that?" Venna, a female of the Rutorian race asked, cringing away from the bar. Her dynamic skin morphed to a deep shade of amber, reflecting her trepidation. Oddly enough, the song flowing through the pub's speakers ended and a more ominous tune erupted.

Sonya gave a wry smile and leaned forward, forearm resting on the bar. "You too coward to try it?"

Patches of red erupted over Venna's skin, growing in size and overtaking much of the amber. It reminded Sonya of how her own dark demon horns became molten when enraged. Hell, even mild anger would sometimes do the trick.

Eyes narrowed, Venna snatched the glass off the counter and held it close to her mouth. She hesitated for only a moment before tilting it to her lips. The instant the liquid hit her taste buds, her face twisted in disgust.

Sonya laughed. "Tastes like shit, doesn't it?"

Venna gagged. "What evil sludge is this? Why would you offer that to me?"

Sonya poured, or rather, plopped, a glass for herself and took a hefty gulp. "Because this little baby'll do the job of five large ales. I call it cosmic oblivion. You get used to the taste."

"Don't bet on it. I'll take something else."

Sonya's delicate tail flicked, and her shoulders sank. "Fine."

No one appreciated her more unique mixes.

However, with her supplies dwindling, she had no choice but to dig down deep and conjure up some creativity. The ship had been in transit for weeks now and, under the current contract, no one was allowed to enter or leave the ship. Not until after the precious cargo delivery.

The irony of it all was that the ship's pub, which Sonya had aptly named The Demon's Punchbowl, was more crowded than ever.

"You know I'm running low on everything, Venna. I can make you something sweeter, but it will be weak."

"That's fine. I'd prefer anything other than that…muck."

Sonya shrugged, admitting to herself that it did taste pretty awful. She'd save it for Marik or one of her brothers.

As she mixed Venna's drink, she thought back to the mysterious cargo. So much trouble over such a small box. She wished she knew what it was they were freighting across space, but she wouldn't dare jeopardize the contract for a peek. Something like that could instigate a war between *Marada* and the Serakians who had commissioned them, as well as with the pirates who were to receive the package.

Sonya had been aghast, and not a bit horrified, that her

brother, Sebastian, had even agreed to deal with such filth as the Pirate King—a most ridiculous title that Ethanule, leader of the pirates, had probably given to himself—but the pay was too generous to refuse.

"How's this?" Sonya handed Venna a pale-colored drink made from various liquors and a good deal of juice.

Venna took a sip before replying. "The flavor is adequate enough."

Sonya nodded and then turned to straighten her backsplash of liquor containers, taking pride in the well-organized array.

Anya appeared moments later and claimed a stool at the bar, her typical sweet smile in place. "Good evening, Sonya. How are you?"

Sonya took in the lithe female's odd blue eyes and lengthy blond hair. She reached out and gripped the point of Anya's ear between her thumb and forefinger and gave a playful tug. It was possible that the rest of her people boasted ears like this. If only they knew who, and what, they were.

"Your hair is up today," Sonya said, dropping her hand.

A soft pink entered Anya's cheeks as she shrank in her seat a little. "I believe Sebastian likes to see my ears."

Sonya couldn't help but smile. Sebastian was smitten for his little Anya, and most of the crew privy to demon culture assumed she was his destined mate, though he had yet to claim her. "I'm sure he likes you any which way."

Anya flushed darker, but concurred with a wobbly nod. "You're probably right."

"I know I'm right, but the style looks good on you nonetheless."

"Thanks. I wish I had your dark hair though. It shines beautifully."

"The grass is always greener," Sonya replied.

"What does the color of grass have to do with hair?" Anya tilted her head.

"Never mind, hun."

Anya was as naive as she was sweet. Often it was endearing, but at the same time dangerous. Space could be treacherous, from the gritty space cities to wandering ship. Threats lurked constantly, especially for one such as she. Lucky for Anya, she had fallen in with a protective and ruthless group of demons. If Anya accepted Sebastian as her mate, she would forever be safeguarded.

Sonya in no way required protection—badassness ran in the blood—but some nights, the ones that felt colder than most, she did long…for something. Not that she was looking for a mate, just something. But, thanks to her aggressive, overprotective, and all around frightening brothers, males admired her from afar and nothing more.

Sonya caught Anya's studying gaze and tempered her emotions. "Would you like a drink?"

"Yes, thank you."

Sonya bypassed the cosmic oblivion in favor of a lighter mix. They'd found out the hard way Anya couldn't handle a stiff drink. The poor girl hadn't even heard of alcohol till she set foot in Sonya's pub.

After filling Anya's glass with something weaker than even Venna's cocktail, Sonya poured a small amount for herself and raised it in the air before drinking it down—a gesture of trust and friendship among demons, and one of the few rituals they carried on from their despoiled home world.

Anya took the offered drink and sipped it gingerly, then proceeded to compliment Sonya with a string of gratitude and thanks.

"Enough, enough," Sonya chided. "Anyway, where is our oh-so-diligent Captain?"

"Bastian is in the control room. I believe we are to arrive at our destination soon." Anya's shoulders hunched.

"Is that so?" Sonya studied Anya's sullen expression. "What's the matter?"

Anya's frown deepened. "He said once the contract is complete, he would leave to hunt down Darius." Her lip quivered. "You must talk him out of it."

Sonya already knew of Sebastian's plan and was in full support of it. Darius seemed intent on reclaiming Anya and enslaving her once more.

He obviously didn't realize one simply did not pursue a demon's mate and expect to live.

"I'll talk to him," Sonya lied.

"Good." Anya's expression lifted a bit before turning stubborn. "And if he goes anyway, then I'm going with him."

Sonya clamped her teeth together, struggling to school her features. No way would Sebastian allow Anya to go with him, but this wasn't Sonya's battle to fight.

Sonya decided to change the subject. "Why don't you come with us when we deliver the package? We could all stand to get off this ship for a bit."

Anya considered that a moment, then nodded. "I would like that."

Chapter 2

The crowded control room buzzed with anticipation as *Marada* reached the rendezvous point where they were to meet the pirates. However, beyond the protective walls of the ship, there was nothing except endless space.

No sign of Ethanule or his pirates.

Sonya shared a wary look with Cale. What if he was right and this was nothing more than a trap? If so, it was an overly elaborate trap beyond the cognitive functions of a common pirate. And really, to what end? It wasn't like *Marada* was swimming in riches. In fact, the opposite was true.

But it wasn't like they could cut and run. The cargo must be delivered to Ethanule before the Serakian's wards would dissipate, allowing the crew to finally leave the ship. Besides that, reneging on the contract meant war with the Serakians, and no one wanted that.

The wall-sized front window flashed, and the starry view of space vanished, replaced by an image of the pirate in question.

Sonya glared at Ethanule, her lips peeling back in a sneer. His appearance boasted everything she hated. White-blond hair fell over pretentious dark-blue eyes, framing a face dripping with conceit. The color and cut of his hair matched that of her father's murderer, and she was suddenly bombarded by horrific childhood visions she hadn't considered in ages.

She shook the memories away, but could not unclench her jaw.

His facial features differed, however: even skin tone, straight nose, and sharp jaw. His deep green coat with gold trim and buttons fell open, revealing a black undershirt.

He perched on a chair with a tall back encrusted with red, green, and blue jewels. Intricate gold vines wove around each stone, rising to the top. It looked ridiculous and lavish, and had most likely had been pilfered from some wealthy family on some far-off planet.

Pathetic.

Both of her brothers, Sebastian and Cale, mirrored her disdain for Ethanule. Pirate blood was only worthy of staining their boots. Why the Serakians, with all their so-called power and wisdom, would align themselves with such scum, Sonya would never understand.

Sebastian addressed the pirate. "Is this some kind of trick? We've followed your directions. Why are you not here?"

"Well, we've moved, of course," Ethanule drawled, as if that wasn't clear to everyone.

"Obviously." Sonya shifted her stance, resting a hand on her hip.

The pirate quirked a brow and openly scanned the length of her body. Cale stood to his full height, and Sebastian moved to block the bastard's view of both her and Anya.

Sonya pushed him aside and brazenly crossed her arms in

challenge, flicking her tail.

"Nice tail." Ethanule smirked.

Sonya whipped her tail again, irritated, and held his stare with equal contempt.

"What's your game, pirate?" Cale snapped.

Ethanule replied with a wave of his hand, "There's no game. The move was unavoidable. You'll see when you get here. I'm sending you a secure signal. Trace it. I'll expect you soon."

The screen switched off.

Sonya coughed in disgust. "What a pompous ass!"

"Well, that pompous ass is going to get us our pay and get these wards down so we can get the fuck off this ship already," Cale replied.

"Captain," Aidan, the pilot, called from his console. "I have a trace on the signal. I'd say we can be there in two hours."

Sebastian replied, "Good, let's finish this. Approach cautiously. Keep your eyes open for anything."

Anya turned toward Sonya and mouthed, "He looked nice."

"Sweetie," Sonya replied, eyeing both Anya and Sebastian, "your record with men is one-in-zero, and your taste is questionable." She ignored Sebastian's humph, but couldn't do the same with the crude gesture he gave her. She returned the gesture before continuing. "Trust me, that pirate has one hell of an ego on him."

Cale interjected, "His ego couldn't possibly be bigger than yours."

"Bite me, Cale."

"Not if you were the last female left in the universe." He feigned gagging.

She rolled her eyes as she tossed a lewd gesture his way.

Aidan followed the pirate's directions until a thick field of space debris appeared outside the window. The control room became quiet as they all watched Aidan weave the ship through a cloud of scattered rocks and boulders. The boulders grew larger and larger, until they were as big, if not bigger, than *Marada* itself.

Asteroid fields were havens for pirates, who would hide their ships among the space junk and attack unwitting crafts that passed by.

"I think we're here," Aidan declared, bringing *Marada* to a halt.

Sonya scanned the area, but spotted no ship, nor a spaceport, only more asteroids, the largest of which drew her attention. She narrowed her gaze on a suspicious notch in the rock that appeared to have been manufactured. It was big enough to fit a ship three times *Marada's* size.

"His base is inside an asteroid?" Sonya gaped at the sheer size of the thing, then scoffed.

A fitting lair for pirate scum.

Asteroids were considered the trash of the universe.

Aidan guided the ship past the opening into a well-lit docking bay gleaming with smooth surfaces. He set the ship down with only a slight thud.

The vibration of heavy grinding reverberated through the room, indicating the thick metal wall closing behind them. Loud hissing followed as the enclosure sealed and pressurized.

Then there was silence.

"Alright," Sebastian said. "Let's go. Anya stays behind me. The rest follow behind her."

Sonya pushed past the assembly of crewmen and positioned herself beside Anya. Aidan and Cale took up the rear, with Cale carrying the parcel intended for delivery.

As Sonya glared at the small box, a strong sense of foreboding crawled over her skin. Whatever resided inside the package held the interest of this notorious faction of pirates, and that couldn't be good for anyone. She wished Sebastian had refused the contract.

After the group descended the ship's ramp, two grim looking males with light colored hair and deeply tanned skin greeted them. Sonya recognized their race instantly. Denaloid: a unisexual breed where males took on the role of mother and father. Females did not exist.

From what Sonya knew, it was unusual for Denaloids to give loyalty a leader not of their kind, and Ethan was no Denaloid. The Pirate King must truly be no ordinary pirate—probably much more ruthless than she could even imagine.

The men didn't speak, merely gestured for them to follow. They headed into a dim cavern carved into the rock, dirt, and ice of the asteroid core.

A string of lights hung garishly along one side of the cave, illuminating their way. Sonya's boots crunched against bits of loose rock that covered the floor. *Only monsters could live in a hovel like this.*

The two guards led them through a maze of dark passages until they reached a brightly lit room. The ceiling arched high above, and guards lined the walls. Sonya counted twenty, taking note of where on their person they might be concealing weapons.

Against the farthest side of the room, Ethanule sat on that

same ridiculous chair she'd seen on screen. She suppressed a scoff at the ostentatiousness of it, and then narrowed her eyes.

There was something about him, here in person, that she couldn't quite put her finger on. Something that spiked an odd degree of curiosity and made her heart flutter, but not in fear.

She scrutinized him further, tilting her head to one side.

The arrogance was there, of course, on display and unabashed. He seemed to wear it like a second skin. Only now the air around him sizzled with deadly menace, making the hair on her neck stand up—or was that just the disturbing fact that she found him somewhat…handsome?

She clenched her jaw.

The pirate raked his gaze over the group, lingering briefly on Anya, then Sonya, then finally the package in Cale's arms.

His expression lit up. "Thank you. Your services are much appreciated. You have no idea how important these are to me."

These?

That sense of foreboding returned.

Sebastian replied, "You're welcome. I trust the wards were taken care of when we entered?"

"Of course, of course. There is nothing to worry about."

"I assume that our pay is ready as well?" Clearly, Sebastian wanted to get out of here as badly as she did.

Ethanule's lips curled upward, revealing a subtle air of malevolence. Behind her ribcage, her heart called out a stuttered warning.

Too late.

"Bastian, the guards!" Anya cried.

Sebastian bellowed before crumbling to the ground, a tiny dart stuck in his neck.

The fury of the Edge flared as pure rage gushed through Sonya's veins, providing a concentrated burst of adrenalin. Her fangs descended, aching to sink into the flesh of her brother's attacker. Clear thought drained away as she now relied on instinct.

She snatched a hidden dagger from inside her boot and sprinted headlong for Ethanule. A guard threw himself in her way, but she planted her heal hard in his chest and booted him into two of his comrades, sending the three of them to the ground.

Without slowing, she leapt into the air and twirled her body in a wide arc over a group of forward-rushing Denaloids, landing on the other side of them, still zeroed in on her target.

Through her murderous haze, she reveled at the surprise coating Ethanule's expression.

Unexpectedly, her vision blurred, darkening around the edges as if she peered through a tunnel. She ignored it as she lashed out and another guard fell at her feet, clutching his neck to hold back his blood. From nowhere, a long sword cut the air toward her. Bowing backward, she caught her reflection in the face of the blade as it hovered over her in a near miss. Red eyes blazed back at her. Her horns had never burned so bright.

Before the Denaloid could pull the sword back for another strike, she leashed her tail around his wrist and pulled him forward. He let out a staggered cry as her knee made nice with his face, knocking him unconscious.

She scanned for Ethanule. The bastard hadn't even bothered to move? As if he had no doubt she would never reach him.

She started for him again, but stumbled. Her heart pounded in her skull as though it was housed there instead of her chest. A sickening wave of dizziness followed.

They must have darted her.

The thought fed her fury, and she fought against the coursing poison, vowing she would have her kill before she succumbed.

Just before she reached Ethanule, he rose from his seat. She tightened her grip on the hilt of her weapon and stabbed at him. With too much ease, he sidestepped her maneuver, and she cursed her weakened state.

His hand slipped around her wrist, and with the slightest tilt of his fist, the dagger fell from her sluggish fingers. A wave of exhaustion assailed her.

Black seeped over her vision. When she forced her eyelids open, he was towering above her, his face too close to hers. Was he holding her up?

She gnashed her teeth and growled, but the sound was not as terrifying as intended. The poison had won.

Her last conscious thought was meant for Sebastian. *I told you so.*

Ethan gazed down at the black haired female demon in his arms. He'd managed to catch her before the sedative had sent her crashing to the ground. Why had he even bothered? The wench had taken out four of his men and wounded three others.

Her horns still glowed with the fury her kind called the Edge. Amazing. He never could have imagined it would take a triple dose to subdue such a tiny thing.

He plucked free the two darts in her right arm and the one in her left hip.

He may have just tranqued her team for now, but that didn't mean they were saved from death. That would depend if they were the ones the king had warned him of.

Before Ethan had set out on his mission to find the Faieara princesses, King Alastair informed him of the terrible fate that had befallen Princess Analia. Naturally, Ethan assumed these demons were the culprits. After all, he knew their kind to rejoice in barbarity.

But after hearing the way Princess Analia had yelled out her warning to the captain, Ethan now had doubts. There had been a desperate concern in her tone and Ethan's magic had picked up on her strong protective intent.

Ethan looked over to where Princess Analia lay unconscious, draped over Sebastian's body.

"Damn," Ethan muttered, then yelled at his brood, "Whose dart was that!"

Ion stepped forward, jutting his chin. "It was mine."

"Had I not ordered the princess be untouched? It will take days for the serum to leave her system!"

"I thought it best to take them all down and sort them out later. What does it matter if she sleeps a few days?"

It mattered greatly. Not only would he have a harder time smoothing things over with her, but he would have to wait to get to the king's next instructions. He was sick of waiting.

"The problem with that sentence, Ion, is that you used 'I' and 'thought.' I am the leader, and *I* do the thinking." Ion shrugged.

This wasn't the first time Ion had challenged his authority, but it would be the last. Ethan would not risk the life of the princess now that he'd finally found her.

Ethan gently settled the female demon on the rough ground, then stood, drawing his sword. Ion pulled his blade as well, and other Denaloid backed away.

Ethan stood still, using his Faieara gift to anticipate Ion's first strike. Ion's swing was swiftly executed with well-trained arms, but Ethan simply stepped out of the way.

Ethan swiped his bade out so swiftly it left a ghostly trail behind as the metal slashed into Ion's neck. Ion shoved his hand against the thick gash, but blood spurted from between his fingers. His gurgled gasps echoed off the bare cavern walls as his knees hit gravel. His sword fell to the ground in a clatter.

Ethan sheathed his sword and stepped away. He could quicken his foes death, but that was not the Denaloid way. They would wait for his last breath before celebrating the victor.

Ion's torso dropped to the ground, and after a few moments more, choked on his last breath. The Denaloids erupted in cheers. Ethan's second in command, Oxnel, came forward to drag Ion's body out of sight.

Ethan faced his men. "Put the captain and his crew in a cell together. Do it quick. We have no idea how long the demons will remain under. Their metabolism is unique. My bet is they will be the first to wake."

The Denaloids rushed to obey.

Ethan crossed the room toward Princess Analia. Her blond hair tumbled in waves over the dark ground. He pulled the dart from her shoulder and lifted her in his arms. Her hair fell aside to reveal one of her pointed ears, the only obvious Faieara trait.

For a moment, he considered putting her in his bed while she recovered—respectfully, he would take the couch—but he had no doubt that when she regained consciousness, she'd be disoriented and afraid and would most likely try to escape. And, if he and the king were correct in their assessment of her magic, she would need a special cell with a lock that her gift could not breech.

He disliked the idea of locking her up, especially considering what he knew of her past, but he would do what he could to make it as comfortable for her as possible.

Unbeknownst to her, their courtship had already started.

Chapter 3

Sonya awoke to an agonized bellow of rage that spurred the splitting pain in her head. She groaned and mumbled, "Shut up," to whoever was making that awful racket.

"It's no use," Cale grumbled from somewhere close by. "He's been at it all day."

She squinted her eyes open and took in her surroundings. Cale leaned against the far wall. On the opposite side of the room, Sebastian snarled and bashed at the door with his fist. The bodies of the other still-sleeping crew members littered the floor.

One of Aidan's legs rested heavy over her thighs. His light breathing indicated he wouldn't be moving of his own accord anytime soon. She shoved his leg aside and heaved to a seated position, taking in the musky scent of soil wafting off the pebbly ground. Thick stone walls closed in on all sides.

They must still be deep within the asteroid. That bastard had betrayed them, after all.

She stood and hopped over a couple of unconscious crew members, heading toward her raging brother. "Sebastian, where is Analia?"

He responded by bashing his shoulder into the door. His horns gave off a brilliant crimson and if he'd taken a second to acknowledge her, she would bet his irises were the same. The Edge had him in its mad embrace.

Sonya rolled her eyes and turned to Cale. He appeared to be calm, but she knew better. Inside, he had to be seething that they had been so easily captured. Same as she.

"We don't know," Cale said. "Woke up here just like you with no word of her."

She threw her hands in the air. "Didn't I say this was a bad idea?"

Cale gave a bitter smile. "I recall you giving Analia permission to come along."

Sonya slammed her teeth together before countering, "I meant dealing with a pirate." She flung her back against the wall next to him and slid down till her ass met the ground. "I almost had him, too." She clenched her fists.

"Sure you did."

She shot Cale a sharp look, but didn't respond, imagining instead what she would have done to that pirate had the drug given her just a few more moments.

It would have been bloody and oh, so satisfying. Unfortunately, all she could do was play back the moment of her failure and contemplate what she should have done differently. How she could have drenched her blade with his blood.

For some reason, the last image of the pirate gazing down at her intruded on her ruthless fantasy. For an instant, there was something in his expression, something she couldn't fully recall, but at the time—even with the drug slowing her mind—it had made her heart thunder.

It made her heart thunder even now.

* * *

Ethan dropped the small, yet heavy, package onto his desk and set to opening it. He was quite surprised to discover the demons had not tampered with the package. In fact, they seemed to have kept their word on all aspects of the contract.

A second box resided within the first, made from the most exquisite dark wood and inscribed with Serakian strengthening spells. The inner box was secured by a lock that could not be cracked, even by the finest of locksmiths. Only the code-holder could open it.

Namely, him.

He scrutinized the hieroglyphs on the lock before sliding the correct sequence into place. Then he pulled a small knife from his pocket and pricked his finger. After a bead of his blood welled, he pressed it into the Serakian's seal.

A light rumbling of gears sounded, followed by a soft click.

He lifted the lid.

Inside rested a thick leather-bound book, lined with an intricate gold weave.

He let out a breath and smiled. "Finally."

Three hundred and fifty years, and his mission was nearing its end. A heavy dose of gratification coursed through him, and he leaned back in his chair to soak it up.

Then he set to examining the book.

He pulled at the flap, then chuckled at himself when he found it impossible to budge. As with its container, the book had been bespelled. However, no mere code would allow him to open this lock. No knife could pry it free. A world-crushing explosion would do little but apply a generous layer of dust.

Only three people in the universe had the power to unfasten the flap and reveal the secrets inside. Currently, one of those three rested peacefully in a nearby cell, bundled in the finest blankets he had to offer.

The princess had been so young when she and her elder sisters escaped the invasion. He wondered if she even remembered him. Before his constituents had rendered her unconscious, he thought he saw curiosity toward him in her expression, but nothing that might suggest recognition.

A knock sounded at the door, then Oxnel entered. "We've received a transmission from a male named Darius. He demands to speak with you."

Ethan pushed to a stand. "And who is this Darius to make demands?"

"I know not, but he's contacted us by way of the ancient argot."

The ancient argot was created by some of the oldest and most revered pirates in history—the private language of the underworld. It comprised of several tongues, as well as algorithms and symbols, and was used primarily for surreptitious communication. This *Darius* knew something of pirate culture.

Ethan pushed the book aside. "Tell me, have our guests awakened?"

"Only the demons thus far, as you predicted. But I suspect the sleep serum may have had an adverse effect. They are very belligerent."

"No, my friend," Ethan muttered while tapping a code into his desk console. "Demons are belligerent on the best of days."

On the surface of his desk, a panel slid open and a small

screen emerged. Nodding his dismissal to Oxnel, Ethan opened the transmission, bringing up the face of a dark-haired male with a chilling gaze.

"Darius, I presume?"

"Yes, and you are the Pirate King?"

Inwardly, Ethan smirked at the moniker. "I am."

"I seek a female who was abducted from my ship. I suspect she and the culprits who took her may be within your territory."

Ethan noted the male's dark expression and instantly disliked him.

Darius continued. "She is petite with long blonde hair and blue eyes."

"I've seen no such female."

"If you or your...clan...come across anyone who even remotely resembles this female, I am willing to pay a handsome sum for her return. Can I count on your assistance in this matter?"

"For a handsome sum, indeed you can." Ethan forced a grin as realization hit him. This was the swine from the Faieara king's vision—the one who'd been holding the princess against her will—not the demons.

"She may very well be on a ship called *Marada*," Darius went on. "If you encounter this ship in passing, I wish to be notified of their location immediately."

"It will be done, as long as we agree upon proper compensation."

"Price is of no consequence."

Ethan gave a humorless laugh. "Now, I've come to believe people who say things like that are usually greatly overestimating their finances."

Darius leaned forward so his duplicitous face took up the entire screen. "I don't overestimate anything."

"We shall see," Ethan countered, knowing full well he had no intention of finding out.

Covertly, he attempted to hack Darius's location, but his ship was either too far away, or the transmission well encrypted.

Darius continued to prattle instructions until he ended the transmission with an abrupt, "See that it is done." Moments later, Oxnel returned with news that the princess had awakened.

As Ethan made his way through the dank passageways, he caught the tail end of a conversation between the demons and the princess, separated by their cell walls.

"What about *Marada*? What of the people on board?" the princess asked.

"We don't know," the demon female replied.

Three loud bangs echoed from the cell, followed by a succession of snarls.

"What was that?" Analia screeched.

The demoness answered, "Sebastian and Cale have been taking turns getting intimately acquainted with a five inch thick metal door."

Ethan almost chuckled at her blasé tone.

Then a male asked, "Analia, can you...you know...with your lock?"

Ethan stilled.

"No!" a second male snapped. "We'll find another way."

The princess replied, "What do you mean? The locks need a key."

Her statement was followed by a brief silence.

"Your lock isn't electronic?" A male said.

"No."

"Fuck."

"What's the matter?" Analia asked.

"Ours is."

Faieara gifts often followed the bloodline. Their interest in the state of the locks confirmed Ethan's assumption. The princess yielded the same gift as her father's father, just as the king had predicted.

"Dammit," the second male snarled. "Analia, I'll get you out of there."

"Actually," Ethan interjected, entering the cavern housing the cells. "I'll get her out of there."

A string of harsh curses flew from the three demons, all aimed at him. Demons had a talent for creative threats, and Ethan had to chuckle when the female promised to rip out his guts through his anus.

"Energetic bunch you all are." He ignored the rest of their graphic threats, as he stepped forward to unlock Analia's door.

Face to face, she appraised him with a timid eye, taking in his long dark coat, black pants, and thick black boots. The gold bands on his fingers drew her gaze before she settled back on his face.

Ethan smiled and bowed. "You like?"

He actually did hope she found him handsome, but hid the desire with a sarcastic tone.

Her uneasy expression transformed into fierce disdain. "Why have you locked us up?"

"To keep you from leaving, of course."

"Why would you want to do that?"

He shrugged. "To answer that, I'll need you to come with me."

Sebastian bellowed, "Let me out of here, you traitorous vermin. I will rip your head from your body."

Ethan murmured, "Well, now I will definitely not be letting him out." He smiled at Analia. "Follow me. My chambers will provide some much-needed privacy."

Analia stepped out of her cell and took note of the two guards against the far wall. Without another word, Ethan headed back down the hallway.

Thankfully, she followed after him. He didn't want to have to drag her with him as if she were a common prisoner.

Sebastian continued to yell, "If you harm her in any way, you will regret it!"

The other demon added in a controlled tone, "That's not a threat, mate. That's a fact."

"Fascinating. Loyalty in demons is difficult to inspire." Ethan gave Analia an admiring glance and walked on. "I apologize about the tranquilizer. I hadn't wanted you to sleep quite so long, and that particular dart was not meant for you, but…no harm done."

"Thank you for your concern," she replied with a surprising amount of venom. "Why don't you get to the point?"

"Just as impatient as your demons, aren't you?" Ethan stopped and opened the door to his chambers, gesturing for her to enter. When she hesitated, he said, "Come on, I will not harm you."

"You'll understand if I don't believe you."

He quirked a brow at her bravado. Her boldness reminded him of her eldest sister, Kyralyn. "Pirates honor." He grinned.

After another moment of hesitation, the princess entered the room.

His chamber was magnificent. Red, orange, and green linen draped the entire room, floor to ceiling. The ground was not dirt and dust, but a spread of lush burgundy matting. Lanterns lined the walls and hung from the ceiling, giving off a warm glow.

In one corner, three large chairs surrounded a small table. His desk sat against the opposite wall, the book resting on top.

She came to a halt in the middle of the room. Just as he closed the chamber door, she whirled on him, her gaze fierce. She looked as though she were ready to beat him senseless.

"Brave little one." He grinned and stepped forward.

Without warning, she lunged at him, and he almost didn't dodge the attack in time.

He grabbed her wrist and twisted her around so that he was at her back with her hands locked behind her. Securing both her wrists in one of his hands, he raised his other to her face. She flinched, and he paused, not wanting to alarm her further.

Then, slowly, he brushed her hair aside, revealing one distinct ear.

"What?" Her body grew tense. "Never seen pointed ears before?"

He smirked. "I've seen ears like yours more often than you might think."

She stilled, and then gave him her profile. "You have?"

"Yes," he replied, excited to find interest layered beneath her anger. "I'll tell you about it if you like, though I much prefer conversations face to face. If I let you go, will you promise not to attack me again?"

She seemed to consider this for a moment before offering a tight nod. As soon as he released her, she darted to the other side of the room.

He took a seat in one of the nearby chairs and leaned back. "Please have a seat," he encouraged. When she didn't, he added. "I've already given my word that I will not harm you."

"My friends are locked up against their will. Some of them are still unconscious from the drug you shot into them. The word of a pirate does not hold much weight with me at the moment."

"Touché," he said with renewed admiration. She had a fiery spirit.

He wanted to ask about Darius, about what sort of threat he posed, but she seemed too skittish for the moment. There were other matters to discuss first, anyway.

Silence reigned between them, but to his delight, her expression became curious. "Tell me, where have you seen ears like mine?"

"Before we get to that, would you like a drink? Something to eat?"

She raised her chin, but did not reply.

"You must be hungry after two days of restful sleep."

She continued to stare.

"Suit yourself." He stood, and she jumped back. He gave her a chafed look as he walked past her to the desk. Placing a hand on the large book, he said, "This will tell you everything you need to know. All you have to do, Analia, is open it."

Her eyes widened at the use of her name.

"Yes, I know who you are. I know more about you than perhaps you do."

"Like what?" She narrowed her gaze.

"You don't remember your people? Your home planet? What happened there?"

She looked at the book and then at the empty package on the floor. "Is that book what we came to deliver?"

He nodded.

"And it holds the answers that I seek?"

"Yes."

"But you seek these answers as well?" She tilted her head.

"I do."

"Why, then, do you need me? Why not just open the book and see for yourself?"

"It's been enchanted to open for only three people in the universe."

"And somehow I'm one of the three?" Disbelief coated her words. "Where are the others?"

"That's what I hope to find out."

She seemed to digest the information, glancing between him and the book as if she didn't know which one worried her most. Finally, she took a step closer. "How do I open it?"

He nodded in encouragement. "You must only touch the lock."

She ran her fingers over the cover as though it were a delicate piece of artwork, her eyes entranced. Perhaps she felt the power flowing off it.

"Tell me," he said, unable to hold off his curiosity a moment longer. "What do you know of a man named Darius?"

She yanked the heavy book up with both hands and heaved it off the desk. He saw rather than felt the book connect with his head. The ground came next, then blackness.

His eyes fluttered open. He pulled himself off the ground and pressed his palm over the throbbing bump on his skull. A quick survey of the room told him Analia was gone. And she'd taken the book.

Remarkable! Her intention had been completely hidden to him.

He pressed a set of buttons on his console to bring up his computer and opened a direct connection to Oxnel's handheld.

Before he could relay the events, Oxnel bellowed, "They're escaping, sir."

Ethan suppressed a groan. "Gather the men and meet me in the docking station. That's where they'll head."

Chapter 4

Sonya leaned against the cell wall, cleaning the dried dirt from under her nails.

Aidan and the other crew members had finally roused from their slumber and groggily paced the small cell. Sebastian continued to work on the door, the skin of his shoulder beginning to crack and bleed from the repeated abuse.

"What happened?" Aidan rubbed both hands over his face.

Sonya gave a harsh laugh. "What do you think happened? Surprise, surprise, betrayed by a pirate. Who'd have thought?" Sarcasm dripped from her words.

"You know," Cale snapped, "That's not helpful."

"Oh? And what would be helpful, Cale? Breaking my arm on a door that won't budge?"

"At least you'd have something new to complain about!"

Sonya bristled and took a step toward him. "Fuck off, Cale. That should be easy enough for you."

Cale responded in kind. "You'd be wise to shut your mouth. Now."

"Make me!"

Aidan barricaded himself between them. "Enough, both of you. Beating each other senseless won't—"

Sebastian stilled, both palms planted against the door, his gaze intent through the small barred window. Moments later, Sonya caught Anya's scent.

She heard shuffling movements outside the door, and then Anya's scream echoed down the hall.

Sebastian's roar reverberated off the walls of their cell. The madness of the Edge effectively dug its claws into him, driving him harder than ever into the thick door. The metal bowed under the onslaught as Anya continued to scream for him.

Sonya felt herself slipping to the Edge as well, wanting more than anything to rip through the walls and introduce her claws to Anya's attackers.

Anya went quiet. Sonya's breath caught.

Sebastian turned wild, clawing and tearing at the barrier between him and his mate. Sonya backed away, and everyone but Cale followed suit.

Terrible urgency beat in Sonya's chest, yet she had no idea what to do.

Then a strange sensation began to crawl across her skin. A pop rang out and the lights flashed bright, blinding her for a moment. The bulbs overhead shattered.

Sonya's eyes quickly adjusted to the darkness. The distinct sound of the lock mechanism clicked just as Sebastian broke through, nearly tearing the door off its hinges.

Anya stood outside the cell, gasping for air, yet smiling triumphantly. Sebastian shot forward to scoop Anya up and squeeze her to his chest, burying his head in her hair. Anya wrapped her arms around him and closed her eyes.

Sonya scanned dark cavern, ready to take on the guards, but they had fled, no doubt frightened by Anya's mysterious power. Or perhaps the raging demons ready to take their heads.

"Let's get to the ship," Cale grumbled from out of the darkness.

"Agreed," Sebastian replied, setting Anya on her feet.

Sonya made her way toward the open corridor, ready to take on anyone who tried to stop them. Hopefully it would be that damn Pirate King.

Anya shouted from behind. "Wait! The book."

"What book?" Sebastian looked around as if he had missed something.

Anya pointed into the darkness. "I left a book on the ground here, just by the wall."

Sebastian roamed his gaze across the floor. "Anya, there is no book."

"There must be." Anya crouched and patted blindly at the ground. Her vision in the dark was not as well defined as theirs. "It must be here."

Sebastian took on a concerned look. "There is nothing, love. We must go."

Anya's shoulders sank, her expression bleak, but she relented.

Sebastian claimed the lead as they made their way through the stony maze, following the familiar scent of *Marada's* metallic tang. He halted his step, placing himself at Anya's front. Sonya paused behind them, sensing it too.

Danger loomed.

"The ship is just up ahead," Sebastian whispered. "But we're not alone."

With a bit more caution, they continued on.

In the distance, a group of dark shadows blocked their way. Sonya steeled herself for battle.

Ethanule stood with five guards on either side of him, weapons drawn. The pirate held a large object in his arms. Sonya tilted her head. Could that be the book Anya spoke of?

"Analia," the pirate began. "We seem to have gotten off on the wrong foot. I apologize. There are things you need to know. Things about our people."

The last few words forced an icy chill up Sonya's spine. Anya had once revealed that she knew nothing of her kind. Didn't even know where she came from or what she was.

"Our people?" Anya gasped.

"We are the same, you and I." The pirate lowered his weapon.

Sonya huffed. "Ha! He's lying." Surely this was a trick. This pirate thought to appeal to Anya's ignorance and naivety—an undergoing that was far too easy, unfortunately.

Ethanule shot Sonya an indignant look and then reached a hand up to brush his white-blond hair to the side, revealing a pointed ear that resembled Anya's. Sonya gasped just as Anya sucked in a breath and reached out mindlessly. Sebastian gently held her back by the shoulder.

Ethanule dropped his hand and continued. "I was about to tell you just before your pesky crack to my head. That hurt, by the way." He gave a crooked smile.

Anya scowled. "Why did you lock us up? Why drug us?"

Sonya jutted her chin, waiting for his response.

"I feared you were being held captive by these demons," Ethanule said. "There are many who develop an unnatural obsession with our kind. I meant only to protect you."

Sonya had to admit, he was skilled at personifying sincerity.

"And the lock on my door?" Anya replied.

"In—which it seems to be the case—you were with these demons by choice, I did not want you able to flee before I could speak with you."

"So you *do* know what I can do?" Anya hissed.

"I have been told, yes."

"By who?" she demanded.

Ethanule hesitated, lowering his eyes. He let out a broken breath and replied, "Your father."

Sonya gasped. A distinct shade of green crawled along Anya's skin, and Sebastian had to steady her on her feet.

Sonya ground her teeth, not sure what to say or do. Her mind screamed that this couldn't possibly be right. He was a despicable, lying pirate, and all this was yet another farce.

Ethanule continued in a soft tone. "I can explain everything if you'll let me."

Anya's throat visibly worked, but she seemed to regain some composure. "Why did you ask me about Darius?"

"What!" Sebastian bellowed, a hint of the Edge returning to his eyes.

Sonya balled her fist. For years, Darius had held Anya captive, used her, hurt her in unspeakable ways. And if these bastards were in league with him, the walls would drink of their blood.

Ethanule did not look as daunted as he should. "He contacted me. Asked me about a woman fitting Analia's description. I didn't like what I saw in his eyes when he spoke of you, so I told him I'd seen no such female."

Sonya studied the pirate in detail, but his expression was true and his stance nonthreatening. Even his guards had lowered their weapons.

"We must go, now!" Sebastian motioned his crew forward despite the armed guards still blocking their way.

Ethanule motioned for his men to stand down.

"Tell me Ethanule," Sebastian growled. "Do you know how far away his ship was when he contacted you?"

"I do not." Ethanule fell in step beside Sebastian as though to debate a plan of action. "Who is this Darius?"

Sonya answered in a scathing tone, "You spoke of unnatural obsession? Well, he's the prime example."

Still looking utterly shocked, Anya began firing off questions so quickly, Sonya could hardly keep up. "What of my father? Where is he? How did he know I'd come to be here? How is it he knew to tell you of me? Does he still live? Does he know where I've been?"

Ethanule edged, "As far as I know, he lives. As for the other stuff, we will have plenty of time to speak of it later. Seems the demon's in a hurry."

Anya halted. Sonya took note of the wild look in her eyes. She wasn't taking this news well. Likewise, aggression and the desire to rip these bastards apart still burned in Sonya's veins.

Enunciating each word, Anya demanded, "Does he know where I've been?"

Ethanule gave a heavy sigh and replied, "Analia, it's complicated." He tried to avert his gaze, but the guilt was clear.

"Do *you* know?"

He paused. "I've been told very little. But what I was told…

I'm…sorry."

Sonya wondered how this male, or the alleged *father*, knew anything of Anya's past. She wanted to rail at him for not doing something about it, if it were indeed the truth.

"It's why I suspected the demons, but now I'm thinking…" Ethanule looked to Sebastian, "Darius?"

Sebastian gave a tight nod, a muscle ticking in his jaw.

"There's much I must explain. It's not as simple as you think. If your father could have done something, I know—"

"Enough," Anya snapped. There was true pain in her voice. "I don't want to hear any more." With a firm step, she stomped past them toward the ship.

Sonya would have gone a step further and knocked the son of a bitch on his ass. In fact, maybe she would do Anya a solid. Sebastian seemed to read her intent and shook his head. Sonya sneered, but kept her fists to herself.

"I'm coming with you," Ethanule informed Sebastian.

Sonya snorted out a humorless laugh.

Sebastian's expression grew dark. "Is that what you think?"

"Remember, I'm the one in control of all the guns." The pirate smirked.

Sebastian spared a glance to a nearby guard and kept moving. Bullets hurt, but rarely packed the power to incapacitate a demon.

"It's important that I explain things to her." Ethanule sounded desperate. "I must stay with her until I can. It's my duty, to my people, my king…"

Sonya scoffed and walked away. There was no time for argument. Not when Darius was sniffing out their trail.

Anya stood by the ship, her shoulders hunched and arms

hugging her torso. She appeared to need her solitude, so Sonya veered toward a smooth wall and leaned against it with her arms crossed. Her gaze slipped to Ethanule pleading with Sebastian.

After a moment, Ethanule headed toward Anya...alone. Sonya nearly lunged to hold him back, but Sebastian signaled everyone to give them space. What could he be thinking? The pirate could feed her any manner of nonsense.

Catching her apprehension, Sebastian again motioned for her to stay back. She threw her arms in the air.

They didn't have time for this!

She narrowed her eyes on Ethanule, hoping to read some of the words he whispered to Anya.

Ethanule smiled at Anya, unaware that he was being watched. Sonya's teeth clenched. She would love nothing more than to slap that grin right off his face.

Her gaze drifted past his straight nose toward his irises. They were blue, like Anya's, but different in shade, deeper and filled with a keen intellect...and something else she couldn't describe.

She jumped as Cale appeared next to her, mimicking her stance against the wall. Sebastian stood nearby as well, not taking his eyes from Anya.

"What do you think?" Cale asked.

"I don't like him," Sonya grumbled. "I don't trust him. He's a damn pirate. Anya has wanted to find someone like her and then *boom*, here he is? It's too coincidental."

Cale nodded. "I would have loved to see Anya crack him over the head."

Sonya grinned at the visual.

Anya's lip quivered at something Ethanule said. Sebastian

lurched forward, reaching them in a matter of seconds. Sonya and Cale hurried after him.

"What did he say to you?" Sebastian demanded, barring himself between the two.

Anya burrowed her face in Sebastian's chest.

Sonya raised an accusing brow at Ethanule, but he didn't notice. His attention remained on Anya and Sebastian's embrace, expression stony.

"I told her that our people are at war, and they are depending on her," Ethanule said.

"I can't think," Anya mumbled. "Ethanule wants to come with us." She looked up at Sebastian with mixture of terror and hope. "What do you think?"

"I think you should at least listen to what he has to say." Sebastian gazed down at Anya.

Sonya opened her mouth to argue.

Sebastian took Anya's chin between his thumb and forefinger. "Then, if you want, I will kill him for you."

Sonya gave a curt nod. That was more like it.

With a crooked smile, Ethanule scoffed. "You could try, demon."

Anya looked him over for a moment and then sighed. "Alright."

Sonya groaned in defeat.

Oxnel pulled Ethan aside, away from the others. "If you leave, you will be relinquishing your status as leader."

Ethan patted his friend on the shoulder. "It was never my plan to stay."

Oxnel's lips thinned. "Think on what you do. You cannot

return and reclaim your position. I could not allow it. You understand?"

Ethan nodded. He would need to challenge not only Oxnel, as the new leader, but also each and every Denaloid for that right. A task that had nearly killed him the first time.

He pointed toward the docked ship. "I wish you luck, but they are my destiny now."

"Then good luck to you as well," Oxnel replied, glancing at *Marada's* crew. "It appears as though you're going to need it."

Ethan smiled. "Indeed." Convincing the princess's entourage to trust him fully was going to be arduous. His gift offered him the impression that each of them wanted to knock him on his ass and leave him here. He supposed drugging them and locking them up may not have been the best course of action, but it was in the interest of the princess's safety. They would have done the same in his position.

He said his good-byes to Oxnel and his men and then joined his new crew.

Cale approached him. "Hey, pirate. Is it true what these Denaloids do to prisoners? I've heard some nasty stuff."

Denaloids observed a strict code of conduct, but what they were notorious for was rendering harsh punishments. "Just be glad you were under my protection."

"Good," Cale said. "We have a male on board who needs some...discipline. He tried to force himself on Anya. Can we dump him here?"

Ethan looked to Oxnel who was close enough to hear the conversation. Oxnel gave an approving nod. Ethan turned back to Cale. "My men would love a *pet* project."

Cale disappeared into the ship and then returned with the

male in question.

Oxnel appraised the prisoner with disgust. He gripped him by the nape of the neck and thrust him toward three waiting guards. As the guards restrained him, the male's pathetic cries for mercy echoed.

Ethan spared him no pity. This miscreant would beg for death long before he received it.

The female demon, Sonya, drew Ethan's attention when she sauntered forward and cracked the prisoner in the face with an artful right hook, rendering him unconscious. Ethan's brows shot up. Then she turned to him with an arrogant wink and a flick of her tail. He got the impression that she wanted to hit *him* just as hard. He smiled at the thought of her trying, and how much fun it would be to thwart her every attempt.

As she ascended into the ship, her outrageously short skirt and smooth thighs demanded his attention. His legs had him closing in before he realized it.

"Nice form," he whispered in her ear, letting the double entendre slip into his tone.

A whisper of her intent hit him just before she whirled on him, but he remained still, not wanting to reveal his talents just yet. He didn't need to look down to know she had a dagger held to his neck.

She took in his amused expression and anger flashed in her eyes. The cool metal of her blade creased his skin. She spoke to her brothers without taking her eyes off him. "What should we do with the pirate?"

Anya spoke up. "I think you should lock him up."

Ethan's jaw dropped, and his eyes darted to the princess. Of all the things he expected, he hadn't seen that coming—from her, at least.

"Sounds good to me." Sonya smirked. "How about you guys?"

Both Sebastian and Cale nodded.

Sonya shoved Ethan down the hall. Still a little taken aback, he stumbled, but quickly caught his footing.

Fine, he thought darkly. It wouldn't hurt to play along for now. He would do his time until the princess came to him for her answers. Curiosity burned behind her eyes. If she wanted answers, he'd make it clear she would get none until he received the respect he deserved.

Anya's voice traveled down the hall toward them. "In sickbay, please."

Sonya rolled her eyes and then looked to Sebastian. He nodded.

"Lucky for you, pirate, Anya's heart is too soft for her own good. The cell in sickbay is too nice for the likes of you," Sonya grumbled and pushed Ethan along once more.

Ethan gathered a calming breath, reminding himself it would not be a good idea to show the she-demon how easily he could disarm her.

Instead, he took in his surroundings as they marched through the wide corridor. Soft golden light feathered over the walls that gave off a pleasant hue of golden-brown. Plush carpet cushioned his step. It was unusual for most ships to offer such luxurious detail.

"Nice ship," he blurted.

"So glad you approve." Sonya shoved him again. He gritted his teeth.

Sickbay was as impressive as the rest of the ship, but not as inviting with sterile walls and too bright lights. A prestigious-looking doctor with dark hair and a rigidly straight posture perched at a desk near the back of the room.

"Sonya, thank the gods!" The doctor shot to his feet. "I feared the pirates had…" He trailed off, his eyes scanning over Ethan.

"Well, the pirates *had*…" Sonya left the rest of the statement open for interpretation. "This one will have an extended stay in your observation cell."

"Is he injured?"

"Not yet."

The doctor raised a brow before expressing a hint of irritation. "You cannot continue to use my sickbay as prisoner quarters."

Sonya ignored the complaint as she heaved Ethan into an alcove containing nothing more than a small cot. Then she pressed a button on the wall, engaging a force field that closed him in.

Their eyes locked through the transparent wall. Ethan countered her ferocious gaze with an arrogant smirk. "My thanks for the escort. I expect you'll be tending my future needs as well." He slid his gaze to her shapely legs.

Her jaw dropped, then she clamped it shut. His lips twitched with amusement.

She scrutinized him for a long moment before commenting, "I always imagined a pirate with your reputation would have more scars, but you look positively dainty."

Ethan merely smiled. "You look pretty dainty yourself."

Her lips pulled back in a sneer. "That shows how little you know about me."

"Likewise."

With one last disdainful glance, she stowed her blade at her waist and headed for the door, giving him leave to appraise her plump backside before she disappeared. She might have a barbaric temperament, but she boasted an outstanding figure.

Chapter 5

"I don't understand why we didn't just leave the pirate behind." Sonya finished drying a glass and then set it with the others behind the bar.

"I haven't even sat down yet," Sebastian complained, sliding onto one of the stools.

With a huff, she set to mixing him a drink. He looked exhausted. Dark stains hugged his eyes, his lips fixed in a scowl. He had probably spent the last two days in the control room, fearing the moment he stepped away, Darius would find them.

The last time they'd faced off against Darius' ship, *Extarga*, *Marada* had not fared well, and Anya had nearly died using her gift to feed energy to the ship's warp drive.

After taking a swig of her new mixture, dubbed bloody screwed, Sebastian finally replied, "Ethanule claims to know how to translate that damn book." Sebastian let out a sigh. "Anya hasn't even opened it yet. She seems wary of it."

"That's understandable," Sonya replied absently. When her brother shot her a confused stare, she added, "Whatever's in that book could change her life…again."

"Aye." He shook his head as if unsure whether he should be encouraging her to open the book or toss it into space, along with Ethanule.

Sonya was rooting for the latter. "What else is bothering you?"

Sebastian hesitated for a moment. "Ethanule is a male of her own race, and I have not yet…" He trailed off.

"Ah. I get it," Sonya said. "You're afraid Anya will choose the pirate over you." At Sebastian's halfhearted shrug, Sonya added, "That will never happen. Have you not seen the way she looks at you? You'd be daft to believe she'd throw you off for another."

"He wants her. I know it."

Some inner part of Sonya, buried deep in a corner of her mind, growled at Sebastian's statement. It would be typical of a pirate to try to steal another's mate. And even though she knew Ethanule would never succeed—Anya was lost for her demon— the idea made her seethe.

For some reason, she felt the need to avert her gaze from Sebastian. "Has he admitted to this?"

"No. I just feel it." He clenched his fists.

Sonya rolled her eyes. "You think everyone wants Anya."

"They do, don't they?"

She laughed, but he wasn't far off. Anya had a way of carving a place for herself in the hearts of everyone she met. "Why haven't you claimed her, anyway?" She couldn't understand the delay. When a demon finds their mate, the matter was usually settled within days, not weeks, as in Sebastian and Anya's case. "What's the wait?"

"Anya has reservations. She fears if Darius reclaims her— which will never happen—that I would be left mated and alone forever."

"But that would be the case even if you *never* claimed her," Sonya rationalized. Most demons held a deep belief that the fates create only one mate for each of them. A single perfect companion, and when found, must be cherished as such.

"Aye, she does not understand. Imagines I could possibly find another." He scoffed at what Sonya agreed was an absurd assessment, though it was true not every race held the same ideals as demon-kind. Tierlocks, for one, believed in many mates, often at once.

And even some demons disbelieved the one mate theory. Sonya supposed that the destruction of one's planet and being scattered throughout space could rock anyone's cultural belief system to its core.

For a long time, even *she* had doubted, what with her perpetual bachelor brothers and Marik unmated for so long. Not to mention her own single status. She'd begun to wonder if they all relied on fate too much and overlooked potential matches due to the lack of life-shattering signs they'd been raised to expect. Then Sebastian had found Anya, and Sonya was again reassured. Then again, perhaps she was merely over-romanticizing the whole situation.

"Would you speak with her?" Sebastian interrupted her thoughts. "Get her to see reason?"

"Sebastian, just let her get accustomed to the idea. It must be her choice, as well as yours."

"Exactly why I want you to speak with her. She will listen to you. And you can tell her how great it would be."

Sonya wanted to yell, "How the hell would I know how great it would be?" She'd never even bedded a male, let alone contemplated taking one as a mate! Instead, she begrudgingly relented while resenting Sebastian anew for his role in her perpetual state of loneliness.

Demons naturally crave pleasure. Without it, they become irritable, or could even slip to the Edge without meaning to, placing anyone nearby in danger.

And they wonder why I snap at them all the time.

Sebastian finished his drink and left. Sonya took his empty glass from the bar and proceeded to wash it in the water basin and then tended to the other patrons seated around the room.

Just as she stepped back behind the bar, Anya entered the pub looking shell-shocked. She had the book nestled in her arms. Sonya motioned her to an empty bar stool and started mixing one of her special Anya concoctions—light and sweet. Anya placed the book on the stool next to her. Then she took the offered drink and gulped it down to the last drop.

"Bad day?" Sonya mused.

"I'm a princess," Anya blurted in a half-crazed tone.

Sonya stared at her for a moment, waiting for the punch line. "Is that so? It's not a bad thing to be, I guess. Unless…do they sacrifice princesses where you're from?" When Anya considered the question with alarming seriousness, Sonya gasped. "No…Do they?"

Anya shrugged. "I don't know. All I've learned so far is that my people are called Faieara, and they may be involved in a war that has spanned four hundred years or more. My father sent me, my mother, and apparently two of my sisters away, to avoid capture. And oh, yeah, did I mention I might be over four hundred years old, if what Ethanule says is even remotely true, which I don't know for sure. And somehow he thinks, at least, I believe he thinks, that I am somehow capable of helping our people." She rapped a finger over her temple. "Did I leave anything out?"

Sonya had begun to worry Anya would pass out from lack of air. She'd never seen her friend so shaken. "Ooookay…. Take a breath, everything will be fine. What about the book, what does it say in there?"

"I haven't opened it," Anya admitted, looking slightly shamed.

"Why not?"

"Because only three people in the universe can open that book, according to Ethanule. And if it does open for me, then… well, that makes everything real. And if it doesn't open…" She didn't finish her sentence.

Sonya could guess the turmoil that was beating a destructive path through Anya's head. She finally had answers as to who she was, where she came from, and why she was isolated away from her people…and it all sounded like one big mess, with the pirate directly at the center.

Yep. Should have left him behind.

Sonya offered an encouraging smile as she refilled Anya's glass. "Either you are who he says you are, or you're not. What-ever you find out, we're still here for you."

Anya's lips thinned into a half smile. "Thanks. It's just, I'm so close to finding out who I am, finally. But what if he's wrong?"

Or worse, Sonya thought to herself, what if he was lying.

* * *

Ethanule lay on the uncomfortable hard mat of his cot with his arms tucked behind his head, staring up at the high ceiling.

As he'd predicted, the princess has come to him seeking answers. He'd been shocked by how ignorant she was of her previous life on Evlon. She remembered nothing of her family or her people, just as he feared. She was even unaware of her true age!

Her father had warned that her memory would be fuzzy, but Ethan hadn't anticipated this complete lack of knowledge.

He had only offered her the basics, then had refused to say more until granted his freedom. He'd been in this cell for two days now. Measure for measure, they had their reprisal.

The enticing scent of cooked meat filled Ethanule's nostrils, and his stomach growled. When he searched for the source, he saw the female demon entering with a plate of food.

He'd have liked to say it was the promise of food that brought him to his feet, but he'd only partly be telling the truth. The she-demon was clad in another of those tight skirts and a form-fitting top decorated by woven laces at the front.

Not only was she a feast for the eyes—even though she was a demon—the strength and bravery she had demonstrated on his asteroid commanded his respect. Not that he would ever tell her that.

She stalked toward him. "Hungry?" Her tone was dangerously low.

He offered a noncommittal shrugged.

"Not hungry?" She hovered the plate over a nearby trash bin. "I'll just get rid of this then."

"Well, if you're just going to throw it away. I don't approve of wasting food." He extended his palm, though the force field was still in place.

"Oh, you want it then?" She held out a piece of meat to him like a master to a pet.

He crossed his arms and raised an eyebrow at her. "Look,

demon, either give me the food or throw it out. I don't give a damn either way." His stomach chose that moment to betray him with a growl, and the sexy little demon quirked a triumphant smile. "Did you only come here to torment me?"

She crossed the room and set the tray on a nearby counter. He tried not to notice her curves under the thin clingy material of her skirt. Her tail flicked when she caught him staring. Her smile vanished, replaced with a hardness that didn't fit her.

"I came to judge for myself," she announced cryptically.

"Judge? I'm a prisoner. I think everyone's made up their minds. What's more to judge?"

"You said a lot to Anya. Maybe it's true." She narrowed her violet gaze. "And maybe it's not. If it's not true, I warn you now to come clean. Because if you fill her head with false hope, you won't live to see what Sebastian will do to you because, pirate, I'll make sure I get to you first. And I'll rip your entrails through your gut and make you watch while your insides are being torn from your body."

"Graphic."

She bared her tiny fangs.

He put his hands up in surrender. "Everything I told her is the truth."

Sonya tilted her head, looking as if she were deciding whether or not to believe him. Then her brows furrowed. "So, she's really a princess?"

"Yes, the youngest of three."

"And what happened? Why was she sent to that place?"

"Like I told the princess, I'll offer no more until I'm freed."

Sonya shifted her weight. "You're a pirate."

"We've established this."

"Pirates in general are untrustworthy. You'll do and say anything to get what you're after. So, pirate, what are you after?"

"I wasn't always a pirate. I'm just trying to save my people."

"How long have you been a pirate?"

"Three hundred and fifty years," he answered without thinking.

"That's a long time of taking what you want with no consequences. You must have grown fond of the lifestyle."

That was true enough. He'd acted the part for so long he was no longer sure if he was a soldier or a pirate. He'd had to do a lot of underhanded things to get into the right position. Was it all for the sake of his home? Or was a little bit of it for him? He *had* enjoyed it more than he probably should've.

"That's what I thought."

"I didn't say anything."

"It's all over your face. Once a pirate, always a pirate."

He'd prove her wrong about that. It had been his duty. He was a soldier, doing a king's bidding. And now he would focus on being a loyal and honorable husband to the princess. The demon turned on her heels without another word, her hips swaying as she went.

"You know, you're not bad looking for a demon," he found himself saying. Maybe he was a little more pirate than he wanted to admit.

She glanced back at him and sneered. "You are not even slightly good looking for a pirate."

Sonya wondered at the fierce beat of her heart as she stomped her way back to the pub. Such a flimsy compliment should not affect her so. Especially one from a conniving pirate, designed to appeal to her vanity.

Yet the pirate's eyes had traveled the length of her body and back again with blatant interest. A traitorous smile crept over her lips. She gnashed her teeth and pressed her lips together until the urge passed.

The ridiculousness of it!

Was she actually intrigued by the attention of a pirate? Her father would be disgusted. More than disgusted! He'd be outraged if he were alive today. And what would her brothers say? She didn't even want to imagine.

Pushing the memory of the pirate's heated expression from her mind, she reentered the pub. She glanced around, dismayed by how many seats remained empty. Now that the wards had come down, the crew was eager to find entertainment elsewhere.

After tending to her only two customers in the place, she wiped down tables and counters, ignoring the fact that they still gleamed from when she'd cleaned them earlier.

As the day drew on, a few more tables filled. Not the rush she would have liked, but better than nothing. Serving them ate up minutes at best.

She briefly considered closing the pub for the evening and heading to the recreation room. For some reason, her body thrummed with pent-up frustration—due to boredom, she assumed. Boredom and restlessness, and nothing else.

Sebastian appeared in the doorway, followed by Cale, Marik, and Anya. They made their way to an empty table in a far corner, and Sebastian motioned for her to join them.

"What is it?" she asked.

Instead of answering, Sebastian turned to Anya. "May I read

part of the letter?"

Anya eyed the piece paper in his hand before giving a tight nod.

He kept his tone low as he read. "Now is a time of great tragedy among the Faieara. Shortly after I had you and your sisters removed from our planet, we were attacked and overtaken by a swarm of destruction. They call themselves Kayadon."

Sebastian paused as Sonya sucked in a breath, recognizing the last word. The Kayadon had destroyed the demon home world.

Sebastian continued. "The Kayadon live only to consume, and our planet is plentiful. They also live for power and have usurped my throne. Our home has become my prison, and I have become nothing more than a figurehead to keep our people compliant while the Kayadon ravage our lands.

"I sent you away to give you and your sisters time to grow into your powers. The reason you must grow into your gifts is because your destiny, along with your sisters, is to return to our home and trigger the rebellion against the Kayadon. We may defeat them yet. I have seen this as a possible future.

"As with all my visions, there are many possible futures. None are set in stone, and for our people, many end in tragedy. But the quest I have sent you on is the only future I must believe in. If our people are to survive, you must find your sisters and bring them home.

"The book you now possess is filled with the information you require for success. Follow my instructions. Find your sisters. Save our people."

When Sebastian finished, he looked up and his gaze met six sets of flashing red eyes. Sonya's mind reeled.

"This letter was found inside the book," he announced. "I don't know about any of you, but I no longer believe in coincidences. Something larger is at work here. Anya came to us for a reason." He placed a hand on Anya's shoulder, whose eyes were cast down as if shamed by the revelation. "Anya will not ask for your help, but I will. This is not an order. It's an opportunity to take our revenge. I'm going to do everything in my power to avenge our people and hopefully save hers in the process. It's your choice to come with us or not."

The entire bar had fallen silent. Sebastian spoke loud enough for all to hear. There was no doubt that Sonya, Marik, and Cale would stand behind Anya, but not everyone held a vendetta against the Kayadon. The rest of the crew would have to choose between joining them or parting ways.

"Of course we're coming," Sonya assured. "We've all dreamt of ripping out Kayadon throats. I can't believe you thought you even needed to ask."

Cale's fists were clenched tight, his red eyes darkening with palpable rage. No doubt thoughts of his Velicia's betrayal swarmed his mind.

Marik mirrored Cale's anger. Amid the Kayadon invasion, he had lost his family as well.

"Well, how do we find these sisters of yours?" Cale growled to Anya, sounding harsher than he had probably meant to.

Anya hesitated, then shrugged uncomfortably. "Part of the text needs to be translated."

Realization struck Sonya like a punch to the gut. "The pirate," she groaned.

"He won't do it. Not while he's locked up," Anya said.

Point Ethanule.

"Oh, he'll do it," Cale assured. "Or he'll become acquainted with my claws."

"We can't keep him locked up. It's not right," Anya continued. "Besides, he wants to help just as much as you do. He lost his home too."

"He'll be freed for his help." Sebastian's voice rang out with the air of a leader, not to be questioned. Yet he hesitated before adding, "He'll be expected to work." Sebastian shot Sonya a meaningful look.

A heavy ball of dread sank into her stomach. "No! Don't even think about it."

"Anya cannot work both in the galley and here at the pub, while continuing her training with Cale and learning about her people. The pirate will take her job in the pub."

"The pirate has a name." Anya sounded perturbed, but she went ignored.

"Damn it, Sebastian!" Sonya slammed her fist on the table. "He can't be trusted. He'll probably just hide out in the back drinking all my liquor like the degenerate he is."

Anya interjected, "He's not a degenerate. He was a soldier—"

"I don't care if he was the freaking king himself! I don't like him, and I don't like this plan."

"Please, Sonya." Anya looked up at her with the most earnest, compelling expression Sonya had ever been subject to.

She wanted to whine and rail and throw a fit—she might have even stomped her foot for good measure—but Anya deserved to possess the knowledge of her people.

"Fine," Sonya grumbled. Surely she could tolerate a pirate for a short time. "But if he doesn't do his job perfectly, I reserve the right to slash his throat."

"No." Sebastian leaned forward in his chair.

She rolled her eyes. "Kidding. I'll just rough him up a bit before I kick him out of my pub."

Chapter 6

Sebastian had allocated a small alcove across the hall for the Anya and Ethanule's research...directly in Sonya's line of sight.

Sonya leaned wearily against the bar and groaned. "Aw, come on, Sebastian. I already agreed to allow him behind my bar. I don't want to have to spy on him and Anya as well. You can't possibly be this insecure."

Sebastian bared his fangs. "Just poke your head out every now and again and check on them. If Ethan tries anything, you had damn well better let me know."

"Okay, maybe you *can* be this insecure."

"Just do as I say," Sebastian snarled.

She gave him an overly dramatized roll of her eyes. "Alright."

He pressed his lips together and offered a tight nod before leaving.

Sonya shook her head with pity for her brother. If he didn't claim Anya soon, she was sure he would lose his mind.

She waited a while before edging towards the door and leaned out to get a better look. Anya was seated next to Ethan, who was hunched over the book, flipping through the pages. Notes and several computers were scattered around them.

Captivating.

Sonya rolled her eyes.

Ethan ran his forefinger down the page of the book. Her gaze followed its slow progress and the need to swallow arose. Something in the motion came across…erotic.

Sonya shook away the errant thought before focusing back on Ethan. His shirt hung loose over his shoulder, and his pants were somewhat baggy. No doubt Sebastian or Cale had lent him some clothes. Ethan wasn't a small male by any means, but her brothers still towered over him.

A single pointed ear poked out from behind his white-blond hair. A simple gold hoop hugged the lobe, refracting light when he turned his head.

His bottom lip drew her attention. It was a bit fuller than the top and there was the slightest crease just under it that cradled a small patch of stubble. How is it the gods would permit a pirate to look so handsome?

He glanced up at her and gave her an arrogant smile, as though he knew the trail of her thoughts. She flushed as anger welled, then stabbed him with a piercing glare before she whirled around and rushed back to the safety of her bar.

Ethan had assumed the demon female would be spying on them. Why else would Sebastian have placed their study directly across from her tavern? His feelings for the princess were obvious. And Anya, as she preferred to be called, seemed to return the attraction.

To make matters worse, she expressed no desire for Ethan

in any respect. To be honest, he wasn't extraordinarily attracted to her either. Sure, she was pretty enough. And kind. But she lacked the fire and sensuality he always imagined his other half would possess.

Still, he had been promised the hand of one of the king's daughters and the title that went with it.

Ethan had felt Sonya's eyes on him for some time before he had glanced up. He'd expected to see disdain in her expression, but instead, she'd been gazing at him intently, chewing her bottom lip. His blood had fired as dark images invaded his mind. Images of guiding her hand to his lower regions as he took that lip between his own teeth.

Then he mentally scolded himself. His future bride sat right next to him, for the love of the gods, and he was fantasizing about a lowly demon? What was wrong with him?

He fixed a blank expression and went back to translating the book. It took a moment to find his place again.

Moments later, he caught Anya studying him. "You're staring at my ears."

She gave a sweet smile. "I've only seen them in the mirror."

He allowed her to look as he focused back on the book. He'd already managed to translate parts of it, but some sections confounded him. It was as though he'd need an entirely differed key to decode it. He marked the section for later evaluation and moved on.

"Ethan?" Anya murmured. "Will you tell me about our home planet?"

He smiled, even as a wave of sadness flooded him. "It's beautiful," he replied. "Towering mountains, deep valleys. Some trees are so large they seem to touch the suns. Do you remember anything at all? Our two suns, and the three moons?"

Anya shrugged. "I get flashes every now and again. Not much to go on. I wish I could remember more."

"Most of our people favor the warm regions. Cold disagrees with us, don't you agree?"

"Yes." She nodded. "What else?"

"Our society is a free society. Well, it was, anyway." He was surprised by how forlorn he suddenly felt. He hadn't spoken of Evlon in a long time. "Used to be that you could choose your own path in life, whatever that may be."

He chuckled to himself. Ironically, Ethan's path was not his own. The king had drawn it out for him, utilizing his power to project himself over space to guide Ethan's journey.

Except, those little visits had ended years ago. Judging by how haggard the king had last looked, Ethan had to accept the real possibility that his liege was now dead. Even before the invasion, Ethan had suspected the king might have been terminally ill.

He decided to spare Anya those details. Instead, he added, "Our markets were rich with traders and merchants and entertainment. You could walk through our town center on market day and not even see a quarter of what was available. As a princess, you would have attended festivals and parties. Your only care would have been what to wear to each." He went quiet, yearning for those times himself. "We'll defeat the Kayadon," he assured, more for his own benefit. "Then, after the wedding, I'll show you everything our planet has to offer."

"Wedding?"

He stilled. He hadn't intended on revealing his plans straight out, but it was done now.

He nodded and gazed down at the book, trying to appear nonchalant. "Once we are wed, I'll take you through the forest of lights, which is actually so thick with canopy that it's shadowed in darkness year-round. It's called the forest of light because the creatures that live there have evolved to illuminate parts of their bodies."

He peeked at her, noting her sickly expression.

"Don't worry, it's perfectly safe," he added, hoping her obvious trepidation was for fear of the dark, rather than of marrying him.

Sonya paused in the pub's doorway, shocked by Ethan's revelation. Condensation dripped over her fingers from the ice-cold glasses in her hands. She wasn't going to enjoy telling Sebastian that he was right.

Ugh, why had she chosen now to bring them water?

"Excuse me, but…did you just say 'we' and 'wed'?" Anya asked, incredulous.

Ethan shifted in his chair. "Well, it was agreed upon…by the king…that once I returned with his daughters, I would be rewarded with the privilege to marry one."

Sonya leaned in to hear better.

"Ethan." Anya sighed. "I love Sebastian. With everything in me, I love him. And I choose him."

Sonya couldn't help but smile.

"But, he's a demon," Ethan replied.

Sonya scoffed and crossed the hall, not bothering to hide her irritation. "I'll take a demon over a pirate any day." She handed Anya one of the glasses.

Ethan quickly covered his surprise at seeing her. "Yes, but

you *are* a demon," he said reasonably, as though he wasn't openly insulting her.

Sonya grabbed her tail and looked at it with feigned surprise. "So I am." She glared back at him. "And very soon, this demon is going to be your boss. Your ass is mine, pirate." She considered the extra beverage in her hand. "I have no idea why I brought two of these," she said and turned to leave.

As she went, she overheard Ethan mutter to Anya, "I have a real talent for pissing off demons, don't I?"

Sonya was in full agreement with that.

She tried her best to ignore them the rest of the evening. After a few hours, Anya left, but Ethan remained, studying the book. Sonya found herself watching him again. Every time she caught herself, she'd forced her attention on something else, but without fail, her gaze would slip back. *Only because I mistrust him so thoroughly.*

All the while, Ethan remained hard at work, switching his attention between the book, the computer, his papers, and then back again. He finally took a break and entered the pub, claiming a stool at the end of the bar.

Sonya considered pretending she didn't notice him, but then he yawned and vigorously rubbed his eyes. She sighed in resignation and sauntered. "What's your poison, pirate?"

Irritation flashed over his face at the moniker. "I need something that will wake me up."

"How late do you plan on working?"

He shrugged. "I haven't even gotten past the first few pages." His brows furrowed and he murmured, almost to himself, "It's like I'm missing a piece of the code."

"Isn't that the whole point of encoding something? To make

it difficult to decode?"

"To make it difficult for others to decode, yes. But I should have the whole key, not a part of it."

"Maybe you're just not using the code right. I could take a look at it for you and see if I can't figure it out. Demons are natural linguists, and a code is nothing more than another language."

"Why don't you just get my drink, demon?" he replied curtly.

"I'll only offer once, pirate. Don't beg for my help later." She turned with a cheeky grin and began mixing an invigorating tea blend.

Glancing over her shoulder, she caught him staring and turned away. Oddly, that look made her feel exposed, though she couldn't explain why.

"Here." She set the cup in front of him. "This should get those brain cells kicking."

He took a sip. "It's bitter." He set the glass down. She was about to point out his faulty taste buds, when he blurted, "Why is this place so empty?"

She glanced around, spotting only one couple in the corner and another on their way out the door. "It's late." She tried not to sound embarrassed by his observation.

Ethan shot her a knowing look.

"It's always slow at this hour," she lied.

"Maybe it's your lack of music." He flicked the edge of his cup with his finger, and the ting echoed in the quiet room.

"Most of the time, there is music playing," she replied. "The speakers are broken, and the tech personnel have been busy with other things."

"Oh. Do you need me to look at them?"

Sonya hissed, showing her fangs. "I can take care of it, thank you."

"Very well," Ethan said, grasping his cup in one hand and sliding off the stool. "But I'll only offer once."

Ethan chuckled to himself as he made his way back to his workspace. Sonya had been pleased enough to try and insult him, but she certainly didn't like the turnabout. If he'd stayed any longer, he was sure to coax a snarl out of her.

After taking another sip of his tea, enjoying the rich flavor, he settled in amongst his mess of research. He'd lied when he called the concoction bitter. In truth, the taste was quite pleasing, and his mind was already perking up.

Before long, he was engrossed in his work again, scrawling on parchment all the lines he could not decode for later reference and cycling data through the computers. It was turning out to be quite a chore. Briefly he wondered if the demon female was correct. Could he be misapplying the keycode?

Searching his memory, he quickly assured himself that wasn't the case. He could still visualize the king's instruction as if he held the directions in his hand.

Could the king have left something out?

Ethan shook his head. It was too soon to jump to any conclusions. He flipped the book back to page one.

He didn't know how much time had passed, but his eyes were beginning to droop when Sonya emerged from her tavern, closing for the evening. She shot him a dismissive glance before heading down the hall. After a few steps, she paused and closed her fists, standing with her back to him as though contemplating something.

Eventually, she faced him, her expression a mix between irritation and reserve. "Look, it's easy to get lost if you aren't familiar with the ship's layout, and having a *pirate* wandering aimlessly is a recipe for disaster." She said the word as if it left a bad taste on her tongue.

"I'm sure I can manage to find my way without accidentally plundering your loot."

Sonya turned away and strode down the hall. "We'll see."

Brushing off her attitude, he continued decoding, growing more and more frustrated with his lack of success. After a while, he managed to make some progress. There were promising leads as to the location of Anya's sister Nadua.

Only when Sonya sashayed toward him, dressed in fresh clothing and her black hair arranged in delicate curls dripping past her shoulders, did he realize he'd worked through the night. She caught sight of him and tilted her head, yet said nothing as she re-opened the tavern and slipped inside.

A moment later, he spotted Anya gliding toward him. She smiled and then paused to study him. He realized then how weary he must look.

"You should take a break. You'll burn yourself out if you continue like this," she chided.

He was about to assure her he was fine when a loud squeal shot from behind. "Oh, my gods, oh, my gods! He finally did it!" Sonya zipped forward to wrap Anya in a tight hug.

Ethan's gut hollowed into a dreadful pit.

Anya sputtered, "You couldn't... You don't... How..."

Somehow Sonya understood Anya's convoluted babbling.

She smiled. "It's a demon thing. We can just tell." Then she bounced in place. "We have to celebrate!"

"No! That's okay," Anya replied, horrified.

Ethan interjected, "I don't want to know what this is about, do I?"

Anya gave him a pitying glance and then averted her eyes.

"Didn't think so." After Anya's declaration yesterday, Ethan had figured it wouldn't be long till Sebastian "claimed" her. What he didn't anticipate was how deep the rejection would affect him. He quickly schooled his features. "Maybe I will get some sleep after all."

One of the computers pinged behind him. He leaned over the screen. He'd been cycling through various galaxies over the last hour.

"This could be it," he muttered, forgetting his wounded pride. "The code seems to be pointing me toward a solar system in this particular galaxy. Five moons, two moons, eight moons, three moons…"

When he brought up the last image, Anya gasped and rocked back on her feet.

Sonya was by her side in an instant. "Are you okay? You're not pregnant, are you?"

Ethan ground his teeth, keeping his face pointed away from them so they couldn't see his resentment.

"What!" Anya choked out. "I don't think so."

She sounded so unsure and frightened by the prospect, reminding Ethan that she knew nothing of their kind. He blanked his expression and met her gaze. "Did you take his blood into you?"

"No, of course not!"

"Then it cannot be." He faced the computer once more.

"So Faieara have a mating ritual similar to ours?" Sonya sounded smug.

"It's not a mating ritual. It's a fertility rite," he explained. "We don't believe in fated mates like you. We choose who we want, but without the fertility rite, which could be likened to your idea of mating, there will be no offspring."

"Idea?" Sonya glared at him.

He was about to inform her that what she called a "mating ritual" was nothing more than a barbaric act, but Anya stepped between them. "This is not important right now. I think seeing that planet is what affected me."

Ethan took in the planet, Undewla, then back at his notes. "Hmm. What a coincidence, this planet is at the top of my list."

Chapter 7

Sonya watched through the wall-sized window as the small shuttle jetted toward the icy planet, Undewla. Not surprising, Anya had insisted on accompanying the group—Sebastian, Cale, Ethan, and Marik—and had managed to convince Sebastian that her gift would help them to find Nadua.

Around the bridge, several crew members bustled at their posts, scanning the icy surface of Undewla for signs of life.

According to records, the planet's inhabitants would deal with outside traders on occasion, but were considered fiercely territorial as well as difficult to locate. The planet was known for its horrendous storms. In fact, more was known about Undewla's debilitating weather than about its people. Sonya hoped Sebastian's party had better luck than *Marada's* scanners.

The small shuttle breached the atmosphere and was swallowed up by the glaring sheen that reflected off Undewla.

Sonya called across the room to the ship's pilot. "Aidan, can you get us any closer?"

"I can, but not much. The…Wait…" Aidan bent over his console.

After a moment of silence, Sonya demanded, "What is it, Aidan?"

He tapped a set of buttons and brought to the screen a magnified section of the rocky asteroid ring that surrounded Undewla. "A moment ago our sensors caught the signature of a ship. Seems to be skewed by all the debris."

Slowly, she scanned the line of floating rocks. Nothing seemed out of the ordinary. "Could the sensors be malfunctioning?"

"Running diagnostics now."

A sparkle of light glinted in the distance, and Sonya leaned forward. A massive ship peeked out from behind a large, slow-moving asteroid.

Aidan let out a harsh curse. "*Extarga*," he announced on a growl.

"Damn." Sonya's heart revved. She realized in an instant that they were being stalked. "Get a warning to the shuttle now. Call them back."

Aidan scowled. "Too late. The surface storm is disrupting transmission. I can't connect to them."

Sonya stabbed her fingers through her hair. "This can't be happening," she muttered. "Why does shit have to go wrong while I'm in charge?"

"Shit!" Aidan spat.

Anxiety squeezed her throat. "Oh, gods. What now?"

"They've sent out a shuttle of their own. It's heading to the planet."

In the span of a few heartbeats, many emotions gripped her mind: Horror at the situation. Fear for Anya and the others. Doubt that she could take on *Extarga* as well as stop that shuttle.

Especially when Sebastian had been unable to take on Darius's ship.

Oddly, she thought of Ethan and the smug comments he would indulge in if she failed. That is, if he were still alive in the end.

Sonya ground her teeth, alarmed by the sudden and violent pang in her chest. When she met Aidan's waiting gaze, she knew her eyes had transformed from their usual soft violet to a harsh red. "Attack!"

Aidan and the others jumped to obey, readying their stations for battle.

"Take out their shuttle first. I want it scrapped. Then go for *Extarga*. We're going to hit and run. Try to get *Extarga* to pursue us."

After that? She had no idea.

Unfortunately, *Extarga* saw them coming and *Marada* rocked from a round of explosions.

Marada's weapons locked on the small shuttle and fired several rounds, none of them a direct hit. *Extarga* let loose a barrage of blasts along *Marada's* hull.

"Shields at eighty percent, Captain," Aidan barked. "We already know we can't take much more of this."

Jarring blasts slammed the ship, causing Sonya to grip her console for support. She looked up with despair as the shuttle disappeared into the planet's atmosphere.

Another cluster of blasts bashed into *Marada's* outer shell.

Sonya let out a boisterous string of curses. Whoever was on that shuttle was Sebastian's problem now. "Aidan, get us into the asteroid belt. We're smaller than *Extarga* and can easily out maneuver them if they follow."

Marada shot for the belt, and *Extarga* followed. To her dismay, the enemy ship matched *Marada* in agility and speed as they weaved through the haphazard patch of over-sized rocks.

More blasts gouged at the ship. The sound of crying metal made Sonya's stomach sink.

"They've hit our main thrusters," Aidan bellowed.

"How's our power?"

"We're running on momentum. I'm controlling us with the smaller secondary thrusters, but that's it."

At this rate, *Extarga* would tear them apart like a child through tissue.

"Then our only option is to hide," Sonya said as another set of expositions rocked the ship. "Is that possible, Aidan?"

Aidan had once run Phase Nine, a deadly space race where contestants were constantly forced into similar situations. Sonya couldn't ask for better at *Marada's* helm.

"It is." he replied, scanning ahead. "I just need to find the right…Ah."

With *Extarga* close on their ass, Aidan twisted the ship through a dense patch of asteroids. The allotted space was too tight for *Extarga*, and they were forced to veer off, putting space between the two ships. Then Aidan doubled back toward a massive rock five times the size of *Marada*, and, with precise movements, hugged the ship to its surface.

Sonya ordered over the loud speaker, "We're going ghost. Shut down all non-vitals immediately."

The bridge light flicked off, leaving them in a faint glow of sun rays reflecting off the planet and floating rocks around them. The bridge fell silent, thick with tension. The asteroid pivoted slowly, taking *Marada* with it. *Extarga*, slow and predator-like, came into view.

"Oh gods, their right there," the ship's navigator gasped.

"The color of this asteroid is not too far off from *Marada*," Aidan whispered. "That's why I chose it. Their sensors would be fouled up by the debris just like ours was. And if they didn't catch where we went, there's a good chance they won't be able to see us at all."

Time dragged on as the crew waited in silence, watching *Extarga* jet back and forth, like a creature that had lost its prey. Most nerve-racking was when the asteroid they had landed on turned, obscuring their line of sight, and any hint of *Extarga's* whereabouts vanished.

When *Extarga* appeared once more it was heading back toward the Undewla. A second object emerged from the gleaming white atmosphere of the planet, glistening. Aidan zoomed in.

It was *Extarga's* shuttle.

"Do you suppose they've captured our crew?" a voice mumbled from the darkness.

Nobody answered, fearing the worst.

A beep sounded.

"It's our shuttle!" Aidan opened transmission.

"They've taken Anya." Cale sounded frantic, and Sonya could imagine the wild look in his eyes. "Where are you?"

She responded, "*Extarga* took out our thrusters. We'll be down till they're fixed. No estimated time as of yet."

"Damn," Cale spat. "Get them fixed and come after us. We're following *Extarga*."

"You can't go after them! They'll—"

"They took his mate, Sonya!" Cale's tone indicated an end to the conversation. He knew what it was to be mated, and now

Sebastian did too, but Sonya never understood how being mated caused one to abandon all reason. If they followed *Extarga*, they'd be captured, or worse…killed.

"We could lose all five of you…" She hated how her voice quivered.

"Not five," Cale replied woefully. "Marik's still on Undewla. The natives captured him."

A breath heaved from her chest as she sank into her chair. Marik and Anya had been seized by two completely different factions. Sebastian, Cale, and Ethan were riding to their deaths. And *Marada* was incapacitated.

"And has the pirate accepted that he's being flown to his doom?" she asked Cale. Maybe Ethan could talk some sense into her brothers.

"The pirate is up for the challenge," Ethan responded, probably seated next to Cale.

Sonya didn't have time to evaluate the odd sense of relief she felt at hearing his voice.

"My princess is in danger," he continued. "If I die trying to save her, then I die with honor."

The pirate was just as daft as the rest of them!

Sonya sat forward. "I want to save her too, guys, but don't you think we should regroup? Form a plan?"

"No time!" Sebastian snarled. He sounded distant and out of breath, clearly fighting the Edge. "He'll take her where I cannot find her."

"But—"

"Enough, Sonya!" Sebastian snapped. "Fix the ship and then follow us, but keep your distance from *Extarga*. Your priority is to the people on *Marada* now. If we cannot… You have to be prepared to leave us."

Sonya shook her head, biting back a wave of emotion that burned her eyes. "I can't leave you."

"Hopefully you won't have to, but… promise me you'll make the choice if it comes to that."

Images flashed through her mind. A body, broken and bleeding, lying motionless in a pool of his own blood…except this time, instead of her father, it was Sebastian, Cale, and even the pirate in his place. "No." Her voice came out small.

"Dammit, Sonya!" Sebastian had never addressed her so harshly.

She quelled her quivering lip. "Promise me you'll come back."

"I…I can't."

Cale jumped in. "You know us better than that, Sunny. We'll be back in no time."

She did know them. Her brothers were two of the fiercest males she'd ever known. She could almost feel sorry for *Extarga* and the bastards on board. Almost.

"Pirate." She forced a sturdy voice. "I expect you to come back as well. You've work to do here."

"Aye, Captain." It sounded as though Ethan was actually smiling.

The transmission cut off. Sonya took a minute to gather herself before barking over the loud speaker, "All mechanics report for duty!"

Chapter 8

It took three full days to repair the thrusters. Another four days were spent tracking *Extarga*.

Space was massive—actually, massive times infinity... squared. Endless. *Extarga* could be anywhere. Could have gone in any direction. For all she knew, *Marada* could be heading away from it.

Sonya drove the crew on, never letting it known that she was starting to have doubts whether they would find the monstrous ship at all. She was running on a mix of instinct, determination, and a heavy dose of delusion.

She wasn't the only one losing hope. She could see it in many of the crew's eyes, but no one wanted to be the first to admit it. The atmosphere on the ship was solemn and quiet. The crew tended their stations without the usual mirth and liveliness.

Aside from the group that had gone after Anya, Sonya worried for Marik. He was alone on Undewla, captured by foreigners who probably didn't even know what they were dealing with when it came to demons—especially one that abhorred captivity as much as Marik. She hadn't wanted to abandon him, but at least she knew where he was.

Once again, her mind drifted back to her family.

Please be okay.

She couldn't lose them. They were all she had left. After her father's gruesome demise, she had been determined to keep the last of her family safe. And her reckless brothers took her to task every chance they got, this being the last in a very long line of rash behavior.

With most of her time spent in the control room, Sonya had closed the pub. The galley had become self-serve, with no one available to take Marik's place as the ship's cook. As it was, Sonya couldn't eat. Demons could go months without food, but doing so siphoned much need energy. However, Sonya didn't feel drained. She only felt the urgency to keep looking.

Yet, in the back of her mind, she knew stress was taking its toll. Sebastian's words repeated in her head, taunting her. "Promise me you'll make the choice if it comes to that." But had it?

No. She'd not leave her brothers, Anya, or even Ethan to the mercy of that madman. She would never stop looking.

What if they're already dead?

Her mind cracked against the terrible thought. She pressed her palms to the side of her head. She pictured Anya and her brothers lying broken on a cold stone floor, just as she had witnessed that harrowing day back in her once loving home.

"You okay, Captain?" Aidan asked from his place at the helm.

Sonya glanced up, erasing the despair from her expression. "I'm fine, Aidan."

Aidan responded with a look that said he in no way believed her.

To lighten the mood, she laughed and said, "I never thought I'd be worried for a pirate."

Aidan responded with a thin-lipped smile and a forced chuckle. "Agreed."

What surprised her, however, was the truth of that statement. The fact that Ethan shared equal time in her mind alongside her family confounded her. Perhaps because she knew if anything bad happened to *him*, the same would befall the others. And he had an arrogant mouth on him that could only invite trouble. Although, wasn't Cale even worse?

The two of them together made for a disastrous scenario.

* * *

Ethan tried to stretch his tired muscles as blood seeped from his many wounds, a task made difficult by the metal straps around his wrist and ankles, pressing him to the wall.

To his left, Sebastian and Cale appeared to be in equally bad shape.

Soon after they'd caught up to *Extarga*, the captain, Darius, had allowed them to come aboard with assurances of ransom: Anya for an extreme amount of space credits.

Sebastian hadn't hesitated to agree, but Ethan had sensed the demon's intention. He would never allow Darius to live.

Over the transmitted conversation, Ethan had been unable to decipher the sincerity of Darius's motives, but he had suspected the male was merely luring them aboard to double cross them in the end.

He'd been correct.

Now they stood, strapped to a wall, bindings around their wrists, ankles, and necks, subject to a regiment of abuse. The psychopath enjoyed causing pain, and had nearly killed Sebastian when he'd refused to cry out from a lengthy punishment. Sebastian continued to flail and snarl like a rabid beast.

Both Cale and Ethan took turns attempting to draw Darius's attention away from Sebastian whenever necessary.

While Darius was running the business end of a blade down Ethan's face, slicing the skin to the bone, Cale called out, "Hey pirate, that looks like fun. Can I have a turn?"

Darius hadn't hesitated to oblige with a succession of hard knuckle-filled jabs to Cale's face.

When Darius had backed off to focus on Sebastian once more, who was still recovering from his earlier attention, Ethan asked Cale, "How was your massage?"

Cale spit out a mouthful of blood before commenting, "Almost tickled."

Cale had no idea about Ethan's ability to heal—a detail he couldn't afford for Darius to learn now—and that it would be in his best interest to allow Ethan the brunt of the beatings. Still, Ethan was surprised by the tenacity with which Cale would bait Darius.

Ethan had been using his magic to heal Sebastian and Cale just enough to go unnoticed. He couldn't heal them completely unless he was physically touching them. But he could send out tendrils of magic that kept their wounds from festering or bleeding out.

He could have easily healed himself. Instead, he kept his inconsequential wounds open to keep from revealing the nature his gift. Darius had already noted his pointed ears with a keen eye, but that didn't stop the asshole from torturing Ethan with the same enthusiasm he showed the demons.

However, something told him that if Darius ever grew tired

of his newest toys, Ethan would be the only one to survive for future study.

Aside from the physical abuse, sleep was deprived of them. If any of them nodded off, an electric current would run through their bindings, choking the air from every cell in their bodies and reopening old gashes. Each of them was coated in a generous amount of dried and fresh blood.

Ethan didn't know how many days had passed, but his exhaustion told him it had been more than a mere few. He worried what had become of Anya. They had not been given any evidence that she even lived.

He found his mind drifting to Sonya with increasing frequency. Fatigue-induced stupors brought on figments of her large violet eyes, flashing with imagined concern—the way she would regard her kin if she were here to see their pain.

The fantasy vanished. Sonya hated his guts, and if her brothers weren't with him, she wouldn't bother with his predicament at all.

Darius entered the room with a threatening gleam in his eyes that brought them all to attention.

"I've got a little treat for you," he muttered.

Ethan stifled a curse. He could read Darius loud and clear, and was instantly aware of the plot. Darius was going to add a new player to his game.

Anya.

Darius smiled at them. The lunatic was practically giddy over the prospect of showing her what he'd done to them, as though she would applaud his work.

Ethan's mind reeled. How could he spare her the pain of seeing them like this? And Sebastian? What special kind of torture would the Edge bring him when he laid eyes upon his mate? When he was unable to reach her, to keep her safe? A demon could go mad from something like that, and Sebastian had already been on the Edge for days.

Ethan spotted a dagger in Darius's hand and mentally cursed. Without even the slightest change in expression, Darius sank the blade into Sebastian's gut. Sebastian didn't flinch. He just continued to meet the bastard's unwavering gaze, as if giving some unspoken guarantee that Darius was looking into the eyes of death itself.

A hint of fear etched its way across Darius' expression, eradicated a moment later.

Ethan couldn't help but to indulge in a taunt. "You *do* realize you've just signed your own death note."

Darius focused on him. Then, with a blindingly swift movement, he slammed the hilt of his blade into Ethan's temple. A deafening ring vibrated his skull before he blacked out.

When he came to, muffled sounds echoed through his head. He opened and closed his eyes a few times and shook away the vertigo. His vision was blurry, but he got the sense that Anya was now in the room and was fighting Darius.

Sebastian and Cale were madly struggling against their bonds. Adrenaline spiked in Ethan's bloodstream, and he tried to pull free, but it was no use. All he could do was hope Anya was able to fend off the much larger male.

Ethan's vision dimmed again. He called up a bit of his magic to heal himself. He looked up just in time to see Darius stab Anya with the same dagger he'd used on Sebastian. Despair ate away at him, darkening his mind and carving out a place in his chest.

I couldn't even protect one girl.

The dagger plunged again. Anya's expression was pained, exhausted. She lifted her arm toward them as if reaching out for something. Then she gave them each one last sorrowful look before closing her eyes.

The bindings that held them began to shake. Magic pulsed through the metal, and he realized what she was doing. Their restraints were mechanized, and Anya could manipulate them just as she had the lock to the cell on Ethan's asteroid.

A tiny clink was all that declared their release. Ethan leapt at Darius, but Sebastian beat him there, tearing into his flesh with unhindered hostility.

The screams escaping Darius were gratifying. Ethan wanted to join in and take a bit of his own revenge, but Cale motioned him back. "Sebastian will kill you too if you get in his way now," he explained.

Ethan moved toward Anya, crumbled to the ground, but Cale once more stopped him.

"Don't get near her either, pirate. Not while Sebastian is like this."

Ethan ground his teeth. There could still be time to save her. But if Cale was right, and Sebastian killed him without thinking, he wouldn't be able to help her anyway.

Sebastian threw Darius' remains to the side and rushed to Anya's side. He pulled her close to him and bellowed, "Please, Anya! Open your eyes!" His gaze flashed between Cale and Ethan. "Someone get a doctor! A healer! Now!" He turned back to Anya. "I will follow you, Dammit! You hear me? I will follow!"

The sight of Sebastian openly weeping for his mate took

Ethan by surprise. Never had he felt such emotion for another.

"Anya, don't leave me!" Sebastian choked, running a blood-ied hand down her pale cheek.

Ethan approached, reaching for Anya.

Sebastian snarled at him. "Get away from her! Find a doctor!"

"No." Ethan made his voice grave. "Give her to me!"

"Do you want him to kill you, pirate?" Cale growled.

"I can help her, if it's not too late already! Give me her body!"

Sebastian's desperate gaze met his. "How can you help her? Tell me!"

"My ability. The root of my power lies in healing."

Sebastian seemed to digest this information for only a split second. "Then do it! Heal her, now!"

"I have to touch her body, so don't kill me. Okay?"

With a clipped nod, Sebastian relinquished Anya, though his eyes still mirrored that of a beast ready to attack.

Ethan pressed one hand to her wound and the other to her heart, drawing magic through his body and into hers. Instantly, she began to heal, but Ethan sensed her soul had already drifted away, leaving behind nothing but a shell. He could heal her body till not a blemish remained, but did he have it in him to call her soul back?

With all his strength, he gathered his magic into the cage of his heart, letting it build until it practically overflowed. The longer it was forced into submission, the stronger magic became. However, magic didn't like to be caged. It liked to run free, and holding on to it for any amount of time would cause it to push back and resist. When it became too much and he could no longer keep his grasp, he unleashed the magic down his arms, over his palms, and through his fingertips it into Anya. Soon he was siphoning more magic than he ever had before.

He glanced up to see both Sebastian and Cale looking dumfounded. Scraps of torn cloth and drops of blood hovered midair as magic charged the room. Anya's body became illuminated by the coursing power. Her wounds were fully knitted, but still there was no soul to fill Anya's shell.

Desperate, Ethan reached out toward Sebastian. "Give me your hand!"

Sebastian did as asked, and Ethan placed Sebastian's palm over Anya's heart and held it there.

"Call her back!" Ethan commanded. When Sebastian gaped at him blankly, he continued. "If you are truly hers, then your souls are linked. She will hear your call."

Ethan had never attempted to reel a soul back from the afterlife, but if anything could aid such a task, it would be the pure devout love Sebastian harbored for his mate.

"What do I do?" Sebastian's voice was gravely.

"Just keep your hand here and imagine her with you. The connection will help my magic."

Ethan closed his eyes and blocked everything out. The pain of his own marred body faded to the furthest depths of his mind. Magic was like a second pulse inside him, surging life into Anya. When he began to grow weary, he called upon his last bit of energy, forcing a blast of power into the lifeless form below his fingertips.

Sebastian leaned over to whisper something in Anya's ear. It sounded both private and intimate. Moments later, Ethan felt something he'd never felt before. An energy that felt like pure life itself.

Then, ever so slightly, Anya inhaled.

Ethan pulled his hands away. Drawing in a deep breath, he swiped a sheen of sweat from his forehead.

Cale slapped his back and let lose a hearty laugh.

Ethan sat back on his heels. "It's not over yet. She's healed. Her soul is in place…for now."

"What do you mean for now?" Sebastian barked.

"Her soul had left her body, her vessel. Her body is in great shock. Her soul is once again connected to this body, but…that doesn't mean she'll wake up."

Sebastian gazed down at Anya, who appeared as though she were only in a sound sleep. "She'll wake up," he said it as if he had no doubt.

Ethan wasn't so sure.

"Let's get back to *Marada*." Sebastian glanced at Ethan. "Don't suppose you have enough juice left to heal us too?"

Ethan shook his head. "Sorry, I'm tapped out."

Cale pushed his shoulders back. "I'm fine, anyway. In fact, I'm ready to do some damage."

"Good." Sebastian stood with Anya in his arms. "You take the front, Ethan take the back."

Cale nodded and dove out of the room. A guard called out in surprise but, by the gurgled sounds that followed, Cale had subdued him easily enough.

Cale peeked his head back into the room and tossed a stolen gun to Ethan. "Here, you'll need this, pirate."

Ethan caught it, and Cale winked before disappearing once more through the door.

"Typical demon," Ethan shouted, following after him.

"Wanting all the action for yourself."

"You called it," Cale hollered back.

Together they fought their way back to the shuttle. The element of surprise swayed luck to their side.

When they reached the docking bay, they took out the overseers and were soon jettisoning away from *Extarga*. As soon as they were safely away, Cale sent *Marada* an encrypted signal, hoping the ship was in range.

Ethan didn't want to bank on it. As he glanced at the flight panel, checking the state of their fuel—not great—he said, "We should head to the nearest station or planet. What's close by?"

Cale charted their position and then a three-dimensional map displayed on a small screen at his front. "The closest planet is Undewla. Nothing else is within reach."

Ethan cursed. The inhabitants hadn't been welcoming, and any fuel to be found on Undewla would be covered by layers of ice and frozen bedrock. But it didn't look like they had much of a choice. If *Marada* didn't come for them, they could either drift aimlessly through space till they ran out of air, or take their chances on Undewla.

Cale set their course, muttering, "Gods, I hate that planet."

Chapter 9

"Sonya," Aidan pleaded from his station. "Eat something and go rest for a few hours. I'll call you the moment something appears on our radar."

"Aidan, I'm fine. Quit harping," she chided.

Aidan's concern was not unfounded. She hadn't left the control room but for a few useless attempts at sleep, and still she could not eat. The churning of her stomach made the thought of food unappetizing.

It was difficult to think of anything else but poor Anya, back in the hands of that bastard, Darius. Her brothers, possibly dead. The pirate likewise.

Unless…

Could Ethan have set them up from the start?

The thought snaked through her mind like a disease taking root. He was a pirate, after all. They'd known him for all of two seconds, and in that time they'd been drugged, locked up, and now separated. Practically gift wrapped and handed to their worst enemy. Ethan had been the one to lead them to Undewla.

"Aidan?" Sonya hesitated before continuing. "Do you think Ethan betrayed us to Darius?"

Conversations from other crew members died down to listen in as Aidan took a moment to contemplate her question. "I don't want to start throwing accusation around until we get the others back and can question them about it."

His answer was far too democratic for her liking. "Do you think it's possible, or not?"

"Of course it's possible. He did admit to having contact with Darius on the asteroid. But Darius had been tracking us long before then."

She felt her fangs descend. "If he did, I will not rest until I'm sure he has suffered ten times what my family may have gone through."

She clamped her teeth together. She was speaking as if they were already dead. But what else could she think? Too much time had passed already. Her brothers would have sent word by now, unless they'd indeed been incapacitated.

Just as the tormenting thought swirled through her mind, Aidan snapped to attention, focusing on his console.

"A distress signal," he announced to the room. "It's from the shuttle"

Sheer elation nearly made her dizzy. Then she grew pensive. "How far out?"

"Not far, a few hours maybe." He didn't wait for Sonya's orders and pressed the ship's engines hard.

As they drew near the shuttle, Sonya inquired as calmly as she could, "Is anyone on board?"

Aidan tapped a sequence of buttons. "There are four life signs."

A smile broke across her lips. She slumped back in her chair, overwhelmed by the wave of relief. "And what of *Extarga*?"

"Our sensors aren't picking anything up, but that doesn't mean much. It didn't show last time till it was too late."

"There aren't any boulders to hide behind now," she discerned. "Alright, let's make this a quick retrieval and then get the hell out of here. Divert power to the shields and bring all weapons online. Any sign of *Extarga*, don't wait, start firing. Open transmission to the shuttle."

Cale's voice echoed through the speaker. "For once, little sister, I'm glad you're such a disobedient pain in the ass."

"Missed you too, Cale. Is everyone okay?"

Pause.

"We're alive," he said in a languid tone.

"I feel like that should have sounded better than it did."

"Anya will not wake. She was hurt badly."

Pain laced a rope around Sonya's throat. "I'll have Doctor Oshwald meet you in the docking bay."

A few stressful moments later, the shuttle docked without incident. She had Aidan set a course in the opposite direction, then added, "Take over command for a while. I'm going to go check on them."

Aidan nodded. "If they're not too banged up, give 'em each a good smack in the face for me."

"Will do." Sonya raced to greet her family, arriving just as the docking bay finished pressurizing. The doctor, who had already been waiting, stepped through the doors first, seeking his patient.

Sebastian gripped Anya's limp body to his chest as though someone might snatch her from him.

And the blood! They were all covered in massive amounts of blood, their clothing stained and torn, but the skin underneath appeared unmarred.

"Follow me to my quarters, Doctor," Sebastian said. "You can examine her there." Before he left, he offered Sonya a tight nod in silent approval.

Cale approached and clasped her on the shoulder—his way of saying she'd done well—and then continued past her. To Ethan, he said, "Come on, pirate. You're buying."

"Next time, demon. I'm done for at least two days. I'm surprised I'm still standing as it is."

"Don't be a pansy. Come take the edge off with me."

Sonya glanced between the two, confused by their unusually chummy exchange.

When Ethan refused to relent, Cale grumbled, "Suit yourself."

She watched as Cale disappeared through the hatch, no doubt on his way to The Demon's Punchbowl to help himself to her liquor. Speechless at the lackluster reunion, Sonya threw her arms wide in a baffled gesture.

"Thanks for not giving up the search," Ethan said from behind her.

Sonya didn't bother to look at him. "It wasn't for your sake."

"Of course, but I'm no less grateful," he responded in that aloof timbre of his.

"Care to explain what went on while you were gone?"

"It's a long story. Perhaps at a later time."

Sonya's rounded on him. "Odd, don't you think? That Darius shows up right as we arrive at Undewla."

Ethan stilled, his eyes narrowing. "What are you getting at?"

"Just that it's quite a coincidence. Almost as if Darius knew where we would be." She didn't hide the accusation in her tone.

He bristled. "Are you kidding me with this?" At her glare, headed, "You're really suggesting that I had something to do with it?"

"Did you?"

He took a menacing step forward. Sonya held her ground, somewhat amused by the idea of his attempting to threaten her. Her smirk seemed to infuriate him further.

Then he paused, his demeanor changing, as if he were disgusted by *her*. Something in that response grated, and she lost her smile.

"I'm not entertaining this ridiculous conversation." He turned to leave.

"Spoken like the truly guilty."

The swiftness of Ethan's attack caught her so off guard that her mind struggled to regain its equilibrium. She found herself pinned to the ground with Ethan on top of her. The bastard had kicked her legs out from under her and trapped her arms beside her head. The shock of it pounded a heavy beat in her chest, and her breaths quickened as she looked at him with utter disbelief.

His eyes blazed with fury. "Do you have any idea what we've been through? Anya nearly died! Still might. And you mean to accuse me of putting her in that position? You must think me wretched indeed." His sneer was coupled with an emotion she couldn't place.

"Get off of me!" Sonya wiggled under his weight.

He tightened his hold around her wrists, leaning in closer, his expression downright dangerous.

She tested her limbs, but was unable to pull free. Panic surged. Refusing to admit how thoroughly he'd subdued her—not to mention how embarrassingly easily—she made her expression nonchalant. Yet she feared he could hear the steadily increasing rhythm of her heart.

Worse, confusion bombarded her as she realized she wasn't only frightened, but excited.

Suddenly, Ethan turned puzzled and his grip loosened. Not quite enough for her to get free, however.

"I'll say this once, demon. Another accusation like that, and I won't be so nice as I am now."

Sonya snorted. "Pirate, if you hadn't caught me by surprise, we'd be in a completely different position right now." She caught the unintentional innuendo in her words and flushed. Unwanted images flashed in her mind, causing a heated pulse to rake up her body. She quickly reined it in, hoping Ethan's mind wasn't as perverse as hers seemed to be at the moment.

To her horror, he smiled. "If I hadn't been tortured and sleep deprived for the last however many days, I might let you test out your theory, *vietta*."

Sonya gasped. "Tortured?"

"Yes. Constantly, and ruthlessly."

She eyed him up and down. "I see no cuts, scrapes, or bruises."

He sneered back at her. "Ah, well, I must be a liar then. I'll be sure to inform your brothers we all imagined it."

Sonya ground her teeth before commenting, "I think you may have a different idea of what can be considered torture."

"I'll remember that the next time a blade is slicing its way down the side of my face while I'm chained down."

Sonya tilted her head in confusion as a sickly feeling churned inside her. Had her brothers experienced torture like that? She searched his face, looking for a hint of a scar and finding no evidence.

"I can see I'll never convince you, so I won't bother to try. Go ahead and believe what you wish." He pushed himself to stand, freeing her from his grasp.

She sat up, but remained where she was on the floor. Without a backward glance, he disappeared into the hallway.

In hindsight, she should have retaliated then and there, while his back was turned, but something in the way she had reacted to being at his mercy tormented her into stunned passivity. She cursed her body's response to him, utterly confounded by it.

That word he had called her repeated in her head. *Vietta*. The way he had said it, she could almost swear it was meant to be tender, but nothing could be more ridiculous.

After a moment, she pushed to her feet and made her way to The Demon's Punchbowl. Cale had let himself in and was seated at the bar, guzzling the last bit of her best liquor.

She approached him. "Tell me what happened."

He blurted out a curse, wiping his mouth. "I was hoping not to recount it so soon."

"So it's true? You were tortured?"

"Aye. And that snake, Darius, had too much fun doing it."

Sonya plopped down on a chair next to him and looked him over. "You've healed from it already? That's quick, even for our kind."

"Turns out the pirate's a healer. He helped Anya first, then was able to heal us just before you picked us up. Lucky break he was there, too, or Anya would have died on that ship." A crease formed between his brows, and he stared into his glass as though concentrating on a single thought. "Sebastian would have gone mad."

Sonya wondered if Cale was thinking about Velicia. Shortly after his mate's betrayal and their escape from the war that had devastated their planet, Cale had resigned himself to the Edge. Typically, when a demon loses a mate, an unending trip to the Edge is inevitable. "Sebastian would have returned to us, just as you did," she reasoned.

Cale gave her a somber look. "For some reason, I seriously doubt it."

She supposed he was right. Cale's circumstance had been unique. He hadn't lost his mate through death. In fact, Velicia could still be alive for all they knew. Yet her betrayal had been no less painful for Cale. He had slipped to the Edge, rendered a violent snarling beast. She and Sebastian were forced to keep him confined for many years.

Sonya would visit his cell often and speak with him as though he could understand her and might actually respond. She had never truly expected it to happen, though.

Then, one day, his eyes had cleared, and his manner returned to normal, surprising them all.

She couldn't imagine how devastated Sebastian would have been if Anya had died, and she couldn't assume that they'd be so lucky as to revive another demon from that kind of madness a second time.

Perhaps she owed the pirate some gratitude after all.

* * *

Ethan entered his room, fuming. Even after a lengthy shower and an attempt to rest, he couldn't get Sonya's accusation out of his head. Had she really thought him capable of handing them over to a madman like Darius? The disgust in her tone every time she called him pirate said yes.

Irritating female.

Why did he even care, anyway? He *was* a pirate—or, rather, had been—and there were no shortage of individuals who abhorred him for it. Why should she be any different?

Yet when she had accused him with such venom, something in him snapped. He had been overcome by the urge to force her to see him as the honorable soldier he'd once been.

But then he remembered he was no longer a soldier. Hadn't been for a long time. Nor was he entirely pirate. He was some strange mix of the two.

And what was wrong with that?

Nothing, that's what.

He had been sent on a mission and there was still much to do. Nadua needed to be found. Marik too, if it were possible. And only part of the book had been translated. Those pages held the location of Anya's eldest sister, Kyralyn.

Perhaps translating would distract him from the she-demon. Yet, as angry as he was, he couldn't ignore the way her arousal had cut through his mind like a hot blade.

It wasn't difficult to discern what sort of male she preferred in her bed. Incidentally, he enjoyed filling such desires, but it was a moot point. As long as their animosity continued, she would never submit to him.

In any case, it was best he leave her alone. He wouldn't want to cause friction between Sonya and his future bride, whichever one of Anya's sisters that may be.

Chapter 10

A couple days later, Sebastian summoned Sonya to his room. Hope filled her that Anya might have awakened.

Disappointment settled in her stomach when she found Anya still bundled in his bed, unconscious. How long before Anya's body gave up entirely?

Sonya glanced around the room, her eyes landing on Ethan. He looked better than he had the last time she'd seen him back in the docking bay. He was washed, shaved, and dressed in dark pants, boots, and a long coat. White-blond hair hung loose around his face, and he wore several gold trinkets: a few rings on his fingers and an ear piece near the point.

Sebastian, however, looked worse.

"Ethan has translated more of the book." Sebastian's voice sounded guttural and raw. He barely took his tired eyes from Anya as he spoke. "He believes Anya's eldest sister is dangerously close to being discovered by the Kayadon."

"You're only finding this out now?" she asked Ethan, her tone harsher than she intended.

"Translating is proving more difficult than I thought. It's

almost as if the book is bespelled to reveal bits of information at a time. I'm unsure if that's truly the case, but it would make sense if the king needs us to follow a specific path—"

Sonya waved her hand in dismissal. "We can't leave Marik to go after this other sister."

Sebastian agreed. "We've discussed it already," he told her. "Cale will be taking the shuttle ahead of us as while we search for Nadua and Marik. He's preparing to leave today, and I would like you to go with him."

"Go where?"

"A planet named Earth. We know little of this place, and what we do have on record is grossly outdated. It's said to be a primitive place, the inhabitants: under-developed cave dwellers."

"I'll go and pack my things. How long till we depart?" She hid her relief at the prospect of leaving. It was the perfect opportunity to get away from Ethan. The fact that he took her down post-torture and exhausted shook her confidence slightly. More than that, she'd developed a nagging curiosity toward him. She found her mind conjuring images of him throughout the day…and night.

And she didn't like it.

Ethan swept his gaze over her. The look in his eyes made her wonder if he could read her thoughts, but the suspicion was easily brushed away.

"Good. You'll leave in a few hours," Sebastian continued.

"Perfect." Sonya turned to leave, forcing herself not to glance at Ethan as she did.

Ethan was in full support of the plan Sebastian had put

forth…at least most of him was. His lower regions seemed to be protesting after seeing Sonya dressed in yet another of those too short skirts and tight laced up tops. But she needed to go. He didn't want any distractions from translating the rest of the book.

"Has she stirred at all?" he asked Sebastian, who had gone back to gripping Anya's hand and watching over her as she slept.

"Not a whit."

Ethan's heart sank. How long could it take for a soul to reconnect with its body? He feared he had somehow performed the binding wrong.

"Then I shall leave you be."

"I have not thanked you yet," Sebastian muttered, without taking his eyes from his mate.

"Thank me when she wakes," Ethan replied before exiting the room.

He followed the familiar path back to his quarters and buried himself in the pages of the book. It had been relocated to his room soon after their return, the cover cautiously clamped open. If it closed, even by accident, and Anya did not awaken, they wouldn't be able to open it again.

After hours of trying to decode the text, Ethan pushed away from his desk with a discouraged sigh. He'd been ignoring the grumble in his stomach for a while, but now it demanded food.

He stretched and headed for the galley. As he turned a corner, he spotted a furious-looking Sonya stomping a determined path in his direction. She barely seemed to notice him, however, and as she passed, he couldn't keep from inquiring, "Is this your natural disposition?”

“That son of a bitch left without me!” Sonya shouted back at him. “Stubborn, arrogant bastard!”

Ethan shook his head, recalling that Cale had protested when Sebastian suggested he take Sonya with him. Ethan ignored the fact that his own mood lifted slightly and fell in step behind her. He reminded himself that having her gone was the better of the two situations. “Send him a transmission. I’m sure Cale can be reasoned with.”

“I did,” she growled back at him.

“And?” He eyed her backside, enjoying the view of her swaying hips and slender tail, swishing back and forth as she marched with purpose.

“He said he didn’t need his little sister tagging along.” Then she grumbled out a few choice words in Demonish.

He had run with a group of demons a few years back and was surprised by how much of the language he remembered. From that same experience, he could tell that Sonya was nowhere near the kind of anger she was outwardly portraying. Her horns hadn’t even started to redden and her irises kept their deep violet hue.

Amused, and curious to see where she was headed, he followed her all the way back to Sebastian’s room. However, when they arrived, he received a strong impression from Sebastian on the other side of the closed door.

He gripped Sonya’s wrist and pulled her back before she could intrude.

She pivoted around, appearing alarmed by his physical touch, and then yanked her arm out of his grasp.

“You don’t want to go in there,” he informed her.

She held her arm to her chest. "Is that so?"

"I don't think your brother would be too happy about you interrupting his reunion with Anya."

Sonya's eyes widened. "She's awake? Why did no one tell me?"

"Apparently, it was very recent," he hedged. "I believe they'd appreciate some time alone."

Sonya's lips formed an O before transforming into a wide smile. She clapped her hands together. "She's okay! Thanks the gods!"

Sonya threw her arms around his neck as she bounced with excitement. His breath stuck in his throat as other parts of him sprang to life.

Once the shock wore off, he raised his hand to return the embrace, but in that moment, she seemed to realize what she was doing. She backed away, looking momentarily alarmed over her own actions.

She schooled her features. "By the way, Cale told me what you did for them. I suppose I should thank you."

"I suppose you should." He crossed his arms.

She shot him an unamused look, and he returned it with one of blank patience, the exact opposite of what he was feeling.

"There's also the matter of your new job."

Ethan raised a brow.

"With Cale gone, I'll continue to help Sebastian in the control room, so I won't be spending as much time in The Demon's Punchbowl. I'll need to train you to take my place."

"No need. I've worked in a tavern before."

"Even so. The pub is my establishment, and I'd like to be

sure you do things my way."

"There can't be much to go over. Besides, is this really important now?"

"Perhaps not, but what else have you got to do? Cale's on his way to Earth, and we're on our way back to Undewla. What more can the book tell you at this point?"

Ethan conceded she had a point. He'd hit a virtual wall once Kyra's location had been revealed.

He shrugged. "Fine, let's go."

Chapter 11

Sonya squirmed in her seat, wondering what had compelled her to think this was a good idea.

Ethan stood on the other side of the bar, his back turned to her as he reached for yet another bottle. He had removed his coat and was covered in only a thin white shirt and a pair of fitted pants that continued to draw her eye downward.

Not to mention, he had smelled delicious. Enough so, she'd decided to act as a customer just as an excuse to put some much-needed space between them. Instead, it only gave her a better view.

He smirked at her, but said nothing.

Her...attraction—for that's what she finally realized it was—disturbed her to no end. How could she find a pirate desirable? Especially one who reminded her so much of the man who had callously murdered her father—at least as far as his hair and build were concerned.

She shook the thought away. "How many bottles of my liquor are you going to use in this one drink?"

He gave her his profile, and a corner of his mouth quirked.

"Just the right amount."

She prayed someone would step through that door soon. Anyone. Because with every second that passed, she was becoming more and more worked up, her skin heating as though she'd caught fever. Dark temptations swirled: images of tangled bodies spurred by urgent needs.

She inhaled and shook her head. When was he going to finish that drink? "Did you lose your train of thought?"

He looked at her then, and it was as if the same heated musings had been rolling around in his mind as well.

She blinked, and his expression returned to normal.

Had she imagined it?

He stepped forward and placed the finished drink in front of her. "Take a taste."

Had his voice always sounded that inviting?

She snatched the glass and brought the liquid to her lips, ready to slap him with her judgment. The drink went down surprisingly smooth, despite containing some of her strongest brands.

He watched her as she licked off the excess liquor off her lips. Their eyes locked, and his were filled with pure masculine interest. White-hot desire pooled between her thighs.

She made her tone nonchalant. "It's not great, but it will do. Try not to use so much product next time." Unable to stay another moment, she hopped off the stool. "Okay then, I'll leave you to it."

Ethan tilted his head.

On her way out, she called back, "If you treat my pub with anything less than the utmost respect, your ass will kiss the larger end of one of these bottles."

* * *

Ethan gaped as she disappeared through the door, not because of her threat. Throughout the night, her wavering intent had provoked an intense hunger in him, and his lower regions had assembled in full-on attack mode.

For a moment, she'd been determined to leap over the bar and ambush him in the most delicious way. He had waited, giving her every opportunity to do so. The desire, so intense, had swirled around her, and he drank it in, hardening with each bated breath. He had allowed himself to imagine how he would subdue her before ravaging her as he knew she wanted.

But then she left!

Left him harder than he'd ever been in his life,

Left the both of them completely unfulfilled.

Surely she was hurting for release. Her own demon nature should be punishing her for putting on the brakes. So why was she denying herself, and him in the process? She couldn't hate him that much.

There must be another male aboard that she used, someone available to take care of her needs.

"*Vietta*." He ground his teeth as the truth of it emerged.

She was doing this to him on purpose. Rotten little female. She had teased him and then condemned him to this miserable state. She enjoyed making him suffer.

He adjusted himself in his pants, debating if he should go after her.

He cursed as his first customer appeared in the door. One of the ship's mechanics, by the looks of him. As the male called out his order, another individual stepped through the tavern doors.

It was going to be a long night.

* * *

Sonya wiped the sweat from her brow before continuing to smash her fist into the practice dummy. The peaks of her knuckles had finally begun to sting, but hardly enough.

Ever since she'd stepped away from her pub, it was as if she were riding the cusp of the Edge. She drew more power into her next punch.

She had to get her body under control, lest she hurt someone. If she were to allow the Edge to overcome her, those around her would be in grave danger.

When she was very young, she'd witnessed an inexperienced demon reach the Edge. The circumstances eluded her now, but violence had ensued. It had taken several large males to restrain the female until the ignited chemicals diluted in her bloodstream and the effects wore off.

She remembered thinking she never wanted to become like that, a thoughtless monster, mindlessly lashing out.

Later, when her father had been callously murdered, she recalled wishing she'd had the power of that same, formidable female.

At the time, her young age had prevented such strength.

Sonya slammed her fist into the dummy. It swayed with a harsh vibration.

It wasn't till she was much older that she'd found the Edge for the first time, the day she and her brothers had been betrayed by their mother and Velicia. To this day the memory burned the blood in her veins.

The boys had been ready to join the fight against the invading Kayadon, and Sonya had been begging them to let her come along. She had been fairly young at the time, barely seventeen.

Sebastian had refused.

How silly it felt now to recall how she had pouted, when in the end, all their lives had been cruelly upheaved.

The fiendish women she once called family had tricked Sebastian and Cale, pretending to send them off with a hug, only to inject them with a solution that made them sluggish and weak. Sonya had been aghast, outraged, but instead of giving into her violent desires, she had helped the boys commandeer *Marada*—once a Kayadon ship—and flee.

Sadly, soon after, their planet had been destroyed by war, rendered unlivable.

The heel of her boot made contact with her stagnant opponent. The spiral metal base gave a resonating protest.

The second time Sonya had been so near the Edge was for the same reason she was now. A frustrating pent-up desire that went unfulfilled. Shortly after they'd recruited their first crew, a male had taken an interest in her.

Unfortunately, being the only living female in the family, Sebastian and Cale were grossly overprotective. And to this day, they intimidated away any male who even looked sideways at her.

In the beginning, she hadn't cared much for male attention and was comforted by her brothers' protectiveness of her. However, when the next few males were driven away, her appreciation rapidly grew into resentment.

She'd quickly figured out how to take care of herself, however. And when that didn't work, she would come here and beat the living shit out of something.

Sparring with her brothers worked the best, allowing her to take out her resentment on them while keeping herself sane.

Win, win. Well, almost win, win. The problem? She spent so much time sparing and training she'd grown to be quite a skilled fighter, and no one else, except maybe Marik, would dare join her on the mat. She had to admit, no one else had much of a chance against her.

Essentially, they'd be the equivalent of this practice dummy, bouncing around in stunned silence.

She gave a final whack and then grabbed the rag off the floor to wipe her face. *Odd*. She usually felt so much better after hours of vigorous physical activity, but there was still a faint tingle rolling through her. Perhaps a cold shower or little alone time would kill it for good.

Her efforts were for naught.

After having forced herself to come twice, the craving was still there, like a weed that kept growing back.

After dressing, she headed back to The Demon's Punchbowl. She'd left Ethan quite abruptly and now worried he had gone through all her product in a single night.

She found him sitting at a table with a group of men, enjoying a game of cards and sipping a drink. The four other males at the table looked up and smiled at her in greeting. That is, until they saw the dangerous look she was giving Ethan.

Ethan spared her a glance and then focused back on his cards.

"What are you doing?" She stomped toward the table.

One of the males scooted away from the table. "I should get back to Bree. She'll be wondering what's kept me. Alright if I'll pay up later, Ethan?"

"Sure thing," Ethan replied, still not bothering to look at her.

The other three set their cards down and relocated to a table across the room.

"Thanks a lot. I was really on a roll," Ethan grumbled, gathering up the pile of notes and chips in front of him.

"You do realize you're supposed to be working." She crossed her arms.

He gestured around the room. "It's dead. There's nothing to do."

"Then you find something to do." She paused, noticing that music filled the room. So he'd managed to fix the speakers. That didn't give him leave to fool around.

"Like what? Everything's clean, and you are obscenely organized. What's left but to have a little fun and maybe fill my pocket?"

"You really are nothing more than a despicable pirate, aren't you?"

His deep-blue eyes narrowed on hers. Disregarding his winnings on the table, he rose to his feet and stepped toward her till she felt crowded by his closeness. A muscle ticked in his jaw. She stood her ground, clenched her fists, and glared up at him. Vaguely, she noted that the three remaining males watched them in silence, but she didn't care.

Ethan looked her up and down before leaning a bit closer. "And you are a horrible tease, *vietta*."

There was that word again. Insults didn't bother her, but she'd like to at least be able to understand them. "What does that even mean?"

He hesitated, and she wondered if he would refuse to tell her. "Roughly, it means rotten female."

"Charming." Then why did he say it like a term of endearment? "Coming from you, I'll take that as a compliment."

He hissed out a curse through clenched teeth. Sonya grinned, excited to see if he would throw the first punch.

Before either of them made a move, a soft voice pulled Sonya from the argument. "Uh, hi guys."

Sonya's anger drained away, and she whirled around to pull Anya into a tight embrace. Then she set her at arm's length to thoroughly assess her. "How are you feeling?"

Not surprising, Sebastian appeared behind Anya. "She claims to be fine," he answered for her, "but I wish she would spend a little more time recovering in bed."

Anya rolled her eyes. "I'm quite well, thank you. Restless, even. We are on our way to the Sanctuary, but I wanted to stop by to see you, as well as to thank Ethan for what he did for me."

"No need, Princess," Ethan replied. "I'm just glad you're alright."

Sebastian put his arm around Anya and pulled her close, "Sonya, I'll find you later to discuss how we are to proceed with Marik's rescue."

"Actually, I've got time now," she said, relieved that they would finally be going after Marik. "Why don't I follow you to the Sanctuary, and we can discuss it there."

Anya waved to Ethan as she followed Sebastian out the door. Sonya didn't spare him a second glance.

Moments later, the artificial sunlight of the Sanctuary warmed her skin. This foliage rich deck was the most unique and beloved part of the ship, a massive space designed to resemble a patch of fertile land.

Anya took a deep breath and smiled. Then she strolled along

the path that weaved over a trickling rivulet. Instead of following, Sonya and Sebastian remained by the entrance.

Sebastian tore his eyes from his mate and faced Sonya with a frown. "We're nearing Undewla as we speak. Aidan will begin scanning the surface for any sign of Marik." He paused. "Anya and I will be taking the second shuttle to the surface to conduct our own search."

Sonya gaped at him. "Just the two of you?"

"Aye. I would go myself, but she refuses to allow that. She feels responsible for his situation and believes her gift would allow her to sense where both Marik and her sister might be."

"And what am I to do? Sit here like a lump and wait?"

First Cale left without her, and now Sebastian expected her to stay behind—again? A girl's ego could only take so much.

"I can be useful, you know."

"I know. That's why I want you to stay here and act as captain till our return. With both Cale and Marik gone, there's no one I trust more to do the job."

"What about Aidan?"

"I want him scanning for Marik full time, not worrying about leading the crew. You did a fine job before. Please don't fight me on this, Sonya. I'm exhausted from arguing with Anya. The chit can be very stubborn when she wants to be."

"You sure you'll be okay? She was captured the last time."

Sebastian grew pained, and Sonya regretted her reminder. "Darius is dead now, so I no longer have to worry about him. I'm taking more precautions this time as well. Plus, since it will only be her with me, I can watch over her more readily. I won't have to split my attention between her and others."

"Fine," Sonya relented, albeit a bit stubbornly.

"One more thing. I want you to keep the pub open if you can. I see Ethan has already begun taking shifts." At her look, he quickly added, "It's for the sake of the crew. With all that's happened, I don't anticipate we'll be able to get to a space city for some time, and I can already see the strain that's taking on the crew."

Sonya felt it herself. They'd all been running on high gear for some time now, and it didn't look as though that was going to stop any time soon. "But I'm nearly out of product. There's not much left for the crew's entertainment."

"I have a personal stash in my room. Feel free to take it."

Sonya had forgotten about that. Sebastian always hoarded extra bottles of his favorite liquors. "When are you leaving?"

"In a few days. Need to make sure Anya is truly recovered. Also, I want to see if Aidan discovers anything useful"

"And while he's doing that," Anya said from behind them, her arms placed innocently around back as she leaned in to listen to their conversation, "I'll be practicing my gift."

"That's not what I mean by recover." Sebastian shook his head.

"And I've told you I'm fine. I'm not going to lie in bed till you're ready to leave."

Sebastian scrubbed his hand down his face.

Sonya couldn't help but laugh at them both. She nudged Sebastian in the shoulder. "You have quite the mate, brother. She's as fierce as any of us."

"That's what worries me."

Chapter 12

Sonya raided her brother's liquor stash on her way back to the pub. She'd been surprised by the amount Sebastian had accumulated and wondered if she'd find just as much hidden in Cale's room. She didn't doubt it one bit, but wouldn't go through his belongings until she was low on supplies again.

She scowled at Ethan as she brushed past him on her way to the stock room. He lifted his chin and mirrored her expression. Apparently he'd collected his winnings before taking his place behind the bar, but where he'd stashed them, she couldn't see.

Inside the small rectangular stock room, lined with shelves, she knelt down and set her load on the floor to rummage through it.

From the doorway, Ethan said, "What did they say?"

As she proceeded to organize the bottles on the shelf, she relayed Sebastian's plan, informing Ethan that he'd be working in the pub more than previously anticipated.

"I should be there to protect the princess," he replied. "Not slinging drinks."

"You'll have to take it up with Sebastian," she grumbled, ignoring the weird feeling that accompanied his tone. They hadn't resolved their previous argument, but she wasn't in the mood right now.

"I'll do that," he declared.

"Assuming Sebastian refuses your request, and he most likely will, I expect you here for the morning shift. Also, you'll no longer participate in drunken gambling while you're on the job. In fact, there will be no drunken anything, understand?" She stood and faced him.

His expression displayed a mixture of irritation and amusement.

"I know the concept of a hard day's work is difficult for you to understand, pirate, and you're functioning on a damaged moral compass—"

He frowned. "My moral compass may be damaged, but at least I'm not a slave to my baser needs."

She stilled. "You're saying I am?"

"You are a demon, after all. Your kind are notorious for their debauchee and barbarous natures."

She choked out a laugh. "My people are barbarous?"

"You said it."

She crossed her arms. "And this coming from a pirate."

"You know nothing of it!" he snapped.

"And you know nothing of me!"

"I know more than you think. And even if I didn't, I had you pegged purely by the manner in which you dress yourself." He gave her a disgusted once over.

That gave her pause, and she resisted the urge to look down at herself. Her outfit was no more revealing than any other female on the ship. In fact, compared to some, she could be considered downright modest. Her skirts, she had to admit, were on the short side, but that was only to accommodate her tail. Besides, she liked them. Not that it mattered what anyone else thought of her, especially not some hypocritical pirate.

"Get out of my pub before I smash your face into the wall," she hissed.

Instead, he took a step closer, goading her with his defiant expression. Her blood fired in a way she'd never felt before, and the pace of her heart increased with a surge of excitement. She was used to people backing down when she issued a threat. They never willingly opened themselves up for attack.

She tilted her head at him with renewed interest.

He seemed to note the change in her, and something like smugness formed behind his eyes.

"Don't be a moron," she snapped, suddenly unsure how to proceed. "I wouldn't want to damage my newly acquired stock. Go speak with Sebastian. I hope he does take you with him. Then I won't have to suffer through your insolence."

If she didn't know any better, she would think his frown showed a hint of disappointment.

Long after he'd left, Sonya was still puzzling over the fact that she hadn't just dragged him out of her pub and knocked him on his ass. He deserved nothing less. She was also surprised to find that she needed another session in the training room so soon.

Ethan went in search of Sebastian, bewildered by what had happened between him and Sonya. How was it that she hated and desired him at the same time? Her indecisiveness was enough to drive his sanity to the brink.

During their first argument of the night, her contempt had been palpable. Nothing had driven him to anger so quickly. She continued to see him as…what were her words? A despicable pirate. He couldn't figure out why that bothered him so much.

Yet, just now, she had once more become aroused. He knew this because her resolve had shifted wildly between furious violence and carnal aggression. In the end, she had settled on confused avoidance.

He would have preferred either of the other two.

He found Sebastian and Anya just as they exited the Sanctuary. Sebastian caught the look in Ethan's eye, and he held up his hands. "No. You are not coming with us."

"I can't allow you to go alone." Ethan glanced between Sebastian and Anya.

"You can, and you will," Sebastian said. "I'll not risk losing anyone else, and I can only stand one stubborn Faieara on this expedition. Besides, we need you here translating that book."

"He's right." Anya smiled at Ethan and grabbed hold of Sebastian's arm. "I sensed the presence of my sister before I was taken by Darius. I'm sure we'll find her and Marik in no time. Please don't worry, Ethan."

His shoulders slumped. He could tell neither of them had any intention of relenting. "What about the cold?" he asked Sebastian. "Anya and I were nearly rendered catatonic by it. How can you take here there a second time?"

To his surprise, Sebastian grinned. "I found a special suit for her to wear. I almost forgot we had it. It's bulky, but it will protect her from the weather. And if anyone besides me touches her, it will zap them into a coma."

Ethan's brow rose.

Sebastian placed a hand on his shoulder and met his gaze. "I will not let her out of my sight."

Ethan pursed his lips. "If you change your mind, just say the word."

Sebastian nodded.

As Ethan headed back to his room, his mind once more drifted to the little demon temptress.

She had appeared insulted when he commented on her clothing, but how could she be? Her dress was designed to snare a male's attention, and snare it she did. The men on this ship constantly looked her way, and she disregarded their attention as though it were to be expected.

Teasing little witch.

There must be some reason behind her unwavering hatred toward him. Either that, or she just enjoyed tormenting him, which was the far more likely scenario.

Well, if she insisted on accusing him of being a despicable pirate, he was more than willing to show her one.

* * *

The next evening, Sonya entered The Demon's Punchbowl ready to start her shift and make sure Ethan had been respecting her orders. She paused in the doorway to gauge the nearly empty room. A few customers were scattered across the pub, but Ethan was nowhere to be found.

Seeing the stock room door ajar, light shining, she moved in to investigate.

Ethan faced away from her, his head tilted back as he guzzled straight from a bottle.

Fury hit her. "I'll kill you, pirate!" She lunged.

Without even looking, he managed to sidestep her attack,

and her fist almost met with a line of bottles on a shelf.

"Calm yourself, female." He turned to her, one finger hooked loosely around the bottleneck. "I was just sampling the product to see what would be best to recommend to our clients."

"*My* clients!" She growled, cursing herself for not taking care of his attitude problem last night.

"I'll pay for the liquor. It was only a drop."

"Damn right you'll pay for it! And that bottle was nearly full till you got your hands on it."

The bastard had the gall to roll his eyes at her. "Very well, I'll buy you another bottle. What's the big deal?" He brushed a hand through his hair and shot her an uncaring smile. Then, with a slur in his voice, he said, "You know, you're rather attractive when you're pissed off. You should remain that way all the time."

She swung her fist at him, but again missed. How could he be so fast, especially drunk? She blamed the confined space. She wasn't used to fighting in such small quarters and feared trashing her entire stock.

"What's going on?" Anya called from behind.

"Princess!" Ethan greeted with a smile.

Taking advantage of his temporary distraction, Sonya latched her tail around the almost empty bottle still grasped in his hand and flung it hard into the side of his head. The glass shattered, and a smile spread across her lips as he went down.

Anya shrieked. "What are you doing?" She rushed past Sonya and knelt beside his limp body. "Ethan?"

"His head is far too thick for me to do any real damage." When Anya gave her a chiding look, Sonya whined, "He was stealing my liquor."

Anya let out an exasperated sigh. "You two have got to stop fighting. Sebastian and I are leaving for Undewla soon, and you'll be acting as captain. If you want your pub to stay open, then you need him. Everyone else is occupied with their own jobs. Sebastian had to pull one of the mechanics to work the galley."

"Yeah, and the food just isn't the same," Sonya grumbled.

With worry etched in her features, Anya's head dropped. Sonya recalled Sebastian saying that she blamed herself for Marik's situation.

"It's not your fault Mark was captured," Sonya said. "And you'll find him, don't fret. Marik can take care of himself. I'm sure he's fine."

"That was a cheap shot, demon witch." Ethan sluggishly sat up and gripped his head.

Sonya couldn't help but smirk. "But I thought I was oh-so pretty when I was angry? Change your mind, did you?

"Indeed."

He placed his hand over the bloody patch where the bottle had sliced him. Brightness erupted under his palm. Sonya shielded her eyes until the light faded away.

He stood a bit wobbly and pinned Sonya with a dark stare. "That tail of yours is wicked. I'll be sure to keep an eye on it from now on."

"You do that!" Wait, had she just given him permission to check out her tail? "Just keep your eyes on my pub, and if I catch you sneaking drinks again, you might not be able to heal after what I'll do to you."

Anya pulled her from the room and gave her a serious look that didn't fit her sweet face. "Promise me you will not kill him while we're gone."

Sonya raked both hands down her face and let out a frustrated groan. "Come on, Anya."

Anya set her chin and crossed her arms, and gave a hard shake of her head.

"What if it's an accident?"

Ethan stumbled to the door of the stock room and leaned against it, offering a self-satisfied grin in her direction. Sonya couldn't help but sneer at him.

"Promise me," Anya repeated, managing to miss Ethan's half of the exchange.

"Alright. Murder is off the table." That was as much as she was agreeing to.

Anya nodded, giving them both a stern look before leaving them alone.

Sonya stepped behind the bar to begin work as usual, expecting Ethan to take off now that she was there. Instead, he claimed an empty table across the room and waited…as though she should serve him!

She grabbed a damp rag and began wiping down tables around the bar, purposely avoiding his stare. She smiled at a table of customers near him. "You need anything?"

One of the three males raised his bottle. "I'll take another one."

She returned to the bar and popped the lid off a fresh ale before sauntering back. Handing the drink over, she asked, "Anything else?"

The other two shook their heads.

As she headed back toward the bar, Ethan called out, "Paying customer thirsty over here."

The handful of other patrons glanced at Ethan, with a mixture of dubious expressions. No one ever spoke to her like that.

Sonya inhaled a calming breath, barely able to reign in her anger. "When you've paid for what you took, then we'll talk."

"Put it on my tab," he replied.

"This isn't the kind of shit-hole that you're used to. You pay or you go." She pointed to the door.

He didn't budge.

She resumed ignoring him and focused on cleaning the mess he had left for her. Glasses piled high in the sink and along the counter. It looked as though he hadn't cleaned a single dish or counter during the whole of his shift. The mats at her feet were disheveled. She leaned down to fix them, then studied her backsplash. Many of the bottles were in disarray. The expensive stock now mingled with the cheap stuff, and vice versa.

Had he intentionally muddled their order?

As soon as she set to fixing it, she sensed he had relocated to a seat at the bar. Once the last bottle was in its rightful place, she turned to see him studying her.

"You didn't miss a single one." He gave her an apprising glance.

Her ire spiked. "So you did do that on purpose?"

He shrugged and continued to look at her curiously.

Trying not to feel self-conscious by his scrutiny, she resumed straightening. She was still pissed, but taking care of her pub helped to relax her a little. She no longer felt murderous, anyway, though the night was young.

"Why do you care so much about this place?" he asked.

She stilled and then glanced back at him. Was he really attempting small talk?

She gauged his expression, which seemed genuinely interested, but chalked it up to the fact that he was inebriated.

Ethan wasn't sure what had compelled him to engage her in conversation, especially when he had intended to continue to drive her mad.

She remained silent for a long moment, and he assumed she wasn't going to answer at all.

Then she lifted her shoulder in an uncharacteristically shy manner as she lowered her gaze. "It's the one thing on this ship that's all mine."

"Explain."

She glared at him, her eyes smoldering with indignation. One thing he'd learned about her was that she despised being ordered around.

"Please," he added.

She eyed him dubiously, somewhat reserved once more, yet her anger toward him was still bobbing the surface of her emotions.

Finally, she replied, "It's important for me to pull my own weight. Sebastian captains the ship and makes most of the decisions, Cale is his second in command, and I provide a service to bring in money. I pay a monthly rate for this space which helps us to purchase supplies and maintain *Marada* when jobs are scarce."

Ethan leaned back in his chair. He hadn't expected such an honest answer, and without a single insult thrown his way.

"We don't go around stealing whatever we like, as *others* do." An accusatory glance followed her words.

Ah, that was more like it.

"Like I said, I wasn't stealing. I was sampling. If I'm going to work here, I'm going to need to know which flavors mesh well together."

"Yet you're clearly drunk."

He waved his hand dismissively. "A fortunate side effect. And I'm not that bad off. My tolerance is higher than most."

"Or so you'd like to believe."

"I'm sure I'd keep up just fine with a demon's pace."

Her lips curled into a roguish grin. "Is that a challenge?"

"Take it as you like."

"Poor decision making is another side effect of being drunk."

"You just name the time."

Sonya paused and studied him. "You must be joking."

"If you lose, I get to drink free for life."

"And what do I get if *you* lose?"

He shrugged. "I could help extract that insidious metal bar from your ass."

"Impossible, since you're the reason it's there."

He chuckled. "Fair enough. Then I'll work for free."

She grinned like a feline toying with prey. "Then let's do this."

A round of cheers erupted from the other patrons, who had apparently been listening. Ethan turned to the room, catching a few pitying head shakes in his direction.

Sonya disappeared into the storeroom and reemerged with a bottle filled to the brim. He recalled that particular brand had tasted very strong.

"I'm starting off at a disadvantage," he pointed out.

"Not for long." She poured herself a generous portion and

then downed it in a few large gulps. When she lowered the glass, she feigned a sweet smile. "Does that seem about the right amount?"

He jerked his chin to the bottle. "Better have a little more."

Not bothering to argue, she refilled her glass and emptied it just as quickly as the first. Then she pulled out a second glass, filled them both and offered him one.

Ethan lifted his and took in a mouthful. "Are there rules to this game?" he asked.

"We go till one of us falls over."

"Sounds good."

Demons may have a naturally high tolerance for alcohol, but she was just a wisp of a thing. That should work in his favor.

"And to keep us both standing, we'll both be serving customers as we go."

"Very well." Ethan moved behind the bar and finished the contents of his glass, then held it out for her to refill it. "I believe you're behind again."

Sonya laughed, shaking her head before she chugged down her drink. "I'm not carrying you back to your room when you pass out."

"That's fine, He said. "Consequently, I *will* be carrying you back to yours."

She frowned at him. "You'll do no such thing."

"Are you afraid you'll lose?"

"Not in the slightest."

He gave an impish grin and jiggled his empty glass at her.

Before long, he lost count of how many bottles they'd finished. His blurry vision told him five sat on the counter, but three—or maybe four—others had been deposited in the waste disposal unit.

Word of their competition must have spread through the ship because the pub was now bustling. Patrons crowded the bar and called out orders, obviously trying to confuse the both of them. From the corner of his eye, Ethan saw money exchange hands and knew bets were being made.

Sonya and Ethan stumbled around, filling orders and making sure their own glasses never completely emptied. Each time one of them fumbled with their footing, the room would erupt in howls, and both he and Sonya would join in the laughter.

Sonya wobbled on her feet for the seventh time—at least he thought it was the seventh—as she crossed to the other end of the bar to take an order.

By the sounds rolling through the crowd, Ethan determined that the room was evenly split, half cheering for him, and half for Sonya. He would have commented on her near fall, but all his concentration was focused on keeping himself upright. He'd nearly sunk to the ground a dozen times already.

Sonya returned to his side of the bar with a devilish grin and wiggled their shared liquor bottle at him. He glanced down at his almost empty glass.

As she sloshed more liquid to his glass, she leaned over the counter top, braced on her forearm. Her position gave him a clear view of her succulent cleavage. He stifled a groan.

She smiled up at him. "Ready to give up, pirate?"

He frowned. She'd been doing little provocative things like that all night. It was driving him mad, and she knew it.

Abruptly, he took a step toward her, and she straightened. He gripped her by the arm and leaned in to whisper in her ear. "Teasing me with your body will not help you win this, *vietta*."

She reared back, eyes wide. Deep crimson spread over her cheeks. "What? I wasn't..." She skated a worried glance over the crowd as if fearing someone had heard his whispered accusation. Then she narrowed her gaze at him. "Your mind games won't work." She turned to take another order, her movements slightly stiffer than before.

Did she not realize the power of her attractiveness? Could that even be possible? But as he continued to observe her, he started to suspect that might just be the case.

By the time they had gone through another few bottles... each...Ethan's legs were like some kind of wobbly confection, nearly unreliable in their support. Worse, the slipperiness of every surface seemed to have increased tenfold.

Sonya wasn't in the greatest shape either, but she still managed to complete orders while swaying her ass to the music.

When a wave of dizziness splashed over him, he feared he might just lose this tournament—a fear that was confirmed a few moments later when he found himself face up on the ground.

The crowd was a mix of groans, cheers, and laughter.

Sonya leaned over him with a triumphant grin. Her words came out slurred, yet teasing. "I'd appreciate it if you take the first shift tomorrow."

He groaned and let his head drop to the ground.

Chapter 13

Sonya sat at the captain's console, hoping Sebastian and Anya were alright. It had been several days since they'd left for Undewla.

Even though Aidan had found no definitive evidence that Marik might still live, no one was ready to assume the worst.

To Sonya's surprise, Ethan hadn't argued over having to work in the pub with no pay. In fact, he hadn't even seemed angry. He did, however, continue to unnerve her with his frequent prying gaze.

When he had accused her of using her body to distract him, she had been so caught off guard that she had nearly stumbled to her ass. The thought hadn't even crossed her mind, but afterward she felt overly self-conscious of her every move.

Miserable tease, he had called her. The idea of it rummaged around in her brain, and she instinctively realized he enjoyed a little teasing.

She quelled the dangerous presumption.

Unfortunately, her body seemed to clasp on to the notion. Much of her time, lately, was spent in the training room.

She didn't know what, but something was happening to her, something that was changing her to the core…. And it scared the hell out of her.

And now, with both her brothers and Marik gone, she had no one to confide in and no one to pummel but the training dummies.

She let out a harsh sigh and stood. "Aidan, take command. Call me if anything happens."

He offered a thumbs up in response and turned back to his console.

She headed to her room for a quick wash and wardrobe change. Then she surveyed her image in the mirror. The short black skirt rode high on her thighs. Her stocking were black and diamond woven. The purple satin corset, strung with black string down the front, followed the delicate curve of her waist and hips.

She raised her chin. Sure it was provocative, but she didn't don these clothes to be a tease. One would need persistent male attention to be a tease.

She finished the ensemble with a dark choker around her neck, then made her way to The Demon's Punchbowl.

She heard the blaring music long before she reached the entrance.

Her jaw dropped.

Center stage, surrounded by a crowd of hooting males, stood two busty females with Sonya's good ale being poured down the fronts of their white blouses.

Her fingers balled into tight fists as she stomped her way to where Ethan was mixing a drink at the bar.

As he poured, he looked up with a grin. Noting her expression, his smile dropped. Then his gaze traveled her body, and another expression came over him. She froze mid-step. He'd given her that look before, and she'd easily disregarded it as nothing more than a means to irritate her. Now she recognized it for what it was: pure masculine interest.

But surely he wasn't genuinely attracted to her. It must be that he had decided to retaliate for losing their wager by making her as uncomfortable as possible.

His eyes lowered to her bodice where, she had to admit, her cleavage was looking damn good. She stifled a sudden urge to jiggle her torso.

What was wrong with her?

Ethan struggled to school his features as Sonya approached. The damn female was dressed like his living fantasy!

"What do you think you're doing?" Sonya's outrage rode over the blaring music.

Long after her blushing act the night of their bet, Ethan had wondered if she was really so oblivious of effect on the males around her. That barely-there top and skimpy skirt was drawing attention away from the two lovely ladies on stage.

She had to see that.

Cool liquid splash over his fingers and splattered onto the bar. He stopped pouring and handed the glass to the customer who had ordered it. The man blindly grabbed for the glass, unable to take his gaze away from the now soaked women who had begun kissing each other.

"It looks like I'm serving this fine gentleman," Ethan replied without looking back at her.

Sonya banged her fist on the bar. "I am not running a brothel here!"

"That's good, because if you were, you'd be dangerously low on employees."

Sonya pointed to the sexual display. "Was this your idea?"

He lifted his thumb and forefinger together. "I may have made a tiny suggestion."

Sonya grabbed him by the collar, bringing his face closer to hers so that they were both leaning over the bar. "This is not one of your pirate dens. This pub is my life, and I will not have you defiling it."

He couldn't resist dipping his eyes to her chest, even though he knew it would heighten her ire.

She bared her fangs. "You're fired! Get out!"

"Wait, wait, hold on." He reached up and gently removed her hands from inching around his neck. "Look around for a second."

Grudgingly, she obeyed and then shrugged, focusing her rage back on him.

He pointed past the melee of overly excited men surrounding the two females. "Those two are in a committed relationship. They're just having some fun with the boys and putting a little spice into their relationship."

Sonya took that in for a moment. "You're kidding."

"Not even a little. They came in during a lover's quarrel. I got them to kiss and make up. And they just didn't want to stop. Who am I to stand in the way of true love?"

"And how did you get them to kiss and make up?"

"The same way you get any two females to kiss. You get them drunk."

Sonya almost laughed at that…almost. He wished she

would just relax and let him take care of her tavern. Sure, he had pulled a few pranks before, just to aggravate her, but now he only wanted to help. There was nothing better for him to do, anyway. He'd made no new ground translating the book, which was irritating in and of itself, and he was currently useless in the ongoing search for Nadua and Kyra.

He tried to convince himself he had done enough up until this point, and now it was fate's time to put in a few hours, but that didn't sit well with him.

After assessing the full scope of the crowd, Sonya plopped down on a stool. "Fine. You're not fired."

Ethan gave a theatrical bow. That was probably the closest thing to a compliment he would ever receive from her.

"Just get me a drink," she ordered.

"Of course, my liege," he mocked. For someone who hated taking orders, she sure liked to give them. Incidentally, he knew how to cure her of that. Not that she would let him try.

Then again, maybe she would. From the corner of his eye, he found her studying him. He wasn't dressed in anything special, just a loose white shirt and a tan coat adorned with the usual gold buttons and buckles. As he fixed her drink, he scanned her intent and found she did not wish to be caught appraising him.

Curious.

By the time he turned to place the drink in front of her, she had already averted her gaze. She gave the liquid a quick taste and then snapped, "Ethan, you had better not put this much alcohol in everyone's drinks."

"Special for you, my captain."

Rolling her eyes, Sonya took a large gulp. As soon as she

finished it, he started mixing her another.

When the music changed to an encouraging beat, Sonya slipped off the stool and moved to the dance floor. Ethan was relieved to see her actually having a good time. Maybe she'd take a break from being such a hard ass.

She tugged a male onto the dance floor with her. After an awkward moment, the male pulled her close and began gyrating against her.

Ethan's mood took a nosedive, but he wasn't sure why. He'd wanted her to have fun so she would leave him to his job. Right?

Maybe it was because that particular male had recently been seen putting the moves on several other females in the joint. But what did Ethan care? He was sure Sonya could take care of herself. It wasn't as if she actually desired the male. Surely she had better taste than that.

Or perhaps that was *her* male. The one she used to slake her need.

He turned to a waiting customer. The woman was rather cute and seemed to be giving him a come-hither look the entire time he fixed her drink. He'd noticed this female earlier in the night, and many times before that. She was often attached to a different guy, offering them that same inviting smile she displayed now. Jade was her name. And tonight she was alone.

After accepting the drink, she thanked him with a bedroom voice before sauntering off, her hips swaying in an exaggerated manner. He watched with detached interest, wondering why he hadn't made the lewd comment she'd been hoping for.

She turned back to pin him with an enticing glance as she disappeared into the crowd—a clear sign that she was a sure thing, had he the inclination to pursue her.

He glanced toward the dance floor, expecting to see that Sonya had moved on, but that bastard still clung to her. Ethan's eyes snapped to the male's hand as it started drifting toward Sonya's ass. Just as he was about to find his prize, Ethan's mind swelled viciously, cutting off clear thought.

He leapt over the bar, rushed forward, and smashed his fist into the other male's face. The wretch hadn't even seen it coming. Neither had Ethan for that matter. He stood stock still for a moment, trying to figure out why he'd been compelled to attack.

"What the fuck!" Sonya screeched and pushed Ethan away to examine the unconscious man. "Why did you do that?"

"He was groping you!" Gods that sounded lame.

"No kidding! If I had wanted him to stop, I would have hit him myself! Heal him!"

Ethan crossed his arms, loathed to do anything for this inferior male who couldn't even defend himself. "Sorry, sweetheart, my power isn't working at the moment."

A small crowd had gathered around them. Sonya ordered two somewhat sober individuals to take the unconscious male to sickbay. Then she dragged Ethan behind the bar and into the storage room, closing the door behind them. "What the fuck, Ethan! Why did you hit him?"

Ethan was still fighting his own astonishment. "I don't know why I did that. I just didn't think you wanted him touching you."

"You deduced that from the smile on my face?"

Ethan threw his arms out to the side and shook his head. "I just didn't like it."

Sonya tilted her head and eyed him suspiciously. "Did Sebastian order you to keep an eye on me? Keep guys away from me?"

Ethan looked at her, confused by the question. What did Sebastian have to do with anything? And how could she have let that ridiculous male touch her?

The answer hit him.

She did it to drive him mad, just like everything else she did.

And it was working.

He suddenly felt overwhelmed by her presence. She looked so damn sexy in that slip of a skirt, and her heavy breathing was causing the mounds of her breast to billow over her bodice. Her thighs peeked out from under her garments.

His body responded to every bit of it, screaming with fevered demands. Even her violet eyes, doused in anger, helped to fill his cock.

She continued to rail, oblivious to his tempestuous urge to take her where she stood. "It is none of Sebastian's business if I decide to—"

Ethan silenced her with a bruising kiss. He pushed her against the door and held her in place by the back of her neck as he slipped his mouth over hers. She let out a soft cry of surprise, and he sensed she was ready to kick him where it would hurt him the most. Undaunted, he slipped his tongue against her lips, demanding entry. He would teach her what happened when she toyed with a male such as he.

Her breath rushed out and after brief moment, she surrendered, taking him in her mouth.

Ethan's entire body strained with anticipation.

His palm breached the hem of her skirt and found her backside. He gave a gratifying squeeze, and it felt as though he was claiming what another male almost took. His pelvis ground into her, and she let out a soft, urgent sound, encouraging him to roll his hips once more.

Suddenly, she flipped him around to take control, as he knew she eventually would. He imagined she would always fight him for control. With speed and skill that rivaled her own, he twirled her body so that he was poised at her back and attempted to cage her front against the wall, maybe with a bit too much vigor. Without missing a beat, she put her hands up to stop herself from slamming into it.

Taking advantage of the position, he yanked down her bodice and covered her breast with his hands. Her head lolled back against his shoulder, her nails digging into the wall as her body begged for more.

To his delight, she glided her ass against his crotch.

"Ah, fuck," he groaned as his shaft gave a hard pulse. They fit together so damn good. He turned her around and ground his entire body into her soft flesh, claiming her lips once more as he rubbed his thumb over one hardened nipple. Her breaths heaved harsh and hot as he readied to rip of her remaining clothing.

Then she stilled.

He sensed the change in her too late, and before he could pull away to give her the space she suddenly required, she shoved her palms against him.

He stepped back.

She straightened her outfit and wiped her mouth in disgust.

Ethan clenched his teeth, not understanding the shift in mood.

"Don't ever do that again," she warned in a tone drowning with the depth of her loathing. She rushed out before he could muster a response.

Left alone and still badly in need of release, he leaned against the wall and scrubbed a hand down his face, trying to figure out what the hell just happened.

Sonya had never come across anything that unnerved her the way that kiss had. She'd been lost…utterly lost. The feel of him pressed against her, the wall at her back, was damn near maddening.

His clothing had been seconds away from becoming tattered rags on the floor. The feeling had been so much like being on the Edge, only instead of rendering her a rabid beast, she had been turned into some kind of wanton creature.

His touch had been like the sweetest agony, filled with the promise of pure ecstasy and unyielding passion. Thinking of it now had her mouth running dry, and her body quivering with regret. Stopping had been like a vicious strike to the gut, but she'd had to do it. Had to get away.

As he had made her mindless with his kiss, a cold button of his coat had touched her flesh, and she been reminded who it was that kissed her with such passion.

Memories of her younger self peeking through a crack as those soulless pirates slashed her father to death battered her brain. It was as if fire and ice had collided in her body.

In the safety her room, she leaned against the wall, vehemently telling herself she didn't want to go back, though part of her knew it was a lie.

She hissed out a curse and paced around the room, trying to find something to occupy her mind, but her thoughts kept drifting back to Ethan.

She threw open her closet and retrieved her favorite set of daggers, then headed to the training room.

Chapter 14

Sonya had managed to avoid Ethan over the next few days, but her mind wouldn't allow her to prevent reliving that moment every second of every hour. She couldn't get it out of her head.

Damn pirate!

And now, because of him, she teetered on the Edge. It felt as though anything could set her off.

She spent much of the day seeking out a willing sparring partner, but no one was eager to put themselves in the path of a tempestuous demon. She needed a real bout on the mat. Someone who could challenge her. A catatonic practice dummy wasn't cutting it.

How ironic that the one time she really needed them, her brothers were away.

And she was beginning to lose ground on another kind of battle that had been raging inside her since Ethan's assault.

She thought back to the last time she'd been kissed. Surely it had been just as heated, but she couldn't recall exactly. What she did remember was directly afterward, the male had started to grow increasingly uncomfortable around her brothers, and he hadn't stayed on the ship long.

Sonya wasn't sure if her brothers intentionally kept males from wanting to pursue her. They didn't openly threaten anyone. Rather, it was in their manner, and a look that said, "If you hurt her, I'll kill you slowly and with great pleasure."

Eventually, Sonya had given up on the whole prospect, and instead focused on exercise and fighting. It had worked great, till now.

This is all Ethan's fault, she told herself as she stomped down the hall. Hours of training, meditating, and vigorous exercise, all designed to keep her from focusing on such things, shattered by a kiss—a kiss that she had only enjoyed because she'd been a little tipsy. Not because it had been passionate, or demanding, or anything ridiculous like that.

She figured it was only fair that he help her fix this.

In fact, he was probably the only one on board ignorant—or arrogant—enough to comply. And because he was the cause, he owed her a solution.

Sonya entered The Demon's Punchbowl and headed straight for the bar. Ethan's dark-blue eyes followed her with a little too much intensity.

Sonya's resolve faltered as she wondered what he thought of her outfit—a tight purple bodice with a black skirt that fell just above tall boots threaded with purple strings. Scolding herself, she quickly morphed her inappropriate reaction into fury.

His own dress was the usual: an overly adorned, neatly tailored coat hugged a fitted tan shirt, and dark-brown trousers tucked into heavy black boots with thick gold buckles. Typical pirate. She would use it as a reminder of why she hated him.

"Captain," he greeted with his usual cavalier smile, as if nothing had happened between them. "What brings you to my fine establishment?"

"My fine establishment," she corrected.

"Don't worry." He turned away and headed several feet down the bar to collect a set of empty glasses. "For you, drinks are on the house."

"They better not be for anyone else."

"Oh, only the most important people."

A nearby table of crew members raised their glasses and cheered at Ethan's words. Sonya shot them a piercing glare. They silenced and looked elsewhere.

She faced Ethan, ready to give him the usual threats to his life, but he had moved to the other end of the bar and was pouring a drink for Jade.

As with most people who chose to enter space, Jade didn't like staying in one spot for too long. She was one of the few people aboard the ship who didn't work as part of the crew. Instead, she paid a hefty sum to be ferried around. *Marada* provided a safe way for her to travel, with a little more excitement than a standard cruise ship.

Jade took hold of the drink Ethan offered, allowing her hand to linger on his a little longer than necessary. The sight made Sonya's teeth gnash together.

When Ethan finally came back to Sonya's end of the bar, she ground out, "This ship has rules, you know. Didn't Sebastian tell you? There's no consorting with anyone on the ship."

"Was I consorting? I recall it being a little more involved than that. Anyway, I thought that rule only applied to the crew? Jade just informed me that she is merely a passenger." He paused thoughtfully. "I do believe she was flirting with me actually, which I know must be alarming to you. Me being the lowly creature that I am." He grinned. "I will go straight to her room after work and let her know how off her judgment of character is. I'm sure she'll be grateful for the warning. Would you like a drink?"

The harsh sound of her teeth grinding rumbled in her ears. With effort, Sonya loosened her jaw, only to allow a string of Demonish curses to run past her lips.

"That sounds sweet," he interjected. "But I don't think you should be coming on to me like that. You know the rules."

"The only reason I'm not pulling your spleen out through your eyeball is because I promised Anya I wouldn't kill you."

He placed his hand on his chest. "I am truly blessed."

"But she didn't say anything about not hurting you."

"Mm, I do like it rough."

Barely holding on to the last of her control, Sonya continued, "Look, you ass, I'm going to give you the opportunity to prove you're more than just a waste of air."

Ethan's mind hissed, reminded of how repulsed she had been by his touch, but he kept his composure.

The effort was monumental.

He had spent that entire evening trying to forget how hungry he had been for her—how hungry he still was for her. How bringing himself relief multiple times had done little to dissuade his need. And she still brought him to full attention just by the sexy sway of her round hips.

"I need someone to spar with, who can offer at least a bit of a challenge," she said. "I'm willing to believe you're not *totally* without skill."

"You want to fight me?" He hadn't seen that coming. The fire in her eyes suggested she wanted something else from him. He tried to read her, finding her innermost desires in turmoil.

"Spar. But yes, I really, really do."

"What do I get if I agree?"

Sonya snorted. "A sliver of respect."

He rolled his eyes. "Not really high on the list of things I want." The lie was easy enough to push through his lips, despite the fact that this female's opinion of him was quickly becoming his top priority. He knew it was wrong. He was destined to wed one of the king's daughters, after all. But something about Sonya's disdain irked him and made him want to demand her respect.

He studied her for a moment. She was acting as though it made no difference if he agreed to sparring with her or not, but a quick scan told him how badly she was in need. If he remembered correctly, demons required one of two things to stabilize their temperaments. Was she asking for one, while wishing for the other?

In an offhanded tone, she asked, "What do you want?"

"I want to be free to run the pub how I want, without you or your minions checking on me."

"My pub has rules. You would still have to follow them."

"How *ever* I want," he repeated.

Sonya glanced around, probably wondering what he had in mind.

"One week," she offered.

The fact she had agreed at all showed how desperate she was.

Looking thoughtful, he added, "And I want you to be nicer to me. That means saying things like please and thank you, and not threatening to kill me every other day."

Sonya opened her mouth to argue, and then closed it. "Fine, for one week also."

"We have a deal then. I'll meet you there after I close tonight."

"No. Now," she insisted, looking a little panicked.

"Who will watch the—"

Sonya turned to the room and bellowed, "Everyone get out! We're closed!"

* * *

Sonya stepped onto the mat. Her skin sizzled with a familiar itch and something inside was screaming to break free.

The entire way to the sparring chamber, Ethan had walked quietly at her side.

How could even his silence sound arrogant?

He'd been watching her, though. Peeking at her from the corner of his eye. She thought he looked pleased, and she assumed he was as eager for her blood as she was for his. But it wouldn't be her who shed it.

Taking his place on the mat across from her, he broke the silence. "So you finally have me alone, what *will* you do with me?"

She pointed to the array of weapons lining the walls. "Pick your poison." She was hoping for something sharp and pointy.

His gaze traveled the selection. "I don't care for poison. Gives me indigestion."

"Fine with me. I love a good brawl."

And to prove her point, she leapt to attack. She put her

full force into her right hook, but at the last second he dodged, throwing her off balance. She realized her mistake too late.

He placed himself at her back, grasped her forearms, and pulled her against him to whisper in her ear. "I know what's going on here."

Her eyes went wide. She slammed her elbow into his stomach. His grip loosened as he huffed out a breath. Pushing away from him, she twisted around and brought her heel up for a high kick.

Again he dodged, and then began circling her with an infuriatingly sexy curve to his lips. Just as she expected the Edge to take over, something else began to happen within her.

"You don't know shit, pirate!" She lashed out again with a succession of jabs and a heel-kick that missed the mark. Furious, she dropped to the floor, swinging her leg wide. A backward flip had her on her feet in the next instant. He evaded her every attempt like a master.

Even with Cale she could land a hit! She lunged again, determined to find flesh with eager knuckles. Then she noticed he wasn't countering. In fact, he wasn't attacking in any way.

"Fight me!"

Bouncing around her, he replied, "Just reading your style, Sweetheart." He smiled.

"Read this!" Now that she was used to his avoidance, she attacked using a wide kick as a diversion, and then wrapped her tail around his wrist to pull him off center.

Her fist connected with his jaw.

Satisfaction filled her as his eyes bulged with the contact. She brought her leg up, but before her knee could find his ribs, he twisted his body away from her.

She reared back for another strike, but he swiped her feet out from under her and had her on her back.

His chest pressed on top of her as he held her still. "Is this fighting really what you want? When we could be doing something much more fun?"

Sonya shifted his weight and pushed him over, reversing their positions. She realized he went a little too easily, and she was now straddling him. Heat pooled at her center, causing her to hesitate. Ethan's irises sparkled with delight, as though he knew the struggle raging inside her.

Determined to keep on track, she pulled out one of the small knives she always kept concealed in a pocket at her side. Knowing how much it would anger him, she used it to pluck free one of the gold pieces decorating his coat.

Ethan grabbed her wrist as the button of his coat flew off. She smirked, and he realized she was only trying to goad him. He knew the battle they were engaged in now was not the only one begin fought. What he didn't know was why she was resisting her natural urges. Did the prospect of being with him, if only for release, disgust her so much?

Perhaps he merely needed to persuade her to feel differently.

"You're playing dirty," he murmured.

"There's no other way."

"Agreed." He reached behind him to unlatch a blade hidden within his coat. In one smooth upward motion, he sliced through the ties of her bodice.

She gasped as the garment slipped open and rushed to cover herself.

Ethan pushed her back to the mat and pinned her arms beside her head. Her torn garment parted slightly with every breath she took.

Ethan locked eyes with her. "I don't think fighting is what you need."

She shook her head, but otherwise did not comment. Large violet eyes were transfixed on his lips, contradicting her weak protest.

"Wouldn't you rather I be touching you?" He moved to caress the soft cord of her neck with his mouth. "Tasting you?"

She shuddered. He almost cried out in triumph as he sensed her will becoming his, any trace of resistance now locked away in the deep recess of her mind. He followed the line of her jaw with his mouth, tasting as he went, until his lips hovered against hers.

She whimpered, her inner turmoil flaring up once more.

Disheartened, he pulled back to gaze into her eyes. Her lids were heavy, wanton, yet fierce, with wavering confusion pooled below the surface. For a moment, he was unsure if she truly wanted this. Was he a cad for playing on her vulnerabilities?

He almost pulled away completely, but before he did, she let out a groan of defeat that called directly to his shaft.

"Damn you," she whispered before pressing her lips to his in a vicious kiss.

Overwhelmed by her sudden demanding need, he blocked his magic and batted away the ruined material of her corset. He palmed her breast. She moaned, making him want to hear more. When he moved to swirl his tongue around one taut peak, she barely stifled a cry of surprise, followed by a river of sweet mewls.

With a new destination in mind, he allowed his hand to skim down her belly, enjoying the shiver that raked over her body. He slid his hand under the hem of her skirt and lazily played there, teasing the soft flesh of her thighs at her apex.

The little moans she made threatened to drive him mad, and all he wanted was to bury himself inside her till they were both panting with satisfaction, but he forced himself to go slow. She would think of him differently after this, and he'd be sure she was unable to keep from grinning when she did.

He pushed aside the thin fabric of her panties to glide a finger over her sex, overjoyed to find how wet she had become. Her body jerked, and her cheeks flushed furiously.

He explored her tender folds, watching with amusement as her breath quickened. The beginnings of her orgasm hit. He continued to stroke her as he dipped his head to lavish attention on her rosy nipples.

When her panting grew dire, he lifted his head to watch as she lost control.

A moan ripped from her lungs as her body arched and an explosion of pleasure crashed over her.

As the vibrating waves began to dim, she looked up at Ethan and understood the hunger in his eyes. He pushed to his knees and tore off his coat. Next came his shirt, while she sat up to undo the buckle of his pants, where his bulge strained against the fabric.

"Finally, I can get you out of my head," he grated, reaching for her panties and practically ripping them off her.

She didn't know what that meant, but his guttural tone sent chills through her. The sight of his thick erection made her body pulse for a replay of the insane pleasure he had forced from her.

He grabbed a hold of her thighs and dragged her lower half toward him, planting her back on the ground. Then in one smooth motion, he kissed her hard just as he shoved into her body.

Sonya cried out from the shock of pain.

With his lips still on hers, Ethan froze and opened his eyes. They grew wide while hers burned with unshed tears.

He yanked his head back to study her, his shaft sliding free. Even before he looked down in horror, she knew he would find blood where they had been connected only seconds ago.

"Fuck!" He pulled up his pants and had them zipped and buckled in no time, then retrieved his shirt and coat before heading for the door. "How could you not have told me!"

His anger fueled her own, but her throat was too tight to respond. She could only glare at him through blurry eyes.

Just before he disappeared, he muttered, "I'm so fucking dead."

A wretched tear streamed down her cheek. There had only been one other time in her life when she had cried, and Ethan would forever remind her of both.

Chapter 15

The sound of Sonya's pained whimper tormented Ethan over the next few days. The last thing he had wanted was to hurt her.

A fresh stream of guilt carved a gully in his stomach.

All he'd wanted was to alter her view of him, soften her aversion, and maybe, selfishly, end his growing obsession with her at the same time. Ironically, the first part of his goal had been accomplished, but not in the way he'd intended. The only thing he'd managed to do was solidify her hatred of him, a hatred that now had a valid foundation.

Aside from raking his mind, trying to figure out how it was possible she had never known a male's touch, he couldn't help but worry what her brothers were going to do to him once they learned of his offense.

His only hope was that Sebastian and Cale might go easy on him for Anya's sake. He'd been indirectly responsible for bringing Sebastian and Anya together, after all. Surely that counted for something…. Hopefully a stay of execution.

He'd contemplated going to Sonya and begging her to keep

quiet, or at the very least, play it down. Knowing her, she would take full advantage of his desperate situation. That's what he told himself, anyway. He suspected the true reason he had yet to approach her was due to an uncharacteristic bout of cowardice.

As deplorable as he felt, he feared seeing if the hurt and betrayal that had been visible behind her eyes was still there.

A part of him was surprised she hadn't sought *him* out, if only to rail at him or demand retribution. Or to finish the fight she had started before he had practically forced himself on her. He would not argue if she did, nor would he fight back. He'd take all the rage she could dole out with silent acceptance. She might label him a nefarious pirate, but he did have some honor.

In a desperate attempt to take his mind off the situation, he tried once again to translate more of the book. Before he knew it, he had spent hours flipping through pages, checking his notes, only to toss away the wasted effort and start over again with not a sliver of progress.

Frustration mounting, he let out a bellow. When that did nothing to diminish his aggravation, he ripped the book from the desk and hurled it across the room.

The book hit the wall with a soft thud, then toppled in a flurry of fumbling pages before slamming closed on the ground.

He cursed, leaning over the desk and digging his fingers into his hair.

It was now clear to him that the code provided by his king was not enough to finish the translation. Maybe Ethan had missed a key element in the instructions. Either that, or the king had become mad toward the end, resulting in nonsensical gibberish.

Ethan had been suspecting the latter since his last counsel with the king's ghostly projection. The king had looked withered, his eyes distant and confused. Evan at the time, Ethan hadn't been sure if the king knew where he was or how he had come to be there. When his empty gaze had landed on Ethan, a hint of recollection sparked, but only for a brief moment. The words he had mouthed next seemed equally odd. "Restore, enhance, sacrifice, sustain. This you must do."

Then the apparition had vanished, leaving Ethan with nothing more than a riddle. He speculated that he was to restore the sisters by bringing them home and possibly enhance their magic through training. He didn't want to mull over what sacrifice might mean, and the last, sustain, was just confusing.

Leaving the book where it landed, he headed to the tavern. To anyone else, it might seem as though Sonya had left him in full control, but he knew the reason for her absence. She wanted to avoid him so badly that she would abandon her beloved establishment to the likes of him.

Any other time he would have loved the freedom, but now it was nothing more than a constant reminder of a shameful act that needed to be rectified.

* * *

Sonya sank back into the captain's chair with a relieved sigh when the transmission came through that Sebastian and Anya were safe and headed for *Marada*. Yet it also caused a sickly feeling in the pit of her stomach. Once on board, Sebastian would again take over as captain, and she would go back to work in The Demon's Punchbowl...alongside Ethan.

She'd been successful in avoiding him since the incident and did not relish the idea of facing him so soon. She'd never been one to avoid confrontation. The fact that she recoiled from the idea of approaching Ethan grated on every level.

Especially when there was no need for it.

Their encounter in the training room wasn't that big of a deal, anyway. Silly, in fact, when she really thought about it.

Though her brothers might not think so.

And Ethan would be so worried about their discovery of his less than honorable conduct, he would mostly likely do anything she ordered. The idea didn't give her as much pleasure as it should. Moreover, merely inviting the image of him into her mind caused her blood to fire…with hunger.

She shivered.

Everything in her came to life when she recalled the beginning of their battle, his easy evasion from her formidable skills. Why that should cause her veins to quicken with a rush of desire, she could not say, but it grew worse as she called to mind the intimate portion of their conflict. Her skin grew heated at the reminder of his touch and the intense ecstasy that had scored her body all the way to bone, and deeper still.

She had been too far lost to warn him of her inexperience. Mindless, in fact. The initial pain had been surprising, but easily ignored, her hunger for more overruling.

But then he had rushed out of there like she was some sort of diseased pile of space junk. The affront sizzled still, burning away every trace of desire.

She lifted her chin, resolved not to let anyone see what an emotional mess she had become.

Aidan called across the bridge. "The shuttle is docking, Captain."

"Good. Keep us in orbit until further instructions. I'll go

and greet them."

"Huh." Aidan's tone was baffled.

She paused. "What is it, Aidan?"

"There are five life-forces on board."

"Five?" Had they picked up a stray? A dark thought filtered into her mind. Could they have been hijacked? "Are there any other ships in the area?"

"No, Captain."

That meant little; pirates survived by the prowess of their stealth.

"Run a physical analysis. Are they calm?"

"No, I'm reading three elevated heart rates and traces of blood."

"Shit. I'm heading to the docking bay. If you detect conflict, seal off the area and alert the crew."

On her way, she stopped to gather weapons from the weapons locker. Because many projectile weapons could be detrimental to a hull, they were generally outlawed on most civilized ships.

However, Sonya had managed to convince Sebastian to stock a few of the safer energy based weapons. The one she was currently strapping to her waist—and had been dying to try out—was a small handheld called a pulsar blaster. It directed a pulse of energy that could knock someone on their ass and crush the breath out of them, while leaving the heavy metal casing of the ship around them intact. Sonya also grabbed a couple of light-weight swords before she hurried to her next stop.

Though she didn't like the idea of asking for his help, Ethan had proven himself to be skilled in combat. And, despite the fact that she was currently in shambles over what had occurred, her family was more important than her pride.

She poked her head into The Demon's Punchbowl and spotted Ethan behind the bar, conversing with a couple of crewmen. "Ethan! Come with me, now."

Ethan looked up, bewildered by Sonya's urgent tone. Was she finally ready to rail at him for what he had done? He looked around the pub. A few of the crew shifted their gazes between him and Sonya.

He turned back to Sonya, noting the weapons in her possession. Was she hoping to finish their bout on the mat? "Uh, do you want me to close the—"

"No time." She motioned him closer.

He stepped out from behind the bar and crossed the room.

She pulled him into the hall and continued in a confidential tone. "Sebastian is docking, and I'm not sure, but there could be trouble."

His mind snapped to attention. What if Anya was hurt again? Dammit! He should have fought harder to join them.

Sonya offered him a sword. He took it and followed her without another word. When they arrived at the docking bay, the shuttle had already settled, but the room was still in the process of being pressurized. They could only wait and watch through a small clear window pane in the bulkhead.

Movement behind the shuttle's front window caught his attention. He spotted Marik, alive yet covered in blood. Sonya saw him too, and her tail flicked in what he assessed as nervousness.

Finally, the door to the room slid opened. Sonya zipped inside, pulling what looked like some kind of gun out of a holster at her hip.

The shuttle hatch cracked open, and a bloodied stranger, sword sheathed around his waist, filled the opening.

Sonya raised her weapon as Ethan tightened his grip on the hilt of his blade.

The unfamiliar male took a step before he noticed they had weapons drawn on him.

His eyes flashed red, and his horns began to warm in color. Ethan paused, surprised by the realization that this stranger was a demon.

Undeterred, Sonya raised her gun.

With a snarl, the strange demon pulled his sword and leapt from the shuttle entrance, his boots landing on the metal floor with a hard thud. Then, rising to his full height, he pointed the tip of his weapon at her.

Ethan's gift went into overdrive. He sensed the male ready to dodge Sonya's shot before countering with his blade. He rushed in front of Sonya and hurled himself at the other male, their blades clashing.

A sharp pain laced Ethan's side. He looked down to see two arrows penetrating his abdomen. From the corner of his eye, he spotted his attacker: a petite redhead covered in an array of animal hides. She had a bow trained on him as she drew back another arrow.

Faster than he could visually comprehend, Sonya sprung at the female, gripping her by the neck and slamming her against the hard surface of the docking bay floor. Brilliantly sharp fangs peeked from under Sonya's full lips. She let out a terrifying snarl as her horns blazed the color of fire.

Ethan couldn't help but take a moment to appreciate the

wild frenzy unleashed. Apparently, neither could his demon opponent.

With her tail whipping the air, she was like some glorious preternatural creature.

Extraordinary.

Marik appeared from within the shuttle, looking equally formidable. His eyes and horns blazed as bright. He dove for Sonya, slamming into her and sending them both crashing across the room into the bulkhead. The protesting wail of crushing metal made Ethan wince.

Marik pulled back to bare his fangs at Sonya and let out a harrowing roar.

Ethan blinked, stunned by the similarity of both attacks.

Sonya's eyes cleared, and she tilted her head at her attacker. "Marik?"

Sebastian emerged from the shuttle and stepped between Ethan and the strange new demon, his arms arranged in a peace-making gesture. Both Ethan and the strange demon still had their weapons at the ready, but were too bewildered by what had just occurred to use them.

Anya raced down the steps and hunched over the redhead, her face drawn tight with worry. Ethan should have felt relief at seeing Anya alive and well, but Marik's unwavering rage toward Sonya distracted him. He stepped toward the two, sensing Marik was ready to rip her to pieces.

Sonya's gaze darted to Ethan. She shook her head and gestured for him to keep his distance.

"Hey, Red," she called steadily. "Call off your boy."

The odd request sent Ethan's attention back to the redhead. It was then that he realized who she was. Her appearance hadn't changed all that much over the years. She was still quite pretty with ice-blue eyes and a fiery mane that framed her face.

Nadua sat up, rubbing her head and giving Sonya a cold glare. Then she softened at the sight of Marik in his rage-filled state. "Marik, it's okay," she cooed.

Marik didn't move as his blazing gaze continued to bore into Sonya.

"Marik, look at me," Nadua pleaded, her tone soothing. "Eyes on me."

Marik's head shifted toward her and the red in his irises slowly faded. Using his gift, Ethan scanned Marik and determined the threat had passed.

Sonya shoved Marik. "Get off me, you jackass."

Marik shook his head as if clearing it and then pushed to his feet. "What the fuck do you think you're doing?"

Sonya reached a hand up to massage her shoulder. "It looked as though you had been hijacked. Why is everyone so bloody? And who the hell is that?" She motioned her head toward the new demon.

"This is Rex," Marik answered while looking over Nadua. "He'd been stranded on Undewla for years and was a great help to Nadua and I. In return, we agreed to give him a ride."

"Maybe you should have mentioned that in your transmission! What am I supposed to think when everyone is bathed in blood?" Sonya pointed an accusing finger at Ethan. "And you! Don't ever get in my way again. I brought you here as back up, not protection."

Ethan bristled. "Perhaps you should take your own advice and inform me ahead of time. It would be nice to know what I'm getting myself into."

She flushed and opened her mouth to speak, but then seemed to notice the two arrows in his side. Her eyes flew to Nadua with renewed wrath.

Ethan canted his head.

Sebastian spoke then. "Let's just get everyone mended and cleaned up. Anya, you can take your sister to our room to wash up and lend her some clothes. Marik, show Rex to one of our empty compartments. He appears about my size, so I'll provide something for him to wear."

"Thank you," Rex said, still warily gripping the hilt of his blade.

Sebastian nodded. "But first, everyone give me your weapons. I won't have you walking my ship armed as you are. Sunny isn't the only one who would jump to the wrong conclusion."

Sonya handed over her weapon and grumbled, "Don't call me that." Then she stormed from the room.

Anya led Nadua away, followed by Sebastian, leaving Marik to shut down the shuttle while Rex waited for him.

Ethan turned to the newcomer. "No hard feelings?"

Rex moved forward to take hold of his entire arm in greeting, hand to elbow. "Not as of yet. Who was that female?"

"Her name is Sonya. A real pain in the ass."

"I can tell." Rex smiled.

At the demon's apparent interest, a flurry of emotions ransacked Ethan's brain.

Rex's gaze swept to the arrows still embedded in Ethan's side, and he pointed to one. "Those are deeply wedged. I'm no medic, but I have extracted my fair share if you need."

Ethan imagined the pain he was going to feel when they were removed. "No thanks," he replied. "I know of someone who should revel in the privilege."

Rex replied with a shrug, then turned back to the shuttle to await Marik.

Ethan found Sonya behind the bar in the tavern, busily scrubbing the counters. As he approached her, one of the patrons called out, "Hey Ethan, nice accessories."

Sonya stilled and then turned to face him. "What are you doing?"

"I was going to get back to work."

Sonya gaped. "Are you just going to leave those where they are?"

"Of course not," he replied. "I can heal instantly, but since you're the reason they're in there, I figure you should be the one to pull them out."

"I'm not pulling them out! Go to the doctor." She waved him away.

"You get me injured, and you won't even help me?"

"I didn't tell you to jump in front of me and get yourself shot, pirate."

Ethan ground his teeth. *And we're back to pirate.*

His reply came out just as cutting as hers. "Maybe if you had proved you could fight—"

Sonya's hand whipped out, and she wrenched one arrow free. Caught off guard, Ethan cried out and slammed his hand down to grip the bar for support. His other hand went to cover the now open wound. His vision blurred.

When he was able to focus, he could almost swear he caught concern in her eyes, but he must have imagined it because when he blinked, that look had vanished.

The room had gone silent as patrons watched the odd

scene.

"There," Sonya said. "Now go have Doctor Oshwald do the other one."

"No, just get it over with," he managed, his head still swimming as blood leaked down his side.

"Why aren't you healing?" she spat.

"I can't heal till the other one is out."

"Damn you." Gripping the other arrow tight, she yanked back as mercilessly as the first.

Though he was prepared this time, the removal of the second arrow was no less painful. He straightened his spine and met Sonya's gaze full on.

"Was that supposed to be some sort of gesture?" she asked in an offhanded tone.

He lifted one shoulder in answer, growing worried. Was it not enough?

"Just heal yourself and get out of my pub." Sonya turned away, but when Ethan didn't move, she snapped, "You're getting blood all over the place! Heal already!"

"Not until you agree that we're even."

Sonya's jaw dropped, and she remained speechless for a moment. "How does this make us even?"

"I hurt you. You hurt me. Hence we're even."

"Is that a pirate thing?"

He shrugged again.

"Well, there's nothing to make even. I'm a big girl, and I knew what I was doing."

Frustration hacked a path through him. Maddening female!

He grabbed her by the arm and pulled her close. "Well, I

didn't! If I had known I wouldn't have...I would have been—"

"Enough!" She pulled away, blushing furiously as her gaze darted around the room. "I don't want to talk about this anymore. So fine then, we're even. Go away." She paused and pointed to the blood-soaked ground. "But clean up this mess first."

With that, she gave him her back and began washing a set of glasses that he had already cleaned earlier in the night. He suppressed a smile, realizing that was what she did when she was unnerved. She obsessed over her tavern.

Ethan called his gift, and moments later, his wounds stitched together.

Chapter 16

Healing such a significant wound drained much of Ethan's energy, and he could feel the strain in his muscles all the way back to his quarters.

He eyed the soft, inviting mattress of his bed for a moment. Then he ripped off his ruined shirt, stepped out of his stained pants, and entered the washroom. He could rest later.

In the shower stall, the warm spray massaged the tightness in his neck and back as he scrubbed the excess blood from his body. He ran his fingertips over the newly healed flesh at his side. There wasn't even a twinge of discomfort, not in that region, anyway. His lower half was a whole other matter.

With his magic fully evoked at the time Sonya had attacked Nadua, he'd read her intention clear as day. Her fierce protectiveness not only piqued his mind's curiosity, his shaft stood at full attention as well.

He hoped his gesture with the arrows was acceptable restitution for his careless taking. It was the best he could offer…for the moment.

Perhaps now they could start anew. He would show her a

little more courtesy, and she? Well, her disdain should be diminished, if only a little. After all, she had chosen him alone as her backup. Counted for something, right?

After drying, he dressed in fresh clothing and headed back to the pub where the others were gathered to discuss the plan to retrieve Cale and Kyra from Earth. Gods willing, Cale had been successful in finding her and both were safely awaiting *Marada*.

Just after Ethan took a seat at the table, he discovered there was another problem at hand. Somehow, Marik had inadvertently claimed Nadua while stranded on Undewla, and neither appeared to be happy about it. They had decided to seek help from the Serakians, whose magic was a mystery even to the Faieara. But if anything could reverse an unwanted matebond, they would know of it.

Ethan should have been furious that yet another of the king's daughters was out of his reach. He waited for a bout of irritation over the fact, but it never came. Curiously, neither did relief when he learned of the plan to break the bond between the two.

Perhaps because he could tell that Marik did not wish to be parted from Nadua. And though his ability to read Nadua was slightly better than his ability to read Anya, he couldn't glean a clear indication of her feelings.

Typically, the longer he associated with an individual, the easier it became to read them to some varying degree. Naturally, some proved easier than others.

Reading Sonya was becoming second nature.

Right now, he picked up her lingering aggression toward Nadua. Whether because of what had happened in the docking bay or because of the unwanted matebond with Marik, he wasn't sure. But at least she wasn't acting on her desire to throw Nadua across the tavern.

The other demons were fairly easy to read as well. They were all deeply worried for Marik. Knowing that, and what he did of demons, he could surmise they feared what might happen to Marik if the bond was truly severed. Losing a mate, for whatever reason, has been known to send a demon to the Edge, permanently. Aside from that, the bond was considered sacred.

When Nadua asked if the Serakians had been contacted yet, tension surged among the demons. Sonya let out a soft hiss before pushing away from the table.

As she stomped toward the bar, Ethan's gaze was drawn to her backside. The sway of her hips coupled with that saucy tail of hers was possibly the most enticing thing he had ever seen.

Her skirt looked particularly soft, and he couldn't help but wonder how it would feel against his fingertips. After a moment, Ethan realized he wasn't the only one interested in the blend of that fabric, and what lay underneath. Rex's eyes were transfixed as well.

A storm of irritation settled over Ethan, but he tamped it down as best he could. Sonya wasn't his. Didn't even want to be. So even if a thousand males appraised her with lust in their eyes, it should be none of his business.

And yet…

As Sebastian took his leave from the group, Ethan caught the sight of Jade passing by the pub. "Jade!" He waved her over.

Her gaze traveled the room till it landed on him, and she sauntered over to greet them. "Good evening, Ethan." She surveyed the table, her eyes coming to rest on Rex like an animal sniffing out fresh meat. "Please introduce me to your new friends."

"This is Princess Nadua and Rex," he offered, gesturing to the demon who was now eyeing Jade with open interest. "Rex hasn't seen the whole ship. Why don't you show him around a little?"

"I would love to." Jade moved closer to slide her hand down Rex's arm before taking his hand and leading him from the room.

Ethan leaned back in his chair and grinned at his own genius. His lips fell when he noticed Nadua's scrutiny. She raised a knowing brow at him. The young princess had always been astute.

"So, Ethan," Nadua said, when only he and Anya remained at the table. "Anya tells me you were involved with a band of pirates." Her tone indicated she didn't find that fact as deplorable as Sonya did.

Anya beamed at him. Ethan smiled back, perceiving a strange sensation coming from her direction. He could only describe it as genuine, heartfelt affection—a bit of her magic seeping into him.

"I was," he replied. "It was your father who put me on that path."

"Is that so?" Nadua tilted her head.

"Yes. Just before I left our planet, he gave me instructions to contact the Serakians. Unfortunately, they are a secretive people and it took me years just to discover a way to pass a message on. To earn a living, I joined what I assumed was a small mining crew ship, but I found myself on a mercenary craft instead."

Sonya returned to the table, bringing with her a fresh round of drinks for everyone. "You couldn't tell the difference?" She gave him a dubious look.

"I was tricked, actually. When I realized what was happening, I tried to back out, but it was too late. It was how that particular group recruited new members. You either agree to work for them, or you die."

Anya placed a hand over her heart. "Did they make you do terrible things?"

Ethan shrugged. "I did what I had to survive. There were about ten of us who'd been abducted. We were considered expendable and were assigned some of the more dangerous missions. I was only with them for a few years when a pirate ship attacked and overtook us. The leader killed most of the others, but I saw an opportunity and convinced him to allow me into his crew."

"And how did you do that?" Sonya asked, surprising Ethan with her untainted curiosity.

"I showed off my gift."

"So you cut yourself and then healed it?" Anya guessed.

"No, I healed one of the men they thought was already dead." *One that still owes me a debt.*

The table went quiet for a moment. Then Nadua broke the silence. "And our father sent you alone?"

Ethan averted his gaze. "There had been four others, each with their own transport off of Evlon. Mine was the only one to escape the atmosphere intact."

Ethan often wondered if the king had known which ship would survive the Kayadon attack. Had the others merely been a diversion so that he could get through? If it were true, Ethan wouldn't judge the king poorly because of it. Not after the things Ethan had been forced to do over the years just to survive.

Oblivious to his musings, Nadua continued. "Father told me once that his visions are never set in stone. That the future is always changing, and even the smallest alteration can carve out a new course."

"That's true. You must have experienced that with your own gift." Ethan recalled Nadua's magic had shown the potential of following in her father's footsteps.

Nadua cringed. "A little. Mine works differently, though. I can see someone's future, and now apparently their past, but I must have some kind of physical contact with the subject first. I haven't had a lot of practice because the people I was living with had skin so cold it would burn me on contact. Needless to say, I didn't touch a lot of people."

"I see." Ethan leaned back in his chair. That meant she probably wasn't as in command of her power as she should be.

"So you're like an oracle?" Sonya asked, a hint of enmity in her voice.

Nadua pretended not to notice. "Sort of, but I can't choose what I see. It just kind of comes, whether it's helpful or not."

"We can work on it," Anya encouraged. "I've been able to evolve my gift quite a bit with practice."

Nadua smiled. "That sounds good." Then she yawned, stating, "I suppose I should get some sleep."

Both she and Anya called it a night, leaving Ethan and Sonya alone.

Sonya stood to clear the table. Ethan rushed to help her, and their hands brushed together as they reached for the same glass. As if he'd burned her, she snatched her hand back, averting her gaze.

For a moment, it seemed as though she might tell him to go,

but she didn't. In fact, she remained uncharacteristically quiet for the rest of the evening.

It made him uneasy.

A loud, vulgar Sonya he could deal with, but this silent version was agonizing. He glanced around the tavern and found it mostly empty. Only a few crew members scattered about.

Thinking this might be a good time to clear the air between them, he started, "Sonya, shall we discuss—"

"I think I'm all set here," she interrupted without looking up from her task. "You can take off for the evening."

Ethan contemplated her stiff visage. "Right. Wouldn't want to risk any meaningful conversations or anything."

She glared up at him for a moment before disregarding him all together.

Ethan stifled his disappointment. "Very well. Another time, perhaps."

Sonya grabbed another dirty glass, relieved that Ethan had left without argument. During his story, she had found herself softening toward him. She thought of Anya, and how early on in her life she had been enslaved and exploited for her talent, used against her will. It was too easy to imagine Ethan in the same predicament. A naive traveler caught up in the darkest society of space.

What alarmed Sonya more was her urge to bash in the brains of a group of males who were already dead, according to Ethan.

She had grown enraged when Ethan had referred to himself as expendable. But what she couldn't understand was why it had bothered her so much, even more than Nadua's refusal to speak her feelings for Marik. Clearly the redheaded Faieara cared for Marik, if even just a little. How could she condemn him to a life deprived of his destined mate? Sure, their joining had been botched, but that didn't necessarily mean it wasn't meant to be.

Then again, maybe Sonya was only seeing what she wished to see. Hoping against hope that Marik, of all people, could find love in this unforgiving universe—every demon, whether they admitted it or not, longed to find their mate.

Well…almost every.

Sonya was starting to wonder if she'd be better off without.

The image of Ethan flashed through her mind and a dark thought tickled the back of her brain. It was a ridiculous notion, and she tried with everything she had to squash it, but before she knew it, a full-on panic set it. Denial waged a war inside her, battling for supremacy. Her heart revved out of control, causing her to gasp for air.

The sound of shattering glass snapped her to attention. She glanced down to see a few shards embedded in her palm, the rest scattered along the floor at her feet.

With shaky fingers, she plucked the tiny daggers free, taking measured breaths and trying to calm her mind.

Then she grabbed a broom to sweep up the rest. She halted as Nadua and Anya rushed past the pub whispering with their heads together.

Sonya raised an eyebrow, putting aside the broom, and followed after them. They turned the corner into the docking bay, oblivious of her.

She entered the room and stilled. The shuttle door was open, and Anya was just about to step aboard.

"What in the name of the gods do you think you're doing?"

Anya and Nadua startled, then shared a desperate look.

Nadua cleared her throat. "I just had a terrible vision. People I love are going to die unless I get back to Undewla and warn them." She paused. "Please, I have to go back. Ava is riding to her death as we speak."

"I can get the ship there and back in no time," Anya added. "You know I can."

Sonya narrowed her gaze at the redhead. "Is this *Ava* someone you love more than Marik? Do you even care about him at all?"

Nadua flinched. "It's not like that."

"Sure it isn't. And Anya, you know Sebastian will kill me if I let you do this."

Anya bit her lip, looking conflicted.

"Please," Nadua begged. "I made a promise to protect Ava. I must go back. None of them know the danger they are in."

Anya gazed at her sister with compassion, and Sonya realized she was reading the Nadua's emotions. Anya lifted her chin and whatever she'd been debating was apparently decided.

Sonya let out a soft curse, recognizing the stern resolution in Anya's gaze. Then she pursed her lips and gave a tight nod. If she trusted anyone besides her brothers, it was pure-hearted Anya.

Resigned, Sonya crossed her arms and sighed. "Well, we'd better hurry then."

They gaped in astonishment.

"You're both going to get yourselves killed. I guess I'll just have to tag along." Sonya moved to gather the weapons Sebastian had confiscated earlier.

Nadua joined her in picking through the bounty. "Thank

you," she murmured.

"I'm not doing this for you."

"Then I'm glad you're doing it for Anya's sake."

Sonya didn't reply, unsure if that was entirely the case. There was no doubt she wanted to keep Anya safe, but a more selfish part of her determined this was exactly the kind of distraction she desperately needed.

* * *

Ethan rushed into the bridge just in time to hear Marik bellow, "What in hell are they thinking?"

"I have no fucking idea," Sebastian replied, equally enraged.

"You wanted to see me?" Ethan asked, alarmed by the commotion.

"Ethan." Sebastian let out a weary breath. "I fear we might need your gift again. Nadua and Anya have taken a shuttle back to Undewla, and apparently Sonya went along."

It took Ethan a moment to fully comprehend what he'd just heard. Still, his reply was weak. "What?"

"Aye." Marik growled. "I'm going to throttle them."

"Get in line," Sebastian countered.

Spikes of dread threaded Ethan's veins "What would possess them to do such a thing?"

"Something about it being important to Nadua." Sebastian replied. "Anya wasn't exactly forthcoming."

Ethan placed his palms on the edge of a nearby console and leaned on it for support. A building panic was quickly eating away his reason. "Can't this bloody ship catch a simple shuttle?"

Sebastian gave a defeated shake of his head. "If anyone but

Anya was guiding that craft, then yeah. But she is feeding it power with her gift. They're nearly twice as fast as us at the moment."

"What about warp drive?"

"We don't have the fuel cells for it."

"Actually," Aidan interjected from across the room. "It looks like we do." He tapped a few buttons. "A third of our previously empty fuel cells appear to be refilled."

Sebastian lowered his head and pinched the bridge of his nose. "Dammit, Anya. Will you never just do as I ask?"

Ethan wondered what it had cost Anya to transfer energy into the cells. That kind of magic always took a hefty toll.

Sebastian sucked in a breath and pulled back his shoulders. "Prepare the ship for warp."

Moments later, *Marada* breached Undewla's atmosphere, careening over the icy land. They'd caught the signal of the hijacked shuttle and were heading in its direction. Thick snow-covered hills, peppered by decrepit looking trees, rushed under *Marada's* belly.

They came over a tall bluff, and the scenery gave way to a barrage of gore and carnage. A sea of lightly blue skinned natives appeared to be engaged in a fierce battle.

Ethan's heart stuttered. Everyone in the bridge stared in awed silence as jagged shafts of ice sprung from the ground, seemingly from nowhere. Some pierced straight through bodies.

"Those are caused by an individual called a Kaiylemi," Marik explained. "They control ice the way Anya controls energy."

"How many are there?" Sebastian asked, gaping like the rest of them.

"I'm not sure. One, maybe two. They are supposed to be

rare among the Cyrellian race."

Ethan was awed by the magnitude of power…performed by a single person? Many of those ice shafts towered over the surrounding trees.

"Do you see any sign of…the shuttle?" He'd almost said Sonya.

"There it is." Aidan pointed out the familiar craft. It had come to rest dead center in the onslaught.

"Take us down!" Ethan demanded. "I'm going out there."

"We're all going out there," Marik corrected.

* * *

Sonya's astonished gaze perused the fierce battle through the cockpit window. A legion of turquoise colored individuals brandished every manner of weaponry. She could practically taste the fierceness, the savagery laid out before her. Smell the spilled blood clashing against the once pristine snow that blanketed the ground.

It called to her.

A massive crystalline dagger shot out of the ground, interrupting a group of combatants.

What the hell?

Nadua searched the crowd and mumbled, "Where is Ava?"

Once again, Sonya surveyed the melee, wondering if it was even possible to pick out a single girl among the chaos. All these people looked close to identical, with hair as white as the snow and dressed in scraps of clothing that couldn't possibly protect them from the cold, let alone the strike of a blade.

While Anya lowered the craft, Nadua jumped out of her chair and began arming herself with her bow and arrows, then slipped a sheathed sword around her waist. Sonya retrieved a sword of her own, and then secured her gun holster to her thigh. She noticing Nadua's quiver only held two arrows. Recalling the accuracy with which the redhead shot, Sonya was sure those arrows would go to good use.

Anya looked drained from using her gift to rush the shuttle's approach. Thankfully, she agreed to stay locked inside while Sonya and Nadua searched out this Ava girl.

With a weary grin, Anya informed them, "*Marada* will be close behind. Bastian will be pushing the engines hard now, and I've been secretly adding juice."

The ferocious sounds of battle outside stroked Sonya's bloodlust. She craved the violence she'd been deprived these last few weeks. "Who are we going after?" She asked Nadua.

"Just follow me. I need to find Ava," Nadua replied.

When the door flipped open, Nadua didn't wait for the stairs to fully descend before jumping out and landing on her haunches in the soft snow. Sonya followed, baring her lengthening fangs.

Nadua shot upright and fired off the last two arrows in her quiver, then discarded the weapon before the projectiles even met their marks. She scanned the field, and her lips curled in a sneer. "Lidian," she breathed.

Sonya followed her gaze to a small girl standing on the outskirts of the field, surrounded by soldiers.

A tremor drew Sonya's attention to another crystal dagger sprouting from the ground and rising high into the sky. Incredulous, she asked, "Does ice always sprout up like that on this planet?"

Nadua replied in an angered tone, "No." She pointed her sword at the girl on the outskirts. "It's her. And we need her taken out. Do you think you can—?"

No need to ask me twice.

Sprinting forward, Sonya yelled, "On it! Don't get yourself killed, Red!" *Or else it'll be my head*, she added to herself.

As she raced for her target, a small group of locals attempted to engage her in battle. However, their apparent and nearly instant fear of her caused them to hesitate, some of them backing off even, their eyes wide. She understood then that her irises had changed crimson. Clearly, to these people she appeared monstrous. She smiled at that, showing them her fangs. It was the most exploited advantage of her kind—ferocious and terrifying, nothing compared to a demon on the Edge.

As several males approached her, she snatched her pulsar gun and fired, propelling them backwards. She aimed next at the group surrounding the ice witch and pulled the trigger.

Nothing happened.

She pulled the trigger again, and again. The gun only gave a dull click.

"A single shot? Piece of shit!" She tossed the weapon aside and gripped the hilt of her sword.

The ice witch spotted her advance, and their eyes locked; Sonya's full of wildfire, the girl's as cold as the ice she yielded.

At once, three of the guards surged forward, swinging their weapons. Sonya blocked the first and dodged the second, but the third blade entered her abdomen just below her ribs, ripping through the flesh of her back.

She let out a harsh roar, yet barely felt the pain. Her mind focused only on the next assault.

As the two flanking guards thrust their blades at her, she twirled her body away, the sword sheathed in her gut coming with her. Her opponents rushed her. She raised her blade to defend. Metal clashed in quick succession. It only heightened her mindless need for violence, sent her further over the Edge where instinct met animal grace.

She rammed the tip of her sword through the neck of the unarmed guard.

As he fell lifeless, she whirled around, her blade arching wide as it cleanly severed the heads off the other two.

Even before the bleeding husks hit the snow, she lurched forward to take out two more guards who had thought to come to the aid of their comrades.

They were easier to dispatch than the first set.

She stood, heaving out white puffs of air, and extracted her opponent's sword from her torso, ignoring the trickle of blood that ran down her front.

The ice witch met her gaze, her lips curling as she raised her hand in Sonya's direction. Sensing the danger, Sonya dove out of the way just before a shaft of ice broke through the ground where she had been standing. No sooner had she pushed to her feet than several cold daggers penetrated her torso as if they had been thrown from the witch's direction.

Sonya lunged forward, baring her fangs. The witch looked around, a hint of panic cracking behind her frigid gaze. Her remaining guards were retreating into the rotting skeleton of a forest. She turned to make a mad dash away from Sonya.

Sonya swiped her claws out to grip the long white tendrils of the witch's hair and yanked back. The witch managed a gurgled cry before Sonya brought her blade to the back of her neck and relieved her head from her body.

Chapter 17

As Ethan raced for Sonya, the ice ceased spiking from the ground. Some of the largest shafts began to crumble. Confusion took hold over the battlefield, and he sensed many of them ready to retreat.

In the distance, Sonya stood like a fierce goddess atop an offering of bodies, her black hair whipping in the wind as she gripped the head of her latest victim.

He slowed his step and approached her as he would a wild beast. Her wounds trickled with blood, staining the white snow under her feet.

Irises filled with liquid fire settled on him. She tilted her head. He put his hands up to show he was not a threat. He had no idea how far on the Edge she lingered, or if she was beyond reason.

Tossing her prize to the side, she strode toward him with the grace of a feline, never dropping her gaze.

"Sonya, you're bleeding. Let me heal you."

She glanced at herself briefly before focusing back on him, continuing her advance, her gaze intense and filled with hooded desire.

Any other time, he would have welcomed the animalistic lust she threw off, and even though a string of alarm snaked through him, he couldn't stop himself from murmuring "Gods, you're beautiful."

Sonya paused at the praise. She blinked, and her irises faded back to deep pools of sunset-purple. She squinted at him. Then, as if nothing were out of the ordinary, she surveyed her surroundings as though ready for another fight. "Where are the others?"

"Sebastian is with Anya, and Marik is looking for Nadua. Are you alright?" He reached out to one of her wounds, but she slapped his hand away.

"I'm fine. We need to regroup."

Around them, the battlefield thinned as rivers of soldiers flowed into the surrounding wilderness. Those who remained tended to the fallen.

Ethan tried one last time to heal Sonya, but she turned on him with a harsh curse. "I'll be fine. Leave me alone!"

From a short distance away, Nadua called to him in a panicked tone.

He rushed toward her. "Are you hurt, Princess?"

"No, Ava is. Please help her." Nadua hovered over a small white-haired female lying motionless, an arrow jutting from her chest.

He swiftly evaluated the wound. It had landed near the heart, but just off the mark. The female still breathed. "I'll need someone to pull out the arrow."

Sonya reached for it and barked, "Got it," before giving the arrow a swift yank.

The female screamed, clutching the wound as blood pooled between her fingers.

From the side, a male hissed out a growl and lunged at Sonya. Nadua flung her body in his way, tackling him to the ground.

"What are you doing?" the male screamed at them.

Ignoring the commotion, Ethan placed his hands on the female's wound, calling his magic into action.

Light sparked under his palms, growing brighter with every breath. With the surge of power, the drifting flakes of snow around them halted in midair, slowly melting and then forming into droplets of water. As if it were his own, Ethan felt the female's skin knitting itself together.

When the wound vanished completely, the light dimmed. Ethan leaned back, feeling slightly drained.

The female blinked twice, touched her fingertips to her chest, and then sat up. "Thank you."

The male who had nearly attacked Sonya gave him a tight nod of gratitude, exuding stunned relief. Ethan returned the gesture before turning to help others who were in need his gift. Their skin was indeed frigid, but with the help of his magic, he was able to prevent the contact burn that Nadua had mentioned.

With each use of his power, exhaustion inched over him and his limbs grew heavy. He couldn't keep this up much longer. Luckily, there were no more dire cases in need of his attention.

He glanced around and spotted Sebastian emerging from the small shuttle with Anya flipped over his shoulder as she tried to justify her actions to him. He appeared uninterested as he stormed his way back to *Marada*. When he passed by Sonya, he said in a clipped tone, "Take the shuttle back to the bay."

Sonya gave him a tight nod, still gripping the oozing wound on her torso.

Ethan hurried behind her as she climbed the small set of stairs.

"What are you doing?" she spat, not bothering to look at him. She planted her butt at the helm.

"You need me. Let me help you." He stepped forward.

She shot to her feet, wary. "I don't need your help, *pira*—"

"You are the most stubborn female I have ever encountered!" He took another step toward her. "There is no reason to prolong your suffering just because you despise me."

Some inscrutable emotion flashed across her face, gone the next instant. "Doctor Oshwald can take care of it."

"Yeah, but I'm here now. I'll make it quick." His voice became guarded. "You won't have to endure my touch for long."

It wasn't that she despised him, or even that she abhorred his touch. Actually she feared the opposite was true, but she hurled that thought from her mind.

When she'd caught sight of him on the battlefield, an oddness had come over her. She'd been swamped by powerful urges, the likes of which she'd never before experience. Her fangs had ached for something other than violence. Her body had burned with a desire so acute it felt like the combustion of a sun flashing into existence where before there had been only a vast emptiness.

The force of it had nearly dropped her to her knees. Yet as fast as the strange sensation had come, she had been able to tamp it down, push it aside and, gods willing, lock it away.

Although, now that she was alone with him, the affliction was creeping back over her, making its way up her spine, over her chest, and then down to settle in the pit of her stomach. "Hurry and get it over with then," she relented, trying not to show on the outside what was tearing its way through her insides.

Ethan eyed her as though she were some kind of rabid beast, claws at the ready. A real possibility. Then his eyes dipped to her mouth, and she pursed her lips, afraid her fangs would re-emerge.

He took a bold step, coming to stop just inches away. As his warmth and scent surrounded her, a spark of desire fired in her veins. She clenched her jaw. Did he really need to be so close for this? Her wounds weren't even that bad. She could have waited for Oshwald to look at them, or even allowed them to heal on their own.

But a part of her—a very twisted, masochistic part—reveled in his nearness, craved it…and his touch.

"Hold still," he ordered in a gravel hard tone that made her heart jump.

He raised his palm to rest just above her hip while his other hand settled on her back. She allowed him to pull her closer till she was pressed up against his chest as they locked gazes.

Where he touched her, heat burrowed under her skin. She swallowed a lump in her suddenly dry throat and had to work to keep her breaths even.

Something in his expression worried her. It was almost studying, as though he were trying to see into the deepest, darkest parts of her mind.

She closed her eyes, but still felt far too exposed and vulnerable. She hated that feeling. Hated him for making her feel it.

She sensed the warmth from his palms the moment he started using his gift. The light from his magic breached the inner walls of her eyelids, and a serene tingle permeated through her body.

The sensation was exquisite.

In the next instant, an extraordinary blast of energy expanded around her. She gasped as all traces of pain left her torso.

Then she felt Ethan's breath across her face and knew that his lips were far too close to hers. She refused to open her eyes. She feared if she did, she would see her desire reflected back at her. And…well, that would be bad.

As if sensing her resistance, he placed his forehead to hers. They were both breathing heavily. She realized she was fully healed yet still remained in his embrace. The strong hand at her hip tightened its grip.

That burning she'd been fighting rekindled into a blaze.

She shuddered, simultaneous urges raging in her mind. She wanted to push him away, yet draw him closer. To surrender to his whims and give herself over to him completely, yet hold onto her control with the unyielding grip of a super massive black hole.

His lips inched closer, hovering with the whisper of a feather's touch. One of his strong arms tightened around her waist, while the other slipped to her backside. His palm clasped down, rocking her forward. The heat from his chest bled into her. She could feel every hard plane of his body where it touched hers.

Her mind went hazy, breaths shaky and ragged. There was no way he couldn't feel the rapid pounding of her heart.

He hesitated, and it almost seemed as though he was giving her an opportunity to put an end to this. She should. She should push him away, take the helm, and fly back to *Marada* as fast as the little shuttle would take them.

She didn't.

He slanted his lips against hers.

His scent flooded her nostrils. Her heart fired into overdrive. With soft urgency, his tongue delved past her lips, tangling and twisting with hers. She leaned against him and deepened the kiss, deliriously fighting for supremacy in the savage kiss.

Soon they were both panting.

He pressed her against the back of a chair, his palm clamping around her neck to hold her still for his assault. The intoxicating taste of him scrambled her thoughts, and she was engulfed by his carnal aggression.

Her fangs throbbed, elongating.

She gasped and pulled away, sucking in shallow breaths as she focused on keeping them hidden from view. Ethan frowned, looking grim and disappointed, yet hungry for more. However, he made no move toward her. For some unfathomable reason, a part of her was devastated by that.

 With silence hanging between them, she stepped around him and slid into the pilot seat. She engaged the engines, and the shuttle sprang from the ground.

He took the seat next to hers, not bothering to hide his studying gaze. Though a good deal of space separated them, she could still feel the heat their kiss had sparked.

Her pulse continued to hammer, her body thrumming with a staggering need. Instinct was telling her to forget Sebastian's order, set the craft back down, and jump Ethan where he sat. Obviously Ethan would be more than happy to appease her.

A bit of reason seeped into her brain. Just as it had in the training room, remnants of the Edge was chipping away at her inhibitions. Yes, that was it. It couldn't have been Ethan's rumbling masculine groans or his sweet invasion as he had plunged into her mouth with expert strokes.

She swallowed hard, utilizing every ounce of her will to keep her butt planted in the seat and focus on her task. It was a shock that she could even fly straight.

After she'd finished guiding the shuttle into the docking bay and shutting it down, she hurried away, putting as much distance between her and Ethan as she could.

Chapter 18

Ethan popped open two ales and handed them to Rex and Sebastian.

Sebastian snatched a bottle and took a long pull, then braced his arm on the bar. "They are all in league to drive me mad."

Rex grunted in detached interest, absently surveying the room.

"Females," Sebastian grunted, shaking his head.

"Indeed," Ethan replied from the other side of the bar. *What an understatement.*

Sonya had not spoken to him since they had returned the shuttle. Subsequently, she'd been absent in the tavern, leaving him to do as he pleased.

If she had abhorred his kiss, his touch, he might understand her avoidance now, but he could still recall the pure, unadulterated lust he had picked up from her. And the delicious sensation of her desire curling against the tendrils of his magic.

She had wanted him. Nothing could convince him otherwise.

The feel of her soft feminine curves against him and her

nails digging into his skin. The smell of her lustrous scent and the sound of her lascivious moans... It had all worked against him. Had snapped the last of his threadbare restraint.

It had been like a planetary collision. No. Greater than that. Like twin galaxies converging in an array of beautiful, disastrous impacts. So significant and mind altering, yet at the same time the most natural thing in the universe.

He frowned.

So then what had he done wrong?

"Anya refuses to listen to me," Sebastian continued. "Says I am being unreasonable. But all I ask is that she vow never to use her gift without my express permission."

Ethan belted out a laugh. "Is that all?"

Sebastian speared him with a glare. "It is not an unreasonable request when she insists on placing herself in harm's way every chance she gets."

"Anya is an extreme empath," Ethan said. "Merge that with her desire to please and her unnatural compassion... I'm sorry, but all you can do is encourage her to strengthen the defensive side of her gift so she can hold her own when the time comes."

Sebastian's shoulders hunched. "That is not an ideal solution." He paused, then added, "But it's not just Anya who is making me question my sanity as of late. Sonya is acting strange as well."

Ethan hid his raw interest behind a mask of nonchalance. "How so?"

"After we left Undewla, she retreated to her room and refused to speak with anyone but Anya. I thought it was a tactic to avoid my ire, but..."

Ethan gritted his teeth, struggling to feign patience.

"Naturally I barged in to rail at her for her part in the scheme, but she merely sat back and accepted the verbal lashing. Not even a peep in her defense! And by the end, I was so discombobulated, I lost all conviction. Even started to feel guilty...Guilty!" He looked up. "So I must conclude, either they conspire to drive me mad, or am I just a dolt for bothering to argue with any of them."

Ethan replied, "Madness is not arguing with a female. It is assuming you might win."

Sebastian cracked a smile. "If that's the case, then we're all crazy, are we not?"

Rex rejoined the conversation with a grunt. "I would gladly dive into madness for the right female."

* * *

"We've stopped for supplies," Anya announced, plopping down on the edge of Sonya's bed.

The apparent concern in her eyes was painful to see. Sonya had always prided herself on being strong, disciplined, confident, but most of all, courageous. *Now look at me.* Hiding out like some coward, unhinged and unsure. But she needed this time. She needed to figure out how to deal with...whatever it was that was happening to her. Unfulfilled desires had never caused her such discomfort.

Anya offered a tentative smile, her gaze too keen. "Don't you need to restock The Demon's Punchbowl?"

Apparently, Ethan had been taking good care of the pub in her stead. She didn't know how to feel about that. "Sebastian knows what to get," she replied. "Just keep telling everyone I'm ill."

"Sebastian is getting suspicious. He says you've never been

sick more than a day."

Sonya shrugged. She couldn't tell Bastian what was really wrong with her, or Anya, for that matter, because *she* wasn't even sure.

Hello denial, why don't you sit right here next to me.

"So, what else is happening around the ship?" Sonya forced a smile. "I know you told me Marik and Nadua have decided to give their relationship an honest shot. Has Sebastian called off the Serakians yet?"

"No. He can't get through to any of them, and whomever they sent is scheduled to arrive any day now. Nadua is upset over the matter."

"*Pfft.* Well, they should have figured their relationship out sooner." She stifled a flinch at her own words. "Anyway, what else is happening?"

"As soon as we're done acquiring previsions and fuel, we'll continue to Earth. Hopefully Cale has found my sister by now." Anya went quiet for a moment. "Do you think there's a chance he'll return mated to Kyra?"

Sonya's heart broke at the thought. "No, hun. Cale has already been mated, remember?"

"But…is there no possibility of a second chance?"

Sonya lifted a single shoulder, hating to dash Anya's hopes. She clearly decided it would be romantic if all of her sisters found love in the demons she cared so much for.

"If it's possible, I've never heard of it. Besides, isn't Ethan set on having one of your sisters for his own?" Saying that out loud caused an odd pang to spike in Sonya's chest. It should be a relief to know that Ethan had his sights set on another, but instead, something like despair clamped her heart.

"I know. It's just you were all so surprised when it turned out that I was Sebastian's mate. And now Marik and Nadua?"

Sonya had wondered about that herself. It was a strange co-incidence. Coming across one's mate was rare these days, what with potential candidates scattered throughout space. And yet it had happened twice in such a short amount of time, with sisters, no less. What were the odds?

Anya brightened. "Oh, before I forget. I asked Jade if she would take a few shifts in the pub like you asked. She said it would be an interesting experience and will start tomorrow."

"Good. Thank you, Anya."

"Why is it you don't want to work there anymore?"

"I need a break, is all." *Technically not a lie.* It seemed as though every part of her life was being flipped upside down, inside out, and backward.

Anya scrutinized her in that way that made her feel like an open book. Yet it didn't seem as though Anya could figure out what was the matter. It probably didn't help that her emotions were off-the-wall chaotic. Although, every now and again, she got the feeling that Anya had finally put the pieces together, her gift garnering any number of damming evidence.

Either way, Anya was kind enough not to press. Or maybe she sensed Sonya wasn't ready to peel back the cover of her mental state and examine the jumbled contents.

* * *

Sebastian waited outside the docking bay as the small craft settled and the room pressurized. Then he stepped inside to greet the petite Serakian female before delivering the news.

"I'm sorry you had to come all this way," he offered. "We had attempted to inform the council that we no longer required your assistance, but we could not seem to get through."

The dark-haired female gazed up at him with a pair of shrewd onyx eyes. An eerie electricity prickled his skin, making him uneasy.

"This is disappointing," she replied, not shifting her glare.

"We will, of course, still compensate you for the inconvenience."

"This is no mere inconvenience," she countered, her eyes flaring. "This is a disaster. It is the season of the dark moon, a time for all initiates to perform their last rite and earn a permanent place among the Serakian. Not only the council, but my entire society is gathered in the sacred ritual of the dark esbat. Even I cannot contact them now. And this assignment was to be my last, to secure my place among them. I cannot go back unaccomplished."

"Again, I apologize. I'm not sure what I can do—"

The Serakian raised her palms over her eyes. "This can't be happening." Then she returned her gaze to Sebastian. Her spine straightened. "You'll provide me with lodgings for the time being, till I can figure out a way to fix this."

"I, uh…"

"A quiet room will do. Nothing near the engines. And a view would be nice. I'll unpack my own things. No one needs to touch anything of mine, and that goes for my shuttle as well, except to refuel it, which can be done any time you see fit."

Sebastian frowned and glanced at the small vessel she had arrived in, dwarfed next to *Marada's* shuttle. "Alright, I can provide fuel, but—"

"Perhaps we can work out the details later. I'm quite weary from my trip."

He blinked twice. "Uh, of course. Then I suppose I'll have a room made up for you."

"Wonderful. Thank you for your hospitality."

* * *

The next day, Sonya convinced herself how ridiculous she was being. Besides being cooped up, her stomach was grumbling something fierce, and she didn't want to keep bothering Anya to bring her food. The burning desire that had overwhelmed her after Ethan's kiss was now a shadow of its former self. She wondered if it really hadn't been all that bad to begin with.

After a long shower, she made her way to the salon. Marik should be back to cooking, which meant the food would be palatable again.

On her way, she ran into Raka, the ship's botany expert, who greeted her with a motherly expression. "How are you feeling?" Raka asked in her deep tongue-rolling accent.

"Much better," Sonya replied. "Starving, actually."

"Well, that is a good sign. Will I see you in the pub later?"

"Actually, I've decided to take a little time off. Jade will be taking over for me."

"Jade?" Raka sounded thoroughly surprised. "The lascivious one?"

"Yeah, she's the only one available. She should be starting today, I believe."

Raka offered a crafty smile. "I'm headed that way now. I'll let you know how she does. By the way, have you met our newest arrival?"

Sonya tilted her head.

"The Serakian," Raka elaborated. "Her name is Portia and she calls herself a witching—a witch in training, or some such. I met her briefly this morning. She seems nice enough, though a little on the small side."

Sonya smiled at that. To Raka, with her towering physique, nearly everyone measured tiny.

"I'm sure I'll meet her soon enough."

As Sonya entered the salon, Marik greeted her with a smile so bright she almost lost her footing.

Marik never smiled!

A bit of Sonya's worry for him eased away. He must truly be happy with his little redheaded mate.

"Nice to see you out and about," he called through the long serving window that separated the galley from the salon. "I'll make you something special."

"Thanks," she replied, grateful that he didn't inquire about her health. Though he wasn't related to her by blood, he could catch a lie from her better than either of her two brothers.

Moments later, he offered her a plate of thick noodles, well-seasoned and covered in sauce. It was mouthwatering just to look at. She claimed an empty seat and dug in, reveling in the rich taste.

Maybe things would finally get back to normal.

"Jade," Ethan chided from across the tavern as he set a drink on the table in front of Raka. "Get out from behind the bar. You know you're not allowed back there."

"What are you grumbling about? Didn't Sonya inform you?" Jade tossed her sleek hair back with the swipe of her hand.

"Inform me of what?"

"I'm taking over her shifts."

Ethan stilled. "I don't believe it." Sonya wouldn't hire a replacement without so much as informing him. Or would she?

He'd suspected she'd been unnerved after what had transpired between them, but was she so distressed that she would allow someone as careless as Jade total access to her beloved tavern?

Raka took a sip of her beverage before responding. "It's true. That's what Sonya told me just a moment ago."

Ethan turned to Raka. "You saw her?"

"Yes. I do believe she is feeling better. She was on her way to the salon."

Ethan watched as Jade explored behind the bar. She picked up a dirty cloth from the wash bin and held it between her thumb and forefinger. Looking appalled, she dropped it back in its place and searched for something clean to wipe her fingers on.

Without another word, Ethan rushed out of the room, heading for the salon. Once there, he spotted Sonya by herself at a table. He knew she caught sight of him too because he felt her unmistakable desire to get away. A desire he would not allow her to fulfill. She'd spent enough time avoiding him, and now they were going to have a real damn conversation.

She stood, pretending not to notice him by brushing imaginary crumbs from her skirt. That brought his already burning temper to a boiling point.

"What the fuck, Sonya!" Fury coated his words.

She gathered a facade of nonchalance. "Morning, Ethan." She proceeded past him to the door. He followed her into the hall, his infuriated gaze burning into her back. "How is Jade getting along?" she added, without even glancing at him.

Frustrating female!

He ran his fingers through his hair, trying to curb his anger. "Jade is standing behind my bar, thinking she's a new employee."

"It's *my* bar, Ethan," Sonya shot back at him. "And Jade *is* a new employee. I hired her yesterday. I need some time off." She turned a corner and picked up her pace.

"That's crap, and you know it. You're using her to avoid me."

She feigned an outraged laugh. "I have no reason to avoid you."

"We need to talk about what happened."

"There's—nothing—to—say," she insisted through gritted teeth.

"I have plenty to say."

She rounded on him, crossing her arms. "Go ahead then."

He slanted a look down the length of the corridor. "Well, not here in the hall."

As if on cue, a small group of children barreled past.

Sonya started walking again. "Look, Ethan, what happened between us meant nothing. Okay?" As if needing to reaffirm the point to herself, she repeated, "Nothing. You did nothing wrong, and I'm not mad at you."

Ethan growled back, "No, *I'm* mad at *you*."

Sonya snorted. "Oh, really? What possible reason could you—"

"You know why."

Sonya stopped again, her tail flicking. As her horns darkened with rage, he couldn't help but smile, ready to sort this out, one way or the other.

"You have the audacity to be angry with me! When you are

the one…" She paused. "Just get back to work, pirate."

He clenched his jaw and ground out, "Stop calling me that."

She leaned with a sneer. "Pirate."

He hadn't even realized he'd moved until he had Sonya pinned to the wall, her wrists locked beside her head.

Her eyes went wide, but then stubborn indignation overrode her surprise. Even before she repeated the taunt, he sensed a shift in her.

Wild desire smashed into him.

Every inch of his body went stiff, focused. They were supposed to talk, but the vixen was distracting him from his purpose. His shaft swelled, aching to punish her in the most delicious way. The thought alone siphoned away the last of his control.

"Demon witch." Unable to restrain himself, he took her lips with rough abandon, pressing her harder into the wall at her back.

A betraying whimper escaped her, and his nostrils caught the intoxicating flare of her scent. He deepened the kiss, swiping his tongue out and demanding entrance. After an agonizing moment, she yielded. Their tongues met, searing and hot, trapped in a sensual dance of submission and domination. Neither wanted to relent.

He groaned, engulfed under a flood of unbridled need that bordered on mindlessness. When she let out an urgent sound that announced she was drowning alongside him, he laced one of his arms around her waist and pressed his body tighter against hers. He undulated his hips so she could feel how much he wanted her. How much he needed her. Her palm wrapped around the back of his neck, holding him in place as her nails lightly scored his skin.

Voices echoed down the hall. It took Ethan a moment to realize whom the deep timbres belonged to, but Sonya had already tensed at the sound of Aidan and Sebastian's approach.

Ethan tore away from her, both of them panting. Something in him thrilled to see she was so overcome with passion that she needed the support of the wall.

The thrill was snuffed out when he caught sight of her tiny fangs peeking from below her glossy upper lip. Icy dread drained the blood from his face.

Can't be.

She noted the direction of his gaze, and the tip of her tongue darted out to lick along one fang as if needing confirmation that it was truly there. Then she gasped and covered her mouth with both hands before taking off down the hall, blasting past Sebastian and Aidan.

"Hey, Sunny," Sebastian said in a surprised greeting.

She pushed off the wall and sprinted past him, not responding.

"Is everything alright?" he called after her, but she was already gone. Sebastian focused on Ethan. "Is she alright? She looked about to vomit."

It had never taken Ethan so much effort to school his features into a blank mask as it did now. "I was just thinking the same thing." With a bit of quick thinking, he added, "Jade's taking on her shifts at the pub for the time being."

Sebastian's brows shot up, and he let out a hearty laugh. "Jade? That ought to be entertaining. Look, if you're heading by sickbay, can you have Oshwald pay Sonya a visit? She can be stubborn, and I know she won't go see him voluntarily."

Ethan bit back a snort at his comment. "Sure thing."

As he walked away, his mind reeled over what had just occurred.

He didn't bother with the doctor. Sonya wasn't ill, at least not in a way that would require a healer.

Chapter 19

Sonya woke from a dead sleep.

The ship shuddered under an onslaught of what sounded like exterior explosions. She threw the covers off her and scrambled from the bed. *Marada* was nearing the archaic planet called Earth, but Sonya had been under the impression that the space around it was virtually a dead zone—vacant of both travelers and ports—and therefore safe to cross. Who would be attacking them in this deserted section of the universe?

Anxiety spiked as she recalled Ethan suggesting the Kayadon were close to discovering Kyra's location. Were those fiends already on Earth? Had they gotten to her before Cale?

She quickly dressed in an easy wrap-around skirt and a loose-fitting top. In the hall, two crew members rushed by.

"What's happening?" she called after them.

"We're under attack," one yelled back.

"No kidding. By whom?" she asked, but the crew members had already disappeared around a corner.

She raced for the bridge. The moment the doors swooshed open for her, she heard Sebastian barking out orders as another blast made contact with the ship. He acknowledged her with a tight nod.

"Ah," Aidan said, staring at his console. He sounded pleased. "That's got it. Bay doors are locked down, Captain."

"Good. Prepare the ship for warp." Sebastian turned to Sonya. "Cale's arrived with two females and may be in need of medical attention. Escort Oshwald to the docking bay and assist him if he needs. And for gods' sake don't attack anyone."

Sonya offered an unamused look before hurrying to retrieve Doctor Oshwald. As they headed to the docking bay, the lights flickered and Sonya felt *Marada's* warp drive engage.

Anya and Marik were already waiting at the bay door. Sonya gave them a quizzical look.

"I sensed them coming," Anya explained with a grin, then she pointed through the window pane. "Look, there they are."

Sonya spotted Cale's familiar spiky blond head as he emerged from the craft along with two females. It was instantly clear which one was Anya's sister. Kyra's features boasted a striking family resemblance with rich light copper-colored hair. The other girl boasted dark hair and looked sickly pale, ready to lose the contents of her stomach.

The access hatch slid open, and the doctor stepped in first. Cale directed him to the pale one.

Sonya was still angry that Cale had left without her, but having him safely back on board greatly reduced her ire. She pulled him in for a tight hug. "Bastian's pissed at you for leaving without me."

Cale gave her an arrogant grin. "I didn't need my little sister tagging along."

She rolled her eyes.

Anya threw her arms around Cale's neck in greeting before turning to Kyra. They had not seen each other for nearly four hundred years. Sonya could practically feel Anya's blast of emotion as they moved to embrace each other.

Nadua rushed into the room, tears brimming and screeching with excitement as she joined her family.

Cale did a double take and then scowled at the redhead. His scowl turned to disbelief, and he shot Marik an incredulous look. Marik exploded with laughter. Sonya smiled at Cale's dumfounded expression over Marik's mated status—something all demons could innately sense.

Humor took a rapid plummet into pity as Cale glanced towards Kyra, his gaze filled with such longing that Sonya's stomach tightened to the point of pain. That look alone, fleeting as it was, held an endless chasm of wishes that could never be.

She averted her gaze so that Cale wouldn't catch the pity in her eyes.

Sebastian arrived then, with Rex following behind.

Cale diverted his attention to the new demon. "Who's this?"

"This is Rex," Sebastian replied. "A new trainee. You've missed a lot."

"I gathered." Cale proceeded to introduce the two females: Kyra, and the Earth native, Zoey. "We didn't intend for Zoey to tag along, but the Kayadon were all over us, and we couldn't leave her."

Kyra appeared to be translating the conversation to the Earthling. When Cale spoke of the possibility of somehow getting her back on her planet, Zoey offered a sound of protest. She and Kyra then proceeded to argue in what was probably the

Earthling's native language.

"We can't go back anyway," Sebastian informed them. "It's too dangerous with the Kayadon behind us. If they have warp capabilities of their own, they could be following us even now."

Cale stretched his arms. "I don't know about any of you, but after a landing like that, I think a drink is in order." He canted his head at Sonya. "Is the pub closed?"

She hesitated. "It's open. Ethan and Jade are working to-night."

Cale raised a dubious brow. "What else has changed? Don't tell me you're mated as well."

She barely stifled a nervous laugh. "Of course not! Don't be ridiculous." Her tail flicked with her irritation, drawing the awed expressions of Kyra and Zoey.

"Pity," Cale replied. "I could have used a new target in the training room."

Exactly why she was glad to be free of a matebond. Any male of hers would endure a never-ending diatribe by her brothers—not to mention continual assaults—and she would be forced to defend him. Moreover, if he were the wrong kind of male—a known reprobate, for instance—a permanent rift could form between her and her family.

She pushed the ridiculous notion from her mind, then dropped parallel to the floor and swiped Cale's feed out from under him with her leg. He landed on his back with a grunt.

She grinned. "That's what you have me for."

Sebastian let out a begrudging sigh as Cale jumped up to retaliate. Sonya tried to slip past him, but Cale caught hold of her waist and heaved her upper half over his shoulder, trapping her legs against his torso with iron tight arms.

"Cale!" Her legs flailed uselessly.

"Now you'll be buying me a drink, little sister."

Sonya tensed as Cale hauled her in the direction of the pub. "No, Cale. I don't want to go to The Demon's Punchbowl."

"Too bad."

* * *

"Jade, less flirting, more working."

Jade responded to Ethan's chide with a withered stare, then turned away from her newest infatuation to engage the impatient crew member waiting at the other end of the bar.

A ruckus near the entrance drew Ethan's attention. Cale lumbered in with Sonya thrashing over his shoulder. Her skirt hem rode up on her thighs as her legs kicked. Behind them, a large entourage chortled.

Cale set her on her feet, and she turned grudgingly toward the bar, her hips swishing seductively as though to torture Ethan alone.

Ethan tempered the lust in his gaze as she approached. Not that it would have mattered. He could have stood there drooling over the floor for all she cared. She didn't even spare him a glance.

Fine with him if that was how she wanted to play it. Their last encounter had been nothing if not a warning. Somehow, even though she clearly detested him in every way, he was inspiring a matebond between them.

How it was even possible, he didn't know.

What he did know, however, was that he would never entertain the idea of becoming a demon's mate. The very notion was abhorrent. Insulting. At the very least ridiculous.

"Pirate!" Cale greeted, crossing to stand by the bar.

"Demon," he responded with a smile, happy that Cale had made it back unharmed. "Just had to arrive with a bang, didn't you."

"I've never been one for subtlety. Brought you a present too." He jerked his thumb behind him.

Ethan turned back to where the rest of the group converged around a large table and caught Kyra's gaze. Relief flooded him.

Kyra's expression turned bright as recognition lit her eyes.

"Princess Kyralyn!" He stepped around the bar and offered a low bow.

"Please don't bow, Ethan. And you can call me Kyra now."

"See," Anya chided, reminding him of the countless times she'd scolded him for addressing her by her title. Nadua too shunned the distinction. He supposed after so long, they no longer related to the ancient ways.

"Apologies. An old habit, I guess," Ethan replied.

"Very old, indeed." Kyra laughed, yet the sound was melancholic.

He took her hand and placed a soft kiss on her knuckles. Apparently another very old habit he would have to rid himself of because she blushed furiously.

His lips twisted with amusement. Now that everyone was assembled, Ethan was sure the book would reveal more of its secrets. Surely the king had envisioned a plan of attack. Ethan could practically taste victory.

Cale dropped a load of drinks on the table, and Kyra jumped. Sonya appeared next with two full pitchers and a set of glasses. By their deep frowns, it was clear the demon's moods had taken a nosedive. What had he missed?

After settling in at the table, Kyra started, "So, Ethan, tell me what happened after I left Evlon."

He blinked up at her. "Starting out a little thick."

Her steady greenish-blue eyes revealed the tenacious young princess he once knew. "Starting at the beginning. I've been in the dark for a long, long time, and now I want some answers."

Ethan let out a breath. "We were all taken by surprise by the attack. None of our seers, not even your father, anticipated it. It was suggested later that the Kayadon had some sort of cloaking magic, but we can't be sure." He let out a slow breath. "I sent you off in that little ship, expecting to see it blasted to a million pieces, but others had started evacuating the planet as well. The Kayadon were distracted enough, and you got through."

He paused, letting his words sink in as the others sat quietly and sipped their drinks. That last day on Evlon was the only time he had ever contemplated disobeying the king's orders. But in the end, he had sent Kyra alone through the atmosphere that had become a chaotic war zone, fearing for her life.

"We sent Nadua next, then Anya and your mother."

Anya had been just a child, barely able to speak in clear sentences, yet she seemed to have grasped the situation as she clung to her mother.

"Your cousins followed, and those who were closest to the royal family. Most everyone else had to fend for themselves. And those who didn't have access off the planet went into hiding or were captured..." Ethan took a drink before adding, "I stayed behind with your father. No one could persuade him to leave. He felt responsible. Felt that his visions had failed him."

At the mention of her father, Kyra's expression turned bleak.

Jade approached with a fresh tray of drinks that Sonya had

signaled for and made her way around the table. When she slipped behind Cale, she lowered her mouth to whisper in his ear, and Ethan noticed a slight tick in Kyra's jaw.

He continued, unfazed. "The King spent the following fifty years sifting through the future and composing the book that helped bring us all together. When he finished it, it was smuggled out and entrusted to the Serakians who enchanted it so that only you three could open it. However, the king charged me with decoding it."

"Why?" Kyra asked.

"Because it holds secrets that can be used against you, against all of us, and he convinced me that I could survive to find you, even though I did not always believe it."

Kyra gave him a grateful smile. "Father was right to have put his faith in you." She kindly placed her hand over his. "It must have been difficult all these years."

He turned his palm up to face her grip, surprised by how much that simple sentiment warmed his heart. "Thank you, Majesty." He couldn't help but smile when she pursed her lips at the title.

Kyra took in a long breath and then let it out slowly. "Well, what's happening on Evlon now? Is Father alright? Are they hurting him?"

"A little after the book started its journey, the king sent me away, and I haven't had contact since." Well, not the kind of contact she was hoping for. "That was three hundred and fifty years ago."

With Kyra's hand still clasped in his, Ethan's magic spiked with the warning that Cale was about to take a mental detour to the Edge and attack.

Interesting.

Ethan released Kyra's hand and filed that information away for later examination. Sonya sat with her arms crossed, eyes turned down and jaw locked. Out of curiosity, he let his magic drift over her. She was on the verge of fabricating an excuse to leave.

Nadua caught his gaze and gestured toward Kyra with her chin. "Tell her your theory."

All eyes turned back to him.

"I believe the Kayadon want something from us. Something they don't have and have been unable to get."

Kyra sat back. "Our magic."

"That's the only thing I can come up with."

Kyra engaged the Earthling in short conversation before turning back to the group. "Zoey agrees."

They all glanced at human, who managed a shy smile in response.

"They're keeping our people alive," Ethan added. "They haven't sold a soul into slavery, like they did..." Ethan stopped himself before he mentioned Marik's name. When the Kayadon had overtaken the demon planet, Marik had found himself in the slave market. "From what I can remember, life went on as normally as possible. People tried to live as best they could. But they lived on the edge of a knife, trying not to be noticed by the Kayadon soldiers that patrolled every village. Any poor soul who drew their interest...disappeared."

Cale's grip tightened around his bottle. "We'll rip every last one of their throats out."

Sebastian leaned forward in his chair, addressing Kyra for

the most part. "We intend to do everything we can to free your people, but I will not lie, our thoughts are on revenge. People will die. Theirs…and no doubt ours. I've made it clear to my crew that they are not under any obligation to join us, and many will end their association with us at the next stop." He paused. "We need allies."

Kyra nodded. "What has been done so far?"

"We've sent out encrypted messages on some underground channels. Anyone who's interested will contact us."

"What if no one responds to it?"

Sebastian shrugged. "There are other options. The Kayadon pose a threat to all the races. There's nothing to say that when they're done with Evlon, they won't move on to the next planet. That should be a powerful motivator."

Kyra nodded. "So where should we start?"

"Spaceports and cities," Sebastian replied.

Ethan interjected, "I could entreaty my old faction and some other pirates I'm acquainted with."

Sonya's muffled rebuff piqued Ethan's ire. He glared at her, and she glared back.

"How about the dragons?" Kyra prompted, seeming oblivious to the exchange.

"Yes, the dragons," Nadua agreed. "They are our allies. Or…they were." She looked at Kyra, then to Anya, suddenly apprehensive.

"I have to believe they still are," Kyra declared. "I spent some time with the clan of Legura, remember?"

"Yes, but…" Nadua trailed off. "Theirs is but one among many. What of the other clans?"

"I cannot say. Perhaps if we get one clan, the others will follow." Kyra glanced at Cale. "Didn't you say you had a dragon pilot on board?"

Cale grunted in affirmation. "Aidan. He's from the Kanisae Clan."

"Could he ask them for support?"

Sebastian frowned, and Cale ran his fingers through his hair before responding, "He was exiled."

"However, we'll ask him," Sebastian interjected. "It couldn't hurt."

The table fell into silent contemplation. After a moment, Kyra suggested they continue the conversation in the morning. Both she and the Earthling looked close to exhaustion.

Sebastian gave a tight nod. "We were only expecting one extra. Do you mind sharing quarters for the time being?"

"That would work out for the best, I think," Kyra replied.

Sonya pushed to stand, finally finding her excuse. "I'll show them the way."

Chapter 20

Ethan watched Sonya escort Zoey and Kyra out of the pub, his ire growing by the minute.

As hard as he tried, he could no longer tolerate her continued repugnance. It was an unnecessary distraction—for both of them. They may never be friends, definitely not lovers, but she would at least show him some respect.

While the others engaged in idle conversation, Ethan slipped away in search of his surly demoness. He found her alone in the hallway, approaching her personal quarters.

He'd had every intention of coming at her in a calm, cool manner, to try for a mature discussion. But the moment their eyes locked, hers narrowed, turning disdainful.

His temper surged. "What is your problem?"

"I figured it was clear," she snapped, sauntering closer to her room as if in no rush, but her inner desperation betrayed her.

He hurried behind her. Once she disappeared inside, it might be another week before she emerged. She whirled on him, her eyes flashing fierce and challenging. She stretched her arm out to block his way.

"What is this grudge you have against me?" he demanded, meeting her gaze with intense resolve.

Sonya only raised a brow in response.

"And do not use the incident in the training room as an excuse. Whatever your deal is, it goes further back than that."

She seared him with a look that, for anyone else, would have been a deadly warning to retreat.

Instead, that look only made his hackles rise. "We are about to go to war! So you and I are going to get past this."

Sonya seemed unmoved. "Did you leave my pub solely in the hands of Jade?"

"You're the one who hired her," he reminded.

She let out a heavy sigh. "Ethan, just get back to work. We've nothing to talk about."

He wanted to roar with frustration. "The hell we don't," he growled, grabbing her arm. Before she had a chance to pull away, he spun her around and seized her wrists behind her back, forcing her into the private space of her room.

The door slid closed behind them.

She made a sound of protest, yet a twinge of her excitement sliced through him. His shaft swelled in response, and lust seized his rational mind.

He pressed forward, caging her front against a wall. He dipped his head to the nape of her neck, just below her ear. Her breath caught.

"Why do I want you?" The words escaped his lips without permission, wrenched from somewhere deep within.

Sonya's voice became a low warning. "If you knew what danger you are in, you wouldn't."

His lips quirked. He knew exactly the kind of danger he was

courting. "Are you talking about your little fang show?"

She gasped, going dead still. "You saw? And still you're here?"

If he were smart, he would leave now before this went any further. Unfortunately, his intelligence seemed to have gone on hiatus. "I know you wouldn't bite me unless I asked you to, and I have no intention of doing so." Not to mention the fact that she was just as disgusted by the idea as he was.

"I wouldn't claim you if you begged me," she hissed, confirming his thoughts.

"Then there is nothing for me to worry about." His teeth found the shell of her ear with a soft pressure.

A shudder racked through her, and ever so slightly, her body arched into him. Her voice came out as a rasp. "I thought you were here to talk."

"I'm finding I want to do a lot of things."

"Do you really think I'm going to let you do *that* to me again?"

His lips curled at her contempt. "Imagine my surprise when the beautiful, flirty demoness turns out to be a virgin. One question has been nagging me, though. How is it possible?"

"It's an easy accomplishment when you have two—make that three—overprotective brothers. Brothers who would show you your own spleen if they saw you now."

He didn't doubt Sebastian, Cale, and Marik would do just that, but the threat was not enough to sway him from his damning course. Her growing desire was like a drug, leaching away reason.

"You must have wanted a bed partner at some point. Demons don't value things like virtue and virginity. Your kind are infamously insatiable."

She snorted. "Even if I did, who would risk their lives for a lay? And those who didn't fear my family—not that there were many—never showed an interest."

Yet another warning he should heed, but the new information only drove his curiosity. "You've pleasured yourself though."

She appeared aghast by his bluntness and floundered for a reply.

He grinned. "I'll take that as a yes. You were too responsive not to have."

Her body stiffened in indignation and then her struggles resumed, but the action only managed to close the distance between them. His crotch nestled snuggly against her backside.

Nothing had ever rattled his control with such cutting precision as the feel of her against him. He was hard-pressed to believe anything ever could again.

The desperation in his muttered words surprised him. "Give me another chance."

She stilled once more. "What?"

"The way we left things, your expression..." It still haunted him more than he had realized.

"And you, what? Want a redo?" Her laugh came out harsh, yet he sensed her wavering. On the cusp of his mind, he wondered if he was once again spurring the situation out of either of their control. But his body hummed with an overwhelming, maddening need, and nothing could stop him now, short of her total rejection.

"I want to taste you," he ground out. "To feel your flesh give way under mine and see rapture on your face as I make you come in my arms. To use your body and teach you to use mine until we are both too sore to walk." When she made no response, he leaned in closer to her slender ear. "Don't you want me to show you how good it can be?"

After a tense moment of silence, fraught with the gravity of her impending decision and all that weighed between them, she gave the slightest nod.

His cock jerked in anticipation, but he released her and backed away, needing to be sure of her resolve.

She turned to face him, displaying a wrinkle of uncertainty between her brows. Her gaze traveled the length of him, her lids growing hooded with the evidence of her hunger, as well as a hint of trepidation. If she gave her approval, he would do everything in his power to relieve her of the latter.

"Take off your shirt," she ordered, then folded her lower lip between her teeth.

He shrugged off the fabric and tossed it away. He remained still, giving her leave to look him over. The intensity of her scrutiny burned bright behind her irises, her billowing desire palpable.

She swallowed hard and then bit her lip again, giving him a glimpse of one descended fang. His shaft pulsed, straining against his pants. He tried not to show his depraved response. Then he sensed her starting to reconsider, alarmed by her own body's reaction.

He stepped toward her. "You won't bite me." He had no idea if that was true, but lust gripped him like a cage of claws.

"Never," she tried to sneer, but it came out husky and alluring.

He inched closer, afraid her doubt was gaining ground. "Tell me you want this."

Her eyes closed as if pained. "Gods, yes."

With that, he closed the distance between them and their lips crushed together. The sharpness of her fangs should have alarmed him, but wild need exploded in his chest, nearly robbing him of breath. He tugged the ties of her bodice, undoing them in a rush and removing her top.

She mimicked his fierce urgency as she fumbled with the clasp of his trousers. Next, her skirt floated to her feet, leaving the rest of her bare except for the sexy black panties that hugged her hips.

He clasped one arm around her waist and palmed her breast, rubbing his thumb over the budding pink nipple. Her eyes closed, and she leaned against the wall as a small whimper of approval filtered from her lungs. Wanting to hear more, he leaned down to take the tiny peak into his mouth.

She inhaled sharply, rewarding him with a feminine moan.

Her wicked intentions were completely open to him now. She was as lost as he, growing urgent and mad with a primal need begging for fulfillment. It was nearly painful to take this as slow as he knew he should, but wanted to please her this time. Needed to.

His palms moved to caress the underside of her breasts and then down her smooth stomach. When his lips followed, she froze and glanced at him. Eyes locked on his, she watched as he continued his descent, her body shaking.

He slipped his thumbs under the waistline of her panties and gave her a roguish grin before tugging them down.

The first taste of her was like a jolt of concentrated bliss arching through each cell, straight to the base of his arousal.

* * *

Sonya tried to stifle a moan, failing miserably as sharp pleasure struck a wicked path to her brain. A quake rippled over her, and she cried out a second time. If not for the wall, her ass would have hit the floor. *This is madness!* How could this feel so good?

He swept along her tender flesh as though he were finding just as much pleasure in the task, savoring her as if she were a delicacy.

Her body quivered fiercely. "Ethan, I'm going to fall," she managed through haggard breath.

"Lie down," he ordered. His tone was so rough it no longer sounded like him.

She obeyed without thinking, forgoing the bed and sinking to the floor. He maneuvered between her legs, gripping her thighs, and continued his assault. Her heart thumped faster, her breath coming in gasps. She couldn't think past what he was doing. Soon, she began to shake again, and her claws dug at the ground. With a cry, ecstasy exploded, taking her vision.

After a moment, Ethan sat back, expression unabashedly smug. She still couldn't move, reduced to a panting, puddled mess on the floor, but she couldn't bring herself to care. A smile crawled across her lips. She couldn't prevent it. That is until she remembered her fangs were on display. Yet, for whatever reason, Ethan didn't seem put off by them. In fact, he looked as though he wasn't finished with her.

Sitting up, she asked, "What next?"

His lips twisted into a grin that screamed of arrogance and triumph, but she didn't care.

"On the bed," he demanded, his eyes darkening with wicked intention.

Normally his bossy attitude would have grated, but at the moment it was strangely appealing. She crossed to the bed.

Warm hands gripped her by the waist from behind, staying her as she was about to crawl onto the mattress. He slipped his hands over her belly and along her torso to cup her breasts. His thumbs teased her already sensitive nipples. She moaned and arched back.

His shaft breached just between the apex of her legs, sliding easily with the help of her dampness. She jumped at the feel, growing slicker still. Slowly, he slid back and forth, not entering, but stimulating them both.

"Bend over," he commanded.

She gulped. At length, her palms moved to the mattress, leaving her in a vulnerable yet titillating position.

Her sudden nervousness must have been evident because he offered, "If I hurt you, tell me and I'll stop."

"Alright."

The tip of his erection brushed her center and she recoiled, remembering their first time. This was different though. He pressed in with slow control, inching forward and giving her time to get used to his girth.

"You okay?" he asked, tone like gravel.

"I'm good," she assured. "It feels…" She couldn't come up with a word. "Okay, I guess?"

"Are you trying to wound my confidence?"

She laughed. "Is that even possible?"

He gave a sharp pump of his hips, and she gasped as a spike of pleasure shot through her. "No," he said and then moved again, silencing whatever retort she was about to spit out, replacing it with a soft moan. Once more, he pumped his hips, filling her and making her whimper.

As he pushed forward again, her hips pushed back. He made a sound of approval and gripped her waist.

A steady rhythm developed, and soon she was panting with fervor as he ground into her with increasing force. But it was wonderful, and with each thrust it seemed only to get better, until she forgot herself entirely, surrendering to the moment. She cried out as a wave of pleasure overcame her, bursting into a million pieces. Ethan groaned as his release came on the heel of hers. After a few heartbeats, he pulled out of her and they dragged themselves onto the bed.

She reached for something to cover herself.

"No, don't," he said, and she paused. "May I look at you a little longer?" He shifted to his side, his head propped on his palm, shamelessly drinking her in.

She chewed her lip, feeling a bit skittish. Her fangs had yet to recede, and she felt exposed in a way that had nothing to do with her lack of clothing. "Only because you asked so nicely."

"Oh, I get really nice after sex."

She bit back a grin. "Is that so?"

"Damn near saintly."

She snorted and leaned back on the mattress. Her body was both relaxed and deliciously sore. After a moment, she had to concede, "That was so much better than before."

"Glad to hear it."

Was he really not worried about her claiming him? She supposed that was why he had taken her from behind, so her fangs were nowhere near him. Not for the first time, she was amazed at how knowledgeable he was about her culture. "How do you know so much about demons?"

He shrugged. "I spent some time with a group of renegade demons before I met up with the Denaloids. They found me amusing."

She arched a brow. Coming across other demons was a rare occurrence. "Do you know where they are?"

He frowned at her. "No. We separated long ago."

"Are you able to contact them?"

"We didn't exactly promise to keep in touch upon parting."

Damn. Any extra help would have been welcome.

"Eager for your own kind?"

From his tone, she couldn't decipher his mood. "Well, sure, but I was thinking to recruit them."

He took a moment to respond. "I have a few channels of communication that may reach them. I can attempt a message. No guarantees."

"By channels, you mean network of pirates." Though she hadn't meant for it to, her voice revealed her disgust.

His lips thinned. "Indeed. Now I've answered your question, perhaps you will answer mine."

She waited.

"What do you have against pirates?"

Silence reigned.

"Were you harmed in some way by one?"

She wasn't ready to delve into that particular topic, still struggling with the idea that she had let a man like Ethan touch her in ways no one else had. She was still reeling from it, her body thrumming with aftershocks. She didn't want to think about his past—or hers, for that matter—but she couldn't seem to stop herself. Briefly, she wondered if Ethan had killed with the same cold carelessness as other pirates would. Had he ripped apart families with a swing of his sword and a smile on his face?

Suddenly weary, she rolled off the bed. "I need to wash up." She paused. "You should too, before you leave. Unless you think you could fend off my rabid brothers."

He gave her a questioning look.

"My scent is all over you," she explained.

His lips curled into a sexy grin. "Then by all means, let's wash up."

Chapter 21

Sonya stepped under the warm spray of water, a little un-nerved. She'd never bathed with anyone before and her lack of confidence in this area irritated her. But Ethan seemed to be having fun teaching her, and damn if she didn't like it too.

As her hair became drenched by the water sliding down her body, he proceeded to lather her heated skin. Slick palms rubbed over every inch of her torso with slow intent. Her head lolled from the attention as a part of her worried how intimate this felt. This wasn't just animal need being sated, this was…sweet.

Thankfully he'd let the subject of her past drop without ar-gument. Although, she doubted he'd resigned to leave it be alto-gether. She'd known him for only a short time, but already she could tell he wasn't the kind of male who gave up on anything he set his mind to. And the more she resisted, the more his cu-riosity would burn.

Part of her wanted to confide in him, as if revealing the truth might help to eliminate the anger and guilt that accompa-nied her everywhere she went. She mentally scoffed, knowing it wouldn't change a thing.

Even if she offered Ethan a hint of the cruelty she'd witness—performed by individuals he might have called brother in arms, had he known them—she had to wonder: would he have joined in their merriment as they'd gouged the life from her father with their swords and knives?

Something in her rejected the possibility, but she wasn't sure why. Perhaps it was the way his fingertips caressed the length spine. His lovemaking had been equally sweet, even after he had taken what he wanted from her.

She lowered her eyes to his chest to watch the beads of water race over his smooth, well-defined muscles, hoping he wouldn't see the conflict residing within.

He stilled, then placed his forefinger under her chin to gently tilt her head up. She schooled her features as best she could, but her betraying lips pursed together as if to hold back a flood of confession.

Studiously, he searched her gaze, concern leaking into his expression.

Was she really that obvious?

No matter. There was a single, heart-wrenching reason why she couldn't tell him of the most devastating night of her life, only realizing it now as she lost herself in the deep serene oceans of his eyes.

She wouldn't be able to handle if he turned uncaring or merely shrugged at her plight. He was a pirate, after all. And as he'd stated before, he already thought her culture barbarous. He would probably think nothing of a random act of violence against one of her own. He might even think her silly for allowing the scar of that night to fester all these years.

"Should I leave you be?" he suddenly asked.

Her stomach churned in a tumultuous uproar, and she was

stricken by a fear she couldn't describe. By his tone, she imagined the question comprised of more than allowing her a bit of solitude to finish washing. She got the impression he was giving her the opportunity to banish him from her bed, her life…forever, if she so wished.

And she should. She should tell him to go and never speak of their liaison again, forget it even occurred. It would be best for both of them, especially since her body seemed afflicted with the urge to claim him as her mate, which made everything that much worse than if they were merely fooling around.

She didn't want to believe it was true that he was hers—wanted to believe there was some colossal mistake—but another thought plagued her mind.

He would never submit to such a binding commitment as a matehood. Not with a demon. The truth was he wanted a Faieara princess, not a crude-mouthed, aggressive female with an ingrained aversion to him.

The idea should have provided some relief…should have.

She opened her mouth to send him away, but her throat locked up at the thought. Her teeth gnashed together as her jutting fangs lengthened in further protest.

To her embarrassment, he noticed.

But instead of looking aghast, he brought this thumb up to graze her lower lip as though entranced. His other hand crawled along her hip and up her side. She resisted the urge to arch into that touch, only to relent a moment later.

Slowly, he guided her back till she met the cool damp wall before lowering his mouth to hers. She was careful with her fangs while returning the kiss, but he didn't seem to pay them any heed as his tongue sought hers.

A fresh wave of desire washed away worry, and anticipation engulfed her body as it readied for his expert attention. If he wanted to leave now, he would need to have a nice long talk with the claws that were digging into his back.

Ethan marveled at her beauty as she accepted his silent commands. Panic had flooded him when he had offered her an out. Fierce indecision had bombarded her, and he thought she might actually take it. He wasn't ready for that. Had only just breached the outer layer of her thick protective shell. He wanted to explore a little more before she shut the door on him completely.

With his body pressed to hers, he hooked the back of her knee and lifted her leg to rest against his hip, opening her up to him. She planted her elbows on his shoulders, folding her arms around his neck as he sheathed himself inside her. They both shuddered at the ecstasy of their joining, pausing to revel in the sensation.

After a few slow pumps of his hips, she pulled herself up to wrap her other leg around his waist, giving him fuller, deeper access. With his palms firmly on her luscious ass and her back against the wall, he thrust his hips, taking pleasure in the fervent sounds escaping from her.

He vaguely noted her tail spiraling down his leg and stifled a laugh. She couldn't be more thoroughly wrapped around him if she were the living embodiment of a carnivorous vine. Which, considering her sexy little fangs, that wasn't far off.

At any moment, she could plant them in his flesh.

And still that didn't spark the sense of foreboding in him that it should. In this moment, she consumed him mind, body, soul, and deeper yet. There was no caution on his part and he didn't bother contemplating why. Instead, he lost himself inside her, letting the deluge of their passion pull him under and then force him to new, erotic heights.

He gave a hard, agonizingly controlled thrust before finding an urgent rhythm that ripped groans from deep within him. She rewarded his efforts with sweet feminine moans born of her own building orgasm as her hips rocked with equal fervor.

Her head flew back on a wild cry as her body shuddered from the power of her climax. His own release followed with an explosive force. A force that seemed to shatter his very soul, breaking it into an incalculable number of shards that made up his entire being, before reforming into something new, something he didn't fully recognize. And as he gazed down at her in stunned amazement, riveted by the drunken bliss in her eyes, his soul cracked and broke again.

All he was, all he had worked for, had guided him to this perfect moment. She was a beacon he never realized he was following.

A dream made real.

The spell broke a moment later as their husky breaths mingled and she met his gaze. The fear he should be experiencing reflected back at him. He scanned her, horrified to find her closing up again.

"Don't," he blurted.

Her expression twisted in confusion, and she lowered one leg to meet the ground. He allowed the rest of her to slide down him, but refused to let her pull away completely. He looped one arm around her midsection, holding her close, and cupped her face in an almost desperate way.

Closing her eyes, she leaned her head into his palm. Her lids flashed open as if the move had been unconsciously done.

"I think you should go," she said. The statement wasn't cruel. Just expressionless. Which was somehow even worse. "If my brothers found you—"

"Would that be so bad?"

Her head jerked back, brows furrowed. "Do you have any idea what they would do to you?"

"You think I'm worried?"

"You should be."

At first he had been, but now? If her family wanted to rip him apart for daring to touch her, they would have a hell of a time fighting him for the privilege. "Aw, are you actually concerned for me?" His lips formed a teasing smile.

"Not at all," she replied, raising her chin.

"Then I don't see a problem. Leave me to contend with the consequences of my actions."

"Why would you even risk it? It's not like…" She trailed off, but Ethan could read what went unsaid. It wasn't as if they were going to be together like this forever. And she was right. That was something neither of them wanted. Wasn't it?

"I've never been one to shy away from a dangerous situation. Besides, I'm having too much fun with you right now, and I don't plan on stopping." He quickly swayed the conversation in a new direction. "Come back to work in the pub. You can't stay cooped up in this room."

One corner of her mouth lifted. "You're changing the subject."

"Jade is awful at mixing. You'd be horrified to know how many have suffered from her attempts."

Sonya laughed, and the sound moved through him like a caress. "I was afraid of that."

Chapter 22

After allowing Ethan to thoroughly *persuade* her, Sonya finally consented to return to work.

Ethan had been right about Jade. The complaints Sonya received over the next few days were staggering. Apparently the chit couldn't mix water and ice without somehow sabotaging the flavor.

But she kept Jade on, for the most part, and simply split shifts with her. Working with Ethan full time wasn't the best idea. Downright dangerous, in fact.

Sonya twisted the cap off a chilled bottle and handed it to the waiting female across the bar. She recognized the girl as one half of the kissing twits from when Ethan had nearly turned her pub into a brothel. Ethan brushed up beside Sonya and rested his hand on the small of her back as he served the second part of the female's order—a strongly mixed drink for her lover.

As the twit strode away, Ethan's hand obstinately traveled lower toward Sonya's backside. She turned her head to glare at him.

He'd taken to doing things of that nature often, such as casting her glances filled with dark promises, even after she'd asked him to not to. If anyone saw the way he leered at her now, her brothers would surely hear of it.

Yet she couldn't muster the proper amount of anger to censure him with any real conviction. That look alone forced a jolt of sexual anticipation down her spine, straight to her core. It didn't help that every night he made good on his unspoken, erotic promises, taking her to a land where nothing but ecstasy reigned. She shivered, recalling how the previous evening he had introduced a length of chain into their play.

Sonya had been instantly wary, had even fought back at first, but the wicked gleam in his eyes had her delirious with hunger and surprisingly submissive.

After he'd won out, rendering her helpless and attached to her own bed, he'd leaned down and brushed his lips over a tender spot of her neck, then gave a soft nip. Sonya had gone wild, her fangs lengthening, throbbing. She hadn't even tried to hide them. Instead, she bared them in a silent warning. But to her surprise, Ethan had offered her a satisfied smirk.

Even now she thought him mad to willingly take her to that dangerous place, but she supposed that's what the chain had been for. Just in case she had lost control. Very clever, as far as tempting a demon went. Although part of her sensed there was more behind it than just caution. She imagined he enjoyed having her fully under his control. And as she had lain there, vulnerable and exposed, he'd taken his time learning every nuance of her body and driving her mad.

He now knew that when he palmed her breast, she would squirm. When he explored between her thighs with his tongue, she would cry out. And when he stopped, she would growl. He always chuckled at that.

Though it had been a touch unnerving to be bound in such a way, she couldn't deny her excitement at discovering what he would do next, the anticipation. The only thing he didn't do was disappoint.

Feeling herself flush at the memory, she clenched her jaw and pushed Ethan away. "Get to work. We have customers who are thirsty."

He leaned in close to her ear. "I'm parched myself, but I guess I'll have to wait till later to have my fill."

She ground her teeth to keep the traitorous smile off her face, but failed in the attempt. "Stop it."

"Stop what? I'm doing nothing but tending to our clientele."

She rolled her eyes. "Go organize the stock room if you can't behave." Loads of new supplies still sat in crates on the floor from when Sebastian had acquired them.

"Very well, but I'm only doing it now because I was going to anyway. Not because you ordered me to."

"Whatever you need to tell yourself."

He gave her a heated once over, lingering a little too long before disappearing. It made her glad she had donned this particular outfit this morning. The tight black top offered a glimpse of her midsection. The auburn skirt hugged the curve of her hips, the hem covering just enough not to flash a peek of her undergarments. Of course, she had to be careful about bending over.

Briefly, she considered following Ethan into the stock room and locking the door behind. Perhaps she'd find a bit of chain of her own to use on him.

"Hi Sonya." Kyra's familiar voice drew her attention. The

Faieara was making herself at home on the ship and, surprisingly, Sonya found her to be quite pleasant. Sweet like Anya, yet not as sheltered or naive.

The fact that Sonya actually liked Kyra grated. Sooner or later, Ethan would begin courting her. No matter what that meant for Sonya, she was determined not to let it bother her.

Zoey appeared next, and claimed a seat at the bar next to Kyra. Zoey was equally likable, if a bit silly. Although that could merely be caused by Kyra's translation of her crude English into the common space language the rest of them spoke.

"The usual?" Sonya asked, grabbing a set of empty glasses. The two had been regulars in The Demon's Punchbowl since their arrival. They both loved to dance, which was probably what heartened Sonya to them in the first place.

Kyra nodded in response, but Zoey asked, "You got anything with bite?"

Sonya paused, hearing the words spoken in perfect Demonish.

Kyra noted her reaction. "What's the matter?"

"Has someone been teaching you guys Demonish?"

Kyra shook her head. "No. Why?"

Sonya glanced back at Zoey. Cale must have taught the girl a few easy phrases. If so, Sonya expected the Earthling had no real idea what she might be saying, which was dangerous, considering the source. No doubt she'd start sputtering stuff like, "My top is too tight. Won't you help me take it off?" or "I have a surprise for you in my pants."

Yeah, that sounded exactly like something Cale would do.

To Kyra, Sonya demanded, "Ask her who taught her to say that."

"No need," Zoey replied, startling both Sonya and Kyra. "I understood you perfectly, and no one taught me to say anything in…whatever it is you called it."

Her diction was perfect, with inflections specific to Sonya's old village.

Sonya growled. "Stop fucking with me. You're speaking it right now."

Kyra shook her head, looking even more confused than Sonya. "No, she's speaking English."

"No, she's not." Sonya glanced around the room, seeking Cale's smug face. She was now convinced that he'd had sent them in to screw with her.

Kyra and Zoey shared a confounded look.

Irritated by the game, Sonya called Ethan from the back.

He emerged a few moments later, greeting them with a smile. "Ladies."

"Ethan, do you speak any Demonish?" Sonya bit out.

"A little bit. Why?"

She turned to Zoey. "Speak, girl."

Zoey leaned back, gaping. "What am I, a dog?"

Sonya faced Ethan expectantly. "Well? Did you understand what she said?"

"Well, yeah, but that's because she's speaking Denaloid." Ethan quirked a brow at Zoey. "For what possible reason would you have to learn that language?"

Zoey's jaw dropped. "It's English. You're all speaking it."

Kyra gasped, her eyes widening. She looked at Zoey. "I think we should ask Portia about that spell she put on you. I suspect when you speak, people will hear it in their most common language. In turn, you'll hear them in yours."

Ethan turned back toward the storeroom, muttering, "The Serakian, huh? Well, that's convenient."

Sonya agreed. The little witch turned out to be useful after all. She realized she had yet to meet Portia. Perhaps she would seek her out a bit later.

"Hey." Sonya gave Zoey a sly smile. "If Cale comes in, do me a favor and mess with him a little."

Chapter 23

Sebastian surveyed the bridge, calculating the number of crewmen he would have to replace after their arrival at Uli Rings. Engineering, security, and navigation. In a few days, the entire ship would feel hollowed out and empty.

Luckily, the core duties could be handled by Aidan, Cale, and himself. Rex, too. He was turning out to be a valuable acquisition. Before he'd been stranded on Undewla, the demon had worked with a crew, much like their own, and knew his way around a ship.

"Aidan," Sebastian called. "How many responses have we received from those transmissions we sent out?"

"Only a handful," Aidan replied. "But several of them are promising. A legion of incubi has already set out toward Evlon, according to their last communication. If we stay on schedule, they'll arrive a few days after us."

The stop at Uli Rings would be a short one. There Sebastian would put the word out that the ship was hiring mercenaries and any other battle ready individuals. After that, they'd meet with the Dragons of Legura, and then head off toward Evlon.

Aidan continued. "Another transmission from the Zerker mentioned possible aid, but I got the feeling they were divided on the matter."

"Let us hope they get un-divided." According to records, the Zerker race was an exponentially fierce, battle-hardened people, maybe even more so than the demons. "What of your clan? Have they responded?"

Aidan let out a heavy breath. "Yeah," he said flatly. "They're not interested." He assumed an air of indifference, though Sebastian knew he must be fuming. A clan he had once gone to great lengths to honor had too easily turned its back on him, and this last rejection was clearly a final slap in the face. Sebastian could relate. His own—once beloved—family had, in a sense, done the same.

"Perhaps the Legura clan will have more scruples, eh?"

The corners of Aidan's lips hitched upward at the snub. "We'll see."

The door whooshed open and Cale entered, a gleaming note in his eyes. He leaned against the wall with his arms crossed and his expression mischievous. "You're not going to believe this."

* * *

The weight of Ethan's impending doom bore down on him as he entered his room and kicked off his boots. He felt drained from the long day. And tomorrow would be even longer, unless the demons came for him tonight while he slept. But he doubted that. He imagined they would want him fully awake when they attacked, for amusement purposes.

Should've been more careful.

Earlier, he'd palmed Sonya's succulent backside while Cale and the others had sat just across the bar, completely oblivious.

To Ethan's surprise, she had responded positively, slithering the tip of her tail to tease his crotch.

Then, Jade, who wasn't even meant to take a shift tonight, had stepped behind the bar and caught sight of their actions. Sonya had offered Jade a dangerous look that, for anyone else, would have been a clear warning to keep their mouths shut.

Ethan supposed he should have gone after Jade when he'd initially read her intent, but for some reason, he allowed her to carry out her destructive mission. He imagined it was because he was tired of hiding his affection behind closed doors. Unfortunately, Sonya felt differently. She'd prefer to keep the liaison veiled from everyone until its inevitable end.

Nonetheless, it was too late. Thanks to Jade's big mouth and vindictive personality, their secret had probably already reached the ears of one of Sonya's kin.

He'd considered warning Sonya about what could potentially be a messy revelation, but he feared she would preemptively end things between them, as well as what she might do to Jade. Besides, there was a chance he'd be able to deal with the situation in a discreet manner. Sonya wouldn't even have to know about it, if he played his cards right.

First thing in the morning, he would approach Sebastian and Cale. If he went to them now, and found the news had put them in a rage, there'd be no talking to them.

He sighed. Even if they had a little time to assimilate the information, there probably would still be no talking to them, but it would be a relief to get everything out in the open. He just hoped he'd survived the wrath that followed.

For now, he intended to spend the night away from Sonya. If her brothers came looking for him tonight and discovered him in her bed, even his magic would not spare him their fury.

He shrugged out of his shirt and relaxed on the cold mattress, letting his muscles sink in and trying not to feel deprived of Sonya's warm heat next to him.

In an attempt to distract his mind, he wondered how Kyra was getting along with the book. He'd lent it to her shortly after her arrival so she could look it over. With no new information being revealed, it was of little use to him. He closed his eyes, worried what that meant.

Was this the end of his service?

The sisters were finally gathered, safe aboard *Marada*. The demons had volunteered to take over the next few steps—rallying allies and supporters to the cause—and the ship was on its way to Evlon with only a few stops at various space cities between here and there. What was left for him to do?

Fight, he supposed. And then possibly die in the process. The king's last words before sending him off planet repeated in his head. He could still feel the regal hand clamped on his shoulder as he'd said, "If you survive to carry out your mission, you will be made a prince among our people." The declaration had brought such honor to him, the like of which he'd never felt since.

From that point on, he had struggled to be worthy of his future bride. As a pirate, he must have been one of the most merciful to be sure, though he spread rumors to the contrary. A pirate needed his reputation, after all. Fear defeated opponents just as easily as warmongering or severing heads from bodies.

But it was the *if* in the king's statement that had haunted him over the years, spreading doubt through him like a virus. Which was why, aside from honing his gift, he'd spent years studying every manner of weaponry and combat.

The king's visions were never certain, and there was neither a guarantee Ethan would survive the insurgent, nor that any of them would be triumphant in the attempt.

But if they did succeed…

He thought of Kyra as his wife, the only unmated princess and the future queen of their people. He searched the depths of his soul for the pride he'd once felt for such an outcome, finding hollowness in its stead. Yet it was more than he had hoped for, wasn't it?

Then why had he not thought of that the moment Kyra stepped foot on the ship? Or, for that matter, informed her of the king's promise and initiated the courtship? He should have been ecstatic…doting on her and winning her affections.

However, when he imagined marrying her, excitement was not what settled in his gut. The weight of all his efforts, a lifetime of struggle, of fighting, with more still to come pressed down on him. Exhaustion plastered his body to the mattress, and his musings transformed into a foggy mist as his body gave over to sleep.

The sensation of others in the room woke him. Two sets of fire-red eyes glowered down at him.

"Get dressed, pirate." Cale's tone was as menacing as he'd probably intended. "We're going to have ourselves a little chat in the training room."

Right. Because that's the ideal location for a rational conversation.

Ethan blinked groggily and rubbed a hand down his face. So much for thinking they would want him awake. At least they hadn't yanked him out of bed and started whaling on him. After scanning them, he found less rage than expected.

He planted his feet on the floor and took a moment to stretch his muscles before making his way to his clothing compartment across the room.

While he rummaged for a shirt, Sebastian said, "I get the feeling you know what this is about."

Ethan turned back and quirked a cocky grin. "I'm surprised it took you so long to figure out what was going on. I thought demons were supposed to be intelligent."

They frowned, expressions turning dark. Cale spit out a colorful curse before taking an aggressive step in Ethan's direction. Sebastian barred an arm across Cale's chest. "Don't cripple him just yet. Marik wants a piece."

"Three on one?" Ethan retrieved a thin white shirt and slipped it over his head.

Cale's lips spread into a menacing smile. "Any last words?"

"Yeah. Don't expect me to go easy on you."

Both demons let out a guffaw.

Cale slapped him hard on the back. "This is going to be fun," he said before escorting him from the room by the back of the neck.

Marik awaited them in the training room with his arms crossed and his lips set in a grim line.

Ethan ignored the deadly stare as he crossed to the other side of the mat and prepared for the onslaught. The demons shared a look as they lined up in front of him. He suspected his calm demeanor baffled them. Most likely they were used to seeing males in this situation cower under their threatening gazes.

"Before we begin…" Sebastian hesitated, seeming at a loss for words. Finally, he said, "You and Sonya?"

It was a simple question with all the hidden layers of complication. Ethan responded with an overly exaggerated shrug. "What can I say? I'm irresistible."

Cale snorted and cracked his knuckles.

"But she hates you," Sebastian continued, somewhat unfazed by Ethan's cavalier attitude.

Ethan knew he shouldn't have responded with his next words, but his mind was still a bit foggy from sleep. Or maybe he was just unable to resist. With a sly grin, he muttered, "Not all of me."

There was a brief paused as the demons processed his response.

Then they attacked as one. Cale's claws swiped out while Sebastian's knuckles sought Ethan's face, and Marik lunged for his entire body. With the three of them coming so fast, Ethan was unable to dodge them all. Marik gouged his shoulder into Ethan's gut, taking him to the ground.

Air exploded from his lungs. As he sucked in a burning breath, Marik wrapped thick arms around him from behind and pulled him upright into a suffocating cage of muscle. Taking advantage, Sebastian cracked Ethan along the jaw. His mind dimmed from the force. Then Marik shoved him toward Cale, who introduced a hard knee to his gut.

Ethan slumped to all fours, grabbing his stomach and gagging for air. When he was able to speak, it came out as a haggard wheeze, "Well, I deserved that."

The demons glared at him, posed for another beat down, but they allowed him time enough to stand.

Marik commented, his tone detached from any discernible emotion, "I just can't believe Sonya would even be remotely interested in you."

Ethan steeled himself for the next assault, this one from Cale alone. He twisted his body away from the demon's powerful right hook, then ducked the vigorous high kick that came afterward. "And why's that?" he asked.

Sebastian rushed him. Ethan gleaned the intention and allowed Sebastian to catch him against his wide shoulder, preparing to heave Ethan over his back. Mid-air, Ethan contorted his body to land on his feet with perfect grace.

Sebastian looked momentarily surprised. "Well, we all dislike pretty much everything to do with pirates, but she's fanatic about it. Actually, I thought she'd end up killing you, not..." Sebastian shuddered, no doubt despising the images his train of thought brought forth.

Ethan now stood at the center of all three demons as they circled like a well-organized pack. He opened his senses to detect the next move.

Cale added, "The two of you together is the most unlikely development any of us could have imagined." He smiled. "A rare bit of fun, though. We don't often figure out who our baby sister is sneaking around with."

That gave Ethan pause, and he straightened his spine. "Sneaking around with?"

Do they not know?

His own question distracted him enough that Cale managed to get in another powerful jab to his jaw followed by a solid elbow to his temple. Ethan growled, mostly at his own carelessness, as the room spun.

"Sorry it has to end this way," Cale remarked, not sounding at all remorseful.

Ethan laughed. "You won't kill me." Just as Cale had said, they only wanted to have a *bit of fun* with him.

"What makes you think that?" Cale huffed.

"You'd miss me too much."

That encouraged a round of deep chuckles from all of them.

"Cale," Marik called across the mat, "he might just have a bigger ego than you."

"Only room for one as remarkable as I on this ship," Cale replied.

Another set of attacks from all three had Ethan pulling out his best defensive maneuvers. Damn they were fast, but he managed to stay ahead of them…barely. Luckily, they were becoming easier to read.

"One question," Sebastian said, looking impressed with Ethan's moves. "I still don't really believe it. How did you get past Sonya's defenses? She was not shy about expressing her extreme dislike for you. I had to force her to promise not to kick you off the ship while we searched for Marik, and still I figured she would wind up ending your life, one way or the other."

"Oh, she still hates me, I'm sure, but she could no more destroy me than you could destroy Anya."

The demons stilled. Sebastian looked completely taken aback, Marik appeared disbelieving, while, oddly, Cale's shock seemed to border on devastation.

Cale cleaned his features of all emotion but for a deep frown. "What do you mean by that?"

Whatever Sonya's reasons were for concealing the truth from her kin, they were bound to find out eventually.

Ethan shrugged. "Tell you what. If any of you can land another hit, I'll tell you."

"Too easy," Cale hissed. He shot forward, but Ethan was prepared and ducked out of the way. Cale stumbled, appearing confounded. Ethan thought he heard Cale mutter, "It can't be true," but didn't think he was talking about missing his target.

The other two sprang into action, coming at Ethan with all their speed. Now that he'd had time to study their moves, and the specific intent behind each one, it was easy to steer clear of the pulverization zone. The demons snarled with annoyance, but after a while, their frustration abated, and they began to see this as a game, rather than an execution.

* * *

All morning, Sonya felt off kilter. Normally she woke early enough to share a quick shower with Ethan before shoving him out the door, afraid one of her brothers might catch him leaving her room. But he'd decided to sleep in his own quarters last night, claiming he was tired.

She'd told him it was fine, but a bit of disappointment had crept into her voice. He'd managed to assuage some of it with a demanding kiss that had her squirming with carnal need.

His mocking grin told her that had been his intention.

Bastard.

Thankfully, after utilizing a few of her old tactics, the madness of her lust ebbed, allotting her at least a few hours of sleep.

She took a bit more care with her appearance the next morning, partly to flaunt what Ethan had missed all night. Well, mostly to flaunt it.

She dressed in an elegant purple and black bodice with brass buckle fastenings, a short dark skirt, and killer fuck-me boots. Next she styled part of her hair in an intricate braid, intertwining a bit of purple ribbon, while leaving the rest to hang in onyx waves down her shoulders and back.

Once satisfied, she traversed the long hallway of the ship's living quarters, coming to stop in front of the witchling's room. She gave a soft knock against the metal barrier and waited. A moment later, the door whooshed open, revealing the small Serakian on the other side.

Sonya introduced herself, unable to keep from peeking inside as she did so. There were multicolored vials lined across every surface in the room—the table, shelves, even along the floor. Each appeared to emanate their own ghostly light, bathing the walls in a vast array of color.

Portia stepped into the hallway, allowing the door to slide shut behind her. "Just a few experiments," she explained, "to keep up with my craft."

Sonya gave a polite, somewhat forced smile. She had no idea how Serakian magic worked and didn't really care to find out. "I came to ask if you would like to share the morning meal with me."

"Very kind of you, but are you sure? Most of the ship's inhabitants have been avoiding me."

It was no secret that most everybody on the ship wished the Serakian away. They were an ominous and secretive people, crafty and inquisitive. Many believed they gathered information like currency. To what end? Nobody knew.

"Just keep your spells off me and we won't have any problems," Sonya replied.

"Likewise, keep your weird mate-boding to yourself."

Sonya grinned. "I can't promise anything. You look like a real catch."

"Well, if that isn't the gods' honest truth. Give me a moment to recess my projects, and we'll be on our way."

As the door opened for Portia, an odd gust billowed from the room. "Uh, I'll wait out here, if you don't mind."

Portia nodded. "Good idea."

After Portia reemerged, they stopped by Kyra's chambers to see if she and the Earthling would like to accompany them. Zoey was nowhere to be found, but Kyra agreed to go along.

The salon was brimming with an unusually large number of people waiting for an empty table as Anya raced back and forth to fill orders, appearing frazzled.

Portia glanced around. "Is there some fantastic dish I should be aware of?"

"Not that I know of," Sonya replied.

Anya spotted them and hurried over, winding around impatient crew members.

"Why is it so busy in here?" Sonya inquired.

"Marik had to step away for a minute. Something about a meeting in the training room."

"A meeting?" Sonya repeated. *In the training room?* That was unusual. "Who's cooking then?"

Anya grimaced. "Myself and Nadua." A loud crash emanated from the galley, followed by a string of curses. "Oh, I think she burnt herself again." Anya rushed away, promising to return with something edible.

Sonya's brow wrinkled. Marik never left his post for a typical meeting—was never called in for one, in fact—and in the training room of all places?

When Anya emerged with a tray of three steaming bowls, Sonya asked, "What's the meeting about?"

Anya's head tilted to one side. "I thought you would have known about it."

"Why's that?"

"Because when Bastian and Cale came to get Marik, I heard your name mentioned."

"My name?" Sonya's chest constricted as Jade's smirking face flashed into her mind. *The chit couldn't be that stupid...*

"Yeah, and Ethan's. I figured..." Anya studied her, probably sensing the flood of rage that was working its way through Sonya's brain. "What is it?"

She balled her fists. "I will kill them."

Chapter 24

"Bullocks!" Cale bellowed after his third attempt at a sneak attack from Ethan's blind spot. Ethan was tempted to tell him it wouldn't matter if they'd blind folded him. He could still pinpoint their positions on the mat.

Like the flip of a switch, the mood shifted, and the demons straightened.

Ethan's attention went to the doorway where Sonya, Kyra, and the witchling stood gaping at them. Sonya's eyes burned fiery red while her fangs looked ready to gouge out all their throats.

What was wrong with him that he found *that* attractive?

"What do you think you are doing?" she snarled.

Sebastian huffed. "Look at you. It's true, isn't it?"

"No!" Sonya countered with a disturbing amount of venom. "It's none of your business."

"Of course it's our business. We look out for you."

Sonya seemed to grow even more furious. "I resent that! I can take care of myself. And I don't appreciate you trying to scare away the only guy who's ever had the guts to sleep with me."

Everyone went still as a heavy dose of shock swept the room. Ethan was now sure none of them had known she'd been untouched before him. Just as he was sure, judging by the fierce protective intent pouring off Sonya, that he was indeed her mate. Not that he'd had much doubt, even if she did wish to deny it.

"What?" Sebastian barked.

"You heard me. You scare away any guy who merely looks at me. And don't tell me it's not on purpose."

"Of course it's on purpose," Sebastian replied matter-of-factly. "But we never thought we actually succeeded."

Sonya frowned.

"Yeah," Cale added. "We just figured you were really discreet."

She reared back, face twisting as though she'd just had the wind knocked out of her.

Her expression pained Ethan. Struck by the strong need to comfort her, he came up behind her and placed his hands on her shoulders.

A sudden and undeniable realization slammed into him.

He would always move to stand by her, even if she rejected him in the end.

The demons studied him for a moment, as if his thoughts were telegraphed all over his face. In turn, they each gave a single nod.

Sonya bristled. "You're approving? You think I'm going to claim him?"

"You're not?" Cale hissed, as if that were an affront to him instead of Ethan.

"Why? So I can end up like you?" she spat.

Cale's lips peeled back, his eyes dangerously narrow.

Sebastian moved between the two and faced Sonya. "You're lucky to have a male who can take on three demons and walk away without a scratch. He's one slippery son of a bitch."

"I don't want that, and neither does he. Why would he, when he's supposed to marry a princess." Sonya gestured wildly at Kyra. Ethan had nearly forgotten she was there.

Kyra's jaw dropped. "What?"

Before Ethan could comment, Sonya replied, tone softer, "Your father made a deal with him. You're supposed to be married when this is over."

Kyra sank hopelessly to the floor, and a heavy layer of guilt twisted in Ethan's gut. To him, the arrangement was moot, but she shouldn't have found out like this.

"I have a theory about all this," Cale declared, drawing the attention of the room. His expression was unreadable, but Ethan sensed a dark roll of emotions billowing through him. "What are the odds that Sebastian and Marik find their mates so conveniently? And now Sonya…with a pirate?"

Sonya opened her mouth, presumably to protest yet again, but Sebastian cut her off. "What are you saying?"

"Our kind may be unnaturally attracted to Faieara."

Sebastian's face hardened. "I *love* my mate."

"As do I," Marik growled. Both seemed to be subtly cautioning Cale to tread carefully.

Cale continued heedlessly. "That may be true, but it doesn't change the facts. Think about it."

"What about you, Cale?" Sebastian challenged. "You were never attracted to Anya."

In a low, somewhat guilty tone, Cale answered, "Not like you were."

Sebastian's irises burned, and his fists clenched, causing the knuckles to whiten.

"Beat the shit out of me later, Bastian," Cale bit out. "Marik, what about Rex? Rex and Nadua?"

A dangerous silence followed the question before Marik replied, "If he was attracted to Nadua, he was wise enough not to tell me about it."

Cale then turned his gaze on Kyra, who was still slumped on the floor, her brows furrowed, eyes unseeing, skin paled. "I want her like I wanted…" He trailed off, but Ethan easily filled in the gap. Like he wanted his true mate. Cale continued, a hint of agony entering his voice. "But it's not real. It can't be. I'm mated and cannot possibly…I cannot truly be as attracted to her as I seem to be. I cannot want her at all."

Everyone was rendered speechless. Ethan knew he should say something to counter Cale's claim, but what?

Kyra pushed off the ground and scrambled from the room. Ethan wondered what had happened between her and Cale back on Earth, and how he could possibly not have seen this coming.

No, he knew how. If he'd been paying attention to Kyra at all, he would have gleaned her feelings for Cale before now, and vice versa. He'd been so wrapped up in Sonya that he'd ignored his other duties. Aside from translating the book, the princesses needed guidance with their magic.

"You should go after her, Cale," Sonya said.

Cale closed his eyes, and Ethan sensed he was struggling with the urge to do just that. "It would be heartless for me to further any contact between us."

"Well, you've got the heartless part correct," Ethan retorted with intentional harshness. "Do you have any idea how many rugs just got pulled out from under her?"

"Enlighten me, pirate," Cale sneered back, instantly posturing for another fight.

"Don't talk to him like that," Sonya snapped.

Ethan's brow rose, and he had to check a weirdly satisfied smile at the unexpected interference.

"Only I can do that," she continued, a little less zealous.

Cale belted out a harsh laugh. "Don't you see? It's happening to you too. You of all people...with a pirate?"

Ethan was growing tired of that word being used as a curse, as if he had some kind of disease. Exactly what was the issue, anyway? "Explain that," he demanded.

"Cale," Sonya said with a warning in her tone.

Ignoring her, Cale replied, "Our father was murdered by—"

"Stop it!" she screamed.

"She was there when—"

Just as Ethan sensed Sonya ready to attack, Sebastian grabbed Cale around the back of his neck and yanked him out of the room.

Marik crossed to follow them out, but paused and turned toward Sonya and Ethan. "Don't listen to him. If Ethan truly is yours—"

"He's not...We're not..." Sonya faltered, shoulders slumping.

Marik shrugged. "Well, whatever this is"—he motioned toward Ethan—"don't let your past influence you." There was an edge of experience to his words. With that, Marik exited the room, leaving them alone.

It took Sonya a moment to face Ethan fully.

He could tell she didn't want to talk about Cale's comments and wouldn't even if he asked. So instead, he decided to lighten the mood. "You rushed to my defense." He grinned.

Her chin jutted upward. "It's not what you think. I just didn't want to have to find a new employee for my pub while your guts were being scraped off the walls."

"Ah, of course. That makes more sense." He moved closer, placing his hands on her hips. He was thoroughly surprised when she laid her forehead against his shoulder and sagged as though relieved.

It felt too right to have her in his arms like this. His mind began to register every nuance of her body where it touched his.

She muttered, "I don't want to talk about it."

"I didn't ask." *At least not yet.*

"You want to, though."

"Yes." Knowing the small bit Cale had revealed made the guilt she felt for being with him understandable, but he wanted more. He wanted to know it all—so they could work past it.

She changed the subject. "Do you think Cale is right? About…"

"It's something I've considered."

"You have?"

"Yes, ever since I figured out you wanted to sink your teeth into me, and not just to tear out my throat."

She pulled back and narrowed her gaze. "That is never going to happen. I'd slit you from navel to nose before that happens."

"I've also figured out, the more you threaten my life, the

more you want me."

"You're delusional. And possibly masochistic," she said, yet she smiled and flushed.

"You may be right about that. It's a good thing I heal fairly quickly."

Her head tilted to the side, expression quizzical. "How is it you're so fast? I've never seen anyone dodge like that."

He grinned. "Another facet of my gift. A family trait, actually." He paused, debating if he should continue. Maybe if he revealed something he'd held private for so long, she would return the favor. "I'm able to read intent."

After a moment of contemplation, she replied, "You cheat?"

"Utilize my advantages," he corrected. His hand slipped to the small of her back to pull her a bit closer.

"Tell me then, what are my intentions at the moment?"

It wasn't difficult to discern. Blaring, in fact. "You intend not to let me kiss you right now, no matter how hard I try."

She smirked.

"And I intend to do a lot more than just kiss you."

Her eyes widened with a hint of desire before they turned calculating. "Game on then."

She twirled out of his grip and moved back with slow, measured steps. He followed, enamored by her adorably sly expression.

"Let's see. How shall I beat someone who can predict my next move?" she wondered aloud.

"An exercise in futility," he declared as he continued his approach, prowling after her in a wide arch around the mat.

"What if I didn't think about it? What if I just acted?"

Ethan smiled. That was exactly why he never told anyone about his special ability. It was too easy to come to that conclusion. "Acting without thinking is difficult to achieve, do you think you can manage—whoa!" He pulled back just in time to avoid a face full of knuckles. "I guess you can."

She circled him as he backed up. That near miss gave her too much confidence and when she struck out again, he saw it coming. He knocked her arm out of the way and then brushed past her, slapping her on the ass as he went.

The surprise in her eyes was swiftly replaced by acute determination. "Okay. I'm going to get this," she muttered.

He understood she wouldn't be satisfied till she did. After a few more attempts on her part, he formed a plan to give her what she wanted so he could get to what *he* wanted. He would let her have one shot to appease the fighter in her. Except, in the next instant, she actually did catch him off guard with a hard kick to his side. Her follow up move was easier to read, but he purposefully didn't dodge.

When she realized he was going to take the full force of her hit, she lost some of the power behind it. Still, it dizzied him for a moment, and he went to the mat.

"Shoot!" She bent over him. "I was sure you would see that one coming."

He clamped his arms around her torso and rolled her to the mat so that she was under him. Capturing her wrists, he brought her arms up beside her head.

"You cheater!" she cried, though she shook with laughter.

"Utilize my advantages," he said, chuckling as she offered a faux growl of protest.

He stared down at her for a long moment, enjoying the humor in her jewel-toned eyes. Had that color ever existed before her? He could believe it was created for her alone.

Her smile died, and she blew out a crestfallen sigh. "Look, Ethan—"

"I'm not asking you for anything," he interjected. "And I can already see the gears spinning in your head. Maybe not now, but soon, you'll latch onto the idea that your attraction to me has been caused by some unseen magical force as Cale suggested." He paused. "Just don't push me away when you do."

She pursed her lips. "It just doesn't make sense any other way."

"There's a lot in this universe that I don't understand, and I can't tell you it's not true, because I don't know. What I do know, is that the king intended for our paths to cross—all of ours, not just you and me. I have to trust he knew what he was doing."

"Well, I don't have to trust some king I've never met," she countered, yet made no attempt to push him off of her. Her head fell dejectedly against the mat. "So you think this is fate?"

"My kind doesn't believe in fate. Not in the way yours does. We believe in choices. Each choice leads us to where we should be. But, whereas one choice could send us on an easy path, another could have us clawing our way there, but the final destination may be the same."

"Isn't that just an abstract version of fate?"

"If that's how you want to look at it. Destiny might be a better word. With fate, you have no choice. What will happen, will happen. But you can always forsake destiny. Deny one, and you'll inevitably be given another. Such is life."

She contemplated that for a moment and then glanced at one of his hands still gripping her wrist. "You do realize you're still holding me down, don't you?"

"I believe you owe me a kiss."

"I thought you wanted more."

"I do." He lowered his head, holding back just before their lips touched. He could feel her heartbeat pick up. "But not here," he said, taking her lower lip between his teeth and applying a gentle pressure. Her eyes flashed, and he suspected her fangs were making an appearance. He lifted his head slightly. "I want you in a position where I can take my time."

She bit her lip, proving him right about the fangs. With a disturbing amount of desire—deranged hunger was more like it—he eyed that sharp little extremity. One day he would analyze the madness behind what he was getting himself into, but not today. He had much more interesting things to do today.

Chapter 25

The sound of general revelry filled the pub. Much of the crew had gathered and were talking excitedly about what they would do when they arrived at Uli Rings. It would be the first large space city any of them had seen in months. The anticipation was palpable.

Ethan remembered Uli Rings well. It was a lucrative spot—for those who knew their way around—and he was looking forward to revisiting his old hangout.

"After the meeting with the dragons, I'd like to show you around," he told Sonya.

"I've been there before," she replied as she washed a set of mugs.

"I know, but you probably haven't experienced some of the more entertaining aspects."

"If you're talking about the sector of bars, brothels, and clubs, then yes, I've seen that too."

He shook his head. "Nope, there's something I think you'll like better.

She huffed out an exaggerated sigh. "I've seen the dancing

ladies too." She wiped a spot on the bar clean before setting the cloth away.

"If I thought you liked dancing ladies, I'd have arranged a stage of them here while you were,"—he made air quotes—"sick." Then he took on a thoughtful expression. "Actually, that's not a bad idea."

"Don't even think about it." She shot him a threatening glare, then turned to engage a disappointed male across the bar who'd been eavesdropping. She raised a brow as if daring the male to say something in Ethan's defense.

"Ethan!" someone called from across the tavern.

He turned to see Kyra hurrying into the tavern. Zoey followed close behind her with a tight grip on the book.

"What's the matter?" he asked as they approached.

Kyra blurted, "Zoey can read the book. I had it sitting there, open, and she, well, she sees it in English. I think it's because of Portia's spell."

Ethan rocked back on his feet and then turned to the Earthling. "Is this true?" When she nodded, he demanded, "Show me." He retrieved the book from her and placed it on the bar.

Kyra provided the way in, and Ethan flipped to the first page that he'd been unable to translate. Zoey began reading something that sounded much like a missive. "Tarians of the dark sector near the dead sun Gizahn. Though our people know not of the other, our fates are intertwined. I, King Alastair of the Faieara planet Evlon, must implore you to take action against a most destructive enemy that will prove all-consuming if left to their own devises.

"The enemy I speak of is the enemy of all. These beings, who call themselves Kayadon, have enslaved my people as they systematically destroy my world, and once finished, will seek out others, such as yourselves, to appease their unending hunger.

"You will require proof, of course. As would I. Truth of their atrocities can be found among the demons, who failed to save themselves from extradition and near annihilation, their planet now barren. Knowledge of their plight is widespread and therefore easily confirmed."

Zoey glanced briefly at Sonya before continuing, "If, by some chance, you still doubt my words, then please ignore my entreaty and pray they do not find you." Zoey paused, meeting Ethan's gaze. "There's a long list of numbers after that."

"Transmission codes maybe," he said. "And possibly coordinates."

She turned the page and began reciting a similar note made out to the Vortian race. And then another to the people of Merose. She read through several more before Ethan stopped her.

"Come with me to the bridge. We must have Sebastian transmit these out as soon as possible." He turned to Sonya. "Do you mind if I escort them?"

"Of course not. Go." Sonya was surprised he'd even asked. Recruiting allies was far more important than slinging drinks. She only felt bad there wasn't more that she could do to help. However, once the fighting started, she'd be worth her weight.

Shortly after Ethan and the girls had left, Cale entered the tavern and took a seat across from where she stood at the bar. She locked her jaw and raised her chin.

"Have you seen Kyra?" he asked smoothly.

Her tail flicked with a flurry of irritation. She hadn't exactly expected an apology for nearly spilling his guts to Ethan, but she sure as hell deserved one. "Yes," she replied simply, in no way hiding her annoyance.

"Well, do you know where she is?"

"Yes."

He let out a peeved breath. "Will you tell me?"

"Nope."

He bared his fangs at her and glanced around as if Kyra would appear before his eyes. Then, with a note of alarm, he asked, "Where's Ethan?"

"Just like everything else, none of your business."

"Is he with her?" A muscle ticked in his jaw.

Sonya shrugged, but had begun to study him a little closer. He appeared more stressed than she had ever seen him. She was loathed to admit how much he resembled Sebastian fretting over Anya—and what that meant. "Does it matter?"

"No," he answered a bit too swiftly. A moment later, he added, "Dammit, Sonya, tell me where they are!"

Sonya tilted her head quizzically. Aggression rolled off him in waves, and she got the impression he was one breath shy of falling over the Edge…over Kyra. "It's true. You really are acting like she's yours…"

And because Cale was already mated, his attraction must truly be magically induced. She let slip a grievous breath, her heart sinking at the implication.

Cale stabbed his hands through his spiky blond hair, which was nothing less than a confession. "It feels like it. Yes."

If she knew he would have accepted it, she would have moved to comfort him in that moment. "Is it just as you remember? Like with Velicia?" The words tumbled from her lips by accident, and she mentally scolded herself.

But Cale kept a blank face at hearing his female's name. "Nearly. What about you? Isn't it driving you crazy that they are together?"

Sonya thought about that for a moment. She could imagine herself in a fierce rage over such a thing as Kyra entirely alone with her male. She stilled. *My male?*

Oh gods, it's happening to me too.

Covering the mental slip up, she shrugged. "Maybe if they were alone, but they're not." Which was nothing short of strange. She kept expecting to find Ethan sneaking into Kyra's room at night, rather than hers, or engaging Kyra in teasing conversation, wooing her, but it hadn't happened…yet.

But if that was what he wanted, she told herself she would let him go to Kyra without reluctance. At the thought, a protest gurgled up from somewhere deep inside, and she had to restrain a possessive growl. Thankfully, Cale didn't seem to notice.

She lifted one shoulder in a half shrug. "Then again, I've decided never to take a mate. It's too much trouble."

Was she trying to convince herself, or Cale?

"You wouldn't be saying that if it were real," he retorted.

Good point. Keep 'em coming.

"Then maybe your theory is correct," she replied, waiting for relief to swell. Instead, an overwhelming surge of sadness accompanied her words. She couldn't possibly wish it otherwise, could she?

A storm of confusion threatened her mind. In an attempt to distract herself, Sonya said, "That Zoey girl found something interesting in the book, so they're all speaking with Aidan and Sebastian about it in the control room."

"Why? What did she find?"

She popped open an ale and handed it to him. "Ethan said something about transmission codes before they left."

That seemed to pacify Cale for now. He took a long swig of his drink and stared at his bottle. After a moment, he mumbled, "It's strange, but if I could have claimed Kyra, I would have done so a thousand times already."

Sonya frowned at the sorrow-filled longing in Cale's expression—so opposite from the excitement he'd exuded when he had claimed his true mate.

Sonya couldn't help but wonder what that might feel like, to claim one's male...mate. Not for the first time, she imagined sinking her fangs into Ethan's soft flesh.

Tendrils of anxiety crawled up her spine, wrapping around her ribcage and clamping her heart like a vice. It wasn't the fear that unsettled her...it was the anticipation. She popped open another bottle for Cale, even though his wasn't quite finished with the first. After setting the drink down, she unconsciously began twirl a lock of hair between her fingers.

"What is it?" Cale asked.

She almost told him it was nothing, but instead replied, "I wanted to ask you something." Her pulse jumped at what she was about to say. "What is it like to claim someone?"

Cale swallowed hard, and she knew she had caught him off guard. Out of courtesy, they never spoke of such things with him. Not since Velicia's treachery.

After a long while, he answered in a steady tone that seemed forced, "It is pleasant. Like you and your mate are joined for an instant."

Pleasant? That's all? Sebastian made it sound like a mind shattering experience.

Cale flinched from the memory she had callously dredged up, and her heart cried for him. "I'm sorry, Cale. You deserved better." Velicia had proved unworthy of her brother—her family—in every way. Like many times before, Sonya wished she had ended Velicia, and their mother, before the three of them had hightailed it off their planet.

She snagged Cale's still-full drink and chugged the contents down. The burn of the alcohol was a welcome distraction from the cluster of emotions churning in her head. Unfortunately, it didn't last long.

She set the empty bottle back down. "What do you think I should do?"

"You know I can't answer that," he responded reasonably.

She wanted to yell for him to guide her, but a confession hissed out instead. "I've never been scared of anything like I am of this."

"I can tell. It's not a good look for you."

She glowered up at him and caught his teasing expression. Jabbing his shoulder with her fist, she grumbled, "Ass."

"Just being consistent," he replied, yet there seemed to be an alternate meaning behind his words.

She set to mixing a stronger drink and then handed it to him. "What are you going to do about your…situation?"

At length, he replied, "I have no idea." He downed the mixture in one smooth gulp, and she poured him another.

Typical of Cale, he brushed away his melancholy and took on an impish mien. "So…you let a pirate board your ship, huh?"

Sonya bristled.

"Plundered your booty, did he?"

"Ugh! You're such a pain!" She swiped her palm at him, but he bowed back, dodging the smack she'd intended to land on his temple.

Cale's grin widened. "Well, you're stuck with me, so you'd better get used to it."

Against her will, her lips curled. He always said that when he knew he was getting on her nerves. But what he didn't know what how much liked hearing it. That phrase eased a bone deep fear that she might one day lose one of her beloved brothers, just as she had Father.

* * *

Ethan leaned against a wall near the entrance of the control room, lost in thought.

In the book, there had been a little over a hundred different messages intended for a wide range of possible allies. All of the old allies had been included. Others were well known, but had never interacted with the Faieara before. And there were even a few new races nobody recognized.

There had also been instructions for Kyra to offer Faieara land in exchange for aid if she saw fit.

It was an odd bit of luck that the Earthling was able to decode what he could not. He considered the possibility that the king had anticipated her being magically gifted with the ability to read and speak any language. Perhaps he hadn't wanted the messages sent out before his daughters were safely retrieved.

It made sense.

If any individual in that long list of contacts decided to inform the Kayadon, then the Kayadon's efforts to find Kyra may have been doubled. Or they may have started seeking *Marada* itself, which may still happen. But finding a single ship in the vastness of space was nearly as impossible as trying to pluck a star out of the sky.

Hopefully the king's messages would bring them help, but Sebastian said he didn't want to rely on the messages alone. Ethan agreed. Within the hour, they were scheduled to dock at Uli Rings to speak with the dragons, a meeting that should prove interesting.

Zoey had pointed out an anomaly in the book regarding the dragon king. There was supposed to be a letter for him in the back of the book, but the page remained blank.

Aside from soliciting the dragons, they would need to recruit as many mercenaries as possible. Most of the current crew would be leaving the ship to avoid becoming involved in a potentially lengthy war.

Kyra sighed and straightened her spine. "I'll be in my room preparing. Please inform me when we are to leave."

Each day Kyra seemed to be closer to embracing the role her title demanded. If things had gone as they should, she would have made him a proud partner. Queen to his king. Still could. He wondered if that wouldn't be best for everyone in the end. The theory that Cale had put forth already hung heavy between him and Sonya. She tried to hide it, but he could see it in her eyes whenever she looked at him. She thought about it constantly.

"Zoey?" Kyra called back as she left. Zoey collected the book and trailed after her.

Ethan rushed after them into the hall. "Kyra."

Kyra halted and turned to him.

"I wanted to speak with you about what Sonya said. I'm sorry you had to find out like that."

She pursed her lips. "Yes, that was a bit shocking. Exactly what did she mean?"

"Only that your father promised me my choice of bride if I succeeded in bringing you all home. Sonya assumes that with your sisters mated that I will want you as my wife."

"And do you?" She raised a brow.

Ethan ran his hand through his hair. "The thought...the status it would bring me among our people...it was the driving force behind all my endeavors." He paused. "Now? I no longer know what I want."

She let out a weary sigh, her shoulders slumping. "That makes two of us."

He offered a smile, but it probably looked more sad than relieved. "Do you think Cale is onto something?"

She shrugged and averted her gaze. "Portia doesn't think it's true."

Ethan had forgotten about the witchling. Serakians could sense magic better than any other race he knew.

"She said love is not an emotion that could be forced. Rather, that it's a state of being."

"Love?" Ethan tilted his head.

Kyra's head jerked up as if stunned by what she had said. "I'm speaking about the demon mate thing, of course."

He recalled the way Kyra had looked at Cale in the training room. Like Cale had just placed a dagger in her heart. "Many demons don't believe love is behind the urge to mate," he countered.

Kyra frowned. "Hmm. To be forced to mate someone you may not even like? Sounds like a bad deal."

The words took him aback, and a dull pang gouged at the

pit of his stomach. He swallowed hard.

"Look, Ethan. I'm feeling a little nervous about this meeting with the dragons. You'll be there, won't you?"

"Of course. But why would you be nervous? You know them better than any of us. Didn't you spend a few years with them on their planet?"

"I did, but that was eons ago, and I never had to negotiate for aid."

"You'll do fine. I'm sure their alliance hasn't changed."

Kyra nodded, but her lips tightened into a thin line. "Alright, I'm going to get ready then."

"I'll stop by your room after we dock and escort you down."

"Thanks, Ethan."

Ethan hurried to his room to wash up and change, during which he could feel the deep rumble of the ship as it docked. It wasn't long before he and Kyra, followed by what looked like the rest of the ship's inhabitants, stepped onto Uli Rings. They were greeted by smiling workers dressed in colorful outfits as a nearby troupe played a happy tune.

The complex was a massive structure made up of three rings that spun to simulate gravity. The first ring was designed to receive ships, register newcomers, and offer quaint shops for those eager to part with their credits. The middle ring was dedicated to travelers, offering a vast variety of entertainment and lodging. The third was mostly staff housing, but there was plenty of fun to be had there as well.

As they crossed toward the registration kiosk, Ethan looked up at the tall arching ceiling that offered a clear view of space. Always an impressive sight.

Moments later, Zoey and Rex joined them in the registration line. The Earthling appeared about to burst with excitement. "I can't believe I'm in a friggin' space city," she squealed. "With...oh, oh, look." She pointed to a couple waiting a little farther up in line before lowering her tone. "Aliens!"

Kyra turned to her. "Technically, we're *all* aliens."

"I know, but they actually look like it."

Ethan regarded the couple's bulbous heads and bead-like eyes. They weren't the most odd-looking species he'd come across, nor the most hideous, but to Zoey, they were probably downright bizarre.

He craned his neck, searching for the rest of their group. He spotted Sonya standing a little farther back in line. Cale, Sebastian, and Anya crowded around her.

Sonya was watching him with those gorgeous violet eyes of hers. He shot her a smile usually reserved for the bedroom, making her flush. She swirled around to wiggle her backside at him as she fluffed her skirt. Then she finished with a lewd gesture and a teasing smirk.

Gods, she was sexy.

"Ethan." Kyra tugged on his sleeve. "Lines moving."

Registering went quickly enough, and they stepped aside to wait for the others. Kyra and Zoey browsed a nearby selection of trinkets, while Rex crossed his arms and leaned against a wall. The demon wasn't huge, but he still emitted a palpable warning for others to keep their distance. It was typical of most demons, as if menace was embedded in their anatomy.

Soon after the others joined them, Ethan noticed two of their group were missing. "Um, where're Marik and Nadua?"

"Nadua is still recovering," Anya replied blithely.

"Recovering? From what?"

"We were practicing our gifts in the training room," Anya explained, looking a little sheepish. "Nadua became overwhelmed, but she's okay. Marik is tending to her now."

"Why was I not informed?" Ethan growled, letting his gaze shift to Sebastian as a wave of guilt settled over him. All their lives the girls had been forced to bungle through their magic. Now they would feel pressure to stretch themselves and advance their gifts as quickly as possible. He scolded himself for not being there to guide them in the process. Pushing too hard could damage the mind, or even the body.

"We did not think of it," Sebastian replied, noting Ethan's outrage. "I will be sure it doesn't happen again."

Ethan gave a tight nod.

They moved to gather in a small transport unit that carried them through space toward the second ring. On either side, similar crafts ferried passengers to and fro. It was the only way to travel between the rings. Well, the only *legal* way.

The interior of the middle ring was just as he remembered: bright and clean, fauna climbing up the walls and dripping from the ceiling. Not many knew that each and every plant had been genetically engineered to be completely unique to all the universe, and that some of the flowers emitted a faint calming agent.

At first glance, the complex looked rather simplistic, but nothing could be further from the truth. Every bit of Uli Rings, from the expansive glossy floor to the placement of the soft overhead lights, had been designed for the specific purpose of making individuals feel privileged. As if merely being here inducted them into high society. And, naturally, those who immerse themselves into the upper-crust fantasy were more likely to spend like the elite.

The establishment, Between the Rings, was packed. Barely dressed males and females—surgically engineered for beauty—danced on raised platforms scattered throughout, while riveted onlookers drooled over the possibility of taking one of them back to their room.

A group of gamblers sat in the corner throwing bones. The combination of cheers and groans indicated the end of a round.

It wasn't difficult to spot the dragons in the corner. A set of guards stood around a table of four individuals, presumably King Mar and his sons. They each resembled the other in some way: regal with broad shoulders and all but one light in hair.

As Kyra crossed to the table, the four who were seated smiled at her.

The one with hair shaved short to his scalp stood and approached her. "Kyralyn, look at you. You've no' changed a whit. Beautiful as ever."

Alarm swept through Ethan, not because the dragon was reaching out for Kyra, but because he sensed Cale suddenly preening for a fight. He shoved Kyra behind him and bared his fangs.

Ethan stifled an irksome groan, knowing the dragons would see his actions as an affront.

Tension surged.

"What's this?" King Mar grunted. "Are we no' allies, Lady Kyra? Are we suspected of some kind of treachery?"

"Of course not, my lord," Kyra replied. "Cale, here, is just uninformed of our intimate acquaintance. Step aside, Cale."

Cale didn't back down. "Like hell I will. What do you mean by intimate? We're here to talk, not to pass you around to a bunch of dragons."

Ethan stifled the urge to shade his eyes with his hand, maintaining his composure. As queen, this was Kyra's show.

"You allow this guard to disrespect you in such a way, Kyra?" the dragon nearest Kyra said. "I could break his neck if you wish."

The shift would have been unnoticeable to onlookers, but the demons steeled themselves for battle. Ethan placed his hand on Sonya's shoulder, claiming her attention. "Calm him. We cannot have him ruin this meeting."

Sonya clenched her jaw, no doubt more concerned with defending her brother. Finally, she nodded.

"I wish only for peace," Kyra assured, maneuvering around Cale. "And he's not my guard. He's not anything, actually. Please, we mean no disrespect."

Cale frowned down at Kyra as if her words had wounded him.

The other male resumed his greeting by scooping Kyra up in what looked like a painful hug. Thankfully, Aidan and Sonya moved swiftly to hold Cale back.

When the dragon set her down, Kyra proceeded to explain how the demons had helped to rescue and protect her and her sisters. This impressed the dragons somewhat, enough that they forgave the slight, anyway.

Ethan observed King Mar focusing on Aidan. Though Aidan too was a dragon, he'd been born to a separate planet in their solar system, which was why his accent differed. Yet Aidan was something of a celebrity among all the clans. He'd participated in the intergalactic race, Phase Nine, and despite the record number of entries that year, he'd won.

After introducing King Mar's sons—Gavin, the firstborn, Tristan, the second eldest, and Lear, the only dark haired male— Kyra and Tristan began to reminisce like old friends. Cale's expression was dark throughout the exchange.

Sonya leaned in to whisper to him, "Maybe you should go back to the ship. We'll make sure she's safe."

"I'm fine," he muttered in a low, curt growl.

Sonya cursed under her breath and then gave Ethan a flippant *well-I-tried* shrug.

Ethan rolled his eyes.

King Mar gestured toward the table. "Sit, and let us discuss the reason for our gathering."

Once settled, Kyra began, "Do you know what's happened on Evlon?"

King Mar leaned back in his chair. "Vera little. We have been unable to establish contact."

Kyra proceeded to relay her family's escape from Evlon and her father's belief that they could win. "We're on our way to Evlon now to liberate my people, and if possible, save my father. Your clan has always been our most valued ally, my lord. We asked you here to implore you for any aid you can provide."

King Mar went silent for a long while. His sons watched him intently, as if they would abide by whatever decision he made. Finally, he spoke. "You know I have been friends with your father, Alestar, since before you were born." At Kyra's nod, he continued. "I am well aware that his predictions canna be counted on as fact. Alestar knew this as well."

"I agree, my lord. Which is why we come to you. We'll need

help if we are to succeed. The strength of your clan could be the advantage we require."

"You're talking war...with a technologically advanced culture."

Ethan narrowed his gaze at the dragon king just as Kyra responded in a reserved tone, "My lord, I never said they were technologically advanced

Ethan tilted his head at the dragons, trying to scan their intentions. It was clear they were hiding something, but he didn't think it was for malicious purposes.

"My King." Kyra straightened her spine. "You've been a cherished friend to me and my family. I've held great respect for you all these years, and I know my father has as well. We have never wronged you in any way, have always shown you graciousness and honor, and in return, you have done the same for us. Or so I believe. Am I wrong?"

King Mar shook his head. "Of course no', lass. Doona vex yourself."

"I call on your honor now, my lord. What do you know of the plight of my people?"

King Mar let out a breath. "It is no' what you think, Kyra love. We are…ashamed. Your father came to me in his ghostly form, long ago."

Ethan raised his brow.

"It must have been just after the attack," King Mar said. "He stayed with me up until the Kayadon found his body, describing what he saw. We know they came in large ships and displayed substantial power. He beseeched us no' to take action, but we could no' ignore the situation. We deployed seven ships. No' one survived."

Ethan recalled that terrible day. Dragon ships falling from the sky, burning to cinders at the hand of Kayadon crafts before hitting the ground. Till now, he hadn't figured out how the dragons had known come the Faieara's aid so long ago. The king had never mentioned contacting them. However, he did recall the king's palpable sorrow over the loss of so many.

"But that is no' what brings us shame," King Mar went on. "The reason your father came to me was to request I hide his bride and youngest daughter. Naturally I agreed, but during the transport, they disappeared. We searched for them but…" He trailed off, shaking his head. "We could no' track them down."

Kyra glanced at her sister. "Analia?"

Anya grew visibly uncomfortable. "It's a long story. One I don't want to get into. It no longer matters, and everything worked out as it was supposed to." She leaned into Sebastian, who put his arm around her and kissed the top of her head.

Kyra turned back to King Mar. "If you wish to make amends, then help us now."

"Our technology has improved since that defeat, but that does no' change the fact that our best ships had been decimated effortlessly. They had no' even made it to the surface of Evlon. How do you expect to defeat such an enemy?"

Kyra claimed the book from Zoey, opened it, and slipped it in front of Mar. "My father has given us information about the Kayadon that we can exploit. Ship schematics, weaknesses. He's mapped out their patrolling schedules and pinpointed windows of opportunity."

And so much more, Ethan thought. He had been floored by the amount of information that had made it into the book: Safe zones where Kayadon did not travel, possible Faieara refugee camps, easy access points to the surface. King Alestar had worked hard to give them the best advantages he could. But what if it wasn't enough? Ethan's eyes darted to Sonya, who was invested in the conversation.

King Mar's expression turned calculating, and Ethan suddenly caught the direction of his intent. Maybe it had been there the whole time, or perhaps only when the king had laid eyes on Aidan. Either way, there was only one stipulation that would sway the king. By the dark shadows in Aidan's expression, he was coming to the same conclusion.

The king hedged, "Still, my people and I would be risking much. If your plan fails, these Kayadon might target my planet, as well as the other clans."

Aidan interrupted in a harsh tone. "Why don't you tell them what you want, Highness?"

King Mar frowned before offering a thin smile. "Aidan Swantel of the Kanasae. Ousted, correct? As I recall, you once rejected an invitation to join my clan."

"I did. As I recall, the invitation came to me with conditions."

"Do you no' wish to reconsider?"

Sebastian leaned forward, placing his fist on the table. "What is this about?"

Aidan answered, "They want me to race Phase Nine in the name of Legura. And to do so, I would need to be a member."

Cale bared his fangs once more. "Is that the terms then?

Aidan races, and you'll offer assistance? With allies like you, it's no wonder the Faieara are still under Kayadon rule."

The dragons shot to their feet, preparing to defend their honor. The demons rose as well. Even the ever stoic Rex appeared Edge bound. Ethan shook his head, ready to kick himself for not anticipating this. Demons and dragons have never been known to get along in large groups. Their ideologies were too different, and they were equally stubborn. He should have finagled the meeting to include only Kyra and himself.

Kyra put her palms up in an attempt to calm both groups. "Everyone simmer down. No offense was intended, right Cale?"

"No, they took it right."

Rex and Sonya both snorted in laughter. Sonya looked as eager as any of them to throw down. If she wasn't involved and his people weren't in desperate need, Ethan would have politely excused himself and joined the surrounding tables that were now placing bets on a clearly impending brawl.

Kyra slumped in her chair with a vacant, lost expression. Ethan didn't know how to get everyone back under control either, but he did know that she needed to be the one to do it. She was the link that connected them all.

"We don't need these amphibians," Sonya announced. "They probably boast little more bravery than their own larvae."

Tristan sneered at her. "And you the intellect."

Ethan balled his fists and pinned the dragon with a death stare. New plan: Cale could hold Tristan down while Ethan punched.

"Enough of this," Kyra barked. "Enough!" But her plea was unable to break through the aggression that had pooled around the table.

"I'll do it," Aidan spoke above the noise.

Everyone went quiet.

Sebastian leaned back to study him. "Are you sure?"

"Yeah," Cale added. "We can proceed without these—"

"I'm sure," Aidan interrupted, probably figuring Cale was about to offer another slight. "I'll join the Legura and race Phase Nine one final time." He stared across the table at the king. "I choose my own crew and my ship, and when it's over you never ask me again. Win or lose."

The king debated, no longer concerned with the agitated demons. Finally, he gave Kyra a nod. "Then you'll have the full backing of our clan."

Kyra blinked twice before commenting. "Thank you."

Ethan nearly sagged with relief and offered Kyra a congratulatory grin.

She smiled back before asking King Mar, "What of the other clans? Would you be able to persuade them to join the fight?"

King Mar shrugged. "I will try, but I cannot guarantee it."

"I trust you'll do your best," Kyra replied. "Oh, there is one other thing." She shared a look with Zoey and then gestured to the open book. "My father indicated that there should be a message for you on the last page, but to us it is blank." She paused. "Do you see anything?"

Ethan leaned in, curious. Earlier, Zoey had mentioned the strange instruction from Kyra's father—a note intended for the dragon king—and they had all been concerned to find the page empty. But Ethan suspected Serakian magic hid an inscription.

The king looked it over. His eyes traveled as if there was indeed a message there. He frowned and then looked at each of his sons. "You canna read this?"

One of them craned his neck to get a better look. His brow furrowed. "No' at all,"

The king turned back to the page and continued reading silently. His face paled further, and sorrow took root in his eyes. When he closed the cover, he stood, appearing resigned. "We will take our leave to implore the other clans for aid. Till next we meet again." King Mar bowed and gestured for his sons and guards to take their leave.

Ethan let out a pent-up breath. All considered, the meeting hadn't ended as badly as it could have.

After the dragons were gone, Kyra threw her arms up and snapped at the group, "What the hell is wrong with all of you?"

"I thought that went well," Zoey said in a sarcastic tone.

"What do you think that message said?" Sonya asked.

"Whatever it was, he didn't like it." Ethan recalled the crease that had developed between his eyes as he'd read.

Rex seemed more concerned with a nearby dancer clad in a gauzy see-through ensemble. "Can we stay for a drink?" he said absently.

"I'm surrounded by madness." Kyra buried her head in her hands, and Ethan nearly laughed out loud. This was the norm, as far as demons were concerned. Their emotions swung like a pendulum. And if he was being honest, that wasn't necessarily exclusive to demons. He still felt aggression over Tristan's comment to Sonya, even if she had goaded him.

As if his thoughts had summoned him, Tristan reappeared without his family or guards in tow. "Is that what I'm getting myself into?"

Kyra's head shot up. "Pardon?"

Tristan claimed the seat beside her. "I've decided to ride with your ship...as mad as it apparently is. Mind if I buy the first round?"

Before another scene broke out, Ethan took Sonya by the hand and muttered, "Come with me."

She didn't argue as he led her away.

Sonya allowed Ethan to pull her out into the hall before inquiring, "Where are we going?"

"To recruit some mercenary friends of mine. If they're still around."

They wound through the crowds roaming the wide corridor. She vaguely noted that her hand was still intertwined with his, and it actually didn't bother her. In fact, she kind of liked the heat generated between their palms.

Remembering what those hands of his could do to her, she stifled a shiver and briefly wondered if there was a dark corner where they could hide away.

Ethan looked at her then, and a knowing smile graced his lips.

"How does your gift work, exactly?" she asked.

His grin widened. "It's not what you think. I can't read your mind."

"Says the man who just did," she countered.

"It's more like I sense them, or the desire behind them."

Oh, he just had to use the word desire.

"Then I play on what I know about who I'm receiving those desires from. For instance, I just got a very strong indication that you wanted to hide. And because I know it couldn't be caused by fear, and because I haven't made you scream my name in a while…" He let his conclusion hang in the air.

"What makes you think it's not from fear?"

"Because you're not afraid of anything, except perhaps things you can't kill."

She rolled her eyes. "What could I possibly fear that I can't kill?"

"Your adoration of me." He ignored her snort of laughter, continuing, "Your utter infatuation. It's okay if you want to idolize me as a god. It really is flattering."

"You are so full of it."

He paused and met her gaze, growing serious. "Of opening up to me."

A jolt struck her in the chest, and her mouth turned as dry as dirt on the surface of a sun.

His gaze shifted past her. "Ah, after you," he said, motioning to a transport unit awaiting passengers.

"We're crossing to the third ring?"

Hands still clasped, Ethan pulled her into the small space. His expression had become teasing again, which lightened her mood a bit. She didn't like that he continued to subtly pester her over things best left unsaid, but was relieved that he'd let the subject drop without much of an argument.

Oddly, that tactic was wearing her down swifter than a verbal blowout would.

The doors closed them inside, and the craft rumbled as it jetted away. A solid bench with a thin cushion hugged either side of the craft, and a ring of windows offered a stunning view. Ethan took a seat and tugged her down so she was perched on his lap. His eyes went directly to her lips.

"Ethan," she grumbled out a soft, yet unconvincing, protest.

"You have me all alone, *vietta*. Is that not what you wanted?" Smugness lifted one sexy corner of his mouth, but she stiffened at the word. What had he said it meant? Rotten female? Then why did he intone it like the sweetest oath?

With his eyelids hooded in that way that made her heart—and other parts—melt, he gazed at her now as if she was his wildest desire…and she loved it.

His tongue darted out to wet his lips, drawing her attention downward. Against her backside, his arousal came to life. Her body responded with a rush of warmth.

The moment he pulled her mouth to his, passion exploded in a frenzy as they drank each other in. With one hand around her waist, he clamped the other on the inseam of her thigh. She mentally urged him to move it a little higher, but he had a secure grip, kneading her soft flesh—which only served to drive her mad! She wiggled her hips, drawing an approving groan from deep inside him. She loved that sound. It meant that he was nearly as lost as she was.

When his palm finally started to inch its way under her skirt, the shuttle came to a stop, making her want to scream with frustration.

"Damn," he cursed, pulling back. Then he warned in a husky tone, "This isn't over."

Not by a long shot!

Disgruntled, she extracted herself from his hold just as the craft's hatch slid open.

Compared to the previous structure, the third ring looked depressed and stale. It was still clean and brightly lit, but there was no view of space, only a dizzyingly long hallway with a white arched ceiling. Windows were placed every so often on one side across from an endless line of doors.

People who Sonya assumed to be Uli Ring staff marched past, ignoring both her and Ethan.

"Follow me," Ethan said, striding down the corridor. The fact that his voice was still rough thrilled her, and she had to mask a self-satisfied smirk.

The hall opened to a large curved room that resembled a common area. A set of plush lounging chairs, a couch, and four small tables occupied the center. All along the inner U-shaped wall were several shops and eateries.

She followed Ethan into a place that looked like a mix between a recreation center and an entertainment room, where people were engaged in hologames and exercise contraptions. A group of four individuals were encased in a clear blocked off room smacking anti-gravity balls with rounded clubs. A soft *thunk* vibrated every time a ball made contact with a solid surface.

Ethan led toward a darkly lit back room. Once inside, her jaw dropped, and she lost her breath.

A grandstand encircled the entire room and led up to the high, domed ceiling filled with multi-colored lights. In the center of the cavernous space was a great circular ring with two massive...mechanical beings...locked in a gritty scrimmage. The sounds of metal smashing against metal hummed in the air, stroking Sonya's carnal nature.

Why were there only but a few individuals seated in the stands, watching these two towering beasts go at it? And most of them looked...bored! *When I would pay just to watch this!*

Was that why Ethan had brought her here? Was this his idea

of a date? *Because if so, nice choice, pirate.*

On the sidelines, two small opposing groups grew ravenous over the action. Well, that was more like it.

"What in the world…" Sonya trailed off as the larger of the two mechanical fighters landed a bone shattering hit against the other.

Crunch.

Sonya shrieked with delight, her tail dancing in anticipation for more.

Ethan smiled. "Fights are staged here sometimes, but this is more of a practice area for those who hope to enter the RCFO."

"RCFO?"

"Robot and Cyborg Fighting Organization. The real stage is back on the center ring."

"Are those cyborgs then?"

"It doesn't look like it, but it's hard to say. Some enthusiasts have gone so far as to have almost all their body parts switched out for prosthetic. I knew a fellow who was nothing more than a brain inside an artificial shell. Great fighter though."

The smaller robot heaved the other into the air and then sent it to the mat in a harrowing crash. When the larger robot failed to get up, Ethan pointed out a cluster of males near the edge of the ring with their arms raised in a victory cheer.

"Those are our guys."

Sonya looked them over. They all had somewhat short, dark hair and physically fit physiques, though they didn't appear to be related. The one that seemed to be displaying the most aggression, with chest bumps and congratulatory slaps on the back, wore a sleeveless black shirt. A scruffy jaw full of dark stubble flanked a fat stogie resting between a set of straight teeth. Four other men stood next to him, and from what she could tell, they all sported a similar tattoo high up on their left arms, although two of the male's arms were concealed by dingy jackets.

Mr. Stogie caught sight of them. "Hey!" He threw his arms out wide, as he crossed the room with long strides, but the gesture was not exactly welcoming. "What've we got here? I know that can't be the Pirate King. Because after skipping out with about ten thousand of my credits, the Pirate King would be a sodding idiot to show his face here."

Sonya shot Ethan a look.

He was utterly relaxed. "Didn't I pay you?"

"No." The male stopped just feet away, his entourage close behind. Sonya balled her fists. After the volatile dragon meeting, and then Ethan's teasing, she had quite a lot of pent-up aggression to let loose. These men were practically signing up for a beating.

Ethan replied without a shred of concern. "Must have slipped my mind what with that angry mob chasing after us and all. Why was that again? Oh, yes, you got us pinched for cheating at bones."

"*I* got us pinched? You were the one fixing the deck."

Ethan paused, looking thoughtful. "Oh, yeah. Too bad you failed to pocket the credits before you started fleeing in terror. By the way, you scream like a little girl. I've been dying to tell you that."

Stogie narrowed his eyes.

Sonya waited to see who would make the first move. If it was Ethan, she would let him do his thing, but if it was the other male, she would be happy to relieve him of his spleen.

No one moved. For a long while, they stared daggers at each other.

Then the harsh planes in Stogie's face eased into a smile. "You *todger*! What are you doing here?" His arms flew out and he forced Ethan into a tight hug, nearly lifting him off the ground.

Instead of answering, Ethan said with a grunt, "Nice fighter you got there. Is it a contender?"

Stogie released Ethan and then stepped back. "Getting there. Only a few more practice rounds like this, and I'll catch the attention of the RCFO."

"I wish you luck."

"So what's with the unannounced visit?"

"Remember, you still owe me a debt." Ethan paused, as if letting the weight of that statement sink in as he glanced back at the ring. The defeated robot was being hauled aside with the help of a crane-bot. "What if I had a better deal for you, with a bigger payout?"

Stogie arched a brow. "I'm out of the business," he replied cautiously. "No more pirating."

Sonya ground her teeth. "You said they were mercenaries, not pirates."

All eyes turned to her.

"Who's the tail?" one of the men in the back drawled.

"The incarnation of your darkest nightmares," she shot back at him.

Deep chuckles erupted.

"Girl's got a mouth on her," Stogie said, quirking his lips into an appreciative smile. "A pretty mouth." Then, stupidly, he reached for her.

Ethan swept the barrel of a gun up to rest against the underside of Stogie's jaw.

Sonya's eyes flared. "How did you get a gun past security?"

"Oh, we pirates have our ways," he replied. "Isn't that right, Ivan?"

It was then that Sonya realized Ivan, too, had a gun…and it was shoved into Ethan's gut.

The Edge engulfed her before she even realized. Pure fury ate through her veins.

Ethan spoke in a reasonable tone. "Let's settle down now, boys, or my female is going to rip out your throats."

No one seemed to take his advice.

As Ivan's men moved in, Ethan called, "Baby, try not to hurt 'em too badly."

Chapter 27

Ethan wasn't sure Sonya had heard him, fearing she was beyond reason. Fire had chased away the beautiful violet of her irises, and her small horns burned molten. There was no way she wasn't fighting someone at this point. If he hadn't experienced her prowess first hand, he might have been worried for her.

Ivan shot Ethan a curious look coupled with an intrigued smirk, but did not lower his weapon. He wasn't fooled by Sonya's small stature, if only because he knew firsthand that Ethan would defend any female who couldn't handle themselves.

His men, however, weren't as intuitive. Their expression indicated all they saw was a wisp of a female challenging four large males. Her size gave the impression that she was an easy mark, when in reality, it lent itself to her swiftness. She was faster than even her more physically endowed brothers. However, with Ivan jabbing that piece into his side, it was still four on one.

When Ivan's crew moved into range, Sonya struck first and with intense speed. Her leg came up high above her head, cracking the closest male on his crown with a downward vertical kick. He went to the ground jaw first. She thrust her fingertips into the jugular of the second male before shoving her other palm hard into his stunned face. The third swung his fist out, missing as Sonya craned her head to the side. She twirled her body, bringing her elbow up to slam it into his temple. He fell. Then she kicked off the ground and jumped toward her final opponent, clamping her thighs around his neck. She threw her torso back, planted her palms on the ground, and hurled the male several feet into the bleachers.

In her crouched position, she turned her lava gaze on Ivan.

Ethan openly gloated as he told Ivan, "You're going to want to put your piece away."

He did, slipping it into a holster hidden in one of his many pockets. Ethan stowed his weapon as well before stepping into Sonya's line of sight. She peered around him, still intent on her target.

"Okay. Come back now," Ethan cooed, placing his palms on the side of her face. She scanned his features in an animalistic manner, tilting her head to the side. Slowly, the fire drained from her eyes, replaced by that jewel-tone color. She blinked twice as if coming out of a trance.

"Hooey!" Ivan burst out. "That is one wild female you have there."

With slow movements, his men began pulling themselves off the ground.

Sonya took her gaze off Ethan to glare at Ivan.

Most of the men were laughing off the defeat, rubbing their bruises, all but the one who was gushing blood from his nose. He started limping, as if heading for the door behind Sonya and Ethan, which caught Ethan's attention. Sonya had done nothing to his leg, and his movements were too deliberate.

"So what's this big paying job you're offering?" Ivan coaxed.

Sonya replied, still surly from her trip to the Edge, "At this point, it doesn't look to me like you or your boys would be of any use."

Ivan ignored the insult. "We're known for our stealth work, quick take downs, not hand to hand combat, darlin'."

Ethan kept the male in his peripheral vision as he maneuvered behind Sonya. In the next moment, malicious intent slammed into him, and he moved without thinking.

Cold steel slipped into his gut. Sonya cried out from behind him. Swifter than Ethan's pain-filled mind could comprehend, she twisted around him, grabbed the attacker by the head, and wrenched till a resounding pop rang out. The body fell limp.

Then she flipped to face Ethan, snatched his gun from its holster, and pointed it at the other males as she desperately held him against her, their front smashed together, his wound dripping between them. Possessive claws pressed into on his back.

"Whoa! Whoa! Whoa!" Ivan and the others yelled, putting their palms up.

"I did not sanction that," Ivan added in a rush, glancing at the dead man without any hint of remorse. "That was a dirty double cross. Ethan, you alright, mate?"

Ethan put his arms around Sonya and pulled her tighter into his chest, partly to obscure the light that accompanied his healing magic, but mostly because of the utter relief he felt to have her there. Though that blade had sliced him high in his stomach, and, to him, the wound was minuscule, it would have gone right through her torso...straight into her heart.

She kept one arm around him with the gun still trained on

the men behind him. Her chin could have rested on his shoulder, but she was too stiff in his arms. She was probably back on the Edge, deeper than before. In a confidential voice, he whispered calming words to her, things he would do to her later when he had her alone, all the while breathing her in as his magic went to work on his wound.

After a moment, her body softened, yet her aim stayed true. His wound began the process of knitting together. Once fully healed, he let go of Sonya and turned to the others. "What kind of slime are you recruiting these days, Ivan?"

"He should not have done that. I apologize for his actions and hold no ill will for his death. You're female did right."

Ethan felt the honesty in his words and gave a tight nod, noticing a few spectators were now focused on them.

"They're fine," Ivan assured, following his gaze. "We're all friends here. But can you have her lower the weapon?"

Sonya still looked irate, her finger tight on the trigger. Ethan placed his palm on the top of her wrist and applied a gentle pressure. After only a slight resistance, she dropped her arm.

"Koda," Ivan called to one of his guys. "Get rid of the body, yeah?"

* * *

Sonya willfully disregarded the repeated apologies Ivan offered her, wanting only to get Ethan back to the ship. What was he thinking approaching these low-lives? She mentally cursed herself for not realizing what that reprobate with the fake limping act had been planning. She wished she hadn't made his death so quick. Her blood still burned for revenge.

How could Ethan have placed himself in harm's way like that?

Just imagining losing him to men like these had her wanting to seize that weapon back from Ethan to eliminate the bastards.

But there was an ignorant, inebriated crowd around them now. They'd relocated to a small bar area next to the recreation center, and Ivan had bought them a couple rounds. They were well into their third when Ethan began to explain the situation on Evlon to Ivan, as well as the proposition the Faieara king had inscribed into the book. Patches of land, rich with precious stones, were to be bartered to anyone who required compensation for their assistance in defeating the Kayadon.

Now Sonya realized why Ethan had come here. Anyone he was acquainted with would demand a hefty payment for their services.

"Look, Ethan, I feel for the plight of your people. I do," Ivan said. "But I could either stay here safe and sound, fighting my robot, or I could go with you and potentially get killed. Which would you choose in my position?"

Ethan frowned. "Your skills with a ship are unmatched. Nothing could ever touch you. Tell me you don't miss the action."

"Of course I miss it," Ivan responded with a dismissive wave. "But do you know how long we've been working on that machine?"

"With what I offer, you could buy a thousand bots ten times better than that one."

Ivan sat back in his chair. "But the risk is ten times greater." He shook his head. "I need another drink." He stood and made his way to the bar. More likely than not it was an excuse to consult with his three lackeys who were flirting with the buxom server.

Sonya leaned close to Ethan. "Do we really need these guys?"

Ethan nodded. "Ivan has access to fleets—not *a* fleet—*fleets* of war ships. He's the leader of the largest mercenary syndicate I've ever seen."

"So now he's a mercenary again?"

Ethan grumbled, "We started off together as pirates, yes. That's not the point. With him, our chances of defeating the Kayadon greatly increase."

Sonya rolled her eyes, and Ethan glared at her. She pursed her lips, returning the expression, but she could see the determination behind his eyes. She had to admit, a fleet, or rather, fleets, of ships did sound like a pretty great advantage.

She sucked back the last of her drink and then slammed the bottle down on the table. "You want him, fine. I'll get him."

Ethan raised a quizzical brow at her before his gift informed him of her plan. "Wait. No, no, no."

"No what?" Ivan returned with a fresh drink in hand.

Sonya challenged him with her gaze. "What if you didn't have a robot to fight?"

Chapter 28

Ethan begged Sonya not to do this as Ivan ordered his men, "Tak, Koda, get the bot ready for another battle."

"Who's the opponent?" Koda asked blithely.

Ivan responded with a deviant smile.

Ethan shot to his feet. "Ivan, do not do this."

"The lady has set the challenge," Ivan replied with a tone of finality, and then headed out of the bar with his men.

Ethan turned to her. "Sonya, this is insane."

She shrugged and followed behind Ivan. "What's insane is bringing me among a group of pirates and expecting me to be docile."

He groaned furiously. *Note to self.*

Back in the arena, Tak and Koda readied the machine as Ethan tried once more. "Please, you don't need to do this."

Sonya shot him a sweet smile, and he gritted his teeth, feeling her resolve. "I'm not afraid of a hunk of tin."

Ivan called from the side of the ring, "It's set for light damage only and to pin, not kill." Then he added ominously, "But I'm not responsible if something goes awry. It's designed to battle machines twice its size, not cute little girls with hot arses and killer moves."

Ethan grabbed her by the hand as she moved to enter the ring. "Sonya, please."

She leaned down and planted her lips on his, and chirped, "Kiss for luck." Then she pulled away from his grasp.

The sight of her next to the steely bot had him frozen in fear. She looked even smaller than normal with the hulking machine more than three times her size coming to a stand. His gut flipped and pinched so badly he feared he might vomit.

Might as well have another blade sliding through my organs. The pain would be the same.

The machine took a hefty step forward. Its shoulders were bulky and wide, making the head look small and out of proportion. Its arms and legs were twice as thick as Sonya's body, the metal mechanics exposed and bulging like living muscle. Ivan had attempted to make the thing fashionable with strategically placed purple and black embellishments racing along the few flat pieces of the metal that doubled as body armor, but it still looked gruff with countless nicks and dings, no doubt from numerous battles.

Battles won!

Sonya stood looking up at the bot as if it were just a bug to be squashed instead of an eighty ton death machine, her black hair falling in waves down her back.

This can't be happening!

"You've got one hell of a female there, Ethan. Although, a bit addled, no?" Ivan said from behind him. "I'll give her one round before I stop this."

That did nothing to ease Ethan's mind. He was helplessly

transfixed as the bot began the fight. Its great massive arm descended toward the mat right above Sonya.

A painful bellow stuck in his throat.

Sonya dodged the bot's first strike easily.

The thing was slower up close than it had looked from afar. She determined the only way it could land a strike was if it caught her by surprise.

Gripping a thick band in its still down-stretched arm, she swung her legs up and planted her feet atop the wide appendage. Then she climbed the length to its shoulder, positioning herself by the head. Rearing her fist back, she slammed through one of its orange glowing eyes.

The bot reached for her, metal groaning as if in pain. She knew it wasn't, but it made her feel better to imagine it was so. Dodging its grasp, she shuffled along its upper back to the other side of the machine's thick shoulder, intending to take out the second eye.

This might turn out to be easier than she thought.

In a surprising move, the bot sprang up and flipped itself over to drive the shoulder she was perched on into the mat. *Spoke too soon.*

Just before she was crushed under all that metal, she pushed off with her legs, landing oddly and hastily rolling to a stand.

The bot's free arm arched toward her. She quickly planned her next move, but a burst of flares erupted from the bot's elbow joint, increasing the speed of its swing.

Metal knuckles bashed into her torso. The air jettisoned from her lungs in a harsh burst. Her body was propelled back, landing hard on the mat.

She forced her eyes to focus.

The machine pushed to its full height and targeted her again. Mustering her strength, she rolled out of the way, still gasping for oxygen as its hammer-like fist smashed down where she had just been.

It was easy to call on the Edge since she had so recently evoked it twice, and she embraced the burst of energy it provided. As the machine came at her again, she jumped to her feet in a twisting move that took her from its destructive path. The mat rumbled under her.

Catching her balance, she raced straight at the bot and then slid feet first between its legs, slicing a thick exposed hose near its heel with her claws as she went. Compressed air hissed out of the now writhing tube, but it didn't seem to cause much damage.

She jumped to a stand. The bot turned toward her, its single orange eye boring down where she stood. Raising both of its huge, shining hands together, it brought them down fast and hard. This time, she anticipated the tricky blast of extra speed and dove out of the way. When the blow collided with the mat, she once more leapt onto its bicep, intending to scramble to its back.

The damn thing rose up fast and then shook her off. As she tumbled through the air, she was caught mid-fall by the rocket-induced speed. It was like a one-two punch. Metal met flesh, causing her mind to blank. The second hit came when she bounced off one of the taut oversized ropes of the ring and landed face first into the mat.

Although she was badly dazed, instinct told her to move and move now! She rolled to the side, her vision tunneling. Next to her, the mat vibrated harshly, springing her into the air.

She could hear Ethan yelling from far away, but could not make out what he was saying. He sounded in pain. She realized then that she had left him with those pirate mercenaries. They could be doing anything to him while their bot kept her busy.

While she was helpless.

Her mind was transported to a dark corner inside a small crawlspace where terrible sounds brought tears to her eyes. "No!" she screamed. Loss and regret conspired with helplessness to bring forth a deluge of boiling rage.

Ethan screamed for Sonya to get out of the ring as panic flooded him. She'd taken some pretty harsh hits and was shaking her head hard as if trying to come out of a daze. He couldn't even glean the machine's next moves to yell out at her.

Word of the unorthodox fight must have spread through the complex because the stands were quickly filling up with excited onlookers.

He didn't give a shit about any of them.

"Sonya! Get up!" he pleaded, banging his palm on the mat.

She did, but he didn't think it was because of his desperate cries. She'd gone fully demonic, her horns and eyes aflame, her fangs descending. She met his gaze for only a second as the bot's massive raised foot barreled down on her. She gracefully flipped backward, avoided the crushing hit, and then latched on to its calf. With a chilling war cry, she dug her claws in past the cords of metal. Oil spewed in an arch, coating her to her shoulder and spilling onto the mat.

The bot lifted its fist and brought it down, crushing part of its own leg trying to get to her. More black liquid spewed.

Ethan's heart stuttered, chest squeezing. Then he spotted her holding onto the bot's forearm as it began rising into the air, her body dangling straight down. When she was high up off the mat, the machine pulled its other arm back and engaged the rocket thrusters.

She vaulted her legs up, flipping her body around and coming to rest on top of the bots arm in a squat. With the power of the thrusters, the bot was unable to alter the path of his swing, and the hit flew past where she had been moments ago.

She let out a raging snarl and launched towards the bot's head, thrusting her fist into its remaining eye socket. The machine made a grinding noise of protest. Yanking her hand back, she crawled to its shoulders and planted her feet on either side of its head. Then she cocked her fist and brought it down hard, penetrating the apex of the shiny metal skull. The orange light that still flickered from one of its ruined sockets died out as Sonya ripped free a handful of wires covered in black ooze.

The machine toppled chest first to the mat, and she rode it to a stop, never losing her balance.

The room went silent. Even Ethan had lost his breath. Sonya's chest heaved with exertion as she fisted the machine's innards in her hand. Nothing had ever looked so terrible or so beautiful.

A deafening roar erupted from the crowd, shaking Ethan free of his stupor. He rushed onto the mat and grasped her in his arms, cursing her for making him sick with worry and thanking the gods she was alright.

As Sonya inhaled the deep musky scent of Ethan, unimaginable relief washed over her. He was alright...and yelling at her.

So what else was new?

"Holy crap! I should have charged for that," Ivan bit out as he approached them on the mat. "That was the most—"

Ethan let go of Sonya and turned to crack Ivan hard across the jaw. Ivan stumbled back, landing against the outstretched arm of his broken bot.

"Okay," Ivan said, rubbing the side of his face. "I'll give you that one."

"It could have killed her!" Ethan shrieked, stalking toward Ivan.

"But it didn't. And now I'm out one bot. Tell me there's more where she came from! I mean, I figured she was one tough female, but *that*? That, I was not expecting."

Sonya glanced around. The crowd was still high from the fight, some of them offering a play by play to those who were just now arriving. Noticing the oily wires and goop in her grip, she flung the mess to the mat. It landed with a squishy thud.

"Well, this outfit is ruined," she commented, looking down at herself.

"You're worried about your clothes?" Ethan snapped. "Of course! I must be insane. Forgive me for not asking! How are your clothes? Are they hurt?"

"Just sore," she assured with a rakish grin. "They'll probably have a few nice bruises in an hour."

Ethan pinned her with a hard stare. "Don't ever do something like that again."

She raised a brow. Never would she promise something so ridiculous. Ethan ground his teeth, realizing it as well. Yet something in his expression made her study him closer.

"You were really worried for me?"

He reared back as if she'd slapped him rather than asked a simple question. "Of course. Did you think I wouldn't be?"

She shrugged. "You shouldn't be. It would be easier for you if I—"

"You think I should prefer you dead?" He stepped away, his eyes wild.

Sonya blinked, confused by his sudden outrage. She wasn't sure exactly what she was trying to say. It was all too clear that her body longed to claim him, and that should alarm him. It alarmed her! The fact remained: he would soon begin courting Kyra. And yet, if he continued to gaze at Sonya the way he had been over the last few weeks, continued stroking her desire to fevered heights…she might be forced to cut a bitch.

Even if said bitch was likable.

It would dishearten Ethan if she did anything to harm Kyra. But if Sonya became any more attached…if she allowed herself to fall for him as she feared she was…she wouldn't have a choice. The instinct to claim her mate would become too great. She could feel it creeping over her even now.

He had to know the danger.

She tried again, "All I'm saying is it would just be easier, and—"

Before she could finish, Ethan whirled around and climbed out of the ring, not stopping his retreat till he was out the door. She glanced at Ivan as if this stranger would hold the answer to Ethan's behavior.

However, Ivan was looking at her as if she were the next big thing. "You must fight for me. I'll pay you well, the best of everything."

"Not going to happen," she hissed. "So, your bot's scrap

metal. Will you help us now or not?"

"*Lun feist*, I will follow you anywhere."

* * *

Ethan waited for Sonya to join him at the transport unit, fuming. He couldn't imagine a time when he had been so furious in his life. She thought he wouldn't care if she died! More accurately, that he should be happy about it—figuring he would be relieved to be free of her. Free to court another.

What the hell was wrong with her?

How could she believe he could want another? Admittedly, he hadn't spouted any sappy declarations of love or anything, but didn't he make up for that every time they were together?

A dark suspicion invaded his mind. Was she projecting her own desires onto him? Did she want to be free of him? His fists clenched. Of course she did. She made no secret of that fact. She'd been appalled from the start to find he was her mate.

A lowly pirate.

Peering down the hall, he caught Sonya's approach and hated that he couldn't keep his eyes off the sway of those curvy hips. Hips that were always soft and relenting under his touch. She was still partly soaked with black oil, which had carved out small rivers down her slender arm to her fingertips. Even filthy and fresh from a fight, even as angry as he was with her, she had him standing to full attention.

By the gods, could he be any more pathetic?

Ivan and two others followed behind her like newly acquired pets.

"So, you're joining us, then?" Ethan muttered abrasively.

"A deal's a deal," Ivan replied, eyeing Sonya as though he were in love.

Ethan ignored the violence that stirred inside him. "Then let's go."

All the way back to the ship, Sonya watched Ethan with open curiosity, while he avoided looking at her altogether. She was so used to having his undivided—if sometimes unwanted—attention, being without it caused an odd feeling to bloom in her stomach.

Standing near the ship's entrance, Sebastian spotted them. "Where've you been?" he inquired, then eyed group of mercenaries.

Ethan marched past him into the ship without answering.

Sebastian turned to Sonya with a what-the-fuck expression.

"Beating up a robot," she offered flippantly, then added, "Found some mercenaries in the process." She peered past Sebastian, seeing Ethan disappear around a corner. Absently, she introduced her flock. "Ivan, Tak, Koda, this is your new captain, Sebastian."

Ivan gave a bow with a flamboyant wave of the hand that screamed of insolence. Adhering to authority wasn't going to be the mercenaries' strong suit, but at this point it wasn't submission they needed, it was warriors.

To Ivan, she said, "Sebastian will show you around. Excuse me." She disregarded Bastian's stunned expression as she hurried into the ship, calling after Ethan.

He did not acknowledge her, merely continued on his way.

"I don't understand your anger," she said, closing in on him.

He turned on her, a slew of emotions flexing behind fierce eyes: wrath, indignation, outrage...but the one that sliced through her heart was anguish.

"Would you be happy if *I* were dead?" he snapped.

The question stopped her dead. For a moment, she couldn't speak, and when she was finally able, all that came out was a quiet, "What?"

"If I were gone, out of your life, would you like that?"

A baffling pain shrouded her chest, spreading like the oil slick that coated her right side.

"Well!" he bellowed, his voice so loud it shook her eardrums.

How was it she could have no qualms about battling a massive killing machine, yet this male so easily terrified the courage right out of her?

He waited for her answer, his expression darkening with every muted second.

She wanted to tell him: *Hell no, I don't want you out of my life! I'm hopelessly addicted and possibly falling for you.* But what she managed instead was a lame, "No."

"Then why would I?" He threw his arms in the air.

"It's not the same for you," she countered. The urge to sink her teeth into him with each intimate encounter was great. Controllable, but great. And it was something she would never be rid of unless she finally did claim him. But she couldn't resign herself to such a vulnerable position. If she claimed him, she would be saddled with him alone...while he could go off willy-nilly and be with any female of his choice. A matebond with her would mean nothing to him. And that kind of betrayal would kill her.

His eyes closed tight, and he squeezed his hands into fists. "It's not the same, is it? I'm glad I have you here to inform me of what I feel. I would have no idea otherwise."

Sonya's jaw fell open, but she quickly shut it.

His expression turned merciless. "Oh, please. Keep going. You're on a role. Why don't you tell me next how unworthy I am for being a pirate, or how in love I am with Kyra?"

Her eyes began to burn, but she choked back the tears. She knew their relationship was nearing its end, she just hadn't expected it to end like this, or so soon. "I never suggested you loved her, merely that you wanted her."

"Ah, that's much better. Couldn't possibly want the stubborn, irritating female I've been fucking!"

She gasped, not at his crude language, but the fact that he'd just admitted to wanting her instead of Kyra...for more than a bed partner?

Rationally, she told her she was reading too much into his words. That he couldn't possibly mean what she thought. More likely he just meant to keep their liaison going. But why? And how could it after this?

"For the love of the gods! How can you not see?" His eyes softened, anger draining away, yet a hint of pain remained. It tore at her.

He moved in close, backing her into the cool metal wall of the corridor. She let him, needing what he was about to offer because it would put a temporary patch over the razor-sharp fear that was ripping a hole her gut.

He curled a finger under her chin and then pressed their lips together. Soft at first, testing. Then the pressure increased and the kiss turned desperate, for both of them. Their tongues collided. Sonya reveled in his warmth, his taste, letting it take her mind to a place without thought.

The depths of her soul cried out for more, but a hazy part of her brain sensed others watching. She almost didn't care. Heat expanded over her skin, and the most primitive form of desire settled between her legs.

When Ethan pulled back, she was ready to shove him into the nearest private compartment.

"Is that clear enough for you?" His tone was deliciously rough, yet his face had gone cold. He pulled out of her embrace, leaving cool air in his place as he trudged away.

Sonya glanced to her left. Bastian and the mercenaries stood at the far end of the hall, staring. Had they watched the whole scene? The sympathy in Bastian's eyes irked her. He probably imagined this was just a little hiccup between a demon and her non-demon mate, just as it had been difficult between him and Anya. But her relationship with Ethan was nothing like theirs. And it never would be.

The sad truth brought fury back. "Dammit, Ethan! You don't get to just twist everything upside down and walk away."

He offered his profile without stopping. "Then you'd better come along."

For the umpteenth time, he bewildered her. His tone had been teasing.

Ethan had found it nearly impossible to stop kissing her, especially when she had so thoroughly and eagerly softened for him. But there had been an audience and the things he wanted to say to her—to do to her—were things best done in private.

He didn't know what he would have done had she not followed him back to his quarters.

"What was that about?" she said, after the door to his

room slid closed behind her. Ethan entered the wash room and splashed his face with water. He couldn't tell if she was being obtuse or truly couldn't fathom his feelings for her.

When he reentered the room, he found her standing awkwardly in the center looking more than a bit rattled, her expression perplexed and disconcerted. Outside in the hall, he had felt her ready to break if off with him entirely, and it had nearly dropped him to his knees.

"You make me lose my mind," he ground out.

"Clearly."

Her brusque comment made him crack a smile. But he let the humor die. "I didn't like hearing you suggest that I'd rejoice at your demise. That's the furthest thing from truth."

One delicate shoulder lifted in response. "Okay, but that's not really what I meant."

He held up his palm. "You assume I'll throw you off for Kyra, but I have no intention of pursuing her."

Her eyes flared.

"And I don't want this to end." He gestured between the two of them. Then, for some reason, he added, "Just yet." He wasn't sure why exactly. Perhaps it was the sudden trepidation rolling off her. He got the impression she was ready to run.

Instead, she tilted her head at him. "What about my, um…" She indicated her fangs.

"You don't frighten me."

She averted her gaze, and that's when he felt it—that same urge to hide. Only this time it wasn't from desire. He frightened *her* a great deal.

They stood in silence for a moment, neither sure of what to say next.

Finally, he stepped forward, swiped his forefinger over the muck on her shoulder, and held it up. "You could use a washing."

She gave a half smile. "And a change of clothes."

"Nah, we don't need that."

She rolled her eyes, but her amused smile lifted his heart.

Chapter 29

Sebastian entered the pub, catching a deep blush on Sonya's face as she shoved Ethan's paws away from her with a giggle. Normally, that kind of scene would result in Ethan being dragged over the bar by his neck, but he tamped down the wayward urge.

Sonya's declaration that both he and Cale had frightened away anyone who tried to get near her had speared him with guilt.

While he and Cale were off bedding females without a care, she'd been here—alone—battling a natural demon urge. If he'd been in that predicament, he might have gone insane. Now he had a new-found admiration for her strength and control…and stubborn will.

Rex and Zoey strode in behind him—yet another set of newly acquainted lovers. However, Sebastian got the impression that it wasn't serious on Rex's part. Then again, he hadn't anticipated Sonya and Ethan's unlikely relationship, so who was to say?

When Sonya spotted them, blood leached from her face,

and she slapped Ethan away more vigorously. Ethan frowned. Following her gaze, he noticed their approach and smiled once more. *No fear of the burly older brother, eh?*

The new mercenaries Sonya and Ethan had recruited sat at the far end of the bar, drinking and talking among themselves. In no way did Sebastian trust them, but Ethan vouched for the group, which was good enough for now.

Other brutish newcomers meandered through the pub, gathering in tight-knit groups. Militants, mercenaries, soldiers without a cause. All taking up space on his ship, all either bribed or bored enough to take up a fight they had no vested stake in. As long as they all played nice, he'd let them be a rowdy as they wanted.

"Hey Sebastian, where's Anya?" Sonya chirped.

With all the new roughneck recruits, Sebastian was hard-pressed to leave his mate unattended, even if she was turning out to be more powerful than he could have ever imagined. "She's with her sisters, practicing in the Sanctuary."

That seemed to pique Ethan's interest. To Sonya, he said, "If you've got things covered here, I think I'll go help them with that."

Sonya waved her approval. Then Ethan drew her close and whispered a few oaths into her ear that Sebastian tried very hard not to hear...very, very hard! The last word, *vietta*, sounded foreign, and made Zoey chuckle.

Sonya zeroed in on the Earthling. Zoey went pale and lost her smile. "Sorry, I didn't mean to eavesdrop." It was still a surprise to hear the Earthling speak their native language.

"What did he say just then?" Sonya inquired sternly.

Zoey looked confused for a moment. Ethan smirked and

nodded his head at her. She answered, "He called you a little temptress."

Sonya's jaw dropped, and she faced Ethan. "Why did you tell me it meant rotten female?"

"You'd have had me by the balls otherwise," he replied matter-of-factly.

She grinned, looking ready to offer a lewd retort, but her eyes slid to Sebastian, and she seemed to think better of it.

"You can finish that thought later," Ethan muttered suggestively.

Sebastian couldn't help curling his hands into tight fists. Sonya shot him a death-stare, letting him know she would knock the ever-living shit out of him if he tried anything. He just shrugged and replied, "It's a hard habit to break."

As though sensing it was time to cut out, Ethan gave Sonya a quick peck on the lips before heading toward the Sanctuary. Sebastian had to admire his fearlessness, especially in present company. He was an acceptable male.

"We're closing in on Evlon," Sebastian informed Sonya, taking a seat at the bar. "Ivan has guaranteed more than fifty ships, but I've seen no sign of them yet."

Sonya nodded her head in response, barely listening to Sebastian. She was still holding in her shock over learning the meaning of Ethan's favorite endearment. She realized he had been calling her *little temptress* nearly from the start.

She glanced at the mercenaries, out of hearing range. "I guess all we can do is hope Ivan's not full of shit. Ethan seems to trust him." She set to mixing Sebastian a strong drink.

"Aye," Sebastian replied, sounding unconvinced. "Anyway,

Portia is working on a cloaking spell to use on the ship when we arrive. There's bound to be some Kayadon crafts lying in wait."

"Doesn't the book detail stuff like that?" She put the finished drink in front of Sebastian.

He wrapped his palm around it. "It outlines patrolling schedules, but it's so old, I fear the information might be out of date."

"Ethan believes his king would have taken that into account and adjusted for future events."

"It has also been said that this king's visions cannot be fully relied upon," Sebastian countered.

True enough, Sonya thought. "Portia's only a witch in training. Do you believe she'll do an adequate job?"

Both of them jumped at the soft female voice. "I am confident in this spell." As she often liked to do, Portia had *popped* in, appearing as if from nowhere upon the empty stool next to Sebastian.

Sebastian bristled. "Ach, girl. You must stop doing that."

Ignoring his chagrin, Portia continued, "I've worked this spell many-a-time. We'll be as if invisible." She snapped her fingers.

On the opposite side of Sebastian, Zoey nodded at Portia seeming utterly convinced of the witch's prowess. Rex's face remained impassive.

"Where's the enthusiasm?" Sonya asked him. "For all intents and purposes, we're about to face down some Kayadon scum." He should be as eager as any of them for vengeance.

He gave her a blank expression. "This is me excited."

Zoey burst into laughter, but the demon was so stoic all the time, Sonya didn't think he was kidding. Sonya hadn't seen him smile once since she'd met him, but with Zoey gazing up at him all dreamy-like, she suspected the Earthling might have.

To Rex, Sonya said, "You'd better take it up a notch once we get there."

"If we get there." He took a swig of his ale.

Sonya had nothing to counter that with, so instead, she traipsed to the other end of the bar, toward the mercenaries. "Ivan, you fellas alright down here?"

Ivan jiggled his empty bottle. "Could use a refill, *lun feist.*" Sweet fire. That was what Ivan liked to refer to her as. His sweet fire. It was better than rotten female, though not so good as little temptress.

"Tell me, Ivan," she said as she retrieved a fresh bottle of liquor and popped the lid for him. "What is the debt you owe Ethan?"

"He's not told you?"

Sonya shook her head.

"Well, it's no secret. That rake had to go and save my skin. Won't let me forget it either." Though the words sounded disgruntled, the corners of his lips quirked.

"How did he save you?"

"Dead as a fleck in space, I was. Well, not quite, but getting there. Before my blood ran cold, Ethan…" Lost for words, Ivan put his palms up and wiggled his fingers.

"Oh," Sonya said, understanding. Ethan had used his gift to heal Ivan.

"Even before that, we'd been watching each other's arses. Seemed we were alike back then, at least when it came to wrong place wrong time scenarios. Brothers in bad luck, as it were." He shrugged. "We'd been swindled onto a ship and forced to work under a tyrant's rule. Bastard got what was coming to him, though. Unfortunately, I caught the overflow. Bad day, that."

"Pirates almost killed you," Sonya said, remembering Ethan's story.

"Ah, so he did mention me. Been squeezing favors out of me ever since." Ivan took a long gulp. "Better believe this is the last one."

"I couldn't care less if it's the last, as long as you're fully invested in this one. What of the ships you promised?"

"Don't you worry, *lun feist*. On their way."

* * *

Ethan relaxed on the soft tuft of grass where he'd been sitting for the past hour.

The Sanctuary was teeming with magic as Anya sent out tendrils of energy, purposefully messing with the bright overhead lights.

Kyra lay back next to Ethan, unable to call her gift for fear of losing control of it—which, from what Ethan could discern, would most assuredly mean death to anyone close by, perhaps even the entire ship. But she remained attentive to Ethan's teachings.

Nadua sat with her legs crossed, still looking shaken after the recent influx of power that had bombarded her the other day. Ethan imagined the experience had been harrowing for her. As a result, doubt in her own abilities ran rampant in her mind. She wasn't putting in the effort that she should.

"Try again," he encouraged, facing her. "It took me a long time to learn to block my power so as not to become overwhelmed. Now I can pick out an individual intent without calling to mind every single one in the vicinity."

Nadua pursed her lips. "I don't want that kind of pain again. It felt like my brain was turning to mush."

"Too much information can do that. Next time it happens, choose one thought—or image—something solid and dear to your heart, to keep an anchor in reality."

"And let the magic flow through me," she muttered, reciting one of the ancient teachings. Then she shared a look with Kyra.

"Precisely," Ethan replied. "Now, try again." For the last few hours, Nadua had been attempting to pick through the deluge of future and past events to single out one for study. Specifically, one of Ethan's memories.

To make it harder, he'd challenged her to seek out a specific one—the moment he'd finally held the book in his hands. For Nadua, it would be like walking through a forest in search of a single tree among millions, but if her gift was anywhere near as powerful as her father's, Ethan was confident she could manage.

Nadua closed her eyes and settled deeper into her seated position. After a long while of nothing, her head canted. "I see..." Her brows furrowed. "Lost it, hold on."

Ethan scanned her intentions, finding determination. He waited patiently.

When she spoke again, her voice came out even and smooth, as though she had entered a trance. "There are people in a room, angry...focused on you." Her head turned as if witnessing something from behind her closed lids. "Violet eyes, no, red, coming at you with furry. My gods, she is going to kill you."

"Take everything in. Where are you?" Ethan said.

"Large room...inside of a cave."

His asteroid base. She was very close to their goal. He debated telling her to move forward in time, but she was doing so well, he was afraid to interrupt her again.

"She's down now. She looks ill or something. You can't stop looking at her eyes. They're so…beautiful. You're saying something to her, but she looks to have fallen asleep. *Vietta Anu*."

Ethan stilled. Little temptress *of my heart*. He hadn't recalled saying that. He did recall how long he'd indulged in staring at her before reluctantly shutting her in the cell with the others.

"Move forward, Nadua. Find the book."

Her head tilted again. "There's a box…on a desk. I feel your excitement as you open it. There's a code to unlocking it." Nadua smiled. "The combination of our birth years: Mother's, Kyra's, mine, and Anya's. You retrieve the book from within, and…relief is extensive." Nadua's eyes flashed open, and she clapped her hands together. "I did it!"

Anya and Kyra both offered excited congratulations.

"Very good, Nadua," Ethan said. "Now try again."

Her expression fell, but after a moment, she let out a slow breath and closed her eyes.

* * *

A squeal of laughter burst out of Sonya as Ethan tossed her to the bed. Her hair was wild, spread over his pillow like rays of a dark sun.

How had this female enchanted him so thoroughly?

She watched him, heavy lidded, as he crawled over her. Just before dipping his head for a sensuous kiss, he caught a glimmer of her little fangs. A beautiful snake, waiting to strike. So then why was he drawn to her? Every day he wanted more.

Worse, every time he envisioned her fangs sinking into his

flesh, he found himself unconsciously nipping at her...actually encouraging her. What not too long ago he had considered a barbaric act, was now the most erotic idea imaginable.

Some part of him realized what was happening—*Vietta Anu*—but he wasn't ready to admit it aloud. There were things between them that needed resolving. And even though they'd been unable to keep their hands off each other over the last few days, Sonya was still as tight lipped as ever.

He pulled back to look at her. Undisguised desire pooled behind her hooded lids. A single fang nibbled at her bottom lip, mesmerizing him for an instant.

He moved in to claim her lips once more, maybe brush a fang with his tongue, but she turned her head. "Don't. I...I need a minute."

Her breath heaved, and he was drawn to the rise and fall of her breasts under the tight bodice, its loosened strings dangling haphazardly over her chest.

Pulling at them, he finished undoing the knots, freeing her from the garment. When he bent to take one taut peak between his lips, she moaned softly, arching for him, but the change in her mood finally penetrated the haze of his mind.

He positioned himself by her side and pulled her into the line of his body. "What is it?"

Again she nibbled her lip, looking far too sexy and... guilty?

Then it hit him. "Ah, you want to put those pretty fangs in me."

Her eyes flared wide, but she didn't deny it. Just as she'd done many times before, she asked him to confirm that wasn't what he wanted—and he did, even though he secretly wasn't sure. He feared how she would react if he put it on the table. Would she finally push him away for good?

She hid her fangs behind tight lips.

"Tell me about your home," he asked, hoping to get her mind off whatever was causing her anxiety.

It didn't work.

She frowned and rolled off the bed.

His eyes followed her movement, but he remained on the bed as she glowered at him.

She knew he wasn't interested her home world. Not really. It had been obvious, ever since Cale's outburst, that his curiosity festered. Every now and again, he would pick for information she wasn't ready to give. She had caught him speaking with Sebastian just the other day, inquiring about their family's history. He hadn't known she'd been listening from inside the stock room.

Sebastian hadn't revealed much. In truth, he didn't have much to reveal. She hadn't discussed that night with her brothers. Not fully. All they knew was that Sebastian had come home to find their father's bloodied, lifeless body on the floor; her, huddled in a compartment under a set of window seats, frozen in shock.

After all this time, she still wasn't ready to relive it.

"First, tell me about Evlon," she hedged.

He bent his arm and propped his head on his palm, offering one of those looks that made her feel all too exposed. "Two suns orbit my world," he started. "Our ancient ancestors worshiped them, believing that, united, they fuel the magic that encompasses Evlon."

Her anxiety began to wane. She rejoined him on the mattress, her curiosity piqued. His arm opened in welcome. When she settled, he rested his palm on her hip, caressing lightly with his thumb.

"Is it true?" she urged him on.

He responded with a sly smile. "Your turn to tell me something."

She hesitated. "We didn't have royalty like you. Instead, we had village councils. Elders who presided over each town. They mostly just settled disputes between landowners and discussed matters that pertained to everyday life. Pretty dull stuff, to be honest." She glanced up at him, "So, is it true?"

His lips thinned, but amusement curled the corners. "Partly, I believe so. For example, twice a year, the suns align in the sky. Somehow it causes a…unique effect on us." He paused thoughtfully, as if remembering. "I haven't felt the power of it in so long. I can't imagine how it would overwhelm me now." He gave her a meaningful look.

"Well? What happens to you?"

"Uh-uh. Your turn."

She frowned, not liking this game. "There isn't much to tell," she replied. "We lived simple lives, only starting to delve into science and technology when the Kayadon arrived. Very few of us had ever been off planet before that, though we'd been aware of the outer races for some time."

"Hmm." He leaned back on the mattress and clasped his hands behind his head.

She waited for him to speak. When he didn't reply, she whined, "Well?"

"Well what?"

She poked him in the side. "Tell me!"

He rolled on top of her, capturing and bringing her arms above her head. She jutted her chin, growing irritated, yet aroused at the same time.

He smirked. "At twilight, the sky turns violet, with streaks of crimson. It will forever remind me of your eyes."

She blinked twice, taken aback by the sudden tenderness in his voice.

"I love you, you silly woman. Why won't you let me in?"

Her breath caught, and her heart jerked into overdrive. "You what?" She became acutely aware of the hard muscles of his body over hers, keeping her in place.

"I love you," he repeated irefully. He hadn't intended to blurt it out like that, but he could no longer hold back. Her stubbornness was never ending.

"But...you can't," she insisted, eyes going wide.

"Can't I?" he said. He could tell if he wasn't partly restraining her, she would have bolted. Was the idea of mating with him so revolting to her that she would deny her very nature? Yet still her fangs advertised her desire.

"You're the one who doesn't want to be with me like that. You just said so."

"You misunderstand. What I want is for you to be upfront with me. This pirate thing hangs between us. How can we overcome it if you won't talk to me about it?"

Swiftly, she fired off, "It's nothing. I'm over it anyway. I don't want to talk about it."

"That sounded convincing."

"Shut up! Get off of me!" She bucked, but he held fast.

"I just told you that I love you, and you want to run away?"

"Do you think I should love you back just because you're supposedly my mate?"

"Pretty much. Yeah."

"Well, sorry to disappoint you."

A muscle ticked in his jaw. He didn't believe for a second she didn't love him. "Why are you being so stubborn about this?"

"Because, since you couldn't trick it out of me, you're trying to force it. You're always making me do things I'm not ready for!"

Her words sliced through him, and he released her.

As if she couldn't get away from him fast enough, she scrambled off the bed, refusing to look at him as she laced up her bodice. He could tell she was going to leave without a word. Probably wouldn't talk to him for a full week or two, maybe ever.

"Wait, Sonya."

She paused halfway to the door, keeping her back to him.

"You're right. I'm sorry. Please don't go. I can tell you keep me at a distance, and it's driving me crazy, but I won't bring it up again. Alright?"

Her shoulders hunched, and he thought she might be wavering. An agonizing moment later, she turned to face him.

"You keep me so off balance," she admitted. "I have no idea how to deal with"—she gestured between them as if the right words escaped her—"all of this."

He pursed his lips, unsure how to proceed. Finally, he said, "If you come back to bed, I'll tell you what happens when the suns align."

Repressing a grin, she replied, "Resorting to bribery?"

Already he knew he'd won. "Usually the best course of action."

He sensed the debate warring inside her. She wanted to resist, yet she wanted to submit. He imagined she had never experienced those conflicting emotions at the same time, at least before he'd come along.

Taking the choice from her, he pushed off the bed and crossed to her. Her gaze followed him cautiously, as if she thought he might attack.

"No longer curious?" he drawled in a husky voice.

She averted her eyes, and one smooth shoulder hiked nonchalantly.

He cupped her face and trailed his thumb over her cheek. "It would be better for me to show you."

He dipped his head, and their lips drew together like a pair of magnets. After a few strokes of his tongue, she melted into his arms. He untied her bodice and let it fall to the floor. Her skirt joined it seconds later. Then he lifted her into his arms, bringing her back to lie on the mattress. She looked glorious, clad in only a pair of black panties, like a feast prepared for him alone. His cock jerked with a hungered response.

He left her to cross to the opposite side of the room. She rose up on her elbow, looking ready to protest his absence, which pleased him.

When he revealed a length of chain and returned to the bedside, her breath hitched, and she met his gaze. That war was back behind her eyes. He didn't wait for her to decide which side of her instincts to obey. He looped the chain several times around one of her slim wrists, then the other before binding them together and fixing the other end of the chain to the crude metal headboard.

He stood for long moments, giving himself leave to admire her body. With his forefinger and thumb, he pulled hard against the fabric at her hip and let it snap back into place. "You drive me mad, but I think you know that by now," he grated, his voice no more than a rumble in his chest. "I think it's time I drive you a little crazy."

She narrowed her gaze and pulled at her restraints, testing them. He hooked one arm under her knee and lifted her leg, exposing part of her backside. His other hand, palm open, came down hard against her.

She yelped. "What are you doing?"

He smacked her again, his palm lingering against her soft flesh to massage the tender area. "Ah-ah, no talking." He tightened his hold on her leg.

"But—"

Smack.

She let out a soft part-growl, part-groan of pleasure. He smirked.

Looking disgruntled, she rolled away from him. He let her go. The chain had enough give that she wasn't trapped on her back. But when she made it to her stomach, he crawled over her and pulled her hips up, fitting her ass against his crotch. Her forearms on the mattress held up her torso.

"Giving me better access?" he teased.

"No!"

He smacked her plum ass once more, but only enough to provide a titillating sting. Her head flew back with a clipped feminine moan. The sound of it gave him the impression that she was shocked by how much she was enjoying this, which was probably infuriating her too. His palm connected once more, before he pulled the elastic of her panties taut. The material creased into her slick folds. After she let slip another moan, he let it snap back against her hip.

"Ethan." Her voice was little more than a plea, her hips rocking.

He rubbed his palm over her ass, and she knew what was coming. Her head craned around to watch him.

Smack.

Another moan, this one louder.

Then he ran his fingers over the fabric between her thighs, reveling in her growing wetness. Her body undulated against his touch. He played there for a moment, until she was panting mindlessly. Then he pulled away. She groaned in protest and met his gaze again, glaring daggers at him. She'd figured out his game. But the sexual torment was backfiring on him, making his cock painfully stiff.

He flipped her to her back, keeping himself between her legs, and trailed his hands over her thighs, her hips, her waist. She squirmed with every inch he took. Farther up he went till his thumbs met the hard peak of her breasts. He bent down to rake his tongue over one pert nipple, loving the mews of pleasure that came from her. Her back arched and her body rolled, seeking his shaft. Her legs clamped around him as if to keep him from backing away again.

He chuckled and extracted himself from her death grip. Then he snapped her panties again. She growled at him, her arms straining against the bindings.

"Be a good girl, and I'll let you come," he said in a grating tone that telegraphed his own maddening lust. When she stilled, he dipped his head to her inner thigh and nipped her with his teeth. Her body jerked, and she let out a whimper, yet she wet her lips in anticipation. He moved closer to her center, giving another nip. The sound she made came out utterly desperate, driving his own lust past the point of insanity.

He yanked down her panties and rolled his tongue against her tender flesh. Matching moans escaped them both. Leisurely, reverently, his tongue circled her clitoris. She cried out, and her body shuddered. Soon enough, her moans came faster, more urgent. Her thighs boxed him in as if she was afraid he might move. She was right. When her body began to shake from an oncoming release, he pulled away.

She cried out, her climax thwarted. If she took it as more punishment—which by the looks of her fiery eyes, she did—then she was wrong. He wanted her to come…fiercely. And now she would, but he wanted to be inside her when it happened.

He rid himself of his clothing. She opened her legs for him and wrapped her ankles around the backs of his thighs.

He plunged into her. The wicked heat of her sheath encased him. There was no slow build up as he pulled out and rammed back into her, again and again, in an almost violent taking.

They both watched the other with cool anger, both refusing to look away. His thrusts came fast and hard, giving her body a kick every time he slammed into her. Her hips moved to keep pace with him, deepening each drive. Her fangs lengthened, catching his attention, but she didn't hide them as she usually did. Perhaps he could take that as a small triumph.

Their pleasure built into something savage. Beautiful and overwhelming and almost agonizing in its ecstasy. It burst through them with the force of a thousand suns exploding in quick succession, reverberating for long moments, as though it would never end. Finally, they grew still, yet their breaths remained harsh.

Ethan's mind felt like it had shattered from the inside. He rolled to lie on his back next to Sonya, who was still tethered to the bed. She didn't complain, just worked on capturing air, same as him.

After the fractured chunks of his mind began to reform, he reached up and set her free. He feared he had gone too far, shown her a darker side of pleasure that she would resent him for, but she curled her body around his and laid her head on his chest.

He hooked an arm around her. "Do I need to apologize for that?"

He felt her lips curl into a smile against him. Then she shook her head. Neither of them said a word, and soon, sleep took over.

Chapter 30

The surface of Evlon

Portia had been right about her cloaking spell. *Marada* had no problems reaching the surface of Evlon, a planet literally blooming with life.

Puking it up was more like it. Sonya practically couldn't turn her head without being smacked in the face by some biological extremity. All around her were dizzyingly tall trees with bloated trunks. Their adjoining roots arched high before digging back into the soil. Plants with shoots as thick as her leg stretched over head. The connecting leaves could wrap her body twice over. Even the rocks glittered with life. Their surfaces appeared to shiver as light refracted off countless faucets.

A stick cracked under her foot. She mentally cursed and swept a wary gaze around, as did the others. There was no obvious path to follow and with the snake-like vines disguising the ground and slithering up any stationary object, it was almost impossible to watch her footing.

Every time a crunch rang out from one of them, the group

would pause and listen for trouble. Who knew what manner of creatures might be tracking them from behind the forest's camouflage.

Kyra, Nadua, and Ethan continued to assure everyone that they wouldn't likely cross paths with a predator, but that didn't mean Kayadon weren't lurking about. Or their horrendous looking pet-creatures of which Sonya had seen sketches of in the book. Only Cale and Kyra had encountered the beasts first hand. Back on Earth, the two had been attacked by a pack of them.

Sonya noticed both Sebastian and Marik kept their mates close, though neither Anya nor Nadua appeared nervous. In fact, both were wide-eyed as they marveled at their old home world. Cale was the same with Kyra, his attention constantly glued to her, regardless that they weren't mated. Again, Sonya's heart broke for her brother. And yet, even though Cale was unable to claim Kyra in the traditional sense, Sonya hoped the little Faieara would accept him—somehow make him happy—if that was what he truly wanted. By the heated looks they gave to each other when they thought no one was looking, Sonya had to assume it was.

After a few moments of silence, the group moved on. They'd left the ship behind, guarded by Aidan, mercenaries, and Portia's magic, to seek out a group of Faieara supposedly hidden nearby. The book had indicated a possible location, but they'd been walking for hours now, with no signs of intelligent life. However, numerous strange animals scurried about, unnerving everyone but the Faieara.

When Ethan attempted to educate her on the local critters, Sonya had put her hand up and replied, "I don't care. Just tell me when I need to kill them."

Every so often, the thick canvas of trees broke to reveal a vast horizon of high mountain ridges, painted in every manner of color. The scene was so beautiful as to be nearly unreal, like an artist's rendering.

Nestled within a deep valley, at the base of one particularly high mountain, sat an elegant chateau with a large village circling around the front.

Ethan followed her line of sight. "The palace," he informed her. "It's overrun by Kayadon now. If we are captured out here, that's most likely where we'd be taken."

Judging by the distance, it would take a full day's hike to get there, if not more. And there was no telling what obstacles lie between here and there. Sonya indulged herself for a moment by imagining that piece of land engulfed by a fiery explosion.

As if reading her thoughts, Ethan lowered his voice so that only she could hear him. "That's where Anya's father will be kept. The *king*."

That doused any immediate plan of attack. Sonya would never hurt Anya by taking out her father, even if a slew of Kayadon went with him.

Ethan continued, "When we're ready, I hope to reclaim the palace and rescue him, as well as anyone else being held there."

She raised a brow at him. "Anyone else?"

He gave a thin-lipped nod. "The whole town had been turned into a prison camp before I had left. No one could get in our out without the Kayadon's knowledge."

"How did *you* get out?"

His lips quirked smugly. "A little instruction from the king, my magic, and a small child who'd managed to hide her gift for invisibility from the Kayadon. She escorted me straight to my escape shuttle."

"What happened to the child?"

His expression fell. "That, I hope to find out."

"You didn't take her with you?"

Another twig snapped from Marik's direction; another pause by the group.

While glancing around, Ethan answered, "I wanted to, but she was young. She didn't want to leave her parents. At the time, I thought it would be safer for her to come with me, but when I tried to explain that, she disappeared." He paused, looking thoughtful. "Now that I think of it, it was probably for the best. I was barely able to keep *myself* alive in the beginning. I could never have taken care of a kid. A female at that."

"What do you mean, *a female*?"

He rolled his eyes. "Like your brothers, most Faieara males take on the role of protector over the females in their charge. Even capable females," he added at her indignant look. "I would have been so overly concerned with keeping her safe that she probably would have gotten me killed."

"You mean you would have gotten yourself killed," Sonya countered. "I imagine an invisible girl could have easily avoided danger. In fact, she might have even helped you out."

Ethan shook his head. "Imagine one of those immoral mercenaries I told you about discovering a child who can make themselves disappear at will. Her life would have depended on total secrecy, lest she end up like…" He glanced at Anya.

Sonya gnashed her teeth together. Anya might be coming into her gifts now, but she'd been brutally exploited from the time she was a child.

As the group continued on, Kyra and Cale's flirting increased in frequency, which was entertaining to watch, but also—for some odd reason—made Sonya feel awkward around Ethan. She almost felt guilty for not engaging in similar behavior. But, while Cale had decided to make no secret of his desire for Kyra, Sonya was doing everything she could to keep her eyes off Ethan. To tamp down the fierce instinct that demanded she keep by his side, weapon palmed, ready to defend. She reminded herself that the boy could take care of himself. Besides, she was still thrown by his unexpected declaration of love.

How could he have just blurted it out like that? With no warning?

She knew he had wanted her to return the sentiment. But she just...couldn't. Because when—*if*—she did, she would inevitably claim him, and there was no going back from that. She didn't want to be heedless about something so permanent—permanent only on her part.

Afterward, he'd clearly been angry—or hurt—that she hadn't reciprocated. Since then, the sex had been aggressive...punishing.

Well, the joke was on him, because she liked it.

And what did that say about her?

Sebastian motioned for everyone to stop, but no one had made a sound. His eyes were trained on something ahead of him. She moved forward to investigate.

Blocking their way was a wide, rounded gorge with a flat base, slathered by vegetation.

"This is the landmark indicated on the map," Ethan announced excitedly. "Some of our people should be nearby."

Anya anxiously glanced around. Was she was sensing something that the others weren't?

The wind shifted, and Sonya caught a strange fragrance. Something—or someone—was nearby, possibly watching them from the dark depths of the forest.

A soft, delicate sound tinkled in the air. Her fangs descended with instant aggression.

But in the next moment, the tune surrounded her, comforting her like the caress of a feather's touch. The tension in her body eased, and a dim smile conquered her lips.

So beautiful…

"I know that instrument." Ethan announced, sounding oddly horrified by the lovely sound. "Everyone! Anything you see or hear in the next few moments will not be real. Someone is weaving an illusion—"

Terror invaded, tearing through the walls of her mind and chasing away serenity.

Mustn't make a sound.

She curled her knees into her chest and wrapped her little arms tightly around them. The old damp wood that made up her hiding place added to the muggy staleness in the air. Her mind was filled with trepidation, body frozen in a ball. Her eyes were trapped wide, yet seeing only darkness broken by a single shaft of light through a fissure in the wall.

Father had told her to stay put, "no matter what." The urgent tone he'd used frightened her into obedience. With shaky fingers, she clutched the necklace he'd given her in her fist. It was still warm from its usual place around his neck. The metal-woven talisman was a symbol of protection.

No sooner had he closed her inside the small compartment than a blast of loud noises made her jump. Outside her hiding place, her father snarled, the sound trailing off into a horrific gurgling that made her mind go wild. Her stubby fingers dug into the calves of her bent legs.

After a moment, she peeked through the fissure, adjusting her position with slow, deliberate movements, so not to make a sound.

Her breath seized.

Father was on the ground...not moving! A stain of red grew from beneath his torso, while three men stood over him, grinning at their work. She recognized them as off-worlders. "Pirates," Mother had called them. Sonya's gaze dipped back to her father's lifeless body.

They've killed him!

Her mouth opened wide in a silent scream, choked back by suffocating despair. Her throat tightened as devastation sucked the air out of her.

Frozen in place, she watched as the men continued to circle the corpse. For some reason, she expected them to leave now. Something felt off. She shook her head and looked again.

Why aren't they leaving?

Sebastian entered the room, lumbering over the pile of broken wood scattered in the threshold. Cale followed behind. Enraged, they lunged at the pirates as their eyes and horns flashed red. But the three pirates were too fast. Blood splattered, and the strong physiques of her older brothers fell to the floor.

Sorrow clutched her heart in a painful squeeze as tears fell freely. *This isn't right,* her mind screamed, fighting against the scene. Yet it wasn't over.

Marik burst into the room next, roaring as he attacked, but the sound was cut off as a blade easily severed his head from his neck. The culprit wiped the blade clean with his shirt-tail just as Anya appeared in the doorway, looking horrified by the gruesome scene. Her eyes flashed silver, and a wild gust of wind swept through her blond hair. She rushed the closest pirate, going for his throat, but the man cut her down with a swing of his sword.

Another male came into view, this one a stranger, beautiful and deadly. A fourth murderer? And he was looking right at Sonya, as if seeing her through the wooden shield. His unyielding blue eyes drew her in, forcing recognition.

Not a stranger. Mine!

"Ethan! Run!" she screamed, pushing against the compartment door. Yet it didn't budge against her weight. She pushed harder, banging with her fists. It still would not relent. She turned to kick at the blockade with the heel of her tiny boot, while crying, "Get out of here!"

Scuffles of movement outside made her look again. Ethan had placed himself defensively in front of her nook, squaring off against the three invaders.

"No! Please go!"

Ethan turned his head to look at her then, resolution set in his deep-blue eyes. He gave her a look of such devout love it tore through her like white-hot lightning. Too painful, yet she wished for more.

A terrible slick sound drew her eyes to his chest. Blood coated the tip of a long sword jutting from his chest.

The anguished scream that ripped from her lungs shook her world, cracking her mind so fiercely that any semblance of sanity couldn't possibly survive…only rage, poised for violence, vengeance, and a furious rampage.

She scratched desperately at the door with her little claws, ignoring the splinters that jabbed deep into her fingertips. The points of her fangs bit into her bottom lip, craving the feel of torn flesh from the necks of those murderers.

Alarm stunted her breath when she saw Ethan's eyes growing dim. His knees hit the floor, followed by his lifeless torso.

Infused by a mindless frenzy, she dug at the now jagged daggers of wood. Seconds before she breached the door, a feminine voice rang out—*Kyra?*—commanding with the authority of a well-versed leader for someone to stop.

The scene suddenly vanished in an array of dizzying sparks, replaced by a wall of vegetation.

Still immersed by the Edge, confusion welled. Thwarted vengeance festered, rotting away reason. She clenched her jaw as the need for violence crashed through her. Her eyes darted wildly for a target.

The only person in the universe with the power to quell the overwhelming madness materialized at her front. His look of concern confounded her.

"Sonya?" Ethan reached for her, and without thought, her arm came up to slap his hand away. He frowned. "It wasn't real, whatever you saw," he said.

She turned away from him, wrestling with the Edge and craving the truth of his words. Not dead? It had been so damn real that *this* now felt like the dream.

She spotted Sebastian a few feet away, holding Anya in his big arms. The others were near as well, unharmed save for the strain in their faces.

"Hello, Siella. I see your power has grown," Kyra called out to someone.

A green haired female emerged from atop a massive stone. "Blessed gods! It *is* you!"

Realization slammed into Sonya. Somehow, this female had morphed her father's murder into a new kind of nightmare. Sonya tensed to attack, but Ethan moved to block her.

She hissed at him.

His eyes went wide, and he drew back. She cursed, realizing she needed to rein it in and crawl her way back from the Edge, lest she lash out again without meaning to.

"You need to leave me alone," she quietly warned. Her body still thrummed with fresh mourning as her mind tried to rationalize that her loved ones were unscathed.

For the span of a heartbeat, Ethan's expression appeared pained before he scrubbed his face blank, turning inscrutable. Sonya's heart sank by the sight, but there wasn't much she could do about it now. She was barely able to ward off the Edge and keep from throwing herself at that female, fangs first.

Chapter 31

One of Evlon's two suns had already set as they made their way back toward the ship, with the other soon to follow. Shadows stretched long, offering an eerie atmosphere among the forest. The entire trip was a silent endeavor, allowing Ethan to mull over everything that had happened.

At first he had been furious with Siella, but the girl had only been protecting her group. Undoubtedly she had saved them from discovery countless times with her power. While her victims were emerged in their own personal horror show, she could dispatch them by whatever means she deemed fit.

His own illusion had been strangely surprising and yet expected. There'd been nothing in the vision about his people, his world, or the fate that might befall both—something that had been his driving force and greatest fear for so long.

Instead, he was assaulted by his new greatest fear.

Losing Sonya.

After ending her illusion spell, Siella had used the power of her flute to hail a group of Faieara, whom she called her guild brothers and sisters. Because most in the group wielded blood magic, they referred to themselves as the Alliance of the Blood. They were led by a dark-haired male named Azule.

Ethan had recognized Azule from long ago, although he looked older now with experience set like stone behind his shrewd, grey eyes. Before, he'd been a young guard, eager to serve his king. During the initial invasion, he had helped to smuggle folks away from the palace prior to the Kayadon assuming command.

Azule had acknowledged him with a tight nod, clearly trying to place his face. Experience had taken its toll on Ethan as well. How differently he must look now: white-blond hair to his chin, braids swept throughout, his tailored clothing foreign to his own people who were dressed in lose fitting garb painted in colors of the forest.

After quick introductions, accompanied by wary glances at the demons, Azule had extended an invitation into their cleverly hidden underground lair. The entrance had been situated at the base of the large crater, precisely where the book had indicated.

Once inside, Azule and his lighter haired brother, Luric, had proceeded to explain how the free people of Evlon had broken into groups called guilds, all most likely veiled by magic. There was no way of knowing how many existed, or where any could be found.

Ethan frowned, stepping over a patch of rock. His glance skimmed over the lavish forest. Were there less free Faieara now than he'd imagined? Would they even be able to find another guild?

Sonya marched ahead of the group, seeming not to care about her loud footfalls, as if daring something to attack from behind the thick brush. Considering her mood, Ethan pitied anything that tried.

Back in the guild's den—just as with now—Ethan had found it difficult to focus on anything but Sonya. She had stood stiff, eyeing the new group with her arms crossed. She was completely closed to him, and he feared whatever she'd seen in Siella's illusion spell had encouraged a huge step back in their relationship. Possibly for good.

Gods, why can she not be easy?

Ethan's pleasure at seeing the large group of thriving Faieara had been muted by Sonya's continued gloom and stubbornness. She'd barely looked at him once since she'd ordered him to leave her be, a trying effort on his part. All he wanted to do was hold her and beg her not to push him away again, though he knew it would be moot. Once they returned to the ship, she would no doubt escape into her room.

A deep sorrow clamped his chest. He glanced at her ahead of him on the trail. Was his vision about to come true?

No. He would not allow it.

As they'd exchanged more information with Azule, many of the guild's inhabitants had peeked around corners to lay eyes on the princesses, surprised and ecstatic to see them alive after so long. Yet some had been apprehensive, mostly due to a foreboding prophecy regarding the king's heirs. According to Azule, the return of the princesses ushered the end of Evlon as they knew it.

Ethan paid it no heed. Prophecies were always plentiful among his people, and most were so cryptically undecipherable as to be useless.

However, Ethan had managed to learn two important things from Azule and Luric before they'd started heading back to the ship: The Kayadon may be weakening, and they'd been gathering healers.

A correlation, perhaps?

When Luric had divulged the last bit of information, Sonya had gone tense before asking, "What do they do with the healers?" giving Ethan the impression that she might yet care for him, even if she didn't quite realize how much.

Azule had been the one to reply, offering the only information he could, via a couple who had recently managed to escape the palace city. "According to Ina and Ru, once a healer was taken, they would never be heard from again."

Sonya's eyes had swept to Ethan for only the briefest second, and he thought he'd witnessed fear overcome a bit of her cold anger, but couldn't be sure.

"We should be there already," Sonya announced gruffly, interrupting his musings. She had pulled her hair back into a tight braid to keep it from getting caught on the occasional low branch, revealing the delicate slope of her neck. He yearned to kiss her there and bury himself in her feminine scent. "How are we to find the ship if Portia has hidden it from sight?"

"With this." Sebastian held out a glowing auburn stone. "Portia gave it to me before we left. It glows brighter the closer we get. Once we pass through her wards, the ship should appear."

Moments later, the air around them shivered with magic. They paused, awed by the sight of *Marada* emerging at their front as if from a billowing, grey mist. A few mercenaries stood guard, not trusting of the witchling's powers. One of them called out after spotting the group, bringing the others to attention. In the next instant, recognition put them at ease and they went back to scanning the woodland.

Sonya wasted no time climbing the ramp into the ship, while the others lingered to watch the final sunset.

Ethan moved to follow, but Kyra stopped him. "I'd like to return tomorrow and speak with Azule about joining us. I'd appreciated it if you accompanied me, since you knew him from before?"

Cale took a step closer to Kyra, silently indicating that he would be there as well. Kyra glanced at him and gave a tight nod, seeming to understand the unspoken proposition. Ethan felt a twinge of jealousy for their natural synchronicity. Meanwhile, he had no idea what was running through Sonya's head, his magic proving useless at the moment.

"Of course," Ethan replied. "But we were not exactly close associates back then. He'd been but a fresh trainee, recently inducted into the guard."

"You may not have known *him*, but I'd be surprised if he hadn't known you. There's a reason why Father chose you, Ethan. You were a legend among our people."

Though he covered it well, Ethan was taken aback by the sudden praise.

"Still are, it seems," she continued. "Those Faieara were just as eager to get a glimpse of you as they were any of us."

He hadn't noticed, too distracted by his capricious demoness. Cale caught it when Ethan's gaze slipped to where Sonya had disappeared, and when Kyra moved away, he pulled Ethan aside. "I've no right to offer advice, pirate, but I'm going to anyway. There's not a lot in this universe that frightens my sister—"

"I've noticed."

"But if what she saw in that nightmare was anything like

what I saw…" Cale shook his head and slanted a telling glance in Kyra's direction. "It's not hard to imagine what she's feeling right now."

"It isn't?" Ethan replied.

Cale offered a pitying grin. "Not for me. I've lost one mate already, and there's nothing worse."

Ethan raised a brow at his words. "*One* mate?" Does he believe he had a chance at a second? Had Cale accepted Kyra as his? "What about your magic theory?"

Something like regret flashed across Cale's face. "The witch confirmed otherwise. And…so did Nadua."

Ethan cocked his head, encouraging him to continue.

"She had witnessed something from Sonya's past, something Sonya was far too young to remember, or even comprehend. But she had been there when our mother and Velicia, my mate, plotted to trick me into a matebond using some kind of elixir I hadn't even known existed. I've told no one of this," Cale added with emphasis. "It would only hurt them to know that it had been used on our father as well."

Ethan digested the information before commenting, "You had said pirates killed your father?"

"Aye, but I'll say no more on the subject. Sonya would go ballistic on me."

Ethan had no doubt on that score. "I understand, but had he found out about this elixir?"

"I've wondered that myself. Knowing my mother…as I do now," he growled, "she wouldn't have wanted this information discovered. She might have had him murdered to keep her secret." Cale paused, as if taking a moment to mourn the loss, or perhaps to berate himself for being duped by his mother. Finally, he continued, "The Serakian informed me she can do nothing to break my bond with Velicia, but I won't let her treachery keep me from what I want, bond or not."

The stalwart intent behind Cale's words slammed into Ethan, and in that moment, they were connected by a similar resolve.

"And your advice?" Ethan prompted.

Cale smiled.

* * *

Sonya yanked open the drawers of her reading desk and dug through its contents. Next she went to the floor and attacked the adjacent trunk, rummaging through some of her most treasured items of memorabilia, tossing them away as if possessed.

She sat back with a curse when the trunk was emptied and she hadn't found what she sought. She glanced hopelessly at her effects now scattered around her.

Tendrils of the Edge were finally beginning to wane, her emotions settling, only to be replaced by a frantic need to locate her father's talisman. She'd made sure to always keep it with her, buried somewhere in her belongings. Usually out of sight.

Where did I put it?

She stood and crossed the room, throwing open her closet doors to sift through every pocket of her wardrobe.

It must be here!

She knew it was a silly adolescent superstition. A hunk of metal, nothing more. But still…

She retrieved a small music box stowed near the back and lifted the lid. "Ah, ha!" She hooked her fingers under the chain and lifted the talisman. It was heavier than she recalled, but then, she hadn't allowed herself to feel its weight in so long.

The chain was thick, made for a male. Along the flat coin-like pendant, the raised symbolic flourishes gleamed against a dark backdrop.

She whirled around as Ethan barged into her room, a slew of emotions contorting his features. Apprehension, anger, determination. But it was only the concern that affected her, reminding her that, in some form or another, her nightmare could yet come to fruition. If the chance arose, he would die for her, she knew it. Dammit, he had already tried once! And every time she thought of that day, she wanted to kill Ivan's cohort all over again.

"Ethan—"

"Don't!" he yelled, his tone harsher than she had ever heard it. "Don't you dare order me away. You're stuck with me, so you had damn well better get used to it!"

At hearing Cale's words through Ethan's lips, her mouth curled. "Is that a threat?"

He cocked a perplexed brow. "Uh, yes?"

She crossed to him and threw her arms around his neck. "Good. I'm going to hold you to that."

He seemed dumfounded for a moment, even as his arm hooked around her waist. "One of us is addled, and I can't determine which."

She laughed and pulled back. "Let me know when you decide."

"You. Definitely you."

"Then what would you do to ease this addled mind?"

"Anything." He turned wary. "What do you have in mind?"

Handing him the talisman, she replied, "Two things. Wear

this."

He studied the symbol for a moment, and she imagined he knew what it meant. "Very well. What else?"

"If I am ever in danger, you must promise not to risk yourself for me."

He scoffed. "I will wear your charm."

"Do you have any idea what would happen to me if I lost you?" She tried to cover her desperation as best she could.

He wrapped his palm around the back of her neck and brought their foreheads together. "Yes, because the same would happen to me."

She shook her head, but did not respond.

"*Vietta*," he whispered, sounding almost pained. "You are all that matters."

"No. You could move on. I..."

"What do you think I witnessed in that illusion spell?" he said. "My people eradicated? My world destroyed? No, none of that. Nothing but you, taken from me every which way."

She met his gaze, her eyes dampening; his darkening to that deep blue only seen in the darkest depths of a fathomless ocean.

"I'll never leave you, no matter how much you demand it."

Molding herself against his body, she hid her face in the crook of his neck, lost for words as tears began to stream down her cheeks. Strong fingers laced through her hair, cupping the back of her head as she fell apart in his arms. All the while, he murmured loving oaths, making her throat tighten all the more, like a sweet torture.

The lovemaking that followed was just as sweet, both of them a little desperate for the other as they stripped off their clothing, haphazardly landing on the bed. As their limbs tangled in fitful passion, Sonya's fangs throbbed and it no longer embarrassed her. She didn't hide them. In fact, Ethan seemed to enjoy the sight. His eyes darkened with unmitigated lust as he drove into her with maddening slow movements.

She cried out from searing pleasure as her orgasm barreled through her. Two more quaked, delving her into exquisite bliss, before Ethan shuddered with his own release.

He rolled to the side, pulling her across his chest. She curled into him, feeling the rise and fall of his heavy breaths and running her palm along the delicious planes of his chest.

After a moment, she said, "You haven't asked me what I saw."

"Because I know you wouldn't tell me. But I think I've gathered the gist of it."

"Is that so?"

"Mm." He sounded drowsy. "I think I have you all figured out."

"Oh, please do enlighten me."

"You're extraordinarily surly when you're upset. You were eager to get that pendant on me. And you tried to finagle an impossible promise from me. What's not to get?"

"Guess you've got it all figured out then, don't you?"

"Indeed." He hesitated. "Your aversion with pirates, for instance, is not exclusive to you alone. Your brothers have also displayed a dislike for them, but your rage runs deeper."

Sonya's body tensed, but he pressed on. "Your father was murdered in your presence." He waited to see if she would respond. Deny or confirm. She did neither. "I can only assume a pirate was the culprit, or perhaps a hired assassin that resembled one."

Sonya remained quiet for long moments. It was a small success that she wasn't rushing away from him as fast as her nimble feet could take her. Perhaps she couldn't tell him exactly what had happened, but his guessing might be enough to thin down her walls. Any interest in the details had left him some time ago. He merely wished for her to trust him enough to confide in him.

"I'm sorry. I wish I could have been there to spare you that pain."

Her head snapped up, something like dread bursting through her expression. When her lip quivered, he thought his soul might shatter.

"Why would that hurt you?"

"I…you *were* there…in the vision, I mean. You…died. They killed you too, and I couldn't…" Her throat worked furiously.

"They who?" He sensed her reluctance, and added in a soft tone, "You don't have to tell me."

"The ones who killed my father. There were three. Father hid me as if he knew they were coming. At first everything had played out like I remember, until everyone else I love showed up and I couldn't do anything…" She swallowed hard.

He pulled her flush against him, understanding. "Shh. It's alright. It wasn't real."

"But the helplessness was. The fear. I lived it."

"It sounds to me like you were very young at the time, correct?"

She responded with a minuscule nod.

"Then you can't blame yourself."

"You can say that a thousand times over, just like everyone else has. And a part of me knows you're right, but words can't erase guilt so easily."

Idly, Ethan trailed his fingers over the soft flesh of her arm, wishing it were otherwise, but her point was hard to dispute. The worst kind of guilt, the kind laced by grief, often stuck like a twisted black sludge.

"So this is why I had to work so hard," he mused. Little did she know he would have worked thrice as had to get half as far where she was concerned. Her awkward half-shrug sparked his intuition. "Is there more?" He was ecstatic that she was finally opening up to him.

"You—at least in the beginning—reminded me of them. Well, the leader, anyway."

He frowned as her words sank in. "How do you mean?"

"Clothes, hair, build. Almost everything about you, to be honest."

His brows furrowed. "So, when you look at me, you see your father's killer?"

Her lips pursed, but she didn't reply.

Ethan let his head drop back. No wonder why she hated him. With his visage tied to such a traumatic scar? How could they ever get past something like that?

Chapter 32

The morning hike back to the guild seemed shorter than the day before. And while dealing with Cale's considerable questions about the land, accompanied by his obsessive protectiveness over Kyra, Ethan had little time to reflect on Sonya's disturbing revelation.

When Kyra had leaned against a tree trunk choked by ivy, Cale had remarked, "Tell me that ivy's not poisonous."

Kyra had rolled her eyes. "Do you think I'd be touching it if it were?"

Apparently, Kyra had informed him of the dangerous plant life—most of which resided near bogs and other swampy areas—in order to relieve his anxiety about the wildlife that often popped out to observe them. Her plan had clearly backfired. Cale now ignored the pack of three-tailed Nax and the flying lizards, instead pointing out each offending leaf, "What about that?"

Ethan had lost count of how many times Kyra had sighed, "It's fine, Cale."

Ethan traced the raised lines in the amulet around his neck, feeling a great deal of pride for his new acquisition. Cale had taken one look at it, offering nothing more than a nod of acknowledgment. The etched symbol signified many things in demon culture, including protection from those who meant to do harm. Most races had their roots in superstition, eventually shrugged off by the advancement of science, technological, and civilization. Sonya was much too intelligent to put stock in ancient beliefs, yet when he had donned the amulet, a bit of tension had eased from her shoulders. She'd gifted him a smile so radiant it was now branded in his memory.

Siella spared them the nightmarish greeting when they arrived at the guild's hidden entrance. She ushered them inside where Azule waited, along with several members of his guild, including Luric.

"It's a pleasure to receive you again, Majesty." Azule motioned them to sit near a hearth where several fire crystals warmed the air. An array of food and drink was spread over a table across the room. Azule poured them each a goblet of sweet wine from a tall pitcher.

Ethan could see he was doing his best to honor Kyra with the bounty, even knowing it was a far cry from the feasts once held in the palace.

As she accepted the goblet from Azule, she offered her thanks before inquiring, "Have you given any thought into joining us against the Kayadon?"

Azule claimed a seat and took a long drink. "Those in my guild rely on me to keep them safe. All due respect, but I don't see how we can go up against such a powerful foe without severe casualties. Assuming any of us survive at all."

"My father has gone to great lengths to gather us here. He led us to your guild. I must know if you are still loyal to him, to us."

Azule's spine straightened. "Of course, Majesty."

"But you are loyal to your guild as well," Ethan observed. He could feel Azule's reluctance, the conflict waging inside.

"It has been only us for so long. What can you expect?"

Nothing less, Ethan thought. He drained his drink, creating an excuse to approach Luric, who had remained across the room next to the buffet of offerings. "You're Azule's brother?"

"Younger, yes."

"Born before the invasion, I assume."

Luric nodded. "I was planning to follow Azule into the guard, had only a year left of training. We lost our family early in the attack. This small group is all we have left."

"It doesn't have to be that way. I believe we can take back what once was ours."

Luric speared him with a steely gaze. "I believe that, too. Azule is not so sure."

Siella entered the room, bringing with her another male and female. "This is Ina and Ru, the two who had managed to escape the palace city."

Hands clasped, the two bowed, and then Kyra waved them over. She was eager to question them about their escape and about the state of the palace. When she directed the conversation toward her father, Ethan stifled a cringe. He had yet to inform anyone of the king's condition, a condition he suspected had worsened over time.

Ru hesitated only slightly before divulging what he knew. "The king resides in the palace. We are allowed to see him once in a while, from a high balcony, though many begin to question if it is truly him or an illusion." Ru became uncomfortable. "He does not look well, Majesty."

Ethan returned his attention to Luric just as Azule crossed the room to join them. "You've carved out an impressive shelter here. I expect you could hole up till the end of time and never be found, if you so wished."

"*You* found us," Azule commented.

"Not without a great deal of guidance."

Azule stiffened. "Yes, from the book you keep referring to. Apparently we've been chosen by the king."

"You resent that. Does your loyalty to your guild supersede that of the king?"

"If the king's visions are so infallible, how is it he allowed us to fall to ruin in the first place?"

"His magic is impressive, but not infallible. None of ours is. And I won't lie, there is no guarantee we will succeed."

Azule and Luric shared a look.

"But not trying is the equivalent of failure."

When Azule frowned, unconvinced, Luric added, "Is this all there is to be, brother? A life in a hole, cut off from the world? This isn't living. This is hibernation. It's cowardly."

Azule narrowed his eyes. "It's survival. Could you so easily lead our people to their demise?"

"If you'd merely ask them, you'd find many are willing to go."

Azule let out a frustrated sound.

Ethan interrupted before the sibling dispute drew the attention of the room. "We have others coming to our aid. The dragons, for one." After he detailed the full list of allies, Azule fell into disquiet.

"A battle the size of which you speak could destroy our planet. There could be nothing left to claim."

"What is there to claim now?" Luric countered.

"Enough, Luric. We will speak of this in private."

"Don't stop on my account," Ethan replied. "I'm so rarely on the outside of an argument these days."

* * *

Sonya flicked a small beetle from her shoulder, sending it careening through the air. It thunked against the base of a tree before dropping to the ground. "Gods, I miss space."

"But isn't it so beautiful here?" Anya practically sang. Her exuberance had yet to wane. Sonya smiled as she watched Anya examine every leaf and flower within the bounds of the cloaking spell, circling the ship again and again.

Being back on one's home must be amazing, Sonya mused, slightly forlorn. As it was something she would never experience for herself, Sonya tried to ride Anya's happy wave. But she couldn't keep from feeling wary of this place, so bright and colorful…wild.

A foreign, high-pitched sound from the forest's shroud set her on edge. It echoed for a moment before dying out. Something on the opposite side of the ship returned the call.

Yet even though this world was new to her, she was already developing a strong protectiveness over it. She could practically smell the Kayadon's stench invading every surface, attempting to lay claim, and she itched for action.

Sebastian emerged from the ship, his eyes seeking until they fell upon Anya. He smiled as he approached. "What are my two favorite ladies up to? Keeping the mischief to a minimum, I hope."

Anya rolled her eyes. "I've not stepped outside the lines, if that's what you're asking."

Anya was proving to be overly curious with her home world,

having been too young when she'd left it to remember much. Sebastian had ordered Sonya to watch over her while she explored, emphasizing that she was not to leave the witch's protective boundary.

Sonya had amused herself, teasing Anya by jumping back and forth across the line. Her fun hadn't lasted long. She found it bothersome when the ship just up and vanished from sight, and Anya along with it.

"Are the dragons close?" Sonya asked Sebastian.

"They should be here any day now. Your acquisition of Ivan has proved valuable. His fleet, too, will arrive within days. The only problem is Portia does not think she will be able to conceal them all. Said she was working on some kind of portal that will allow her to speak with her people about providing assistance." Sebastian shivered. "Merely walking past her compartment unnerves me. As if the very air is altered by her sorcery. But if she can persuade them, their help would be invaluable."

"Sounds like everything is coming together," Sonya observed.

Sebastian nodded and then scanned the area. "Where are the others?"

"Ethan and Zoey are going over the book to see if they missed anything," Sonya replied.

Anya added, "Marik and Nadua are hunting for game. Marik wants to put together a large meal to celebrate our achievements. And Cale and Kyra have gone off to work on Kyra's magic."

Sonya didn't know much about Kyra's magic, only that it could be destructive when out of control. "She'd better get a handle on it fast."

* * *

The fire roared under Marik's catch: a great beast that, according to Nadua, had been served at every royal function. Marik had been so elated by the prospect of fresh meat that he had insisted on cooking it on a spit, just outside the ship. He'd motioned to the forest, saying, "We cannot waste such glorious scenery."

The first sun was low in the sky, threatening to set in a matter of hours. It looked as though Sebastian might protest, but then Anya had bounced with excitement, giving him a look that Sonya knew he could never resist.

After that, Sonya had recruited Sebastian and Rex to help her retrieve a decent array of refreshments from her bar, while Ethan, accompanied by Ivan and his crew, had set off to invite the Faieara guild. They'd returned with only a few as the meal was nearly ready. Azule and his brother greeted them respectfully. Two others whom Sonya did not recognize from the previous meeting followed behind. When Siella came into view, Sonya bit her tongue, determined to keep her residual anger to herself.

No doubt sensing her struggle, Ethan eased up behind her, clasping his arms around her torso. She leaned into him, loving that his gift could so easily tell him what she needed.

Ivan grumbled, "*Lun feist*, you ever tire of this one, you just let me know. I may just be able to quench that fire."

Sonya gave him a rueful smile. "You couldn't handle me."

Ethan laughed. "Might be amusing to watch him try. Ivan's ego could use a swift kick in the balls."

She turned in his arms. "Are you suggesting I've kicked your ego in the balls?"

"Repeatedly." Ethan's grin widened. "And with relish, I imagine."

She stifled a guilty expression. "Well, you continued to ask for it."

"I'll be sure to evaluate my requests in the future."

"Ugh, tell me you are not about to let him kiss you, *lun feist*. And with me standing right here?"

Ethan tightened his grip around her. "Go flirt with someone else's female."

"Do you send me to my death to cull the competition?"

"Merely to silence you."

"I'm not one for suicide. These demons hold the same fire as she, but none as sweet. For hers, I would die."

When it looked as though Ethan was losing patience with his friend, Sonya angled his face toward her and brought her lips against his. He offered a soft groan of approval before deepening the kiss.

Ivan grunted out a sound of protest, though his words were droll. "Cannot watch this betrayal. My heart weeps, *lun feist*."

It was possible he left then, but Sonya was too immersed in Ethan that she didn't care either way.

Vaguely, she mused that it should have been strange to be kissing Ethan with Sebastian, or even Marik, so close, but nothing felt more natural. And the other's disregarded them as though they'd been openly affectionate from the start.

It was only when Marik called out that the food was ready that they pulled apart. One glance at Ethan's heated expression told her he wasn't hungry for food. As a debate raged in her mind, Ethan smirked.

"Mind your balls," she warned as she dragged him toward the fire.

His responding frown made her laugh.

Chapter 33

Sebastian burst into the room, rousing Sonya and Ethan from a dead slumber. Her first instinct was to protect Ethan, and tendrils of the Edge began to creep through her.

Ethan displayed a more rational presence of mind. "What's wrong?" he asked Sebastian.

"Cale and Kyra have gone missing. Get dressed and meet us outside." Then he left as quickly as he'd entered.

Sonya cursed as she scrambled for her clothes. Moments later, she and Ethan joined the others outside. As she disembarked, she overheard Aidan speaking with Sebastian, Marik, Rex, and Tristan near the ramp. "The dragons are nearly here. And many others are just behind them. Without the Serakian to shield their crafts, the Kayadon will see them coming too far in advance."

"I've sent Zoey to retrieve Portia," Sebastian replied coolly. "She will have to do what she can without her kin."

Farther into the field, Nadua consoled Anya, both of them looking sick with worry.

"Where were they last seen?" Sonya asked.

Anya raised her hand. "They told me Ru had directed them to a secluded area yesterday where Kyra could practice her magic far from the ship. That was the last I had seen of them. I assumed they had returned, and I had just missed seeing them." Guilt riddled her voice.

"Then we should begin with Ru," Sebastian replied, placing a reassuring palm on his mate's shoulder.

Anya lifted her head. "It's possible the day became late, and they stayed the night at the guild." She finished with a tight smile.

"Let us hope so," he said.

Zoey rushed from the ship, gasping as though she'd run the entire length. "Sebastian," she called. "Portia is...well, I don't know how to explain it exactly. Her room is like a black hole or something. I don't know what to make of it."

Multiple curses rang out.

"Aidan," Sebastian said. "Return to the control room and see about delaying out allies." When Aidan obliged, Sebastian lowered his head and muttered under his breath, "This war may very well be upon us before we're ready."

Unconsciously, Sonya's hand reached for Ethan's. He took it and pulled her close. Sebastian's words resonated with her own sense of intuition, and she feared chaos near.

"We cannot wait for the witch to be done with her magic," Sebastian continued. "Ethan, Rex, and Anya, you three come with me to fetch Ru. The rest of you, begin searching, but do not stray too far from the ship. I'll not have the rest of you go missing as well. We will return shortly."

Releasing Ethan's hand was like ripping a piece of her soul free. She was torn between wanting to stay with Ethan and wanting to find her brother. Ethan gave her a steadfast look, filled with everything that did not require words. They were both strong fighters, both capable of taking care of themselves without the other. Still, their separation would be brief and nothing could stop them from reuniting.

As she watched the party march into the thicket, she turned to her group and assumed command.

* * *

Ethan hurried behind Sebastian, who rushed ahead with long strides while Anya clung tightly to his back. A part of Ethan resented that Sebastian had separated him from Sonya while keeping his own mate close, but then he reminded himself that he and Sonya were not mated.

Sonya still hadn't even broached the subject.

He shook his mind clear. None of that mattered now, not while the future queen was potentially in danger. He'd held onto the slim hope that Anya was correct, and Kyra and Cale had holed up at the guild overnight, but somehow he knew it was just a fantasy. Cale would never be so reckless with Kyra as to keep her out past dusk. Not if he cared for her even half as much as Ethan did Sonya.

His theory was confirmed when they greeted Siella at her post. "I've not seen them," she announced.

"What of Ina and Ru?" Ethan asked.

"Ru hasn't returned from his hunting trip yesterday." Siella turned thoughtful. "I've not seen Ina in a while either. Why? Is something the matter?"

"Yes," he declared. "Kyra and Cale appear to be missing."

Siella gasped, "Missing?"

Sebastian added gruffly, "We've come to believe Ru might

be privy to their last whereabouts. We must speak with him."

Siella called for Azule the same way she had the day before. When he appeared, she quickly relayed the new.

Azule's gaze slipped to Ethan. "It's not rare for Ru to hunt far from the guild and wind up spending the night in the woods. Ina went in search of him this morning."

"Alone?"

"She assured me that she knew where to find him. She seemed not the slightest bit worried, so I had no reason to question her."

"Do you know where Ru might have sent Kyra and Cale," Sebastian asked.

"I've no idea. There are too many places in these woods where one could lose themselves, but I will gather some men to help in the search."

* * *

Nadua had climbed high in the trees to see if she could better assess their surroundings, while Marik paced near the base, glancing up with an irritating amount of impatience.

Sonya wanted to scream, "At least you're *near* your mate." But she held her tongue, knowing her surliness would not help the situation. She was tempted to have Tristan fly around in his dragon form, but that would be like sending up a flag that read, "Attention all Kayadon, please won't you come kill us."

Each of them was equipped with a sword as well as an energy gun that could either debilitate or dispatch an enemy, depending on the chosen setting. Sonya prayed they wouldn't require the use of either. Nadua also carried her customary bow with a quiver of arrows strapped to her back.

After the little Faieara shimmied down the tee, she pointed

into the distance "There's a string of open meadows that way. Aside from that, I see nothing but treetops and mountains."

"Then we'll head that way," Sonya said. "We don't have one of those glowing witch rocks, so I suggest we mark our way." She unsheathed her sword, ready to slash into the bark of a nearby tree, but thought better of it. It wouldn't be only them who could follow such a path back to the ship. Instead, she retrieved a nearby stone and placed it atop a protruding root where it was obvious it didn't belong. That way, they could remove the evidence when they returned.

As they wound through the maze of roots and foliage, they took turns placing a rock in a visible yet awkward location. The hike was lengthy, with obstacles formed by time: tall stones to climb over and thick trees at every turn.

And flowers!

Oversized flowers everywhere, practically dripping from the sky.

Sonya didn't have anything against the obtrusive things, but today their vivid bright colors and sweet fragrance seemed too cheerful for her mood. More than once she swiped her blade out to sever the head of a particularly offensive blossom.

Each time she did this, Tristan would shoot her a perplexed look, but otherwise made no comment.

The first meadow they reached was empty save for a few creatures that scurried away as soon as Sonya emerged from the tree line. The second was not a meadow at all but a crude grave of an old stone foundation. The skeletal ruin was nearly swallowed by encroaching vines, as if the forest was determined to reclaim its land. Busted bricks littered the ground, covered in moss and peeking through tall grass. A single arch doorway and a partial wall stood sentinel, overlooking a slope of turf clipped by the encompassing forest, and yet looked ready to crumble at the first gust of wind.

Sonya glanced at Nadua for an explanation of what this place might have been, but stopped short when she saw sorrow in the female's eyes. Sonya followed her gaze to where burn marks scorched part of a deteriorating wall.

"Someone's home," Nadua said simply, and then steeled herself before moving on.

Tristan bent over the mark. "Does no' appear to be a natural fire. Too localized."

Sonya and Marik exchanged a glance, both of them troubled by the same thought. Nothing else in their surroundings showed evidence of burning. No tree was scarred by fire. It was entirely possible this was the result of a Kayadon attack, the ones who'd lived here either killed or captured.

They headed back into the cover of the forest. Sonya kept her ears open for any sound that might lead them to their quarry. It wasn't safe to yell out their names as she wanted to, but there was something that bothered her far greater. "If they had gone this way, Marik or I should have caught their scent by now. They could be in the complete opposite direction."

Nadua's shoulders slumped. "Should we head back then and start anew?"

"Maybe the others have returned with direction from Ru," Marik suggested.

Sonya nodded. This search was already starting to feel like scouring the universe for a particular rock the size of a fingernail. Just as she turned, a low growl sounded from a short distance away. They all paused before glancing at Nadua.

"I've never heard that before," she said as she drew an arrow from her quiver.

Marik and Tristan unsheathed their swords, and Sonya palmed her gun. Another growl rumbled toward them, louder this time, but it was difficult to tell the exact direction it had come from. Sonya motioned the others into a tight group, their backs to each other.

Several yips mixed in the air with other, more threatening animal sounds.

"I count five distinct calls," Sonya announced. "Maybe six." The scent from the other beings wafted over them.

Tristan jerked his head in several directions. "Whatever they are, they've surrounded us."

Sonya sensed the impending attack and tightened her grip on the butt of the gun, scanning for any sign of movement. Her gaze landed on a pair of eyes so black they looked devoid of soul. The beast growled low, zeroing in on her, and she returned the deadened stare with one doused in red.

The creature took a step forward, pushing through the foliage. A long snout filled with sharp teeth slick with saliva came into view. Another menacing step forward encouraged a second beast to reveal itself. The skin around their bodies was tight and sunken in between the bones.

Three more creatures emerged into the open behind them, eyeing Marik and Nadua. Sonya knew what they faced. The drawings in the book had offered a fairly detailed image, only falling short where the smell was concerned.

The growls turned into guttural barks from all creatures but the one staring her down. Its fierce body was coiled, ready to spring at her throat.

Sonya smiled at the challenge. "Come and get me, you demented little bugger." Then she fired off several shots.

The creature leapt out of the way, and the energy blasts slammed into a thick trunk several meters away. Before she could adjust her aim, the creature bounced off the surface of a nearby boulder and launched itself at her, teeth bared.

She raised her arm to block the attack and hissed when the creature's jaw locked onto her forearm, slick dagger-sharp fangs sinking into her flesh. The action knocked the gun from her hand.

In the back of her mind, she registered that the other beasts had initiated attacks of their own. Marik's blade sliced at one just as Nadua's arrow penetrated the body of a second. Tristan was contending with two at once.

Sonya kicked her knee up, catching the beast in its hard, bony chest. It let out a sound of pain but did not relinquish its hold. With her free arm, she unsheathed her sword and ran it through the beast's body, twisting the blade as she did so. It let out a howl, releasing her arm and falling to the ground.

She heaved her sword up, slicing the creature's rib cage, past the neck, and then directly through the skull. The two halves pulled in opposite directions, spurting black blood as the carcass fell apart.

She dove for her gun. Her body hit the ground as her hand closed around the weapon. Rolling to her back, caught the blur of another creature leaping for her. She pulled the trigger. The beast's head exploded into gory shrapnel. The remains plopped down just inches away.

Then all was quiet.

"Holly hell those things were fast," Marik bit out. "Are you alright?"

Sonya almost answered, but it was Nadua that he'd addressed.

Nadua responded with a nod and then glanced at Sonya on the ground, zeroing in on her bloody arm. "Sonya, you're hurt!"

"I'm good." Sonya pushed to her feet, ignoring Tristan's outstretched arm. After a moment of tense, silent waiting, she decided that there were no more creatures preparing to attack. Moreover, no Kayadon had appeared. Which seemed kind of strange.

As if reading her mind, Marik asked, "Do you think there are Kayadon about?"

"It's possible, but I think they would have joined in the fight." A heavy desire to mete out vengeance raged through her, but she tamped it down. There was one thing she wanted more than to seek out and destroy any Kayadon. "We need to get back to the ship and make sure the others have not been attacked as well."

* * *

"The day comes to an end," Azule announced sullenly as they made their way back toward *Marada* with a handful of his followers behind them. After trekking back and forth so many times between the ship and the guild, Ethan had nearly committed the path to memory.

Sebastian had returned to the ship hours ago to conduct his own search and check if the others had found success, while Ethan had joined Azule and his group.

The ship came into view, blurry at first as the barrier gave way. Outside the ship, Sebastian stood next to Sonya, her back to Ethan as she pointed at something to her right.

Azule placed a hand on Ethan's shoulder, claiming his attention. "We will begin anew in the morning. If Ru or Ina return this night, I will question them immediately."

Something in Azule's expression told Ethan he wasn't confident they would ever see Ru or Ina again. Whether the other male suspected the two had perpetrated a betrayal or had instead, been captured—as they all feared Cale and Kyra had been—Ethan wasn't sure. But for their sake, it would be better if they'd been captured.

Ethan thanked Azule again and said goodbye before watching the group vanish into the forest. As he turned to approach the ship, he took note of the expression on Sebastian's face. Sebastian glanced past Sonya, meeting his gaze and causing Sonya to turn as well. Seeing him transformed her features from a demon prepared to rage to unmitigated relief.

He countered that with a smile, but frowned when her bloodied arm caught his attention. He rushed forward just as she did the same. "What happened?" he demanded, hardly recognizing his own voice.

She threw her good arm around his neck, her body solidly pressed against him, effectively keeping him from examining her wound. "I was so worried for you!" she practically sobbed. The distress in her tone took him aback.

The thought of her in danger sliced right through to his heart. Though he burned to heal her immediately, he could only tighten their embrace.

"Tell me what happened," he repeated, stroking his hand over her hair and struggling to keep his own emotions in check.

She recounted her attack. Yet it was only after she groused

over him splitting off on his own—no matter that he'd been with a large group—that she allowed him to heal her.

When every slash in her silky skin was knit back together, he brought her palm up and kissed the inside of her wrist where much of the damage had been wrought. "Like I said, you're stuck with me. And that's no promise, *vietta*. It's an outright threat."

She let out a sparkling laugh, then became serious. "I take it that Ru wasn't able to help?"

"He's gone actually," Ethan replied. "Along with his mate."

Sonya tilted her head. "They went missing the same time as Cale?"

"It's possible Ru did, but Ina was spotted this morning before we reached the guild. Claimed she knew where Ru was and was going to find him. At the time, no one knew we were missing two of our own. She hasn't been seen since."

Sonya glanced up, gauging the dimming sunlight. Her expression turned sorrowful. Endeavoring to search at night would be too dangerous for any of them, especially after the attack.

"You know Cale is fierce. Wherever he is. I'm sure he and Kyra are in no danger."

Sonya locked gazes with him. "Thank you for attempting to sooth my worries, but I can see right through you."

Ethan pressed his lips together. It was true; even he didn't believe his own words.

Portia's slight figure popped so suddenly into the clearing that they all jumped. "I see you've made a mess of things without me."

"Portia!" Sebastian yelled. "By the gods, where have you been?"

She shot him an affronted look, but her words came out

blithely. "Only doing my best to campaign for your cause. Commence with gratuitous behavior."

"I'll ask you why I should be grateful later. Is there a way for you to use magic to find Cale and Kyra? They've been missing since yesterday."

"I'm aware. Hence the comment about the mess. I can scry for them, but that takes time and concentration, and I won't be able to work spells to conceal the oncoming horde." She pointed to the sky.

"Do it," Sebastian ordered without hesitation.

"Very well. I should hear back from the council in a few hours' time regarding what they are willing to provide. With any luck, they'll send more powerful magic wielders than I." With that, she vanished.

Chapter 34

The next morning, Sonya found herself faced with bad news, followed by terrible news. Neither Ru nor Ina had returned to their guild, and Portia's scrying had failed. So not only were they no closer to finding Kyra and Cale, but more of the *horde*, as Portia had so eloquently put it, were fast approaching, all but announcing to the Kayadon that an invasion was coming.

The only good news seemed to be that far more races had come to the Faieara's aid than any of them could have anticipated. Numerous ships were now stationed around the planet, waiting, and new transmissions were flooding in by the hour.

Unfortunately, with the search for Cale ongoing and no intel on the Kayadon's stronghold, they were nowhere near battle-ready.

Sebastian kept up the pretense of leader, dividing his time between the search and consulting with Aidan, Tristan, and Ivan over battle strategies. All the while, he kept the waiting ships in check and far enough away from the planet that the element of surprise was not lost. Many of the crafts were run by blood-thirsty captains, mercenaries, and pirates who didn't take kindly to being ordered around. They were itching for action.

And Sonya was right there with them.

Each moment that past felt like lost time. Time that could be spent taking back what the Kayadon had callously claimed. This world might not appeal to her taste, but it should not belong to Kayadon scum.

She knew Ethan could sense her urgency, but made no attempt to temper it. She imagined he felt the same. The only thing holding them back was the worry that if they attacked now, both Cale and the future Faieara queen would be put in worse jeopardy than they might already be.

If they were even alive.

Sonya shook the notion from her mind, clinging to the only thought that would keep her from breaking down completely. She knew her brother well, and if he'd been captured or killed, he wouldn't have gone down without a fight.

Sebastian summoned them all to the clearing to perform one last search before he unleashed the legion of eager warriors upon the Kayadon…and this planet. In a moment of uncharacteristic compassion, Sonya worried for the ignorant Faieara who had no idea their world was very close to delving into a fiery pool of chaos.

Would any of them join the fray and take to battle, or would they escape farther into their protective woodland? That is, if there even were any more hidden guilds. It was entirely possible that Azule's band of brothers was an anomaly among an otherwise enslaved race.

Ethan believed there were others. He would have her believe there were hundreds, if not thousands of free Faieara concealed all over Evlon. After he'd insisted it, Sonya had given her best encouraging smile, but feared it looked more patronizing than anything.

Azule had yet to decide whether he would fight by their side or not. Each time he refused to give a definitive answer, she had to bite her tongue to keep from crying, "Coward!"

At times she had to wonder if any from this world had the guts to do what needed to be done. Then she would admonish herself for such thoughts. She only had to remember the bravery Anya had displayed, as well as Anya's sisters. Not to mention, Ethan was more than a fearsome fighter, filled with courage and determination equal to her brothers, perhaps even outshining them in some ways.

"We'll head off as a group," Sebastian said when they were all gathered. "We can't risk splitting up at this point."

Sonya nodded, assessing the rest of the group: Nadua, Marik, Anya, Tristan, and Ethan. If another pack of those creatures attacked, the little buggers wouldn't stand a chance.

A voice called from behind. "What about us?"

They all glanced at Azule, a little surprised to see he was flanked by what must have been his entire guild—Sonya determined forty or more.

"We're glad to have you," Sebastian said diplomatically.

Ethan called out, "Are you here merely to help in the search or to fight when the time comes?"

"I'd hoped just to recover the princess, but my guild has spoken. They're eager to take back their home. And as far as I can tell, this time—with you, Ethan, and your constituents—we may just have a chance."

"About time," Sonya mumbled.

"Very good," Sebastian said more loudly.

Sebastian instructed Azule to split his guild members into two and send them in opposite directions for a wider search. Azule complied without argument.

Then Sebastian turned to his own group. "Rex, Tristan, take the lead. The rest of us will follow behind. Marik, and Ethan, take up the rear."

It didn't escape Sonya's notice that Sebastian had placed all the females, including herself, at the center of the group and she was reminded of Ethan's comment about a male's natural instinct to protect their females. Yet instead of indignation, Sonya felt only affection for her eldest brother. Although, she did give him a swift jab in the arm and call him an overbearing dolt.

He responded with a bemused look before taking his position.

Just as Ethan took his first steps behind the party into the foliage, Portia popped into existence at their front.

She spoke quickly so that no one could get in a word. "Oh, good. I caught you. The counsel sent a few more witchlings. Not what I'd hoped for, but better than nothing I suppose. Anyway, I've had Enaki take over scrying. She seems confident that she can get results. Loralye will help me with other things while Yarrow is attempting to brew up some major concealment. He has some very interesting ideas."

Ethan blinked, and Portia was gone.

Tristan visibly shuddered. "Canna say enough how unsettling all this magic is to me." At their looks, he added. "Doona get me wrong, the Faieara are different. They're born with it, same as dragons. Runs in our blood. Witches, Serakians, whatever they want to call themselves, they use magic in unnatural ways. They go against the natural order, in my opinion."

After hiking for several hours, they took a short break in a thickly wooded area that overlooked the valley. Sebastian and Rex kept watch while the others relaxed. Marik reached into his pack and fished out a bundle. He unwrapped it, revealing a hunk of smoked meat. The sweet scent drew everyone's attention. Without a word, he broke off pieces and passed them around.

Ethan bit into his portion and then settled next to Tristan on the branch of a downed tree. "So, you and the witches on your planet are still at odds?"

Tristan looked at him. "You heard of that?"

He nodded. "My king spoke of your people often."

Tristan ripped of a chunk of meat, chewed, and then swallowed before saying, "A more deceitful bunch I have never met, those witches. Claim to want peace between us, but forever find ways to sabotage it."

Ethan glanced over the beloved mountains that surrounded the deep valley containing his once home; the palace. "Have you or anyone in your clan spent much time exploring off world, or learning of other spacefaring cultures besides the Faieara?"

Tristan raised a brow and shook his head. "We've no' had the need. Our world is plentiful. Would not have even bothered with your lot had your king not sought out and befriended my father so many years ago."

"There are other benefits to be gleaned than forming alliances. It's a valuable experience. I've spent a lot of time away from my people, having to find unique ways to survive. Of course, my situation is extreme, but if I ever need, I can mingle with every manner of foreign cultures without inadvertently causing or taking offense. Once I understood the ways of others, animosity was easily avoided."

Tristan narrowed his gaze. "Now, I know you're no' suggesting there's a lack of understanding on the part of my clan. You doona know what those bluidy witches have done."

Ethan shrugged. "You've shared the same land for centuries, yet cannot get along. I imagine both sides are guilty of something. Could it be pride that keeps you from peace?"

A muscle ticked in Tristan's jaw. He opened his mouth to respond—

A brilliant light flashed over the sky. Seconds later, the rumbling of the fierce, yet distant, explosion rocked the ground at their feet. A shockwave followed, compressing the air from Ethan's lungs and nearly knocking them all over. Ethan sucked in a breath and shot to his feet. A plume of smoke billowed up from behind the wall of trees.

A deafening quiet settled over the group as they all gaped. Even the wildlife seemed to have taken a stunned pause. A light wind filtered through the leaves above.

A second explosion accompanied the first, this one slightly farther away. A heavy ball of dread settled in the pit of Ethan's stomach.

The good news was the explosions were nowhere near *Marada*—they resided in another valley altogether—but they were far too close for comfort.

Several ships shot overhead, made into shadowy figures by the thick forest ceiling.

Sebastian let out a harsh curse. "We must get back, now!" He started to move, but then froze in place and tilted his head to the side.

Sonya retrieved her gun and swung her head around as if hearing whatever had alarmed Sebastian.

"Those creatures are coming," she said.

Ethan pulled his gun, though he could detect nothing out of the ordinary. A heartbeat later, low growls registered. He tightened the grip on his weapon. Snapping of twigs indicated numerous entities approached.

"Not just creatures," Marik hissed. "Kayadon."

"An army of them," Sebastian declared. "Let's go." He ushered everyone in the opposite direction. Their pace started as a jog at first, in order to remain quiet, but before long, Sebastian ordered, "Hurry!" and they all sprinted forward.

The creatures Ethan had only seen in drawings suddenly raced beside him. He had to hold back a gag from the sight. Bony, gray skinned animals with large jaws designed for catching and holding prey. He kept them in his peripheral as he forced his legs faster. When one jumped at him, he was ready with his weapon and shot it down.

Sonya made good use of her gun. Her aim was spot on as she kept a swift pace. Ethan took to counting the yelps as she felled one creature after another, allowing pride to wash over him.

He reached thirteen when all at once chaos threaded through his world. Blast after blast vibrated the ground around them—targeting them—the heat of each explosion scorching his skin. Through the turmoil, he tried to determine if Ivan's fleet or the dragon's ships had moved in, but it was impossible to tell. The trees shielded every craft that flew over.

A plethora of violent noises bombarded his ears. He could only assume the Kayadon had discovered the presence of the enormous army stationed around the planet and initiated the attack.

"They're closing in," Tristan yelled.

Ethan glanced back. Several Kayadon dodged through the trees after them. They appeared a bit more haggard than he recalled, their skin just as tight and devoid of color as their ravenous pets. Several sets of veiny white eyes locked onto him.

"What's the plan?" he asked no one in particular.

Only a few feet ahead, Tristan answered, "We need to find a place to make a stand. Any ideas?"

With a quick glance around, Ethan tried to draw on his memory of the land. After a moment of gauging their position, an idea sparked. "Keep going! There should be a hanging cliff ahead. If we get there, we can keep the Kayadon from surrounding us. I think it's our best chance."

Nadua gasped. "Oh! The cliff! I"—she directed an arrow toward a creature nipping at her heels—"I had a vision once. We were all there on the cliff that overlooks the palace! I'm sure of it now."

Sebastian's feet beat against the ground, his hand locked with Anya's as he pulled her along. "If it gives us the advantage, then I'm all for it. Lead the way, Ethan."

Moments later, they paused just before the edge of the rocky cliff to face their attackers. The cliff was nothing more than an oddly shaped but massive rock that narrowed and then billowed out before dropping off. Perfect for forcing their enemies in a tight bottle-neck and slowing their progress.

From this point, the sky was wide open and Ethan ascertained the battle in its entirety. Ships from both sides sliced through the sky, targeting each other. Many were spewing fire and flames even as they continued their assault. He realized many of the sounds he'd assumed were bombs had been ships ripped from the sky and crashing destructively to the ground, taking out a field of ancient trees.

The city that surrounded the palace in the valley below was in clear view. Ethan's gaze became transfixed; many of his people raced through the cobblestone streets, engaging in battle. Kayadon attacked with fervor, displaying no pity for their physically smaller opponents.

Well-established fires spewed black smoke from most of the buildings, making Ethan wonder if the battle had started long before he and the others were aware.

Grueling doubt scattered his mind.

Were they too late? Had they made a wrong move? Was the rebellion to be squashed even before it began?

The smell of ash coated his nostrils, punctuating his troubled thoughts.

Struggling against his distress, Ethan focused on the approaching Kayadon. He would not stop fighting until he sucked in his last breath. If this was to be the end, it would be an end to remember.

Rex, Sebastian, and Marik took the foremost positions, garnering first shot at the fiends. All the demons, including Sonya, were fiercely on the Edge, their eyes gleaming with bloodlust, horns burning brighter than the flames spreading over the forest.

Nadua pulled back toward the edge of the cliff, using her arrows on the oncoming army. Anya stood by her side, nervously clutching her sword in case she needed to use it.

Sonya planted herself as Anya and Nadua's fearsome defender, rapidly felling the Kayadon's creatures with her gun.

Ethan raised his own gun and proceeded to take out their gaunt faced foes while Tristan joined the demons on the front line.

Soon enough, the Kayadon were climbing over bodies of their own kind to get to them. As far as Ethan could see, Kayadon poured from the thick forest, so many, they were uncountable.

When despair threatened to choke the air from Ethan's lungs, Tristan sounded a triumphant cry. Ethan turned to see several crafts dotting the sky, approaching. When he looked again, he realized they were not crafts at all, but dragons.

Diving toward the sea of Kayadon, the procession unleashed a long stream of boiling fire. Some of the dragons arched back into the sky to engage an enemy ship heading their way. As a well-organized group, they clung to the hull, their claws ripping through metal as though it were as thin as a sheet of parchment.

Two dragons broke off from the group and sailed overhead. Hot air blasted over Ethan as the great beasts flapped their massive wings to slow their progress, looking ready to land. Preternatural magic sizzled in the air, and the dragons transformed just feet off the ground, landing softly on two legs near Tristan.

King Mar and his eldest son rose to their full warrior height, greeting their kin with a nod as they unsheathed thick blades. Ethan burned to know what had initiated the attack, but that conversation would have to wait. Kayadon surged forward, managing to push them all back a few steps.

"Come on!" Sonya ground out encouragement to her group as she fired into the deluge.

The battle seemed endless. Both the Kayadon and their pets appeared to multiply each time she took one down. Even through the fog of her Edge-drenched mind, she understood that they couldn't go on like this. Their enemy's numbers were too great. Eventually the Kayadon would breach the line and tear them to shreds.

A flurry of impossible movement drew her gun to the right. "By the gods, Portia! I nearly took your head off!"

Portia merely smiled. "Brought you a present!"

Sonya glanced at Portia's feet, where three bodies huddled, clutching their stomachs and dry heaving.

"Cale!" Sonya's chest thudded with relief. Kyra crouched next to him, an odd expression on her face. "What's wrong with them?" Sonya asked Portia.

"Side effect of astral dimensional navigation. They'll be fine in a minute."

Kyra and Cale began to rise unsteadily, yet the third body remained on the ground. It took Sonya a moment to rationalize that it was a Kayadon restrained around the torso by thick vines.

Behind Portia stood two individuals Sonya had never seen before. The dark skinned female draped in black exuded a deadly aura by way of her deadpan stare. The male, much like Portia, appeared uncaring about the war waging around him.

"Aren't you going to help?" Sonya inquired curtly.

"We're forbidden to engage in battle," the female replied, her tone almost bare of emotion but for the coldness in it.

Incredulous, Sonya gaped at Portia.

Portia shrugged. "It's true. The counsel has denied my request in that regard. But I've devised a workaround. We're stirring up some big magic that should offer solid protection. Try not to die till then."

Together, the Serakians vanished.

Sneering back at the battle, Sonya squeezed off another round of shots.

From her peripheral vision, she saw Cale clutching Kyra, trying to talk to her. Kyra's eyes were wide as she surveyed the carnage. Cale tried to claim her attention, lightly shaking her. He kept asking if she was alright. She wouldn't be if the Kaya-don broke through.

"Cale, we need you," Sonya yelled over the clatter while taking out one of the two ravenous creatures that had scrambled past Rex. Ethan dispatched the other. She cast him a hooded look, loving the crooked smile he shot back.

Finally, Kyra seemed to come to her senses, and Cale left her side to add his hefty might to the battle. As he retrieved a dead Kayadon's fallen sword, he instructed Ethan to join Kyra and the Faieara farther out on the cliff.

Sonya frowned, but didn't have time to protest. A feral beast had wrapped its jaws around Sebastian's leg. Sonya stepped forward and blasted it through the neck. Sebastian shook it off and then grated a quick, "Thanks," before slicing into the chest of his closest opponent.

Once again, the Kayadon gained ground, pushing Sebastian and the others back till they were all fanned out in a line of gun-shot blasts and swinging blades.

Cale yelled back to the group, "Kyra! What's the holdup?"

That piqued Sonya's curiosity, but she didn't have time to inquire what they were up to. Two gnarled creatures leapt on Cale. The first sank its fangs into his shoulder, clinging to him with lengthy limbs. The other came for his jugular. Sonya adjusted her aim and fired, bursting the skull of the latter.

"Cale, get it together!" she said. Then she swung around and dispatched a group of Kayadon as they lunged at Marik.

Cale snapped the neck of the creature attached to his shoulder. "You get it together! That shot was a little too close to my head."

Sonya laughed.

"What are they doing back there?" Cale asked.

She glanced at the Faieara. They were poised in a circle, hands clasped, eyes closed. "They're holding hands. Maybe they're praying for a quick death."

As if feeling her gaze on him, Ethan glanced her way. Something in his expression gave her understanding. Whatever they were doing, magic was most definitely involved, and might even be the only thing to save them when exhaustion finally overpowered their resolve. They just had to hold the Kayadon back till then.

Sonya turned with renewed energy and a fierce determination to do just that. She squeezed the trigger of her gun so much her fingers were starting to go numb.

Without warning, a heavy blast smashed into her back, throwing her forward. *A bomb*, her mind quickly rationalized, even before her body settled from the jarring hit.

Oh gods! Ethan!

She rolled to a stop and heaved her torso off the gravel, her eyes landing in the spot she had last seen him. In his stead, a blinding light engulfed the entire edge of the cliff.

"What the hell is that?" Marik barked from right next to her on the ground. Everyone gasped for breath, pulling themselves to stand. Sonya dared a look behind her, finding the Kayadon just as stunned, yet recovering just as quickly.

Sebastian noticed the bound Kayadon that had been delivered alongside Cale and Kyra.

Cale ground out, "That one belongs to Kyra."

As what? A pet?

Sonya and Marik shared a look. Then Marik started for the odd light imitating from the Faieara. Sonya took a step to follow.

Cale motioned them back. "I don't suggest getting too close to that."

Whatever was happening, he didn't seem worried, which eased Sonya since his own female was lost in the light.

Sonya turned to fend off the Kayadon, expecting them to take full advantage of the confusion. Yet nearly all of them were motionless, shocked expressions tilted to the sky.

Sonya looked up and sucked in a harsh gasp. "By the gods," she muttered.

A translucent blanket wrapped over the sky above, stretching out and pouring down like water over an upside-down bowl. An array of electric-like veins writhed, morphing from blue to white and back. She couldn't tell if it met the ground or just went on forever.

Her lungs suddenly felt heavy. She fought for breath, fending off a full-blown panic.

The Kayadon seemed equally disconcerted, some of them retreating entirely while others remained transfixed.

"What's going on?" Sonya managed, glancing at Cale.

His lost expression was not comforting. He shrugged. "This is new."

Chapter 35

Ethan clasped hands with Anya and Nadua as Kyra completed the circle. Almost instantly, he could feel their prospective powers tingle through his skin. Rituals such as this worked to intensify the magic of a chosen individual. Each of them would be sifting their energy into Kyra, hoping to merge their gifts as one.

The moment Kyra had suggested it, the king's words had echoed in Ethan's head. "Restore, enhance, sacrifice, sustain. This you must do." Ethan had looked around, expecting to see the king's phantom form watching over them, but all he found was unending carnage as his world delved deeper into chaos.

Was this the moment the king had spoken of? Was something in his actions now imperative? He couldn't help but focus on the suspicion that had haunted him for ages.

Sacrifice?

Using magic extensively, pushing too hard, could harm the yielder beyond repair. This circle could overexert one or more of the princesses, essentially risking their well-being, or worse, their lives—especially because they were still considered novices by normal standards.

With his advanced experience, he could spare them the consequences of what was to come—what they probably didn't even know to expect—and enhance Kyra's magic. But to do that, he would have to deflect the repercussions onto himself. A harrowing—as well as dangerous—task for even the most powerful of his kind.

Could he risk himself like that? Sacrifice himself so that others could possibly live?

He would have liked to say it was the desire to save his people that made up his mind. After all, it was all he'd ever worked for. But when he imagined Sonya dying at the hands of her greatest enemy, the decision was easy to accept.

He turned to take one last look at her and found himself trapped by her gaze. The concern that transformed her expression broke his heart. In that second, he knew without a doubt that she loved him. He cherished the realization, claiming it as his greatest success. He would hold onto the thought with his last breath, and then, if it came to that, beyond.

He consoled himself with the knowledge that he would be giving her a chance at survival, and was oddly grateful that she had not mated him. There was a chance she would be gifted with new love…if the gods were merciful.

He closed his eyes and opened his magic to Kyra. He sensed Anya and Nadua do the same. Then he manipulated the circle to take the magical recoil.

When the pain started like fire in his veins, Ethan pictured Sonya's beautiful violet eyes, her begrudging smile every time he'd managed to force it from her. He imagined her soft skin relenting under his touch and her sexy moans in his ear when they lost themselves in the other's body. He called on every memory they had created together and would use them as a distraction when the energy became too great for his mind to comprehend.

His magic flared, gouging into his energy. He struggled to sustain his efforts. Sustain the circle and the power flowing through it. He could tell Kyra was making progress, taking control of her volatile magic as if wrestling with a feral beast and winning, and then latching onto theirs to feed it.

Satisfaction surged, even as Ethan's essence was crushed by the pressure, his energy being sucked from the very marrow in his bones. Still he forced more magic into the circle, utilizing his gift to revitalize the others.

Without warning, his power was no longer his to command. It now belonged to Kyra, and he didn't resist. As he siphoned all the consequences of calling so much magic, agony nearly brought him to his knees. Lava burned through his veins, and his brain pulsed painfully against his skull. His teeth clenched to keep from crying out. He brought Sonya's calming image to mind once more, focusing on her instead of the anguish.

His last thought: *I'm so glad I had a chance to tell her I loved her.*

Sonya marveled at the vision in the sky, wondering what was happening. A deafening boom rang out, echoing with tangible vibrations that curled through every nuance of her body.

She jumped back in horror when a nearby group of flabbergasted Kayadon began to...melt? No, that wasn't right. It was as if they were disintegrating, one molecule at a time and incinerated by invisible flame. They didn't even have time to yell out a protest. When those few were rendered to dust, the process spread to another group.

At once, dreadful understanding sparked over the battle-field and the purest form of fear spread over the Kayadon. They scrambled over each other to get away. Yet none of them could run fast enough. Eventually, they all succumbed to the weight of the frightening magic. The decimation was staggering.

Sonya, frozen in unmitigated awe. She had to work to gasp in a long breath. She struggled to rationalize what she'd just witnessed.

Nothing but a bit of trampled grass stood as evidence that an army had been there but moments ago.

She turned her incredulous gaze toward Sebastian and the others, hoping someone was willing to break the dazed silence. She was stunned anew to find Kyra's pet Kayadon unaffected, still unconscious and lying in that same spot on the ground.

Small stones rose several feet off the ground around them, hovering. The group collectively tensed.

What now?

Cale gasped, studying a wound on his arm that he'd acquired during the fight. Amazingly, the deep slash was knitting itself closed right before their eyes.

Her own scratches, though she hadn't realized she'd had any till now, were healing as well. She marveled as they faded out of existence, leaving nothing but smooth, healthy skin.

Yet Ethan and the others weren't finished.

The unconscious Kayadon heaped in a ball began to stir, to change. His skin shifted from the dull, dead gray to a warmer hue. His bones began to grind and morph into something less grotesque, almost pleasing to the eye. Dark hair emerged from his newly reshaped skull.

Sonya turned her back, sickened by the sight. Everything in her demanded she take her gun and end his life before he had a chance to beg for it with what she was sure would be a pair of sparkling clear eyes.

Moments later, Cale ground out, "Guess this means I don't get to kill you after all." Where was the malice? Where was the centuries-long hate? He'd almost sounded amused…jesting with a fiend from every demon's nightmares!

And then the bastard spoke back. "Is this an illusion?" Despite his accent, he sounded so…normal.

Infuriating rage brought tears to her eyes. She swiftly blinked them away before becoming distracted by the barrage of falling ships that seemed to be breaking apart from within. The pieces scattered as though no more solid than dust. Any fires that still raged were miraculously extinguished as if by a great breath.

The gust reached her moments later, nearly knocking her over a second time. The radiant light that had encompassed the cliff dissipated.

As if utterly exhausted, Kyra, Anya, and Nadua went to their knees, breathing heavily. To Sonya's horror, Ethan fell back and landed hard against the stony ground, unmoving.

"Ethan!" She rushed to him. She gasped at the bruises, like patchwork over his skin. She cupped his face and rubbed her thumb over his cheek. "Ethan?" she muttered, shoving aside the terror that gripped her chest. "Wake up. You did it. The Kayadon are destroyed. It was amazing."

He didn't even flinch as two of her arrant tears dripped over his face. She wiped her cheeks and pushed through her tight throat. "Please wake up, it won't look good if you pass when the girls have not. You have a reputation, remember?"

No response.

The only reason Sonya managed to hold it together at all was the fact that Ethan still breathed, although shallowly.

To her left, Cale cried out in joy as he whirled a smiling Kyra in his arms. Sonya had to keep from lashing out. Instead, she demanded. "What's wrong with Ethan?"

Kyra turned sorrowful as she focused on Ethan. "He chose to accept all the consequences of using so much magic."

"What?"

"Energy magic costs energy. That's why Anya and I get so exhausted afterward. I didn't realize it till the end, but he sacrificed himself so we wouldn't have to."

Sonya speared Ethan with an accusatory glare. He'd done this to himself on purpose? He knew what would happen, and still he sacrificed himself. How could she have protected him from such power? From something she didn't even understand? And why hadn't she realized before that there had been a good-bye in his final gaze?

"You stupid son of a bitch!" she screamed, struggling to rein in her emotions.

Sebastian asked warily, "Does he live?"

She fought to maintain her voice. "His pulse is faint."

"We should move him somewhere safe." Sebastian turned his attention to Kyra. "I'm assuming the Kayadon are no longer a problem?"

"Only those within the field have been healed or destroyed," she replied.

With that, the Kayadon asked eagerly, "Others are healed?"

Stroking Ethan's hair, Sonya leaned close to him. "I'm sorry

I've been so difficult. I promise to be kinder, easier, but you have to wake up."

He didn't.

She only overheard bits of the conversation between the others. Cale confirmed that Ru had betrayed them, setting him and Kyra up to be captured by Kayadon. When Cale launched into a tirade about what he would do when he found the little shit, Sonya broke in. "Can we discuss revenge later?"

Cale offered a look of condolence, which she stubbornly ignored. There was no reason for it. Ethan wasn't gone yet. Anya had come back from the brink, stronger than ever. Ethan would too.

Everyone began debating options. Returning to *Marada* was out of the question. Even if they could find their way back, the hike would be too dangerous. There was no guarantee that more Kayadon weren't on the way right at this moment.

"Let's go to the palace," Kyra exclaimed. "It's not far, and we can rally my people. There might be healers there too."

They all turned toward the magnificent building residing just beyond their perch. It was mostly unscathed but for a few blackened walls and a crumbled tower.

"Was it cleared of Kayadon?" Cale inquired.

Kyra hesitated. "I...think so."

"Does it matter!" Sonya said. "If it wasn't, it will be soon." She would make sure of that.

"What do we do with him?" Rex said, glaring down at the revived Kayadon.

The Kayadon replied smoothly, "I am no threat." He looked at Kyra. "You have done the thing I believed impossible. I owe you my life and will serve you till my last breath."

"Lying Kayadon scum!" Sonya shrieked. "You think your pretty new shell will make us trust you."

"Bring him with us, but keep him bound," Kyra ordered. "I'll decide what to do with him later."

The others readily accepted her queenly decree.

"Whatever," Sonya scoffed, adding, "If he even breathes wrong I *will* kill him."

* * *

"I think we've hit the motherload!" Oxnel belted out a hearty laugh as Ethan claimed fistfuls of treasure from the deep chest and stuffed it into the hidden compartments in his jacket. Oddly, his pockets seemed to never fill.

This ship must have been an easy mark. He didn't even recall the inhabitants fighting back when they overtook it. Where were they anyway? He stilled at the thought. How could he have taken his eye off them? They could be devising a mutiny as he and Oxnel became seduced by the bounty.

He found himself in a dark room where several unrecognizable individuals huddled in a corner. They feared him, not realizing it was unnecessary. He'd not harm a soul if he didn't have to, but they didn't know that…and that was the point. Fear kept people in line, a tactic that nearly every race utilized.

Despicable? Yes. Effective? Extremely.

He went back to rummaging through the treasure and found an odd necklace that piqued his interest. He stared at it, trying to remember why it looked familiar.

As he debated clasping it around his neck, something drew his eyes to the left. A great field full of brilliant colors merged seamlessly with the ship. A dimensional rift, he surmised. "I don't remember seeing that before," Ethan said to Oxnel.

"Summoned for you, I believe. Been here the whole time, just waiting."

"Should I go there?" It looked so peaceful, inviting. A place without worry or sorrow.

"Isn't that where you've been headed this whole time?"

Ethan's brows drew together. "Have I?" He stepped toward the edge, looking down at an entire world of divine grace. He could feel it reaching for him, soothing him. Yet it was hard to focus on any one thing. A meadow stretched out, blanketing a bundle of endless rolling hills. Beyond that? Well, no one could know what lay beyond that. "I'm not sure. Wasn't there something I was supposed to do?"

"I think you've done all you can. Don't you? Aren't you tired?"

"You have no idea," Ethan said bitterly, feeling the weight of his weariness press down on him. The barest of movements, separated him from calm tranquility. Just a step, and he would know peace.

He stretched out his leg.

Chapter 36

At the base of the cliff, Sonya saw Tristan and his kin standing near burning wreckage, their expressions sorrowful. One of his brothers knelt over the lifeless body of their father. Sonya felt for the dragon's loss, but stayed near Ethan while the others offered condolences.

After a moment of mourning, the group rallied. They utilized ship parts from wreckage and crafted two gurneys, one for Ethan and the other for King Mar's body. Tristan and Lear carried their father, while Rex and Sonya took command of Ethan. The others flanked them, keeping a look out for danger as they headed toward the palace.

Sonya listened for approaching trouble, but the forest remained eerily quiet. The usual chatty wildlife seemed to be stuck on a breath.

As the group trudged forward, her gaze continued to slip to Ethan as worry ate through her chest. His breath was too slow, his pulse too faint. She couldn't imagine what it must have been like to be at the center of such an enormous blast of power.

Her stomach rolled as she looked him over. It had been

enough to render a powerful healer like Ethan unconscious.

Rex had helped her dress his wounds by ripping bits of his shirt into strips, the color of which—once a light grey—was now stained red.

Her insides twisted.

She wasn't in the habit of seeing Ethan bleed without the assurance that he could heal himself right away. Now his wounds gaped, blood soaking his clothing and pooling on the makeshift gurney under him. Too much blood.

Her throat tightened as she held back a sob. Unshed tears pricked her eyes. Her world felt somehow frozen, and a deeply buried part of her brain rationalized she was experiencing a form of shock. Silently, she begged the gods to let him open his eyes, for that sly smile of his to grace his lips once more.

Apparently, the gods were on hiatus.

After what felt like hours upon hours of walking, they found the edge of the forest and entered the village outskirt. Or what once had been the village outskirt. Most of the buildings were now crumbling, carved by fire and destruction. Burning ash rained down. The smell of it saturated her lungs.

Yet the palace was intact, as though separate from it all, a beautiful entity that had declared amnesty. Only a small tower billowed with smoke.

Debris in the street slowed their progress as they made their way through the city. When they were more than halfway to the palace, Anya paused and turned her attention to a ruined dwelling.

Sebastian quirked his chin at her as if asking what she sensed.

Anya tugged at her pointed ear and then gestured to the

rubble. One of her own kind was near?

Anxiety spiked Sonya's heart rate. How many of them were there? Would the onlookers see the mishmash group of demons, dragons, and Faieara as a threat and attack? Her fangs descended in readiness.

"Hello?" Anya murmured in a benevolent tone. "You can come out. It's safe now."

They waited, but nothing happened. Sonya was ready to enter that broken-down shack and yank out whatever resided within, whether it be friend or foe. Anya lifted a finger and glanced sternly at her. Sonya gritted her teeth, reining it in.

Movement drew both of their attentions back. A small child with light metallic-purple hair peeked around a corner.

"Hi," Anya said sweetly.

The child ducked away.

Cale grumbled, "Do you want me to go get it?"

Kyra swatted him in the chest. "He's not an it."

He shrugged while Anya corrected them both. "She."

The child peered at them again curiously yet frightened and then hurried away.

It looked as though Anya wanted to chase after the girl, but Sebastian caught her by the elbow. "Let's move on," he said. "We'll worry about rounding up survivors later."

The closer they got to the palace, the more impressed Sonya became by the sheer size of it. It towered over the town and looked to have been partially built into the side of the steep mountain at its back.

Anya slowed her pace and grabbed Sebastian's arm. "There's more," she whispered.

Sonya jerked her head around, only seeing plumes of smoke

and falling ash.

Sebastian replied, "Can you tell how many?"

"There are a lot of them."

Sonya and Rex shared a look, setting the gurney with Ethan off to the side. When she again surveyed the area, she caught multiple sets of eyes gazing at them through windows and behind broken carts and walls.

She drew her weapon and bared her teeth. Her only thought was to protect Ethan.

Kyra motioned for her to put the gun away. Like hell. Not when her mate was so vulnerable.

"We're surrounded," Cale murmured, unsheathing his own sword.

Rex and the dragons gripped the hilts of their blades.

Kyra put her palms up. "Stop, everyone. Just calm down. They're probably just scared."

"My sister is right," Anya said, stepping forward. "I feel their fear, but there is no aggression—from them, anyway." She shot Sebastian an accusatory look. Just like with Sonya, the Edge loomed, driving his instinct to douse any threat to his mate.

Whispers erupted around them, and Sonya strained to hear what was being said.

"They're speculating on who we are," Cale announced.

At that, Kyra straightened her spine and ordered them all to stow their weapons. Cale and the dragons did as she asked, but Sonya and Rex hesitated. Kyra may be queen of this realm, but Sebastian was still their Captain.

After only a slight hesitation, he gave a nod and they both obeyed.

Kyra took a step forward. "Hello!" she called out. "I am

Princess Kyralyn, daughter of King Alestar." The whispering grew in volume, fanning out in all directions. Kyra continued, "With me are my sisters and allies to our people. You need not fear us."

After a tense moment, a brave young male popped his head out from behind a building. His wide eyes said he was terrified, but his strong voice carried toward them. "Where are the Kaya-don?" he asked.

"They're gone," she replied. "For now."

"They are never gone."

"Well, they're not here."

An older gentleman appeared from behind the rubble and hesitantly approached. Sonya stepped back and crouched over Ethan's unconscious body. She didn't get the sense that the old man was a threat, but tendrils of the Edge were muddying her mind. Nothing and no one was to come near him until she felt it was safe.

She watched with a narrowed gaze as Kyra spoke to the old man and it became apparent that they recognized each other from before.

The old man grew ecstatic and turned to yell, "It's true! They have returned!"

More Faieara emerged to investigate, and the whispering grew to a roar that slowly dissipated as the news made its way through the city. Sonya's mind raged as they neared in growing numbers.

She felt a warm hand on her shoulder, and bared her fangs at its owner.

Rex remained undaunted by her display. He peered down at her, offering a reassuring expression. "It's alright. Your male is safe."

It took a moment for his words to register, and another moment to fight of the madness off the Edge. Slowly, she stood and shot him an appreciative nod, which Rex returned.

The old man went to one knee in front of Kyra and bowed his head. Those near him followed his lead, and then in a wave the rest of the Faieara knelt.

Astonishing, Sonya thought, that their loyalty still remained with the king and his royal line after all this time.

Chapter 37

The Palace
Twelve days later

Sonya reluctantly unwrapped her arm from around Ethan's torso and eased out from under the covers. Wearily, she crossed to the hearth and studied the pile of flickering fire crystals. When intact, they provided a continuous source of light. Once cracked open, they offered heat for a time. And when drained, their bright red-orange hue turned clear, and their surfaces almost cold to the touch. During the first few days after arriving at the palace, she'd taken great pleasure in smashing them against the back of the fireplace. Now she merely tossed one in with enough force to rend it in two.

A little over a week had gone by with no change in Ethan's condition. His wounds still weren't healing.

A soft knock sounded at the chamber room door. Sonya knew it could only be one person. Apparently, Anya was alone in her ability to endure Sonya's surly demeanor, probably because she could sense the underlying dread that caused it.

"Come in," Sonya called, cringing at the scratchiness in her own voice. The sound would only give Anya cause to encourage her to get some fresh air, or worse, join the festivities that persisted throughout the palace and surrounding village. The Faieara had been celebrating the return of what was left of the royal family nearly nonstop, preceded by a time of mourning for the fallen king.

According to Anya, her father had been very ill, surviving only because the Kayadon had forced healers upon him, or so one of the restored Kayadon had claimed. And with no available healers, he'd succumbed to death quickly.

Anya tentatively peeked her head in, and then stepped inside. She wore a gloriously deep purple gown created solely for her by a miniature army of fawning seamstresses. Seamstresses who had also attempted to take Sonya's measurements...once.

It always shocked Sonya to see Anya actually looking like a princess, a far cry from the little Faieara's ragged beginnings and skittish demeanor. It seemed like only yesterday when she'd been hoofing it by Sonya's side through the forest in dirty, battle-torn garments, racing for the palace. At the time, it had felt like an eternity before they'd reached the palace. Looking back, it had probably taken less than half a day.

What Sonya and the others hadn't known then, was that Portia and her cohorts had utilized some of the power from the Faieara's bubble of destruction to weave a strong protective ward around the palace, the city, and beyond. They still weren't sure how far the shield stretched, but no un-healed Kayadon had been seen within since the battle.

They were out there, however. Not all the Kayadon had been eliminated—or healed from the disease that coursed in their veins, mangling their bodies and slowly killing them. Some had been too far away to be affected at all.

Anya offered one of her trademark smiles, full of loving concern coupled with a fair amount of beseeching. "I came to see how you're doing."

"Same as last time," Sonya snapped, regretting it instantly. Seemed she always regretted her harsh tone as of late, but Ethan's condition made her more churlish than ever and she couldn't keep from snapping at everyone who spoke to her.

Anya strode forward to stand beside the bed, glancing down at Ethan with a crestfallen expression. "He will come back to you."

A mixture of feelings battled within Sonya: Irritation, because no one could know for sure. Sorrow, because it hadn't happened yet. And a heartsick, soul ripping hope that pained her more than the other two combined.

As always, Anya gave her a knowing look before changing the subject. "You need to eat, Sonya. You need to get up and be around people who love you."

Thus far, Sonya had divided her time between sleeping next to Ethan, sitting near the fire, and pacing the room. When she was alone, she tried begging Ethan to wake up, pleading with all the pain that filled her heart. And when that didn't work, she turned to empty threats, such as biting him against his will.

Food and conversation had no place in her routine. And seeing the joy in others, the happiness, merely served to strengthen the bitter misery that was her only companion.

She shook her head.

"Please come join us, just for a little bit," Anya continued. "You should not be mourning him as if he is already gone." She lowered her gaze, affected by own words, and Sonya grew guilty. Anya had watched her father's passing not but days ago, and Sonya hadn't even been in the right state of mind to be a source of comfort for her friend. Still wasn't.

"Have any healers come forward?" Sonya said, staring into the blaze of the fire. Turned out every available healer had been kept in the palace dungeon, courtesy of the Kayadon. However, the lot had escaped sometime during the scuffle, disappearing into the forest to only the gods knew where.

Anya gave a slow shake of her head, and then glanced sorrowfully at Ethan's still form.

Sonya pelted another fire crystal into the pit. It shattered on impact.

Anya jumped, but made no response.

Sonya wished she could blame the healers, whoever they were, but after hearing what they'd endured over the length of their captivity, well, she would have clawed her way free too.

Anya turned to a more manipulative tactic. "If you don't take care of yourself, you won't have the strength to care for him."

Sonya produced her most murderous glare, but Anya just gave a thin lipped smile, knowing she had won a small victory.

With a heavy sigh, Sonya relented. "Fine, I'll be out in a moment."

Anya gave a nod of approval and then left, no doubt to warn the others.

Sonya sat on the bed next to Ethan, struggling to harden her emotions for the task ahead. She brushed a strand of his hair behind his beautifully pointed ear and leaned down to kiss the tip before whispering, "I love you, you stupid pirate. You promised I was stuck with you, and that means all of you. So you had better damn well come back to me soon."

She kissed him softly on the lips and then crossed to the door, prepared to defend against the depressing barrage of happy she was about to immerse herself in.

* * *

Ethan took a step back from the inviting fields, smothered in that ethereal warmth, and turned away as a heavy bout of anxiety assailed him. "I don't know," he said to Oxnel. "It doesn't feel like that's where I belong. Not yet." When he tried to meet the other male's gaze, the world rolled and twisted into something new.

"Ivan?" Ethan's voice rippled from his lungs.

Ivan tilted his head up and smiled. He stood alone in a darkened meadow, hands stretched out over a burning fire. Three moons fanned out over the sky. Beyond the darkness, veiled behind a wall of surrounding forest, several sets of red eyes sparkled.

"I was wondering when you'd get here," Ivan declared.

"Am I late?"

"You had me worried. I was about to send out a search party."

For some reason, Ethan took offense. "You know me better than that. I don't need saving."

"Don't you?" He rubbed his hands together as if the air around him was freezing and then placed them back over the fire. "Ah, *lun feist*."

Suddenly intrigued by the blaze, Ethan stepped forward. The flames surged higher before transforming from a fluid red to a tranquil purple. Atop the embers lay a delicate chain attached to a familiar pendant. Unconcerned by the heat, Ethan reached through the flames to retrieve the item, and then slipped it over his head.

"What have you there?" Ivan asked.

Ethan followed his friend's curious gaze toward the pendant around his neck. Confused, he lifted it in his palm for closer study. It took him a moment to recall. "Somebody gave this to me."

"Who be giving you gifts then?"

One by one, in a wave, the glowering eyes from the depths of the forest shifted in color, from burning red to a soft violet. Compelled to find those onlookers, Ethan left Ivan and entered the dark forest.

Shadows whisked past him, taunting him with harrowing noises as if to ward him off. The forest became dense and before long he was shoving past thick repressive branches.

Vines tightened around his arms and legs, holding him back from his goal. The moment he pulled himself free, the ground grew damp, cold, and then pliable, swallowing him to his waist. His legs burned from the effort of forcing himself forward, trudging through the muck. Exhaustion chipped at his resolve, and eventually he could go no farther.

"Stuck…" a voice whispered from the darkness.

His head jerked around to survey the area, but he caught no sign of the speaker. "That's right!" he challenged. "What are you going to do about it?"

Silence.

"Don't you dare go!" he yelled. "I need you!" When still he received no response, he doubled his efforts, yanking his body into action, digging his way out of the mud. Finally, he managed to crawl free and raced through the moonlit forest, over the slimy ground faster than it could suck him back down.

A part of him realized his lungs should be scorching with fatigue, yet he felt nothing but the urgency to keep going. He was close. *Just a little farther.*

He came to a dark area and paused. Thick rock encased him in a large chamber. Several passageways branched off from the main room of his asteroid lair, each leading to a very different destination, equal in darkness, and each more ominous than the last.

As he approached the center of the room and surveyed his options, light refracted through one of the entrances, offering a clear view of endless fields bathed in warmth.

He knew he would find nothing but peace beyond that threshold, but something made him hesitate, an odd sensation against his lips.

He fisted the pendant around his neck. In a flurry, the room flooded with vibrant hues of violet bleeding with red. It took him a moment to realize where the windstorm originated from; it poured from a passage to his left.

When he gazed into the vortex of color that faded into the darkest blackness, it was not fear that clutched him. It was clarity.

He was not meant to go quietly into death. The ultimate sacrifice was not his final mission. Destiny called him.

He still had a purpose.

Chapter 38

Not surprising, Anya was the first to spot Sonya as she descended the stairs into the great hall. After reaching the bottom, she meandered through the crowd, crossing the large, ornate room toward the table where she, Sebastian, Nadua, and Marik were seated. They all greeted her with pitying glances, concealed by plastered smiles.

Under normal circumstances, the assorted dishes of food gathered at the center of the table would've enticed her. As it was, she only filled a plate to appease the others and keep from being nagged. She proceeded to pick at the items blindly chosen and imagined the grub was delicious, if only her taste buds weren't as numb as the rest of her.

Around the room, Faieara danced to the beat of the music performed by a lively band. The singer's voice was enthralling as she spouted the tale of a lonely patch of flowers, squatting in the shadows at the base of a tree. Sonya sensed there was an underlying meaning to her tune.

After a moment of watching the blurred, faceless crowd, Sonya began to recognize some of the individuals. Azule was there, smiling and laughing, surrounded by a small pack of his guild.

Anya had mentioned that they'd decided to move to the village and help rebuild as well as to seek out Ru. The bastard had betrayed Kyra and Cale, practically handing them to the Kayadon for a two day torture-fest. Ina had been captured, however, and claimed not to have known of the plot perpetrated by her mate.

Ina now resided in the dungeon alongside two fully healed Kayadon—the one from the cliff and another that had been found within the palace. Sonya had heard through Anya they were repentant for their actions and had even offered to serve the Faieara, swearing allegiance to Kyra as queen. Thankfully no one was ready to trust them just yet. If Sonya had her way, they'd be relieved of their heads directly.

Anya nudged her and then motioned for her to continue eating. She must have been staring off into space. She did that a lot lately.

Another familiar face caught her attention. Ivan raised his glass at her from across the room. He and his men looked to be getting acquainted with a fawning group of females. Their smiles were radiant as the men animatedly regaled stories of battle.

Ivan sent her a questioning look, subtly asking about his friend. Sonya shook her head. Ivan frowned. The room blurred from a wave of billowing tears. She quickly blinked them away.

"Ivan's fleet was a godsend," Sebastian announced, following her line of sight.

"Oh?" Sonya replied. It was an effort just to keep that tiny word from shaking its way out of her.

"Aye. Not that the others were any less integral. According to reports, the Kayadon had been expecting a rebellion. Had been preparing for it, in fact. They had seers of their own, I suppose, and they might have even caught a few of our ships on radar. But they hadn't been expecting the sheer force of our defenses." Sebastian grinned smugly. "Albeit late, the arrival of Ivan's fleet took the Kayadon by surprise and confused their efforts."

Marik guffawed. "They didn't know their asses from their elbows."

Sonya forced a smile and scanned the crowd. "I don't see the dragons."

"They took their fallen back to their planet," Sebastian replied. "Aidan went with them."

Sonya fumbled with a hard chunk of food on her plate. She recalled Aidan coming to check on her and Ethan, offering positive thoughts and saying how glad he was to have met them both. She hadn't realized it was a goodbye. She also hadn't realized how attached she had become, and it hurt to think she might never see the dragon again.

The room erupted in lively cheers. Sonya turned to see Kyra and Cale enter through a large archway, the Earthling and Rex not far behind.

Sebastian groaned and rolled his eyes. "Cale is going to be impossible to deal with now. I don't give a fuck about all this royal crap, and I am sure as hell not calling him *Your Majesty*."

Sonya actually cracked a genuine smile at that. Since Cale was Kyra's chosen, he had been inaugurated alongside her. Sonya had missed the entire affair, but Anya had detailed it out for her later. There had been vows and everything.

Her smile lasted until Cale and Kyra neared. Confusion twisted her features, just as her heartbeat stuttered.

They are mated!

Sebastian and Marik gaped at them as well.

"How is it possible?" Marik breathed.

Cale offered an arrogant smile and placed his arm around Kyra. "My little mate is remarkable. That's how." Then he delved into a tale about how their mother had discovered a drug that induced matebonds, even against a demon's will. It had been used on Cale because Mother wanted Velicia in the family. He'd only learned of the plot recently when he'd approached Nadua to help him look into his past.

Sonya would have been horrified at this new bit of information if she wasn't fighting off a sick, selfish wave of jealousy. She tried to tamp it down and rationalize her way out of it, telling herself she only felt fury growing because of Ethan's condition, but then Cale's next words snapped something inside her.

"Kyra healed me when she healed Ginn and that other Kayadon."

"You mean Ethan healed you," she hissed, shooting to her feet and knocking her chair back in the process. "And now he can't heal himself."

Cale appeared to be momentarily stunned. Then he averted his gaze as he rubbed the back of his neck. Tension exploded into thick silence. She could tell they were all scrounging for something to say, some way to comfort her, but she was on the verge of losing it. Great...now guilt over her outburst mixed with the grief that had already settled in the pit of her stomach. It wasn't Cale's fault, or even Kyra's.

Sonya pushed away from the table and mumbled, "I'm sorry," before rushing from the room. She needed to remove herself before she sullied everyone's good mood. They deserved to be happy and to celebrate. Hell, Cale should be screaming his joy from the towers. He'd been gifted with a second chance. Sonya could only wish to be so lucky.

She pushed open the heavy wood door to Ethan's room and froze. Icy dread vaulted up her spine.

The bed was empty!

"Ethan?" she croaked.

Oh gods, why had she left him alone?

The adjacent washroom door that she'd left open was now closed. Pulse pounding, she crossed the room and flung the door wide.

Unmitigated relief surged, and she almost crumbled to her knees.

Ethan stood looking into the mirror, a pair of sheers in his hand as he clipped the last of his long hair short. Severed white-blond tendrils lay along the counter top and at his feet.

Her entry made him jump. Warily, he turned to her.

Unable to temper her emotions, she threw herself into his arms and burst into incoherent sobs as she tried to ask if he was alright. He stood frozen for a moment, and then slipped his arms around her. Her crippling elation was complete, and she gripped him for support.

Ethan threaded his fingers through the hair at her nape. "I woke, and you weren't here. I assumed…" He paused. "I feared you…" His voice sounded scratchy and unused, with a hint of sorrow.

She lifted her head to gaze at him, brows furrowed. "What? That I had died?"

He shook his head, closing his eyes as if pained. "No. Not that."

She frowned. "That I didn't care?"

He grimaced.

"Nothing could be further from the truth," she assured, alarmed that he'd come to that conclusion. "Waiting for you to come back to me was the hardest thing I'd ever endured. I have never felt such dread. I was afraid I'd never be able to tell you how much you mean to me."

Ethan's mouth parted slightly as he studied her expression. "And how is that?"

She leaned in to capture his lips with hers. He responded instantly, molding his mouth against hers. His warmth chased away a fraction of her anxiety.

"You set my heart on fire," she rasped.

"And you command my very soul," he countered in an equally husky tone. He bent to kiss her again, breathing her in as she did the same.

She tightened her arms around his neck, and he recoiled slightly. "Are you still hurt?" She yanked herself away, but Ethan stayed her, his palms splayed across her back.

"Just a little sore," he said. "My magic is still replenishing. I can vaguely sense the kingdom is in the midst of celebration, but I'm healing the old-fashioned way."

"You should go back to bed. Oh, and food! I should bring you some food! Are you hungry? And blankets, if you're cold. Or more fire crystals, perhaps?" She paused at his amused expression.

"Just you. That's all I want."

She knew her responding grin probably looked ridiculous and a bit drunken, though she'd had no liquor, but she didn't care. "Well, you have me. And you'd better believe you're stuck with me."

"Good." He claimed her lips once more, hard and demanding, delving his tongue past her lips. By the time he pulled back, her breath had become labored and liquid desire pooled between her thighs. Then his tone turned rough. "How about we make it official."

She stilled. "You mean claim you?" Her throat went dry as her body thrilled at the idea.

He nodded, his eyes darkening with lust. She loved the way they did that. The more he wanted her, the darker they'd become. And right now, his irises were nearly black.

She shivered, her fangs making an appearance. His hooded gaze turned rapt as she slid her tongue over one. Then she eased backward, delighted when he followed as though unable to take his eyes from her.

"I think we should get you cleaned up first. You have hair all over you. Why did you cut it anyway?" She crossed to the shower stall and turned the water to a pleasantly warm temperature.

"So as not to resemble someone horrid from your past," he said from behind.

She jerked her head around, her throat thickening from a wave of emotion. "Oh, Ethan, you didn't have to do that."

He shrugged. "It was by far my least painful sacrifice."

"Speaking of, I forbid you to ever do anything like what you did on that cliff." She undid the buttons of his white shirt and slid the fabric over his broad shoulders, marveling at his muscular physique.

"Haven't even made me yours and already making demands?" He smirked.

"I'm serious. You nearly died. Please promise me."

"How about this?" He unlaced the strings of her bodice. "I promise to never knowingly do something that would take me from you, if you agree to the same."

She agreed without hesitation, her breath coming in spurts as he freed her of the bodice. Their remaining clothing soon joined the puddles of cloth on the stone floor.

He guided her under the shower spray, his hand caressing its way down her spine and over the swells of her backside. She allowed her fingertips to roam the hard planes of his shoulders and chest, committing every crevice to memory. White-hot desire made attempting to wash a bumbling endeavor.

She gripped his engorged shaft, loving the heavy shudder that ran through him. While stroking him, she leaned in to nibble his earlobe, pulling another rumbling moan from deep in his chest. The sound was like a drug, dulling her mind and yet strengthening her senses. His scent was more acute, his heartbeat like the rush of wind against her eardrums.

Her fangs throbbed, begging to sink into his flesh. It was almost like being on the Edge, but all she wished to contrive was pleasure.

She sank to her knees and took him into her mouth, being careful with her fangs. He let out a guttural moan and, almost as if he couldn't help himself, thrust into her mouth. But then he stilled and allowed her to slip her tongue over his soft flesh at her leisure. She teased the tip for a moment before drawing him deep.

Foreign oaths escaped him as his body shook from her efforts. "You're going to make me come if you keep that up," he warned.

She shot him a wry look, and then sucked him deeply, relentlessly.

"Ah, gods, Sonya. You wicked female." Hot liquid spurted

the back of her throat, and she drank him down, wringing every last drop, reveling in the rolling shudders that raked over his body.

He pulled her to stand and their lips connected under the spray, the water cascading over their heated skin. His thick finger slid between her legs, and he groaned in approval when he found her slick. He pressed her against the damp wall and teased her budding clitoris.

"I want to hear you scream," he growled.

His forceful actions called to a primal corner of her brain that begged for more. Yet she was already on the verge of coming. He dipped his head to her neck and latched on with his teeth. The orgasm burst through her like a mini-explosion and her lungs rumbled as she cried out.

Roughly, he pulled her into his embrace, branding her with a devastatingly blissful kiss that rendered her mindless for more. His thickening shaft was hard as stone against her stomach.

She wasn't entirely sure how they'd reached the bed without tripping over every item on the way—there may have been a crash that went ignored by both of them—and they were still covered in a patchwork of suds.

She had, however, registered Ethan's unusually stiff movements. Bruises and cuts still marred his body.

"Sit against the headboard," she ordered. When he did, she crawled across the mattress to straddle his lap, resting her elbows on his shoulders. They gazed at each other for a moment. Then Sonya inched down, impaling herself on his rigid shaft. Rapture surrounded them both, their eyelids sliding to half-mast.

"You feel so damn good," he ground out as she began moving atop him.

Again a muddled—profoundly euphoric—version of the Edge had overcome her. Her fangs descended, throbbing painfully.

"You want to put your pretty fangs in me?"

She nodded, nearly whimpering with the need. Her hips undulated faster as if to punctuate her answer. He gripped her hips, his fingers digging into flesh as he gave one hard thrust. She moaned. Then his palms came around to cup to her ass as his shaft slid in and out of her. Her movements grew frenzied, her craving ravenous.

Ethan watched her in riveted anticipation.

Her heart fluttered wildly as her panting turned urgent. She leaned close, bringing her lips to hover over his neck. He turned his head to give her better access, the only encouragement she needed.

His flesh gave way to her sharp little fangs.

Exquisite ecstasy blasted her mind into oblivion, submerging her body into pleasure that was so intense it bordered on agony. Succulent, anguishing, merciless pleasure.

She drew greedily from his pierced neck. Bliss bombarded her senses as the deluge bombarded her every cell.

The great rumbling moan that came from him vibrated through her. His hips now drove into her with savage abandon, his shaft thick and invading.

He let out a harsh groan, tensing for his impending release. She threw her head back on a rapturous scream as a succession of erotic spasms assailed her.

She went limp, nuzzling her forehead against his shoulder. He hooked his arms around her and pulled her to him as they rode the tremors and fought to catch their breaths.

Everything was changed.

Chapter 39

Sonya stretched out beside Ethan in utter contentment. His fingers lightly grazed her side and along her hipbone while she ran hers over his chest.

They hadn't spoken as their bodies descended from the impossible high of their passion. Sonya snuck a glance at him, finding his lids closed, a small curve to his lips. He peeked an eye at her.

"How do you feel?" she asked.

"A little sad." His widening grin contradicted his words. "What a tragedy that can only be experienced once."

Sonya snorted. "If that happened every time, we would never get out of bed."

"A meager sacrifice."

She laughed.

With a hungry rumble from his chest, he rolled on top of her and planted kisses in the crevasse of her breasts.

Sonya arched into his touch. "Again? You must be starving."

"Indeed." His lips roamed lower, over her mid-section.

Her tummy grumbled, and he tilted his head back to look up at her. Her cheeks flushed. "I've only eaten slightly more than you over the last couple of weeks."

He hid his surprise with an admonishing frown and stood. "Then let's get you fed so I can have you back in bed with your body's full attention."

She rolled off the mattress and slipped into a fresh skirt and top. After stepping into her boots, she ran her fingers through her disheveled hair.

Ethan watched her with dark eyes as he buttoned his white shirt. He'd already donned a pair of black pants that had been neatly folded by the palace servants and placed alongside her clothing in their shared dresser.

Then he escorted her into the hallway. As they made their way to the great hall, Sonya realized she actually felt nervous, but as they came to the top of the wide staircase, it was like seeing the space anew. No longer annoyingly miserable—filled with too many happy party-goers—it was brightly lit, ordained with intricate, architectural nuances that added an old-world and elegant atmosphere. Columns lined the walls, their smooth surfaces decorated by vine carvings in the stone. Tall windows on one wall cast shadows along the geometric notches in the high ceiling. Even the music sounded more jubilant.

They had but reached the bottom of the stairs when Anya cried out with glee and raced toward them. She threw her arms around Ethan, and he stumbled back from the enthusiastic embrace.

"I'm so glad you're okay," she sputtered.

The others approached, not far behind. Sonya caught the knowing look in both of her brothers' features and flushed. She lifted her chin.

Alarm spiked when they moved in to greet Ethan. "He's still healing," she warned. Cale's palm halted mid-air, seconds from planting a harsh congratulation on Ethan's back. Instead, he gripped Ethan's shoulder and pulled him in for one of those quick masculine half-hugs. Sebastian and Marik did the same. Rex just offered his hand. Zoey, a kind smile. And Nadua and Kyra fretted over his still visible bruises.

"I'm fine now," he assured them all. "Just hungry."

With that, the group ushered them across the room to the table they had been occupying. Immediately upon sitting, the Kyra and Anya began filling plates for both of them. Sonya was about to protest, but Ethan leaned in to whisper, "Let them fuss. It'll help to ease their residual worry."

Impishly, Sonya teased, "You do realize you're being served by the queen herself."

Ethan's eyes widened, and he paled slightly.

"Oh, hush," Kyra chided before Ethan had a chance to respond. "It doesn't really count within our group, anyway."

"Like hell it doesn't," Cale disagreed.

Sebastian slapped him in the back of the head.

"I could have you charged with treason for that," Cale spat, although his eyes held too much amusement.

Sonya glanced around at the makeshift group of merchants, pirates, royalty, and warriors. This was her family, and she loved them all. And if anyone thought to take them from her, she would unleash a wrath the likes of which had never been seen before.

"I'll be right back," Kyra exclaimed and then disappeared into the crowd.

Sonya picked up a fluffy white ball from her plate and bit into it. The fruity middle tingled her taste buds.

"Those are my favorite," Ethan declared. She snatched another one and held it out for him. He bent forward and took it into his mouth, along with half of her finger, and then sucked lightly before pulling back.

She gave him a roguish look as heat pooled between her legs. It would be just like him to keep her hot and bothered all evening.

"Ugh," Cale grumbled, leaning back in his chair. "I can't watch this."

"Then don't," Sonya shot back.

Kyra reappeared then, seeming a little out of breath. "Ethan." Her voice sounded too sweet. "Follow me, please."

Ethan's brows knit, but he stood and following Kyra to the stage that housed the band.

"What's going on?" Sonya swiveled her gaze around the group.

A secretive smile played on everyone's lips, but no one responded.

Kyra motioned for the music to cease and called for the crowd's attention. Then she addressed the room in a loud decisive voice. "We have all sacrificed something during these last dark days. We have lost homes, loved ones. And there is still much strife ahead.

"My father, King Alestar, had the keen insight to designate one among us as his champion, Ethanule of the Guard, otherwise known as the Pirate King. Without Ethanule, we would never have made it this far, and the Kayadon would still be strolling our palace halls. He has worked tirelessly, risked his life on more than one occasion, and never lost hope. His courage and devotion to the Faieara nation leaves me awed even now. There is only one way I can think to honor his unwavering dedication and loyalty." She turned to Ethan. "Kneel, Ethanule of the Guard."

Brows still creased, he sank to one knee. She opened her palm to reveal a thick gold ring with a square red stone. Ethan stared at it for a moment and then shot Kyra a questioning look.

"Give me your hand," she ordered, smiling down at him.

He hesitated, then raised his hand. She slipped the ring on his finger.

"I offer you my father's ring, and from this point on, you will be addressed as Prince Ethanule, and I would call you brother."

Ethanule's mouth gaped as though to speak, but no words emerged.

"You may rise, Prince Ethanule."

He stood, but remained speechless. The crowd erupted in a roar of cheers, and Kyra pulled him in for a hug. He seemed to come to his senses then, his lips curling into a roguish grin.

As they left the stage to rejoin their group, the band started back up, belting out an enthusiastic tune that mirrored the excitement unfurling around the room.

When he returned to his seat next to Sonya, she inquired, "What's with the grin?"

He shook his head and chuckled. "I should have never doubted the king. That sneaky old man told me this would happen. He just muddled up the details."

"Well, congratulations, but I'm not calling you prince." She lifted her chin.

His eyes sparkled in challenge, and a shiver raked through her. She got the very distinct impression she'd be doing just that later tonight.

"What about you?" he said. "Technically we aren't wed by Faieara standards, but still. How do you feel about your new title?"

"What title?"

"Princess, of course."

Her head jerked back, and she shot to her feet. "Ugh. No one is calling me princess. Got it!" She aimed her finger at everyone in turn.

They all burst out in laughter.

Ethan put his arms around her waist and tugged her onto his lap. A rumbling groan reverberated through his chest. He whispered into her ear. "My sweet Sonya, you are the temptress of my heart."

She slipped her arms around his neck and met his gaze. "You've just plain stolen mine, pirate."

He placed his lips against her in a tender kiss that spoke of dark promises to come. Then he gave an arrogant smirk. "And I don't plan on ever giving it back."

About the author

Kiersten Fay has been a fan of the paranormal all her life,
from watching sci-fi and supernatural television shows
with her eccentric mother, to reading almost every type of
romance she could get her hands on.

Her Shadow Quest series is just getting started. To learn
more about Kiersten Fay, or to get info about upcoming
releases, go to
www.kierstenfay.com

Or follow her on Twitter @KierstenFay,
and on Facebook. www.facebook.com/KierstenFay

CPSIA information can be obtained
at www.ICGtesting.com
Printed in the USA
LVOW12s0907220816
501337LV00002B/9/P